LOST VEGAS SERIES, VOLUME TWO

ARTHUR, BLACK WOLF

LIZZY FORD

CAPTURED PRESS

ARTHUR

ONE

ARTHUR'S SENSES AWOKE SLOWLY. First the crackle of a fire, then the heat against his left side contrasting against the cold chill numbing his exposed right cheek and hand. The comforting scent of burning wood was followed by an ache radiating throughout his body. He was sore, and the intensity of warm pain left him wondering if he had been thrown off a horse several times. The middle of his chest felt unusually hot, and he was not able to immediately assess whether he was injured there or not.

Unable to awaken fully, he slid again into the lingering vision, which played from the beginning once more.

Tiana wore the blue dress and bracelet he had envisioned in every iteration of the dream. Her blond curls bounced around her shoulders as she sprinted through a field and towards the sunrise, which had painted the sky pastel shades of pink and yellow. Unlike former versions of the possible future, this vision was different. Arthur saw more of her location. She ran away from a forest and towards the mountains, and four steps behind her, reaching out to grab her, was someone other than the skinwalker Arthur had envisioned every other time.

This time, their father, Edwin Hanover, chased Tiana.

Seeing the skinwalker in all his beastly forms pursuing Tiana had once terrified Arthur, but the expression on his father's face alarmed him more. Perhaps because he knew that look, and he understood what it meant to be on the receiving end of it. No one who incited his father's anger survived the day.

Arthur could not know, from this tiny glimpse, what had changed in their lives for this version of the future to materialize, but he did not doubt the message behind the vision.

Tiana remained in danger, except the skinwalker was no longer the greatest threat to her life.

The vision faded.

Arthur's senses gradually pulled him from semi-consciousness into the real world. As he became acquainted with his body once more, he sought some memory of why he was unconscious in the first place.

TIANA LEAVING HIS SIDE ... the skinwalker walking into the middle of the village ... the black wolf's cold nose against his hand ... darkness.

ARTHUR'S EYES SNAPPED OPEN. "TIANA," he breathed. His sister was alone, vulnerable, facing down a creature that had ripped through hundreds of lives in the short time Arthur had known him.

"Don't move!" Marshall Cruise's urgent whisper came from the other side of the fire.

Arthur froze. His senses picked up no danger, but his mind had not yet cleared of the fog left over from heavy sleep. What was the threat? The skinwalker? Natives? Ghouls?

Marshall knelt beside him and stretched towards the warm spot on Arthur's chest.

"What is it?" Arthur demanded quietly. "Am I badly wounded?"

Marshall snorted. "No. I was using you as an incubator."

Arthur's brow furrowed.

Marshall gently lifted a bundle off his chest, removing the source of pressure and heat. He leaned away and placed the bundle on the ground.

"Why?" Arthur asked.

"Another surprise from our magic wolf." Marshall unwrapped the cloak.

Arthur sat up with a grimace. He had not been interrogated and beaten in two days, but he certainly felt as if he'd just left another round with Diving Eagle. "What ..." His question faded as he peered over the edge of the bundle. His features softened into a smile. "How beautiful."

Several tiny puppies with eyes and ears not yet opened and pink stomachs slept in the bundle. Their coats ranged from white to gray to black, with one of them covered in brindle fur. They were small enough for two to fit in his hand, if he dared pick one up.

"Six," he counted. The number resonated within him, and his head shot up. "Where is the beast?" His heart began to race, and he stood.

"Not here," Marshall assured him. "The magic she-wolf whisked us away from danger."

"What do you mean?" Arthur noticed their surroundings for the first time. They remained in the forest – but no village or bonfires or people were visible in the night anywhere around them. Darkness fell outside the ring of light provided by the fire. His eyes went to the chains Marshall had pried off both of them and deposited at the edge of the firelight and settled on the wolf. "What happened to her?"

The she-wolf had turned whiter than starlight. She lay on the opposite side of the fire, unmoving, except for the steady rise and fall of her chest.

"You are more comfortable with this magic than I will ever be," Marshall replied curtly. "When I woke up, she was in labor, and we were all here. You were unconscious and would not respond when I tried to wake you. She was this strange shade of white. I helped her birth her babies, and she fell into a slumber from which she had not awakened. So I took her babies and wrapped them up to keep them warm."

Arthur went to the wolf and knelt beside her. Her breathing was steady and deep. She was alive with no labored breathing or twitching or any other sign her rest was imbued with discomfort.

He could not recall the last time he slept this deeply, and no wolf would survive past infancy if it slept in such a way it was unaware of the world. Though he did not feel connected to the wolf on an energy level, he could not help wondering if he were somehow.

"Even witnessing it, I cannot understand how we came to be here," Marshall said, unease in his tone. "And I do not know how far she took us."

"I can ask her when she wakes up."

"Oh, so she speaks to you? You forgot to mention that earlier."

Arthur was silent. He had explained, in as few words as possible, his gifts to Marshall while they sat in a cage in the Native warriors' village. He had also avoided speaking in too much detail of exactly what he could do, and had only provided general information. It was never wise to trust a Cruise with information that could send Arthur and his entire family to the stake.

No sooner did the thought cross his mind, than he recalled what news Tiana had brought him shortly before the skinwalker appeared.

Marshall's family was no longer a threat to anyone, here or anywhere. Arthur shifted the sleeping wolf closer to the fire and dug his hands into her thick fur, pensive. He had not wished to tell Marshall the truth about what the Hanover patriarch had done to the Cruises earlier, until they had escaped. Now that they were free, Arthur hesitated again.

They possessed one cloak between the two of them, which was being used to keep the wolf's puppies warm. Arthur saw no weapons or tools or anything he could use to hunt with, and even if they had something of that nature, neither he nor Marshall could spend more than an hour from the fire without freezing. They each wore a single, thin layer of clothing and boots.

He glanced at Marshall, who was carefully cradling the sleeping puppies. Guilt fluttered through him, along with an acknowledgment he and Marshall needed one another to survive the forest alone.

He could not reveal the truth now.

The silence between them weighed as heavy as his conscience.

"I can speak to her," Arthur said. "Rather, she speaks to me. Usually in one or two word sentences, no more. I can sense danger as well, in a way unlike any skill a normal man possesses, and I have told you already of my visions of the future."

"You said you have few and they are as solid as dreams."

"That was not entirely true," Arthur admitted. "I cannot control when the visions come, but they are in great detail. My directional sense is not just for determining which cardinal direction we face, but can guide me anywhere I tell it to take me."

Marshall raised his eyebrows. "And you choose now to tell me this because why? You think we will die out here, and you feel the need to confess to your deformities?"

Confess, yes. "Take it how you will." Arthur did not like how it felt to lie to the man who saved his life more than once, and who chose to value the lives of the magical she-wolf and pups when he did not have to. If this kindness were not an indication of Marshall Cruise's nature, buried beneath his skepticism and resentful façade, then what was?

No matter what Arthur's father claimed about the Cruises, and how differently Marshall and Arthur saw the world, Marshall Cruise was a good man.

What other lies of my father's have I adopted without questioning? Arthur did not know this answer, which left him more troubled. Truth had little value to his father, or in their household, and he had never realized how skewed his perception of the world had to have been before this moment.

"What do you recall about the moment before we left?" he asked. "My sister was with us, and yet, she is not here."

"I heard someone shout and woke up in time to see you and the wolf vanish. All of the Natives were in the center of the village and your sister ..." Marshall drifted off. "Is she special, like you?"

Arthur did not respond.

"You lied about why we were hunting down that skinwalker in the first place, so I do not expect absolute honesty. I will, however, assume she possesses deformities of a different nature than yours," Marshall said shortly. "A commotion among the Natives awoke me. When I turned to talk to you, you were already gone. I saw Tiana lift the skinwalker into the air with magic and start to crush him."

It was Arthur's turn to be disbelieving. "Tiana?"

"Yes. That waif with the ghoulish eyes."

Arthur ignored the flush of heat inside him. It was hard to be angry with Marshall, even when he used such a disrespectful tone.

"She flung him against a tree and was crushing him when the wolf appeared out of nowhere and took me away," Marshall said. "I awoke here, beside you."

Arthur was silent. Tiana had never been permitted to allow her deformities to manifest. Their father forbade it, just as he secretly trained Arthur how to use his. Even so, Tiana trusted her brother more than anyone else and had revealed to Arthur a couple of her gifts. She used telekinesis to move her furniture and sometimes glimpsed the future, though not with the detail Arthur did, and she had admitted to crushing Matilda Cruise's head by accident when their stepmother tried to kill Aveline. It was *possible* she could lift a man.

But to lash out at a stranger? Some of the Native women had hit her, and Tiana did not complain or attack them. If she were going to hurt someone, self-defense was the rational time to do it.

"You are certain it was Tiana who did this and not some other deformed person?" Arthur asked, puzzled.

"I have never seen such an act in my life. It is stuck in my head." Marshall tapped his temple. "I know what I saw, Arthur."

"My sister has such deformities, but not the temperament. She would never hurt anyone for any reason," Arthur said.

"If she decided to make an exception, I am glad she chose to murder the skinwalker, or we would all likely be dead. As much as I despise pointless Hanover violence, I would also like to live to see my home again."

Arthur ignored the dig at his family, more interested in determining what motivated Tiana to act rashly. If he foresaw the skinwalker threat, had Tiana as well? He could not otherwise account for what she had done.

He rose.

Tiana, he ordered his magic silently. A faint breeze nudged him, and he faced the direction it indicated.

"Before you make some valiant claim that we need to save your sister, consider the fact we are stranded with a magic wolf and six puppies and little else in the middle of the forest," Marshall told him. "She is safer where she is than we are stranded out here among the Ghouls and wolves, assuming she destroyed the skinwalker as she appeared to be doing."

Without a vision proving Marshall right or wrong, Arthur did not feel nearly as comfortable making such an assumption. His sister had rarely been permitted outside her room and never left the city. She had no way of understanding the threats the Natives and forest posed to her or how to navigate them.

But ... he had seen her running from their father in the latest vision before he awoke. She was alive, though he was unable to guess in what shape.

"We need food and water," Marshall added. "I do not think you will want the wolf or her babies to die out here."

Arthur faced away from the direction in which Tiana was. "Of course not," he agreed. "She saved us again, and apparently, at great expense to herself."

"Then it is your turn to watch the pups while I sleep," Marshall said and stood from his place beside the fire. "They have eaten once and will probably be hungry again soon. I know I am." He approached and held out the bundle of pups. "This cloak is of spring quality, not winter. You will need to hold them to keep them warm."

Arthur accepted the bundle, once again disturbed by Marshall's compassion. Marshall did not coddle the animals but accepted the duty to care for them without question. Being good, *doing* good, was second nature to him.

No one in Arthur's family practiced or valued compassion, either.

Arthur watched the Cruise heir return to the far side of the fire and curl up on the ground, his back to the flames. Arthur sat and unfolded the cloak to peer at the tiny puppies again. Two white, one black, two gray, one brindle. They were piled atop one another, sleeping.

"I wonder if they are magic, too," he murmured.

"It they tell you, let me know," Marshall grumbled.

Arthur replaced the cloak and sat back, cradling the bundle as Marshall had. He shivered and moved closer to the fire. The early spring night was clear and crisp. His breath rose to the skies in visible clouds, and he mulled Marshall's claim about what happened before they were teleported way from the Natives' camp.

Why had the wolf saved them, if her master were in danger?

Why would she save them at all?

Too concerned about his sister to sleep, Arthur shifted the bundle of puppies to the side of the fire where their mother lay. If the wolf were ill, or did not wake up, he would face a difficult decision come morning. They needed to move, for fear of Ghouls or the Natives or hungry cats and wolves catching their scent, but would not go far if they were forced to carry the massive wolf.

Arthur waited until he heard the deep breathing and soft snores of Marshall before creeping closer to the wolf.

"Hey," he whispered and stroked her head. "Can you hear me?"

He stilled his hand and held his breath, waiting. No words emerged.

"I need to know if you are well enough to travel, or if you can heal yourself," he tried again. "I do not possess the healing magic. I know you do. You saved my life at the river."

Tingling, warm energy tickled his fingertips. She did not speak, but a faint vision entered his thoughts. It was too elusive for him to capture. Arthur closed his eyes to concentrate.

This time, he caught the quick, faded image of puppies in his mind.

He smiled. "They are all well and healthy," he reported. Withdrawing his hand, he picked up the bundle of sleeping pups and placed them on her side. "Maybe you can hear their hearts? Or feel their warmth?"

The fur beneath the bundle flushed black. The color blushed outward, darkening her unnatural white fur. The black circled the bundle and extended several inches out in each direction before it stopped.

Was this the magic of the wolves? A sign of some sort? Arthur had no way to explain her coat's return to its normal color in the area surrounding her babies. He rested his hand on her head once more and closed his eyes.

"All of us will be in danger if we remain here," he told her. "Of all the questions I want to ask you, only one needs to be answered now. If you have strength for more, we can talk for as long as you have the strength. But first, I must know, will you be well enough to travel soon?"

The image of a sunrise floated through his head before vanishing.

"Good," he said and released a sigh. His eyes went to Marshall, who slept soundly. Arthur had no intention of leaving his sister alone in the forest, even if what Marshall claimed was true. Arthur would rather hunt down a skinwalker and angry Natives than tell the man quickly becoming his friend what happened to his family.

TWO

ARTHUR DOZED OFF AND ON, too concerned about being exposed in the forest to sleep for long. When dawn crept through the clouds and past thick layers of branches, he roused himself fully. The bundle of pups in his arms was squirming. He shifted closer to the wolf and unwrapped them, setting the pups down close to their mother's belly. Despite their closed eyes, they sensed her and climbed over one another and the cloak to nurse.

He watched, smiling, then draped the cloak over the wolf and her babies to keep the morning chill from reaching them. The she-wolf remained silver-white, with the exception of the bloom of black from where he'd placed the pups on her side. He glanced at the wolf's face then back.

Her eyes were open. She didn't move, but she watched him.

"Good morning," he whispered. "Are you well enough to travel?"

Food.

Arthur sighed. "We have none and no weapons to kill game. We will find food today," he said firmly.

She did not respond, and he wondered if the self-sufficient wolf was irritated with humans who could not hunt for themselves.

Arthur stood with a grimace. His muscles were stiff. The cold morning carried a warm breeze, one he hoped meant the winter was finally ready to give way to spring. Shivering, he crossed to wake Marshall. The Cruise heir was trembling from cold in his sleep.

"Marshall, time to go!" Arthur said and shook his friend awake.

Marshall groaned. He stretched onto his stomach and then sighed loudly. "My stomach is eating itself!"

"Mine, too," Arthur said. "That is why we need to go ..." He tilted his head and paused with a glance at the wolf.

The image in his mind was not the direction he had wanted. Not towards the city, not towards Tiana.

"North," he said.

"North?" Marshall asked and pushed himself onto his knees. "Is that not the opposite direction of anywhere we want to be?"

"It is." Arthur looked away from the she-wolf.

Marshall caught his glance and looked between the two. "Whose decision is this?" he asked.

"Hers."

"Why are we considering going north?"

Safe. Babies, she answered

"We cannot take her with us to the city," Arthur reasoned. "She cannot travel alone with her babes. We will situate her somewhere safe with her pups, then rescue Tiana and go home."

If Marshall doubted Arthur's plan, he did not show it. "We will need your father's army to rescue her. Our enemies will not free her willingly."

"If that is the case ..." Arthur trailed off, unwilling to promise anything. Neither Marshall nor Tiana could return to Lost Vegas, or the Hanover leader would hurt them both. Arthur did not know how to protect his friend, especially when Marshall was ignorant of the danger. Traveling north would give him time to think.

Marshall shook his head. "If you had told me a month ago I would be at the mercy of a Hanover and a dog, I would have thought you madder than your father."

Arthur said nothing and hopped in place to keep warm.

The she-wolf had sat up, tugged off the cloak, and was grooming her babies. When they were clean and fed, the pups piled up next to her for warmth. Arthur collected them gently and replaced them in the cloak.

The wolf stood and shook off the leaves clinging to her fur. She gave the men a long look before turning and walking into the forest.

Arthur hastily kicked dirt over the embers of their fire. Marshall followed her, hugging himself and grumbling about the cold, lack of food, and the cursed Hanover's. Arthur trailed and listened to him with newfound patience – and a great deal of dread.

"Will we ever go home?" Marshall asked.

"Yes, we will," Arthur answered. It was inevitable that he would return to his home, and inevitable that Marshall discovered the truth. Of every thought on Arthur's mind, he could not help wondering if he had the power and influence necessary to save the remaining Cruise from his father. Marshall would hate Arthur for hiding the latest Hanover massacre, but this would not deter Arthur from protecting him.

Marshall grumbled more quietly this time.

Cold and miserable, Arthur focused on formulating the explanation he would have to give Marshall eventually. For once, his father was not present to give his side of the story, even if his side was often an excuse. Arthur had accepted all his father's excuses, not because he did not know better, but because he hoped one day to make a difference in how the city was managed. He could not do that, if he challenged his father and lost his position as heir.

As they walked through the awakening forest, Arthur could not help realizing there was no excuse he could accept for what his father had done and what his father would try to do to Marshall and possibly Tiana. He was beyond choosing blind obedience, beyond towing his father's line to those who already knew better. He could not see himself returning to the role of dutiful son and ignoring all he had chosen not to see before. Neither did he see himself walking away from the city that had suffered long enough under the rule of mad Hanovers'. He had always intended to become the leader his father was not, to help the city rather than punish it.

Where did that leave him? If he wanted to help the city and repair the damage done by his family, did he not have to return to his father's nest and play the role expected of him?

His eyes went to the back of Marshall's head.

What if returning meant sacrificing his friend and sister?

He could think of only one way to protect them, an option he had not wanted to entertain for weeks.

"Tell me again about this alleged plot to overthrow my father," he spoke quietly.

Marshall glanced over his shoulder at him then back. "Are you addressing me or the wolf?" he snapped through chattering teeth.

Arthur rolled his eyes. "You. I may be willing to talk to your ... friends," he said with effort. "You said there were people who wanted to rid the city of my father."

"You want to betray them to your father."

"No. I want to hear their plan for saving the city from him." Arthur was careful not to advocate for the murder of his father, even though he suspected that was the plan.

Marshall stopped and faced him. "Why?" he asked, gaze sharpening as he studied Arthur. "You have been ignoring me for weeks when I tried to address you on this matter!"

Arthur measured his words before speaking. "I have heard you, even if I did not respond," he said. "Something about our adventure to the forest has changed my perception. I do not disagree with you, Marshall, about the city deserving better than my father."

Marshall's eyebrow lifted. "Suddenly, you do not disagree with me? Does that mean you support what I have said, or are you planning to use this knowledge against me? Or is this a moment of weakness you will regret when we return?"

"Perhaps I have had a vision of what may come to be, if I do not prevent my father from acting as he intends to," Arthur said. "How entrenched is this movement against him? Are you the only one in it?"

"No." Marshall studied him until they both began to shake harder from the lack of movement. He spun away and began trailing the wolf again.

"Who else is involved?"

Marshall was quiet for a moment.

"I am sorry, Marshall, but I need reassurances this movement has the ability to usurp my father and is not the daydream of the Cruises alone."

"Many powerful men are involved, including my father, and someone close to your father," Marshall replied. His tone had lost its edge. "And ... Ingram."

"Gavin Ingram? My father's security advisor?" Arthur had not known if this plan extended beyond the Cruises or not, but the mention of the Ingram patriarch, whose prominent family was the third most influential and wealthiest in the outer city, led him to wonder if it were possible to cultivate Marshall's accomplices as allies. He stood a better chance of outmaneuvering, or outright overthrowing, his father, if so.

Assuming his father did not witness his betrayal in a vision.

"The same," Marshall said.

"Then this plan has deep roots in the elite."

"It does. Very deep. There are more supporters for our plan than your father has supporting him. Four and a half centuries of mad rule is enough," Marshall confirmed slowly. "I am supposed to test you to ensure you were not like your father, then sway you to our side, and if I succeed, introduce you to Ingram and the others upon our return."

"What is your determination? About me?"

"You are arrogant, proud and foolish – but you are not your father."

Arthur did not deny the assessment. In fact, he found it sound, even though it came from a Cruise.

"You are truly interested in usurping your father?" Marshall asked with another uncertain glance towards him.

"I want to protect those I care about and my city," Arthur replied. "If there was a way to do it without challenging my father, I would prefer that."

"And if there is not?"

Arthur hesitated. "I am open to an alternative."

"This is more than I ever thought I would hear you say," Marshall said.

Unable to identify a path where those he cared about lived, and he returned to his duty as the Hanover heir, Arthur lost himself in troubled thought.

They walked until midday. Spring came in full force this day, after the longest winter he could recall. By noon, he was sweating from the heat and sun. Seasonal streams formed as the snow and ice melted, and the forest filled with the movement of animals who no longer feared leaving their burrows. Squirrels leapt from branch to branch above their heads while rabbits rustled in the underbrush.

The she-wolf panted and kept several dozen feet ahead of them, pausing on occasion to ensure they followed. Marshall quietly picked his way through the forest, and Arthur cradled the pups as they walked.

Reaching a stream, they all stopped in silence. Marshall dropped to his knees, cupped his hands and drank from the trickling waters. The she-wolf drank for a moment then approached Arthur. She nudged the pups with her nose. Arthur set them down and unwrapped them while the mother wolf nudged his hands to hasten him. He moved aside for her to inspect the puppies.

"From winter to summer in half a day's time," Marshall complained.

Arthur dunked his head and shivered at the icy water before drinking his fill. "I hope this holds out."

"Me, too."

The she-wolf fed and cleaned her babies. Marshall gathered the tiny wolves and bundled them up again.

Together, the two of them set out once more, following the wolf as she continued north.

Not far past the stream, she stopped abruptly, head elevated.

Arthur and Marshall froze and waited. Her tail stayed down, her ears forward. She did not growl as she had when she saw Ghouls, and she did not appear alarmed.

Shifting their direction, she walked another half a mile before pausing again at the top of a shallow gully.

Marshall's breath caught, and Arthur hurried to his side.

At the bottom of the gully lay the skinwalker, half man, half beast, unmoving. Two of his limbs were at odd angles. His beast fur was matted with blood and his human skin smeared with it.

The wolf's tail wagged. She trotted down the gully to the still skinwalker and began to lick his bloodied skin.

Marshall cursed.

Arthur was still.

"We should have guessed she would lead us to the beast that's murdered hundreds!" Marshall muttered.

Arthur had a different reaction. "Tiana did that?" he asked, surveying the gashes, crushed body parts, broken limbs and blood of the mangled man.

"Are you not concerned we found the creature that murders entire villages in one breath?" Marshall demanded.

"He can murder no one now," Arthur pointed out.

"Good. I hope he dies here."

"You sound like a Hanover," Arthur said, amused.

Marshall glared at him.

Help him. The she-wolf's whisper was anxious.

Any desire Arthur had to let the skinwalker rot in place was lost when the she-wolf spoke to him. She did not have to ask again, not after saving his life a second time.

"She saved our lives, Marshall, and she brought us here for a reason," Arthur started. "We cannot leave them like this. She is too weak, and he is –"

Before he could finish the sentence, Marshall was striding angrily towards the wolf and skinwalker. "The sooner we are done with this, the sooner we can go home and overthrow your father!" he snapped.

Arthur almost smiled. He asked his magic for help knowing which direction to go in and was pleased with the response. A village belonging to the Newe, their Native allies, was located less than three miles away.

His satisfaction faded when he reached the skinwalker and witnessed his mangled condition firsthand.

The man was alive and blinking, glaring at Arthur and Marshall.

"I ... found ... you again," the Native said in a gravelly voice. His breathing was ragged and irregular, though he displayed no outward sign of pain.

"I believe we found you," Marshall retorted.

Arthur debated how to handle the skinwalker and squatted beside him. "We can help you," he began. "But if we do so, when you are well, you must leave the territory around Lost Vegas for a thousand miles, without causing any further loss of life, and never return. You have hurt too many people."

The skinwalker gave a wheezy laugh.

"You have no room to negotiate right now," Marshall seconded in a hard tone. "I am usually the diplomatic one between the two of us, but for once, I find myself agreeing with a Hanover. Either do as Arthur says, or we leave you here to die."

"I ... agree," wheezed the dangerous Native.

Arthur assessed the beast that was half transformed. "You are a mess," he said. "Can you choose one form? Preferably human, as you will be easier to carry."

The skinwalker closed his eyes.

Arthur waited for a response and then witnessed the beast changing slowly into a naked, fully human form.

"A word," Marshall said to him.

Arthur stood.

Marshall moved a short distance away. "How exactly are we going carry him and the pups? And where are we going to find help? His wounds are beyond our ability to dress without the proper supplies."

"There is a friendly village three miles from here. We can have him there by sunset," Arthur said.

"Sunset? Three miles?"

"We can build a stretcher out of branches."

"And use leaves and fairy magic to bind his wounds?"

Arthur sighed. "Do you have a better idea?"

"I do. One of us goes to the village and asks for help then returns with a healer and enough men to carry him."

"Very well, Cruise. We will adopt your plan," Arthur said, surprised Marshall had an answer that was sound. "Your plan, your choice on who goes to the village."

"I do not want to be left with that thing," Marshall admitted quietly, eyes on the skinwalker. "Agreement or not, I do not trust it. But you have the ability to navigate that I do not."

"Take the she-wolf. She can do what I can."

"Will she leave him and her pups to go with me?"

Arthur approached the wolf, which continued to lick the skin-walker's wounds.

"Would you accompany Marshall to a Native village to fetch help?" Arthur asked the animal, ignoring the native.

The wolf lifted her head.

"You would have to leave your babes and your master. But we need the assistance of the Natives in the village. Marshall can speak to them on your behalf. They are allies of my family," Arthur stated.

The wolf gazed at him for a long moment, not blinking.

"You will be back by the pups' suppertime," Marshall added. "I cannot navigate the forest alone, and we cannot leave your pups and master exposed. One of us must stay. Arthur is more adept than I at treating the wounded. He is a Hanover. He does not mind blood on his hands."

Arthur rolled his eyes.

The she-wolf looked between them then at the skinwalker.

Yes, she answered.

Arthur nodded to Marshall.

"Do you know the place you seek?" Arthur asked the animal. He formed a vision of the path and the destination.

Without answering him, the wolf spun and loped in the direction of the village.

Marshall hurried after her.

Arthur watched them go and then moved closer to the skinwalker. He sat down on a log and placed the bundle on the ground between them.

"How are they?" the skinwalker wheezed.

"Healthy from what I know," Arthur replied. He peeled off his shirt and began tearing it into strips. "How is it our paths continue to cross?"

"You ... hunted me," the skinwalker responded. "I hunted you."

"You hunted me?" Arthur asked. "You did not seem interested in me when I was stalking you all those days."

"Did not know ... your name."

"Ah. You did not think my father would allow his heir to wander the forest like a lost dog. The secret is, he did not know." After a quick assessment, Arthur shifted forward to bind the worst of the wounds. He started with the Native's right leg and then paused. "Have you always been missing your left leg?"

"It will return."

Arthur studied the skinwalker's features. They were tight, and an unhealthy gray shaded half his face. "Because it is magic," he said. The skinwalker was the man in the world he least wanted as a companion, but as long as the creature continued talking, he would not fall asleep and die from his substantial head wounds. "The legend I heard claims your magic lives in your leg." Arthur shifted forward to look at the stump. "This was not a wound. You were born deformed?"

The skinwalker did not answer.

Arthur moved on to the other wounds. When he ran out of shirt, he removed the pups from their cloak and tore it in half. He left half for the pups and ripped the rest into strips.

"Who did this to you?" he asked, wanting to hear someone other than Tiana had.

"A little girl with Ghoul eyes."

Arthur was quiet for a moment. "I did not know she was capable of this."

"You know her?"

"My sister. The one you swore not to harm."

The Native gave another rattling, shaky laugh. "I have been lying here ... planning her death. Nothing has given me ... this much pleasure in years."

"Unfortunately for you, you already agreed to spare her," Arthur reminded him. His thoughts went briefly to the changed vision.

The Native grimaced as Arthur cinched tight one of his wounds.

"I do not know how she could do this to any living creature or how you are alive at all."

"She did not want me dead ... or ... I'd be dead," the skinwalker said.

"There is that." Arthur's hands paused, and he recalled what Tiana had told him about murdering Marshall's sister, who had been Tiana's stepmother. Had her first experience wielding her power scared her out of murdering anyone else? "I hunted you, because I had visions of you killing her. How is that possible when she can do something like this?" The question was more for him than the skinwalker.

To his surprise, the skinwalker answered. "What did you see? Exactly? Tell me again."

Arthur's hands paused. He remembered how interested the skinwalker had seemed when he mentioned the vision before, at the frozen river. He began to wipe and bind the wounds again.

"You were chasing her across the grasslands ..." Arthur murmured and told him the scene he had witnessed nightly for months. When he finished, the skinwalker was silent.

Arthur shifted forward to ensure the man still lived.

"Then you did not see me kill her," the skinwalker said.

"No, but why else would you be pursuing her?" And why was their father now in the vision?

"I do not know," the skinwalker admitted. "But what you saw was ... what you saw. It was not more or less than this."

"You think I should not assume you were trying to hurt her?"

"What you saw was what you saw."

The skinwalker had a point, and Arthur was not certain he liked taking advice from a beast that had slaughtered every living being in three villages.

"You said you were hunting me?" he asked. "Why?"

"Paid to hunt people."

"Who paid you?"

The skinwalker smiled.

Arthur's family had never been beloved. His father uncovered at least one plot a year to assassinate him and another to assassinate his heir. "For once, I do not blame someone for wanting my family dead," he said, thoughts on Marshall.

"He wanted you ... alive."

"Ransom is a good motivation as well. My family is wealthy, and my father powerful," he said. "Who is this man? How did he come to have enough money to tempt anyone to kidnap a Hanover?"

"My price is never money," the skinwalker reminded him.

"He must have had something of value."

"Every man has something of value."

Arthur waited, dissatisfied with the response. When the skinwalker did not elaborate, he pressed for an answer. "Where were you supposed to take me, assuming you succeeded?"

"Not far from here."

"So he is local."

The skinwalker was quiet.

"Does it matter now who it is?" Arthur prodded. "You have failed. Why not tell me?"

"It is not a matter of failure that keeps me quiet," snapped the skinwalker moodily. "You will not believe me if I reveal who he is."

Arthur leaned forward in interest. "Who is it?"

"A man with a mark like the one you bear."

Arthur touched his shoulder, where the tattoo of an eagle was located. The sacred mark was born only by Hanover's. "My father?" he asked, surprised.

"No."

"No one else bears this mark, except for my sister."

"I told you. You would not believe me."

It was hard to think when his mind was fatigued and his body starving, but Arthur could only draw one conclusion. "Another Hanover? One outside the city?"

"He tracked me down when I was two thousand miles away," the skinwalker explained. "Hired me without asking my price."

"Interesting tale, but to my knowledge, no other Hanover is alive at the moment. Who was it really?"

The skinwalker muttered something under his breath and dropped his head back, falling silent.

Sensing he was done speaking on the topic, Arthur tried another topic to encourage him to stay awake. "Your wolf. How did you come by her?"

"Not wolf. Guide."

"Guide? She leads you places and you murder everyone in them?" Arthur asked, confused.

The skinwalker laughed hoarsely. "No. She is my spirit guide."

"From the spirit world."

"Yes."

"Hmm. A spirit wolf. Well, I cannot deny she is no normal animal."

"She has been too weak to heal or travel far," the skinwalker said.

"Her pups are spirit babies?"

"One may be. It is rare for more than ... one to possesses the gift she does."

Arthur looked at the pile of warm, fuzzy puppies. "Is their father a wolf or spirit or ... you?" he asked.

"No father."

"Interesting." Arthur finished binding the last of the major wounds and sat back. "Knowing what you do now of my sister, why do you think you were in my vision?"

"You said I was in this form for most of the visions."

"That is correct."

The skinwalker gazed at the blue sky visible through the pine needle canopy above. "I rarely kill in this form," he said at last.

"You do not believe you were pursuing her to kill her."

"No."

"Why else would you be pursuing her?"

"It was your ... vision. Not mine."

Arthur dwelled on this tidbit of information. The discussion changed his initial interpretation of visions he had of the skinwalker chasing Tiana. He was less clear as to why his father would be in a field outside the city, since no Hanover leader ever left the city after ascending to his place in charge, but his father's fury was unmistakable.

"After you promised not to hurt her, when we were at the river, the visions ceased," Arthur said. "I cannot imagine you were not chasing her for good reasons. Thus your promise must have stopped that version of her future. I did nothing else in the span of that day to affect it."

"Maybe she did."

"For a murderous beast, you are rather wise," Arthur stated reluctantly.

"I have lived ... two, maybe three lifetimes. You owe me for granting this promise," the skinwalker reminded me. "More so after your sister tried to tear me apart."

"I will uphold my side of the deal," Arthur said. "What is it you want?"

"I will tell you when the time is right."

Uneasiness twisted Arthur's empty stomach. The skinwalker had not said he would reveal the price when he decided what it was. Which meant, he already knew. What was he waiting for? Did he have visions as well?

What could a man evil enough to slaughter babes in their mothers' arms possibly want from Arthur?

Who is worse – this man or my father? Arthur contemplated with no small amount of surprise his father had competition.

The skinwalker's eyes closed.

"You must stay awake. I do not care if you die, but our common friend does. She has been too good to me for me not to act in her favor." Arthur gathered up the pups and shifted back to the log. "What is your given name? I have heard several variations."

"The man who bore ... my given name is dead. I call myself Black Wolf, in honor of my guide."

"You murdered my friends, Black Wolf," Arthur said. "Good men. Men I have known my entire life."

"They are here with me."

"What?"

Black Wolf smiled coldly. "All the spirits ... all *my* spirits ... they stay with me forever. Say farewell, if you wish. Your friends are standing behind you."

Arthur whipped around without seeing anyone. He relaxed. "You are hallucinating."

"You believe in your magic but not mine," the skinwalker observed.

"Your magic is terrifying. Nonetheless, you have lost too much blood not to be delirious." With no food for two days, Arthur was growing too uncomfortable to continue the discussion. He huddled with the pups on the log, feeling ill himself.

The skinwalker's eyes closed once more, and his breathing became deeper.

"Awake." Arthur nudged him with his foot.

Black Wolf's eyes opened again.

"My ... friend," Arthur started. "One of those you attacked. He did not die, but from my understanding, he is badly wounded. My sister claims you inflicted him with a wound that will not heal."

"Maybe."

"It is not outside the possible?"

"If I hurt him in this form, the wound is like any other," the skinwalker explained. "If I was in my other forms, then the wound was made with magic."

"How is a magical wound healed?"

"Only I can heal it."

"And in return, you would want something from me," Arthur said. "If I promise to pay it, will you heal it?"

The skinwalker peered at him closely for a moment then relaxed his head to the ground once more. "No."

"No? Why not?" Arthur prodded, mind on Warner and what Tiana had revealed about his lover's condition.

"When I reveal the price for not killing your sister, you will understand. It's rare when anyone can afford my services twice."

A chill ran through Arthur. "I would do anything for him."

"You may have the opportunity to prove this."

What could Black Wolf ask of him that would make him unwilling to pay a second time?

It seemed too simple for the price to be his life. Why would the skinwalker hide it if so?

Arthur surveyed the skinwalker's body, not at all convinced the creature would survive until sundown. With his attention split between Black Wolf and his own misery, he shifted to sit on the ground with his back to the log and rested his head back. The pups stilled soon after he did. He began to doze fitfully and soon forgot his efforts to keep the creature awake.

No visions formed, and the hunger in his belly turned to pain.

No more than three hours later, however, he felt the warm lick of a rough tongue against his cheek and opened his eyes. Too distracted by his own misery, he had not heard the wolf's approach.

"Hi there," he said and shifted to sit up straight. As if sensing their mother, the pups began to squirm. She nudged the bundle. Arthur set it down and then glanced around. "I hope you brought help."

Slow. She replied and then settled onto the ground beside him to feed her babies. Her fur was marbled black and white.

Arthur rose and went still, overcome by dizziness. When the spell passed, he returned to the skinwalker's side. "Are you dead?" he asked.

"Not ... yet." Black Wolf's eyes cracked open.

"I would recommend you not reveal your identity as a skinwalker," Arthur advised with some amusement. "You decimated one of the Newe villages."

Black Wolf grunted in response.

"Arthur!" Marshall's call came from several hundred feet away. "I lost the damn wolf!"

"Here, Marshall," Arthur croaked loudly.

Minutes later, the Cruise heir appeared, trailed by four Natives. Marshall had been provided a change of clothes and carried a satchel across his chest. He reached Arthur and pulled the satchel off to hand to him.

"I brought their healer and people to carry him," Marshall reported.

Arthur reached into the satchel and felt a canteen and something wrapped in canvas. He pulled it out, smelling the food before he opened it and unwrapped it to reveal a thick venison sandwich on flatbread.

He ate it as fast as he could, oblivious to the movement and discussion going on around him. When he was done, he drank all the water in the canteen and lowered it then threw his head back with a satisfied sigh.

"I could eat a herd of buffalo," he said.

Marshall moved closer to him. "They were reluctant to help. I promised them our fathers would compensate them well."

Arthur nodded. "I can imagine our allies are uncomfortable, given the recent events. Skinwalkers, Hanover's ..." He shook his head.

"The Natives believe your father means to burn the forest down to find his heirs," Marshall said. "Even our Newe allies are preparing for possible war."

Arthur watched the healer strip off the skinwalker's bandages, clean the wounds, and re-bandage them. Two of the Natives stood waiting with a stretcher.

"I know you wish to find your sister, but we need to return before your father does something rash," Marshall urged him. "The Natives claim the smoke from the city is so thick, it hides the city at dawn and dusk, and he is calling in favors from every ally he has to amass weapons and food."

Arthur listened, his stomach sinking. Even he did not know what his unpredictable father would do in this circumstance. The Hanover hold on the city would be threatened by the loss of both his children, and the political challenges were likely to mount. Tiana was safe outside the city, as safe as she could be. Arthur could return safely, but Marshall could not, and he would not allow the fiery fate to befall his friend. Not yet, until Arthur had bargained for Marshall's life or found support among his father's detractors.

Arthur glanced down at the pups, which were being cleaned by their mother, then at the men loading the skinwalker onto the stretcher. "We both need rest and food. We can discuss our plans to leave in the morning," he said, aware Marshall was waiting for his decision.

"Your sister will be safe. She can take care of herself," Marshall said, sensing his hesitation.

Arthur nodded. He did not believe for one second he should abandon Tiana, no matter how many people claimed she had great powers. But neither did he want Marshall's compassion directed at *him*. The guilt sliding through him was enough without his friend's understanding look.

He moved away from Marshall to gather the pups. The wolf stood and then carefully watched over the men carefully moving her master. Arthur cradled the pups and fell into step behind Marshall, ahead of the stretcher, and behind the Native leading them back towards the village. His stomach growled again, but he did not hear it, not when his mind was raging between telling Marshall the truth and leaving before the Cruise heir could stop him. He could not save his friend and sister unless he reached his father before either of them.

THREE

AVELINE AWOKE RAVENOUS AND FEVERED. Sweat rolled down the sides of her face, and she pushed off the blankets trapping her to the narrow bed. One of her arms was heavy, clumsy, probably wounded, though she experienced no pain anywhere.

"Finally," Tiana's soft exclamation was followed by the touch of her cool palms against Aveline's cheeks.

It was not the warmth of her surroundings alone that caused Aveline's discomfort, but the eerie charge radiating off Tiana, usually present when she used magic or was agitated. Her head throbbed, and her thoughts were laced with the heaviness indicative of some medicines.

"Air," Aveline croaked. She opened her eyes – and saw only darkness.

The charge lessened, and she heard Tiana shift and move around her. Seconds later, a cool breeze touched the exposed skin of her legs and feet.

"Am I blind?" Aveline asked.

Tiana laughed. She lifted a cloth off Aveline's face.

Aveline blinked rapidly. She didn't feel hurt or tired – but something was off about her body. Tiana's smile distracted her. The Hanover girl sported a yellow bruise around one eye and along one cheek and wore the traditional dress of the Native enemies of the city: fleece, fur and leather.

A Native peered down at Aveline with a sharp, assessing gaze, leaving her with no doubt this was a healer.

"Can you sit?" the middle-aged woman asked.

Aveline did so, frowning when she caught herself careening to the side of her heavy arm. She steadied herself and looked around. She was inside a small, round tent that smelled of herbs. The tent flap was pinned open, and she glimpsed the cloudy sky and trees outside.

She shook off the blanket covering her arm.

"Wait!" Tiana stretched across her to stop her from flinging off the blanket completely.

Aveline stilled, but Tiana did not let her go.

"What do you remember last?" Tiana asked her, black gaze studying her closely.

Aveline thought back. "Jose, Rocky and I arrived here and ... there was a commotion." Most of her memories were a blur after arriving to the encampment. "I remember feeling hot and sick during our travels and more so when we arrived. Am I diseased? What happened?"

"You are suffering from a deformity," the healer said.

"You transformed into a skinwalker," Tiana said simultaneously.

Aveline looked between the two of them. "What?"

"Half skinwalker," Tiana corrected herself. "Leaving the city may have caused you to try to transform. But because you are only half skinwalker, you could not transform fully. Your body tried and it almost killed you."

Aveline started to laugh. "Have you been reading your fairy tales again?" she asked.

"No, Aveline. I am very serious," Tiana said. "But you know what this means? We are both very special. I always knew you were and now I know why." She appeared pleased.

"I'm not deformed. I'm not magical. I'm not ..." Aveline lifted her heavy arm as she spoke and reached up to scratch her head.

From the elbow down, her arm resembled that of a bear, down to the massive paw and four inch talons.

She stared.

"You have to stay calm!" Tiana said. She hurried around the bed and draped the blanket over her arm again. "You cannot change on your own, but your body tries when you are distressed."

Aveline stared at the blanket, unable to believe what she had seen. She began to tense, and panic fluttered through her. As if in response, thick fur crept up her expanding bicep.

"Calm," Tiana said again.

Aveline met her gaze.

The Hanover girl was not at all alarmed by the sight of her deformed arm.

"Tiana, what's wrong with me?" Aveline managed.

"Nothing," Tiana said firmly. "We are both special. Did your father or mother not murder a thousand people in three days?"

Aveline nodded and swallowed hard.

"This is how. As a skinwalker. You are only half, so you are not transforming fully. When you had nightmares, half of you turned into a bear and the other half either remained human or turned into a great cat," Tiana explained. "It was quite confusing for us."

Aveline shook off the blanket again and lifted her bear claw. She flexed her hand and then released, dismayed when the bear paw responded to her commands as if it were really her hand. She squeezed it closed.

"It will make you an even better assassin," Tiana added. "You can cleave a person in two with one hand."

Aveline was silent. Deep down inside, next to the panic subdued by pain medication, was the acknowledgement of what she had always known: she was different. She had spent her life aware of her devil's blood and the curse she inherited, without ever expecting it to manifest into her physical body.

"Do you not agree?" Tiana asked. "Your claws are larger than my fingers." She took the paw in both hand and tugged Aveline's fist open to display the talons. Aveline felt her cool palms again, this time through the fur and skin of her bear claw.

It really was *her*.

"I guess it will make me more effective," Aveline allowed. "But how do I live a normal life with this?" She waved the bear paw. "I'm deformed!"

Tiana's smile was warm, understanding. Peering into the Hanover girl's Ghoulish eyes, Aveline realized what she had said.

"I didn't mean ... Tiana, you've always wanted to leave the city anyway, to go somewhere where you would fit in. I just want to stay in Lost Vegas and be like my father," Aveline said weakly. "I cannot exactly blend into a crowd with a hand like this. I am sorry if I hurt your feelings, Tiana, but I don't want to be deformed."

"You did not," Tiana assured her. "You are appalled to be different, but I am happy not to be alone anymore. I am happy my closest friend is like me. I am the selfish one. I should apologize to you."

Tiana Hanover did not have a selfish bone in her body, and Aveline knew it.

"You can wear a glove," Tiana suggested.

This time, Aveline reviewed what she wanted to say before speaking. There was no hiding a deformity this size and no glove that would accommodate four-inch claws. The transformation turned her lower arm from its normal size to the thickness of her thigh. "Maybe," she said for Tiana's sake.

"We are like sisters now," Tiana said and smiled again.

Aveline had a hard time finding any good in her circumstances. It would take a lot of work to hide her deformity in the city, where she was likely to be burnt at the stakes by Tiana's father, if discovered. With another look at Tiana's smile, Aveline kept her concerns quiet and studied her massive paw.

Tiana was right about being able to slash a person into pieces, she admitted. It would help her coerce people into doing or saying what she wanted. People like the man who betrayed her.

Aware of Tiana's hopeful gaze, Aveline released the breath she held and nodded. The fur crept down her arm, and her bicep returned to its normal size. "This can be useful," she said. "Once I'm used to it."

She did not need to look at Tiana to feel the Hanover girl's excitement.

"Where are my clothes?" she asked and glanced down. She was naked beneath the blankets.

"You have been sleeping for two days. Every time you trans-formed, you tore apart the clothing you wore," Tiana explained and twisted to see the healer. "Will you examine her again?"

Aveline gritted her teeth in irritation. She was headachy and groggy from the medication the healer had given her. The skin of her bicep started to stretch again in response to her emotion. Forcing herself to relax, she sat with tried patience as the healer examined her quickly.

With a brisk nod, the Native moved away from her.

Tiana stood waiting, Native clothing in her arms. She appeared comfortable, if not outright cheerful, dressed like one of the Diné who had declared war on her family and Lost Vegas.

"My clothing is shredded?" Aveline asked.

"It is," Tiana said and rested the Native clothing on the bed. "But you are one of them. You will fit right in."

Aveline eyed the garb without moving.

"Was your mother not a Native?" Tiana prodded.

Aware both of them were watching her, Aveline nodded. "She died at my birth," she said. *Allegedly.*

Leaving the city had been worse than she ever expected it to be. She had begun to doubt the foundation of her life and now, she was deformed. She had always known the devil's blood ran through her veins. Was this what her father had tried to tell her? Why he taught her to control her anger never to lash out at anyone? Was skinwalking the devil's curse? If so, why had he not told her directly what would happen, if she did not control her emotions?

Why had he never transformed into a beast form in front of her to show her what form her fate would take?

Rocky's insistence that Aveline's mother did not die at birth returned, along with the claim her mother – not her father, as she had been told – had been the one possessed by devil's blood who massacred a thousand people in three days.

She did not want to believe her father would lie to her.

"The skinwalker tribe is said to come from the far north," the Native was saying. "Your mother was far from her people."

Why would her father keep this truth from her, too?

Aveline flung off her blankets. "Yeah, well, maybe she realized skinwalkers are terrible people," she said. She dressed quickly. "Where are Jose and Rocky?"

"They are safe," Tiana said. "Everyone is in this village, except for Arthur and Marshall Cruise."

"Is your brother well?" Aveline asked.

"I believe so," she replied. "I had a vision of him last night. He is alive."

"And *you?*"

"Their chief has been very kind to me," Tiana replied. "They hate my father, too."

Aveline snorted. "But are you free to leave? A prisoner?"

"They are being unnecessarily kind, considering whose daughter I am," Tiana said.

Aveline's instincts, honed by learning to survive the streets, were nowhere near as assured or calm as Tiana's. Even if the Hanover patriarch did not want his deformed daughter back, he would use her to get what he wanted, and so would his mortal enemies. Tiana was at ease and smiling, as if she were a guest, but Aveline guessed that was far from the case, especially since Arthur was no longer in this tribe's possession.

"You even have a feather," Aveline murmured, uncertain why she was disturbed to see Tiana in the clothing of her enemies. The feather was pinned in Tiana's hair, a streak of black against the blond.

"I earned it," Tiana said quietly, solemnly.

Aveline's eyebrows quirked in amusement. "What you have done?"

"I took a life."

Aveline knew nothing of the Natives' traditions and wondered why Tiana had revealed killing Matilda to anyone. Her head ached too much for her to think clearly about everything. "If you want to wear it, then do it," she said. "If they are forcing you to, then don't."

"They have not forced me to do anything."

"I find it hard to believe you are being treated well by your father's enemies."

"You will see. Their chief is very kind," Tiana added. "He requested to speak to you when you were awake, if you feel well enough?"

"Definitely," Aveline said, suspecting she was going to have to help Tiana navigate the politics of this place.

"Thank you," Tiana said to the healer.

Aveline followed her out of the tent into the village. Tiana had no chains, no one watching her at all that Aveline could find. The Hanover girl moved through the village unchallenged and paused outside the largest of the temporary tents located towards the center of the village.

"Sir?" she called. "Aveline is awake."

After a pause, the entrance was flung open by a Native not much older than Rocky.

For the first time, Aveline saw Tiana wilt, as she often had in the city. Her eyes dropped, shoulders hunched, and she stepped aside.

I hate that, Aveline thought. The fur on her bear arm expanded, and she forced herself to breathe deeply.

"Come," the Native said curtly to Aveline.

Already disliking him, Aveline nonetheless obeyed and entered the warm tent. Tiana remained outside, and the flap closed behind her. A fire and a single bulb lit the interior enough for Aveline to see the form of an elderly man seated near the fire. He was bundled in blankets despite the overly warm tent.

"It pleases me to see you well," the older man said and peered up at her.

Aveline started to cross her arms and then stopped when her bear claw interfered. "Am I a prisoner?" she asked.

"You are a guest, until my father decides otherwise," the younger man said in a hard tone. "He wishes to speak to you about the Hanover girl."

Here comes the bad news, Aveline thought and braced herself to learn that Tiana had been lied to.

"Please, sit in comfort," the older man seconded and motioned to a spot near him. "I am Elk Hunter. This is my son, Diving Eagle. We have much to discuss." He paused and coughed hard enough for his face to turn bright red.

Diving Eagle handed him a wooden goblet of water.

"You are her guardian, are you not?" the elderly man asked when he had recovered.

"I am," Aveline replied. "Appointed by her brother and father."

"You entered my village subversively."

She said nothing.

"I wish to speak to you openly about the circumstances you both find yourselves in. I value your honesty."

Aveline hesitated then sat opposite him. "My friends? Jose and Rocky? Are they in these same circumstances?" she asked.

"Jose is an ally, and claims Rocky is his protector," the chief said. "How true this is does not concern me. What concerns me most is the Hanover in our midst. Your friends will remain here, pending your agreement to our terms, and the Hanover carrying out what she has agreed to already."

"They're hostages."

"Yes."

Aveline swallowed hard. "She is nothing like her father or her brother," Aveline said. "She will keep whatever promise you forced her into making. Your grievances could not be directed toward a more innocent person."

"I am aware she is different," Elk Hunter acknowledged. "And we all saw what she did to the skinwalker."

Aveline's brow quirked. In the far reaches of her mind, she saw an image of a Native man and a wolf, a flurry of movement, someone shouting ... but none of the pictures formed completely. "I can't remember anything," she said.

Elk Hunter glanced at his son, who began to speak.

Aveline listened to his version of events, of Tiana using magic to subdue and then throw the skinwalker into the sky, in quiet. She recalled Matilda's death at Tiana's hands, and the magical events Tiana could not control, the telekinesis and mind reading.

"You are not surprised," Elk Hunter observed, sharp eyes on her.

"No," Aveline replied.

"Would it surprise you to know only one Hanover heir every generation is born with this power, which allows him to rule and protect his city?"

Aveline frowned. "But Arthur is the Hanover heir, not Tiana."

"This is clearly what their father used to believe as well," Elk Hunter said. "Though he must have suspected otherwise to assign you as her guardian and to send the messages I have been receiving lately."

"Perhaps he *hopes* otherwise," Diving Eagle said.

Aveline tensed. "Why would you say that?" she snapped.

"Because her mind is not fit to lead," he replied.

She rose. Anger flared within her, warming her body from the inside out. Her shirtsleeve ripped as her entire arm transformed into that of a bear. "There is *nothing* wrong with Tiana!" she growled.

The warrior shifted closer, eyes flashing with challenge.

"My son means no disrespect," Elk Hunter said with a glance at his edgy Native son. "His anger is derived from a different source."

The warrior looked at his father and then dipped his head. "My apologies, Father," he said through gritted teeth. "I did not mean it as an insult. The Hanover views the world through her heart."

"That's a good thing!" Aveline retorted.

"I would agree," Elk Finder said. "It's a gift to view the world as beautiful when most of us see its faults instead."

"But you must admit she cannot do so, if she is to lead," his son said reasserted more quietly.

"Soon, you will see things as I do," his father replied with a warm smile.

"No, Father. You will live many years yet and lead us through what the Hanover's bring upon us."

Aveline half-listened, assessing the elderly chief was too frail to survive the year. Deep inside, she understood Tiana's chances of survival on her own were not good. The Hanover girl was too gentle to use her power to hurt others, which left Aveline puzzled about Tiana's motivation for trying to murder a skinwalker.

Aveline scratched her neck with her normal hand and felt the fur that had spread across her shoulder and up her neck. She grimaced. Holding her temper had always been a challenge. She now had an additional reason to work harder at it.

"Please, sit. We are here to discuss her fate, and yours," the chief said.

The words settled some of Aveline's fury, as she realized the importance of this casual meeting. If she reacted poorly, she likely condemned them all. Rolling her shoulders back, she sat back down.

"You are aware of the nature of the relationship between my people and the Hanover's?" Elk Hunter asked her.

Aveline nodded.

"You understand, then, that I cannot release her." He glanced at his son again. "My behavior towards the daughter of the enemy of my people has been lenient enough for my own people to doubt me. She is being treated as an honored guest and has her freedom, as long as she remains within the village. After witnessing what the skinwalker did to another of our villages, this one filled with families and children, I did not believe it right to confine her after she prevented the skinwalker from doing the same to this village." He shifted and sipped water before continuing. "Those outside the village, who did not witness her actions, do not understand how I could grant our enemy life, let alone regard her as a guest. The tribal council arrives today to review my decisions, and I have entrusted them with a recommendation, and ultimate decision, of how to handle both of you."

Aveline listened, startled by his candidness. Her arm returned to normal, until her bear claw was all that remained of her deformity. "Why are you telling me this?" she asked warily.

"I am recommending Tiana's life be spared, under three conditions."

Aveline braced herself for the bad news. "What are they?"

"The first, that she helps us trap the skinwalker."

"I thought you said it was thrown into the sky," she said.

"It landed five miles away – alive. Barely, if the amount of blood found around its landing place is any indication," Elk Hunter replied. "However, his body was not there. As long as the creature is loose in our lands, and we hunt it, our focus is elsewhere than on our traditional enemy, who becomes a larger threat each day."

"You want her to capture it?" Aveline asked.

"We will track it, but only she can contain it," Diving Eagle said.

"Why not kill it?"

"We intend to use it against our enemy."

Aveline was not at all opposed to witnessing a skinwalker kill – or try to – the Hanover leader. "That man will not die easily," she said. "I don't think even a skinwalker can stop his madness. But I will not stop you from trying. After all he has done to the city and to his own daughter ..." She shook her head.

"You will have the ability to speak to it as well," Diving Eagle said.

"I don't care to."

"Don't you wish to understand more of what you are as well? It can teach you about your mother's people and your heritage," he pointed out.

"I don't want to know more," Aveline snapped. "I am content knowing what I do and carrying on my father's legacy. Now, what's the second condition?"

"That she and her successors will never harm a member of our people."

"Basically, peace with a Hanover," Aveline said. "What of her brother?"

"We did not have a chance to discuss this with him before he vanished. But when we have him again, he will agree to similar terms, or they both die," replied the warrior firmly.

It was not hard for Aveline to believe the siblings would have no problem agreeing to peace, unlike their mad father.

She heard the soft patter of rain begin to fall against the tent and looked upward.

Had Tiana ever been out in the rain? The errant thought distracted her, made the silence stretch uncomfortably. "What's the third condition?" she asked and refocused.

"She can never return to the city," Elk Hunter replied.

"I'm sure she didn't argue with you there, either. She's always wanted to ..." Aveline stopped suddenly, registering the condition. As Tiana's guardian, if the Hanover girl did not return, neither could she.

"You anticipate a problem?"

"Not with her," she answered. "Do these conditions apply to me as well?"

"They do," Elk Hunter confirmed. "You are part skinwalker, a danger as great as either Hanover."

"You want to banish us."

"That is the goal," Diving Eagle said. "In exchange, you and the Hanover live."

"It is more than I ever thought I would offer a Hanover," his father said.

"I am not a Hanover," Aveline retorted. "Tiana does not belong anywhere her father can reach her, but I belong in that city. It's my home."

The two were silent.

"You of all people understand what it means to want vengeance," she continued. "You have not walked away from a war spanning centuries! The man who betrayed my father and me remains in Lost Vegas, and I *will* find him!"

The warrior shifted at last and approached his father. He bent and whispered quietly before straightening once more. Elk Hunter appeared to think on the request before he nodded.

Diving Eagle looked at her hard. "She can never return. You may, if you agree to carry out our business inside the city," he said.

"Business?" she repeated.

"You are an assassin?"

In training. Though no one seemed to care she was not an official member of the Guild.

Aveline nodded.

"And a skinwalker. You would stand a better chance of surviving an assassination on the Hanover chief than any others we have sent to subvert him."

Aveline had never heard of any Native challenging Tiana's father but doubted said Native would have gotten far before he ran into someone who decided to burn him at the stake. Surviving Lost Vegas was an art in and of itself. A stranger to the city would not know that.

"You will be given ten days," Elk Hunter said solemnly.

"Ten days?" Aveline echoed. "Most assassinations take months to plan!"

"If you fail, Tiana's life is forfeit," Diving Eagle said. "As are yours and those of your friends."

It was a compromise of sorts, one that would allow her to enter the city again, even if she carried the burden of executing vengeance on behalf of complete strangers. Then again, was that not what she had always wanted to do? Become a professional assassin? Why did this feel like more strings were attached than would be in a paid job?

Her life, Rocky's, Jose's and Tiana's were in the hands of the men awaiting her answer, people who, for reasons she did not fully understand, seemed to genuinely wish to spare them. What made the mortal enemies – who were involved in a centuries' old blood feud with Tiana's family – risk angering their own people to protect the Hanover girl?

Because she's special. Aveline had always understood this, but something other than her heavy bear claw felt off about this situation.

"I have no real choice here," Aveline said. "I'll do what you ask."

"You are wise for someone so young." Elk Hunter smiled. "We cannot take the city while he is in charge." He exchanged a look with his son. "The Hanover agreed already to the three conditions. Before you leave for the city, you will both have to testify before the council this evening."

"We have to see the council?"

"They will be interviewing everyone in the village, including you."

"Are you certain you should send her?" Aveline asked. "Tiana will only tell the truth, and if your people are angry with you for treating her well, they might be even angrier when they see the extent of it."

"The truth is expected," the chief said.

The rain fell harder against the leather ceiling of the tent.

Elk Hunter began to cough again and was soon doubled over.

"You're dismissed," Diving Eagle snapped at her and dropped to his father's side.

Aveline glared at him again before whirling and striding out. She clenched her bear paw and shifted her weight. Her unnatural hand was heavy enough she had to constantly correct her posture to keep from overcompensating and leaning.

The rain was cold and dashed what warmth the early spring day had held. Aveline shivered. As she mentally reviewed the discussion with the chief and his son, dread slid through her.

Had they manipulated her into a suicide mission? Had she let her emotion cloud her judgment?

Did it matter? Not only did she have no choice, but Aveline always intended to return to the city.

Aveline had promised to help Tiana, and breaking this promise would dishonor her father and everything he stood for.

But ... Aveline had always suspected the biggest threat to Tiana was her father. Someone wealthy enough to pay off Karl had tried to hire her to murder Tiana anyway. Who was in a better position than Tiana's father?

Unable to make sense of her situation through her headache, Aveline sighed.

Tiana had not gone far from the tent. She stood near the bonfires located at the center of the village with a scrawny Native boy whose head reached her shoulder. They were hand-in-hand, their faces tilted upwards towards the sky, as if they both enjoyed the rain Tiana had never felt against her skin.

"Views the world through her heart."

Aveline had not heard the chief's son follow her but turned when he spoke. "That will never be a bad thing," she told him.

"Not for her. Perhaps for those around her," Diving Eagle retorted. "If she loses her faith in the world, she will destroy everything she touches."

His words left Aveline colder than the rain. She could think of no comeback and watched him stalk away. The Native's glance lingered on the two figures enjoying the rain before he barked an order. The boy with Tiana dashed to him in response, and the two left Aveline's line of sight.

The longer she stood in thought, the more she understood his words. He saw the threat Tiana could become, if she ever saw the darker side of life. Tiana could become something worse than her father.

Except Aveline knew what Diving Eagle did not: Tiana had lived in the shadows her entire life and still glowed with light, hope and optimism. The shadows had not tamed and twisted her spirit. The darker the experiences, the brighter Tiana would glow, the way the moon overpowered the light of stars, no matter how dark the night.

The only danger to Tiana, if her abilities were as powerful as the chief claimed, was the fear of men who misunderstood her – and her father.

Aveline approached Tiana, concerned and overwhelmed by the complexity of their situation.

"I have never felt rain on my face before," Tiana said. "Is it not wonderful?"

"It's cold," Aveline said grumpily. Her irritation could not dampen Tiana's excitement at her world, and the Hanover girl stretched out her arms, as if trying to drench herself in water. "We need to talk about something. Where is Rocky?"

"This way!" Tiana whirled and began walking back towards the direction they had come.

Aveline trailed. She found herself more troubled about what was to come than how she could ever pass as normal sporting a bear claw.

Tiana waited for her at the front of a tent. Rocky emerged and caught Aveline's gaze. He inclined his head to the side.

"I need to talk to Rocky," Aveline said to Tiana. "Stay right here. I'll be right back."

Joining Rocky, the two of them walked a short distance away.

"How are you?" Rocky asked, searching her features.

"I feel like I fell out of a tree." Aveline touched her pounding head. "Is it true what I've been told? Tiana tried to murder someone?"

"It was pretty impressive," Rocky said with a smile. His eyes went from her to a passing Native. "I have the feeling we're in trouble here."

"We are. Lots of it," she agreed. "They want me to kill someone in the city. In exchange, they won't hurt any of you."

"Sounds suspicious to me."

She nodded, eyes on the forest. "None of this feels right." She lifted her bear claw. "I want to find Karl but not like this."

"Go," Rocky said easily. "I can take care of your friend."

"I made her a promise. My father would not approve of me leaving her."

"Then come back," Rocky said. "Nothing will happen to her while I'm here. You deserve closure, Avi."

She had not expected him to agree with her. "You haven't heard who they want me to kill yet," she said ruefully.

Rocky waited.

The second she said his name, his expression changed from open to shuttered.

Rocky listened, concern on his face, as she filled him in on the conversation that had transpired with the chief and his son.

When she was done, Rocky rocked back onto his heels and gazed towards the clouds.

"What would you do?" Aveline asked. Never had she had to ask this question of anyone.

"You have ten days?"

She nodded.

"Don't worry about anything out here," Rocky said. "Find Karl. His brother Wilhelm lives in the old place where Karl used to live. You remember visiting him there when we were little?"

"Yes."

"Get what you need from Wilhelm and Karl, and you meet me in nine days. I'll bring Tiana and Jose, and we'll all go somewhere."

"You don't think I should try to kill the Hanover leader at all?" Aveline asked.

"I think every assassin who has tried to kill a siting Hanover leader for four centuries has failed for a reason," Rocky replied.

"Would you try?"

"No."

Surprised by his quick, honest response, Aveline considered her position on the matter. All she had ever wanted was to follow in her father's footsteps. What better way than by murdering the Hanover leader?

"What if ..." She looked at her bear claw. "What if I'm the one person who can do it? Because of what I am?"

"You're only half-beast," he reminded her.

Aveline was quiet, considering. What if she could save Tiana and the rest of the city from her father? If Tiana was safe, then she could go to the Freelands, and Aveline's oath would be fulfilled. She did not want to part ways with her friend, but the two of them had two very different goals in life.

"Let's look at this logically," Rocky said. "Do a dry run. Go through the motions you would go through if you were serious about it. I guarantee you will walk away from him when you realize it's impossible."

"Smart. As always." Aveline lowered her deformed arm.

"Your father always said an assassination is successful here first." Rocky tapped his temple. "You have that look on your face. Promise me you will think about it before you do anything."

"I will," Aveline promised. "And if it seems impossible, I won't try."

Rocky appeared to accept her words, for which she was grateful. Deep down, she knew she had already made her decision to carry out her promise to Arthur and Tiana by protecting Tiana from the man Tiana feared most in the world.

Impossible or not, Aveline was going to find Karl and then kill Tiana's father – or die trying.

FOUR

TIANA'S DREAD and fear had been building since the discussion earlier with Aveline, who believed they would be condemned to death or slavery by the council. By the time Tiana stepped into the hot tent to meet the tribal council later that night, she was overwhelmed and fighting back tears.

Eight women sat in positions of importance on a dais at the far end. What looked like half the village had crammed itself into the small space to watch the interviews, which had been going on all day long. The talk fell silent when she entered, Aveline at her side. Whether it was the charged energy of the tent, the heat that caused sweat to drip down her face before she reached her position standing in front of the council, or the stares, or a combination of all the sensations, Tiana was claustrophobic and felt sick to her stomach. The space in which she stood, before the council of middle aged and elderly women wearing severe expressions, was as confining as her old room. Her father had regarded her with this same expression every time they met. Disapproval, if not disgust, was clear on the faces of the women.

I cannot do this, she thought. *I cannot go back.*

Her only conscious thought was of returning to the hellish room, or worse – a cage, where she would spend the rest of her existence. Her ears began to ring, and her hair lifted wildly into the air around her.

"State your names," one of the women boomed.

Tiana's attention snapped to her. Aveline nudged her, and Tiana cleared her throat. "Tiana Hanover," she replied.

"Aveline Gerard."

Tiana sank into her mind and senses, unable to follow the discussion occurring on the dais when she was struggling to draw a deep enough breath. The women talked, Aveline responded, and murmurs went through the crowd. The pattern repeated itself, until silence fell.

Aveline nudged her again. "Say *yes*," she urged.

Tiana blinked and glanced from her friend to the council. She did as Aveline said, trusting her friend with her life. Her breathing grew shallower. When tunnel vision formed and the drink ware and other belongings of the council members began to lift into the air and spin, Tiana panicked.

She raced out of the tent, desperate for air and to feel the great outdoors. Tiana stumbled twice in the mud left over from a day of rain and continued onward, heading for the peace and quiet of the forest.

Tears stung her eyes and blurred her path. She ran until the terror she experienced whenever she thought of returning to her father released her. When nothing but the patter of rain against leaves filled her ears, and the cold water dripping down her face penetrated her frantic escape, she slowed and then stopped. Tiana sank down onto her knees and leaned against a tree. Her hands shook, and her mind would not focus on any one thing let alone clarify the fog surrounding what had been said by the tribal council.

She had not had a panic attack since leaving the city. Tiana waited for the vise around her chest to release its hold. She found herself gripping the small knife Red Moon had given her and pushed up her sleeve.

Slicing into her skin, Tiana released a breath. Pain penetrated her thoughts, giving them some cohesion among her chaotic emotions. Her hair, along with the loose branches and rocks in her surroundings, lowered and returned to their natural positions.

She sagged. Matilda had been wrong about bleeding out her magic, but the sensation of cutting her skin and the pain that followed always grounded her when nothing else seemed to.

Tiana cut the scarred skin of her inner arm again and relaxed further. Warm blood streamed down her arm and mixed with rain. She drew her first deep breath and lifted her face to the night sky. The rain was cold, the mud beneath her numbing her exposed skin, but she could imagine nowhere else she wanted to be. She dropped the knife and let herself dwell in the dull pain until she was shaking and soaked.

A pool of warm light lifted the gloomy night from the area around her. It was red light, not harsh enough to disturb her sensitive eyes yet bright enough to guide someone's path.

"Why are you bleeding?"

She tensed at Diving Eagle's terse voice. He was always angry with her or seemed ready to strike her. Tiana hunched her shoulders, waiting for him to hit her, now that they were alone and his father was not there to protect her. He crouched in front of her and gripped her injured arm, turning the soft skin of her forearm upward so he could assess the damage in the light.

Tiana twisted her arm away, but he held it tightly. "These are not animal bites or scratches from trees," he said.

"I did it," she whispered.

He glanced from her forearm to her face then back. His normal disapproval was clear on his features, and he pulled out a small roll of bandages from the pouch at his waist.

Why would you do this to yourself? She read the question in his mind.

Tiana feared demonstrating another of her capabilities by answering. She watched him wrap her arm in a bandage. "Your father is not here. You do not have to pretend to tend to me," she said.

"My father taught me to do what I believed to be right for my people, no matter who is present to see it."

"My father taught me to suffer."

His hands paused. "You wish me to pity you?" His tone hardened.

"I speak only the truth," she replied. "You have a good father. I hope you cherish him."

"He is the most honorable man in the world." He continued with the bandage. "He is gifted. Like you."

"He is?" she asked, interested for the first time in anything this man had ever said to her. "What is his deformity?"

"It is not a deformity," was the curt response. "It is a blessing."

"Mine is not," she said quietly, distraught.

"No," he agreed. "Yours is not." He was quiet for a breath before he spoke again. "My father is a peacemaker. He has negotiated treaties and trade agreements with tribes who have been enemies of my people for hundreds of years. Every single one – except for the Hanover's."

"I have heard us called blood enemies," she said.

"We had several blood enemies at one time," he replied. "My father met your father once, twenty years ago." He dropped his hands and replaced the bandages in the pouch. "My father went with the intention of offering peace, because peace is the legacy he wanted to leave after our people have suffered through four and a half centuries of war. He looked into your father's eyes, and he left the meeting without speaking."

Tiana listened, fascinated by an account of her father she had never heard before. "Why? What happened?"

"My father's gift is the ability to see the spirit of everyone he meets. He can read intentions, and he knows when someone is good and when someone cannot be salvaged," Diving Eagle said. "When he saw your father, he saw a man with a spirit not of this world, born of evil so great, even my father declared that my people must always be at war with him and any Hanover who possessed this ... thing inside him."

Tiana's pulse raced. She feared asking the question at the tip of her tongue. Diving Eagle was quiet, and at last, she whispered the words. "What did he see in Arthur and me?"

"Not that, or you would be dead," Diving Eagle replied. "He did not share with me what he saw, but he has defied everything we stood for to protect you." Diving Eagle gripped her arms and rose, lifting her with him. "He is never wrong, and I do not question him."

Tiana rested her palms against his warm chest to catch her balance and just as quickly snatched her hands back. He was close enough for her to smell his masculine scent. She braced herself and waited for him to leave.

Diving Eagle released her. "The council is debating whether or not to accept my father's decision. They understand his insight is unique, but the war between your family and mine extends centuries before any of us were born."

"Do you share his gift?" she asked. "Can you see my spirit?"

"If I could, I would not have invited a skinwalker into the midst of my warriors," he growled. "And I would not be indebted to a Hanover for saving them and my father."

"I was not trying to save your warriors," she said before she could stop herself. "I did not even kill the skinwalker like I wanted to." Reminded of this fact, she reached up and plucked the feather from her hair. "Red Moon said I earned this, but I did not." She handed it to him.

Diving Eagle accepted it with a glance. "Your intention is not in question. My failure to protect my people is. My father is the greatest chief since the Old World fell. His health is failing, but it is my judgment that almost ended his life."

That Diving Eagle experienced any emotion other than anger

surprised her, and she ventured to look up into his features. "But it did not," she said. "You could not know what he was."

"I should have."

"No," she said. "You should not have. I saw him in a vision where he destroyed everyone I love. You do not have my deformity, for which you should be grateful. You will never have to flee your family and home because your father wants you dead, and you will never fear what you are, and what you might do if you are distressed or cornered, because you already know what you are capable of."

"Is that why you fled the council? Because you feared what you would do?"

"No. I felt ... trapped. Like I did under my father's guardianship," she replied. "I want to be free. I cannot go back to being trapped. Ever."

"Free." He repeated the word as if trying to decide what it meant.

"I want to go to the Freelands and stay there forever."

"They may not exist."

"And if they do? No one can say with certainty they do not."

He shook his head and stepped away from her. "Your dream is foolish."

Tiana breathed deeply, relieved not to be confronted by his intensity any longer. He was not the first to call her desire this. Aveline and Arthur thought her foolish as well.

"I imagine it is better to be foolish and free than enslaved to your father," Diving Eagle added. "The council is debating your fate. You may return to the tent you share with the assassin." He waited.

Tiana looked around but could not identify which direction either of them had come from. She had run far enough for the smell of smoke and well-lit tents to be hidden by the forest.

"Come on," the Native warrior said. He turned and began walking.

She trailed him, shivering but grateful to be cold and wet and in the forest instead of confined with the council in the warm tent. She dared not ask what he thought the council would decide for fear of the answer.

Diving Eagle led her through the forest, back to the mobile village and left her at the tent without a word. Sensing them, Aveline shoved the tent door open.

"What were you thinking, Tiana?" she exclaimed and gripped her arm to tug her into the warm, cozy tent they shared. "Where did you go?"

Tiana was ready to cry when she noticed that the thick bear hair had crawled all the way up Aveline's neck and jaw and half her cheek. The image of Aveline with a beard made her smile instead.

Aveline rolled her eyes. "Change clothes. The council will decide at any moment what to do with us." She tossed clean clothes at Tiana. Her eyes lingered on Tiana's bandaged arm, but she said nothing about the self-inflicted wounds.

"I am sorry for leaving you, Aveline," Tiana said after she had changed. "I should have stayed. You might have been in danger. But I ..." She sighed.

"I can handle myself," Aveline said and then added. "I understand. I wanted to run, too. That was one hostile bunch of women."

"Do they trust their leader enough not to murder us?" Tiana joked weakly.

"The only thing clear to me is that they hate your family and everything you stand for," Aveline said and sat beside the cheerful fire at the center of the tent.

Tiana's heart sank. She silently berated herself for not being strong enough to conquer her fear and remain.

"But I have a feeling we are useful to them, and they know this," Aveline added. "They would be foolish not to use us, especially when we are willing to help."

"Did they mention Arthur?"

"Once, and I got the impression they know where he is but cannot get to him right now."

"Hopefully he can ..." Tiana trailed off. She did not know how to finish this thought or sentence. The Natives had been torturing her brother, and she had no desire for Arthur to return to their father. "Hopefully he is safe."

"Arthur has decent survival sense," Aveline said. "You both have been sheltered from the world, but I think he understands how to navigate people better than you do. He did not spend his life locked in a closet."

Tiana braided her wet hair and sat beside her friend. The brilliant glow of Aveline's pendant – a gift from the electrical engineer in the basement of the pyramid – made her glance down at the matching necklace she wore. Aveline was fidgeting, tugging at the hair of her bear arm. Tiana suspected her friend was not as thrilled by her new-formed deformity as Tiana had been.

"Are your friends okay?" she asked.

"For now," Aveline said, frowning. "I hope it stays that way. It'll probably depend on what the council decides." She shook her head. "Something weird is going on, Tiana. I mean ... relatively weird." She lifted her bear claw. "The council seemed to think you are your father's heir, not Arthur."

Tiana laughed. "Never!"

"I know. But the way they talked about you was weird."

Tiana leaned back to grab a blanket and wrapped it around her shoulders. "My father hates that I am alive."

"I told them that. And told them their village wouldn't have been spared if not for you."

Tiana glanced at her friend at the mention of the incident in which she had tried to crush the skinwalker. "Do you think I'm evil, Aveline?" she asked quietly.

"You? No. There is not even an evil thought in your head."

"What about my deformity? Could it come from an evil source?"

Aveline gazed at her claw, features drawn. "I may be half-skinwalker, but I don't have the urge to wipe out villages like the full skinwalker did. I don't think our deformities are good or evil. I think *we* determine that. You could never be evil, not even a little, and I'm content being ignorant of whether or not an assassin would be considered evil."

Reassured by Aveline's confidence, Tiana began to relax. Diving Eagle would not agree, but Aveline knew her better. "I am happy we met, Aveline," she murmured and hugged herself.

"I am, too."

"And I like your bear claw."

"It's growing on me," Aveline said with less enthusiasm.

"Literally," Tiana said with a soft laugh.

Aveline pushed her away with a smile. "Go get some sleep. Whatever happens next will happen quickly."

Tiana rose and crossed to the bed she had claimed as hers. She lay down facing the fire and closed her eyes, happy Aveline was there to protect her.

Tiana's vision flared to life soon after her eyelids closed. It occurred in the same place she had witnessed the skinwalker brutally murder everyone she loved except this time, no one else was present aside from her and the skinwalker.

THEY STOOD in the quiet forest near the lodge she had yet to find in real life. He was unarmed and in human form, his lean frame supported by one natural leg and one that was clad in black. Behind him, spectral images of people she did not know milled. There were hundreds of them, perhaps thousands. The only one of them paying attention to her was a ghost boy around the age of ten with a slashed chest. This one stood close enough to listen to their discussion.

Tiana risked a look around her. Forest was on every side without any sign of anyone else who had been present previously.

"We have to do it," said the skinwalker.

"Pardon?" she asked, facing him again.

"No one else can."

"Do what?"

"Stop him."

"TIANA."

She snapped awake at Aveline's voice. The vision remained, and Tiana sat and looked around to ensure they were safe. Light trickled in through the flap across the entrance, which had not been secured.

"It's time to go," Aveline said.

"Go where?" Tiana asked.

"You're going to find the skinwalker, and I am going on a mission."

Tiana's breath caught in her throat. "The council does not want us dead?"

"Not yet apparently." Aveline grunted as she pulled on her boots. "We're useful, as I hoped." She laced the second boot and stood. "Rocky's going with you."

"I had a vision about him," Tiana said thoughtfully.

"Rocky?"

"No, the skinwalker."

"Was he savagely murdering everyone again?"

"No." Tiana paused. "It was very different this time."

"Sounds like a good change to me," Aveline said with a distracted glance towards the entrance.

"I do not know for certain. The vision was too short."

"Listen, Tiana." Aveline's hushed voice drew Tiana's gaze. "I don't trust the Natives to be honest with us about our ... *your* fate. They are sending me to the city. I'll be safe. I don't think you will be here."

Tiana frowned. She did not have Aveline's insight into people and had not suspected anything of those around her.

"Survive. Whatever it takes," Aveline told her. "Promise me you will do what you must."

"I will," Tiana said. "But you must promise to return to me."

Aveline hesitated. "I don't know that I can guarantee that, Tiana."

"Why not?"

"Because they want me to assassinate your father, and I don't know if I can." She flexed her bear claw.

Tiana sat in quiet surprise before she spoke again. "They want you to kill my father?"

"They think it'll allow them to attack the city."

"What about the people?" Tiana asked.

"What people?"

"There are tens of thousands of people in Lost Vegas."

Aveline shrugged. "Maybe they will take it over and replace him. It's not my concern."

It was rare when Tiana was dissatisfied with an answer someone gave her. "This sounds like a poor plan. All of it."

Aveline straightened. "I have no choice, and neither do you. We will both die if we don't cooperate, and they'll kill Jose and Rocky, too." Her grave warning silenced Tiana's concerns – for the time being. "If I don't return, stay with Rocky. Your father has survived assassination attempts his entire life by Guild members. I may not have much of a chance."

Tiana understood Aveline's point and chewed her lower lip, pensive.

"I have little time to plan. There must be some point where your father could be vulnerable. Can you think of anything?" Aveline asked.

Tiana sifted through what she knew of her father's routine. It was next to nothing, since she was rarely informed of his doings at all. "I do not know," she said, feeling worthless to help her friend. "Do not face him, Aveline. You do not understand the danger."

"I have no choice. He is the greatest threat to your safety, and I swore to protect you. This is me doing that job." Aveline pulled on a light coat of waterproofed leather and fleece lining. She started towards the door.

"Wait!" Tiana said, panic stirring within her. She threw her arms around her guardian in a bear hug.

Aveline sighed and reluctantly returned the hug.

"I can think of only one instance where I know anything of my father's schedule. Every Sunday night, my father goes into the secret passages," Tiana said.

"You know this how?"

"I heard him one night when I was waiting for Arthur to return. The passages used to lead somewhere, but were walled off. I heard someone moving through a passage on the other side of the wall in the part of the passage bordering my father's quarters. Matilda was asleep, and Arthur had not yet returned. It could only have been my father," she answered. "I listened every day for months, and it occurred every Sunday night."

"That might help." Aveline released her and pulled away. "I'll have to slip by the guards and return to your closet. Is there any other entrance to the passages in the walls?"

Tiana shook her head. "I searched for years to find a way out," she said sadly. "If there is, it must be in my father's quarters."

"Thanks, Tiana."

"You must come back, Aveline," Tiana said. The air around her became charged with energy stemming from her deformities, which responded to her unsettled emotion. No one, especially not her father, would hurt Aveline or anyone else she cared about ever again.

"I'll try." Aveline started towards the entrance again.

"You do not understand, Aveline," Tiana added. "If you do not return, I will come after you."

Aveline paused, her hand on the flap of the tent. "No, Tiana. You could never navigate the city on your own, and your father is too dangerous."

"So am I, Aveline," Tiana responded, thoughts on how easy it had been to fend off the Ghouls and skinwalker. "Or ... I can be."

"Whether or not I return, go be free in the Freelands. It's what you always wanted." Still frowning, Aveline flung open the tent flap and strode into the cool morning.

Not if you and Arthur die. Tiana did not have time to voice her words.

Troubled by Aveline's mission, Tiana was also surprised to find the depths of her own resolve when it came to saving those she cared about. Would she face her father?

The thought of standing up to him terrified her.

Recalling Aveline's news about the council's decision, Tiana dressed quickly and left the tent, anxious to hear what her role in tracking the skinwalker would be. Her vision replayed in her thoughts, and she debated what the skinwalker had been about to tell her before the dream ended. Had she changed the future by attacking him before he tried to hurt her friends?

The morning was cloudy but the rain had stopped. Rocky waited nearby, talking to the second man they had traveled with, Jose. A group of Natives – including Diving Eagle – mingled at the center of the village. They were dressed for travel with saddlebags and bedrolls slung over their shoulders.

Aveline approached her friends. She hugged Rocky and then walked a short distance away to speak to Jose in private.

Tiana hung back from everyone, feeling alone without Aveline. She gripped the pendant hard with one hand. If Aveline did not return, or if her father killed her friend, Tiana would use every last one of her deformities to find justice.

Diving Eagle left the group and approached her. Rocky moved towards her simultaneously and stopped beside her.

Tiana dropped her gaze to the ground and waited.

"We will leave as soon as the horses are brought to us," Diving Eagle informed them both.

"Can't wait," Rocky replied. "Let's go find us a skinwalker!"

Tiana peered at him from the corner of her eyes, curious. Around her brother's age, Rocky wore assassin blacks. His smile was quick for a trained killer, his dark eyes warm and sharp. While he appeared at ease, she picked up a similar subdued tension that Aveline possessed.

Even when her friend relaxed, she was always ready to leap into action, and so was Rocky.

Diving Eagle appeared neither impressed nor irritated by Rocky's genuine enthusiasm. That he tolerated the assassin was probably the most pleasant he was capable of being with his enemies.

"My father asked me to give you this," the warrior continued and handed Tiana a pouch the size of her hand.

She accepted it without a word and waited for him to turn and leave before she opened it. Inside was the feather she had returned to Diving Eagle, along with a bracelet of turquoise beads, separated by wooden spacers carved in the shapes of animals. She smiled, touched by the gift from the man who had sought to protect her despite his hatred for her father. She slid the bracelet over her wrist but left the feather. Red Moon had told her only warriors who killed in battle were allowed to wear the feathers, and she had failed in her first battle with the skinwalker.

She tucked the pouch in her satchel.

Her second surprise of the day: Red Moon and other young men from the village brought them all mules instead of horses. The scrawny youth she befriended brought hers and Rocky to them with a smile. Her mule was chubby, smaller than the others, and furry with its winter coat.

"His name is Bear, because all he does is eat like a bear before hibernating," Red Moon told her.

"He is beautiful," she said and accepted the reins. "Are you coming with us?"

"Not this time. I'm staying here to help Father with a trade agreement," the youth said with confidence she had never held for anything in her life. "But I'll be here when you return with the skinwalker."

"Mount up!" Diving Eagle called.

"Thank you," she said to Red Moon.

Tiana mounted and saw Rocky do the same. They guided their horses to join the group of five accompanying them.

"We are headed north, where the last sign of the skinwalker was found," Diving Eagle said. "I sent word to our neighbors not to engage him, if found, and to let us handle him."

"You mean let Tiana handle him," Rocky said with some amusement.

"She is the only one who can."

Not expecting Diving Eagle to agree, Tiana hid her smile. He was reluctant in his praise of her, even when everyone understood how ineffective normal weapons were. She guessed he remained angry with himself for not knowing about the skinwalker when he brought the creature into camp.

Diving Eagle trotted his horse to the front of the column to lead the search party into the forest.

"Funny how hard he tries not to admit what's in front of him," Rocky said for her ears only. "Stay close, Tiana. We're not safe here, no matter what they tell you."

"I have been treated well here," she replied.

"But have they told you what happens when you do what they want? When you become disposable?"

"They said I can go wherever I want."

"How? Do they intend to provide an escort? A map? Will they fund your journey? Because traveling that far will be expensive."

She studied him then looked towards Diving Eagle. "They said nothing about any of this," she said.

"When someone makes a promise but offers no details, assume they are lying," he advised. "I know you can smash us faster than we smash flies in summer, but that power only works when you know to use it."

I see why Aveline trusts him, Tiana thought. Rocky possessed the same street and people sense as her friend. "I am ready," she told him.

"Good. Let's go catch us a monster." Rocky lifted his chin to motion her to follow the chain of warriors.

No sooner had the group begun to file out of the village than a rider on horseback barreled into the otherwise quiet area. Tiana heard his shout and glanced over her shoulder. His gaze swept past all of them and settled on Diving Eagle. The rider cantered down the line and stopped beside the chief's son.

Their procession stopped.

"I'd say that's bad news," Rocky said quietly from his position on the horse following hers.

Tiana studied the two at the head of the column, who spoke too quietly for anyone else to hear. Diving Eagle's face remained expressionless, but his jaw clenched. He gave a terse nod then waved the Native on the horse behind him to approach.

"Really bad news," Rocky added.

Tiana waited, trusting his instincts and taking note of Diving Eagle's mannerisms. He was difficult to read, more so considering she had rarely spoken to anyone before a few weeks ago. Their exchange the night before lingered in her mind.

There was more to him than anger. He cared for his people.

He did not seem like someone who could care for anyone at all, and this insight left her wondering if her own father – who had often wished her dead – might also care for her behind his cruel façade. He normally spoke out of anger or disappointment, but what if those emotions did not cloud his behavior when he dealt with her?

She had never thought him possible of anything more than what he displayed. If she were learning one thing about people, it was that there was more to them than she could possibly know.

The messenger left the head of the column to return to the village. After a moment of discussion, Diving Eagle turned his mule and walked down the line towards her. Rocky edged out around her horse to hear.

"We know where he is," he reported.

"Shortest hunt ever," Rocky said with a smile. "What's next?"

Diving Eagle shook his head, and his gaze grew distant for a moment. "It will be complicated."

"A large raid? Or do you need my assassin services for more discretion?"

"Neither. We are allied with the tribe who has him," Diving Eagle said. "You and I are going." This he directed to Tiana.

"Not alone," Rocky said instantly.

"If you insist." Diving Eagle addressed her still.

"I do," she said quietly.

"Then the three of us will go." He spun his horse and started off once more, this time not followed by the group of other Natives.

Tiana glanced at Rocky. He gave no indication he thought this was a bad idea. She squeezed her mule with her legs and followed Diving Eagle.

FIVE

ARTHUR SAT up straight before he was fully awake. His mind clung to the lucid dream that woke him, and the muscles of his body were tense enough to ache. He opened his eyes and blinked rapidly to ground himself from the vision.

He lay on one of the beds in the small medical clinic belonging to the Natives who reluctantly agreed to help him and Marshall. In the bed beside his was the skinwalker, who appeared to be swaddled from head to foot in linen bandages. Marshall lay sleeping in the row of beds across from him, while the she-wolf had stretched out on the floor between Arthur and the skinwalker.

Grainy, pre-dawn light filtered through the windows of the clinic. Arthur wiped his face, alarmed as much by the vision as by his heavy sleep.

"How long have I slept?" he asked the Native tending the skinwalker.

"A day and a half."

Arthur sighed. "Too long!"

"You were talking in your sleep. Nightmare?" the Native healer asked.

"I wish." Arthur shivered and twisted away to hide his face. He spotted the basket at the end of his bed and threw off the blankets carefully to avoid disturbing the pups sleeping within.

A nightmare would have been better than the vision lingering in his thoughts. Arthur had witnessed the city collapsing in on itself and being swallowed by the earth. In the middle of it all, standing on the edge of the abyss, watching it happen, was his father, who had left the city to find his children.

No Hanover had ever left the city once he became the leader. If this dream were the reason why, then Arthur would never again question this custom. He did not understand fully why this was the case, or why Lost Vegas had appeared to collapse the moment his father stepped outside.

The skinwalker had told Arthur the day before that the visions were exactly what they appeared to be. Unlike most of Arthur's visions, which appeared to have some room for interpretation, this vision did not. There was no second-guessing what he had seen.

Edwin Hanover had always said there were secrets to leading, and to the family history, he would pass down only upon his deathbed to his heir. Arthur had to believe the history of their deformities was one of these secrets but could not fathom what else his father hid. A secret powerful enough to destroy the city?

His mind worked fast, and he recalled the strange rumors the Natives believed about his father. He had always dismissed the strange talk of an unnatural army raised from the dead, or in some cases, an army of shadows that prevented any force from taking the city. He had viewed this talk as nonsense, the kind of tales told to children by their parents to scare them into behaving.

Until a few weeks ago, the skinwalker had been one of these tales.

"Are you hungry?" the healer asked.

Arthur shook his head and stood. "I have to leave."

"Your friend is not well enough to go with you," the Native said.

"That man is no friend of mine," Arthur said with a glance at the skinwalker.

"Not him." The healer pointed to one of the private rooms at one end of the small medical bay.

Not certain who he meant, Arthur nonetheless approached the door and pushed it open.

His breath caught in his throat, and his heart flipped over in his breast. "Warner!" he exclaimed and hurried forward. He dropped to his knees beside the low bed of his lover and friend and scoured Warner's features.

The dark-haired man was paler than usual, his skin clammy. He was unconscious. Warner's upper body was exposed, and a white bandage spotted with black wrapped around his body.

Arthur gripped Warner's calloused hand, thrilled to find his friend after weeks of wondering if he had survived the skinwalker attack. "I cannot believe you outsmarted that thing," he whispered proudly. "If anyone could defeat a skinwalker, it is you."

Warner was unresponsive to his voice, and Arthur's happiness shifted. He glanced again at the wound, frowning when he saw more black spots soak through the bandage. He touched one and lifted his hand, able to make out the combination of blood and black.

The skinwalker claimed it was a magic wound. The coloring was indeed unnatural.

"No salve or medicines will stop his bleeding," the healer said quietly. "It was always said that a wound inflicted by the skinwalker does not heal. I never believed it, until now."

Concern spun through Arthur. He had been hoping the skinwalker was lying about being the only person who could help Warner.

"He has been in this state since bringing his sister here."

"His ... ahh." Arthur recalled Tiana's tale of pretending to be Warner's sister so no one knew she was a Hanover.

Arthur sat in silence, studying Warner's face. The sense of urgency, left over from his vision, fueled his blood with adrenaline, but he was having a hard time leaving Warner's side despite knowing the storm headed their way.

"I will waken your friend and bring you both breakfast," the healer said.

"No," Arthur said quickly. "I am leaving. Marshall will not like that, but he and Warner must remain here. Actually, all three of them must stay."

"You may wish to speak to Chases Deer before she leaves on her hunt. She was undecided what to do with all of you, the last time we spoke."

It took Arthur a moment to place the name of the Newe chief's daughter and heiress, a warrior said to possess the agility of an antelope. "Very well. May I have some clothing?" Arthur asked. "I do not wish to disrespect her dressed like this." He glanced down at the smelly, torn rags he had been wearing in a cage for several days.

The Native nodded and left the doorway.

"Hang in there, love," Arthur whispered to Warner. He leaned forward and kissed his lover's forehead. "I will return with a way to heal you."

He left the room, fidgeting and distressed to see his friend lying motionless in bed. The Native was out of sight in one of the rooms on the other end of the bay, and Arthur crossed to the wolf.

"Hey, wolf friend," he said and crouched beside her.

She cracked an eye open and wagged her tail. Her fur was a patchwork of black and white this morning.

"I need to leave. It is urgent," he said. "The others must stay here, but I am uncertain what their circumstances will become after I leave. Can you safeguard them? For a short time at least?"

She lifted her head, glanced towards the mangled body of the sleeping skinwalker, and snorted, as if to remind him she could go nowhere so long as her companion was hurt.

"We always end up with me in your debt," he observed. "One day, I will repay you for everything."

She dropped her head back to the wooden floor. Arthur lifted her basket of pups off the bed and placed them beside her then stood, gazing down at the skinwalker.

The only reason the Native was alive was because of the wolf. The tangled relationship among the three of them left Arthur frustrated and upset when he allowed himself to acknowledge how much damage was left in the skinwalker's wake – to include Warner's unhealing wound.

Why did the wolf choose to accompany the creature? From what Arthur had experienced, the wolf had compassion and an understanding of how to relate with humans, unlike the skinwalker she safeguarded. What benefit was there to her in their friendship? Why was a good spirit staying with a rotten one?

Worry about Warner, Marshall, and Tiana caused Arthur to fidget and then pace. The healer returned with clothing and an apple and handed them to Arthur.

"Thank you," he accepted the clothes and stripped off the rags he wore. Arthur's thoughts moved too fast for him to catch, and his hands fumbled with the clothing. He drew a deep breath, aware both the wolf and healer were watching him, and then tried again to tug on his clothing.

"You should wait to leave until the doves come," the healer said.

"Doves?" Arthur echoed, his voice muffled by the shirt he pulled on.

"Every day, your father sends out a hundred doves carrying his demands."

Arthur cursed his father silently. Too mad to understand how many ways he had placed his children in danger, Edwin had long since destroyed the respect any Native in the vicinity of the city would otherwise have for the leader of the city. Arthur finished dressing.

"Where are these messages?" he asked.

"Chases Deer."

"Very well. I will stop to pay my respects and read my father's demands before I leave." Arthur smiled. "Thank you for tending to us despite my father."

The Native returned the smile. "You always bring us meat during the annual hunts. We do not do this for your father," he said.

Arthur nodded, suspecting as much. "I will bring you more than meat when I return," he promised. He did not need directions. He had come to this very village more than once over the years since he began leading the annual Winter Hunt.

Arthur stepped out into the cool morning and strode through the village, past the oldest tree in the forest, bedecked in lights, and into the permanent part of the village. During late winter, when hunting parties returned to this area to hunt, the village swelled to three times its size. The semi-permanent tents along two sides of the village marked the presence of the hunting parties, while the more permanent family homes were tucked deeper into the forest.

The chief's ambassador to the village during the hunt was a trim woman Arthur had met on two occasions. One of the rare female warriors, she was revered for her agility and ferocity in battle.

Arthur navigated the quiet village, eyes roving each home he passed for the familiar mark of the chief: a hawk carrying a feather. He found the pennant pinned outside the home he sought and knocked at the door.

Chases Deer opened the door fully dressed, down to her boots, and carrying a warrior's weapons: a rifle and knives. She was his height with dark hair and eyes and a birthmark on one cheek.

"I apologize for disturbing you so early," Arthur said.

"You do not disturb me," she replied. "We are riding out early today to search for elephants."

"Really?" His eyebrows lifted. "What is the occasion?" Elephants, rare in this part of the country, were prized by the Natives of some tribes and viewed as signs of stature and luck.

"My father believes he has married me off," she replied somewhat tartly.

"Ah." Arthur smiled. "I know that pain. My father has tried on more than one occasion to marry me off as well. It is the curse of the firstborn, is it not?"

"A great curse," she agreed. "Come, Hanover." She pushed the door open wider and stepped back.

"I wanted to thank you for your hospitality before I left," he said and walked into her lodging. "And ask another favor."

"Have I not done enough for you?" she challenged.

"More than enough. But this will benefit us both, I believe."

"Go on."

"Keep my companions here until I return."

"If the Cruise heir is as rich as he claims, then I am happy to ransom him to you," she said with the cunning Arthur remembered.

"He is, and I am happy to pay the ransom for him and my injured companion, Warner. Just please do not put them in a cage," Arthur replied wryly. "We have had enough of cages for a lifetime."

"We do not share our neighbors' fervor with interrogation and torture. The Diné have developed a reputation for their conduct in battle. The promise of coin and goods are all I require," she said and crossed to collect two canteens and a satchel. "I thought you would ask for assistance ransoming your sister back from your enemies."

Arthur was quiet for a moment. If not for his vision, he would jump at the chance to work with Chases Deer to help his sister. As it was shaping up to be, Tiana was safer outside the city, in the hands of their traditional enemies, than she would ever be within reach of their father. "Perhaps when I return," he said slowly. "Does everyone know of the state of Hanover affairs?"

"That your father blames the Natives for kidnapping his children and is threatening war with every tribe between the city and ocean?"

"Is that what he claims?" Arthur could not account for his father's increasingly erratic behavior. While true, Chases Deer's father was a longtime ally, Edwin Hanover was recklessly risking losing the cooperation of the very tribes with whom the city shared a symbiotic relationship. The city was not an island, as much as Edwin tried to make it one. The citizens of inner and outer cities depended upon the trading partnerships between city and Natives for basic staples.

Arthur was beginning to find it more difficult to overlook, or ignore, his father's negative impact on the world around them.

"I have no explanation for you," he said pensively. "I don't understand my father's motivations anymore."

Chases Deer studied him for a long moment. "You are not like the other Hanover's."

"I should hope not." Arthur opened his mouth to point out how his grandfather and great grandfather had been different but stopped himself.

No ruling Hanover had ever possessed his right mind, not according to what Arthur knew of his predecessors.

"But you cower in your father's shadow," Chases Deer pointed out.

"Do we all not do the same?" he challenged softly.

She rolled her eyes at him in irritation. "My father asked me to explain how you were permitted not only to live, but to escape the Diné."

Arthur forced a laugh. "I cannot explain it myself," he admitted. "Diving Eagle wanted me dead, but his father intervened."

"It is not like Elk Hunter to pardon his blood enemy, and definitely not characteristic for Diving Eagle to spare anyone who displeases him."

"I understood that about him, too," Arthur said and touched his bruised eye.

"Yet you lived."

"We did."

She waited for more.

He shrugged. "I am not hiding anything from you, Chases Deer," he said. "I am not in a position to defy you when the lives of my friends are in your hands. I cannot explain why I was spared any more than I can explain my father's actions of late."

Her hard features softened. "You are lost."

"I am."

She glanced towards the door, as if concerned someone would interfere, then moved closer to him and lowered her voice. "My own father wants to free you as well, against my wishes."

"I am grateful to you and your father," Arthur said with eloquence that would impress even Marshall.

She snorted.

"I understand what the Hanover heir is worth," he added. "I have nothing of value to barter with you, and no weapons to fight you. All I can do is give you my word I will do all I can to spare your people the wrath of my father."

Chases Deer was quiet for a moment. "I do not know what tales to believe about your father, or why every Native chief fears him. Is he not a man like you?"

Not exactly, Arthur answered silently. Sensing there was no safe response, he waited for her decision.

"Your father's messages are over there. You may view them, if you do not already know what lies he tells, and then you will leave before any other tribe finds out you are here." She pointed to a trunk. "I will even give you my fastest horse to ensure you make it to the city. I cannot promise you that my people will not track you and capture you for ransom, but you are fortunate that I chose today of all days for my elephant hunt."

"The alliances are shifting," Arthur observed and went to the small wooden trunk. "Are we still allies at all?"

"We were never allies," she returned.

"Then why did my father favor your people?"

"Favor!" she snapped. "Threatening us every time the wind changes is not favoring us!"

"You never hesitated to trade with us."

"We had no choice," she allowed. "Lost Vegas is known even among the Natives for its metal workers and luxury goods, the benefit of controlling all trade on this side of the country. Your father's focus has always been on the city. He charges his allies a tenth the price it costs for him to import many of the rarer goods your city is known for. Spices from afar, silk, ore. His threats towards us have been hollow, and he never followed through with any of them as long as we respected the treaties. You being here has turned his focus to us, and no one is pleased, least of all my father, whose fears run too deep for me to believe they are without merit. The Hanover chief has already broken two trade agreements in the past week."

How did his father come to this point? How could anyone in their right mind believe angering the Natives surrounding the city was a good idea? Arthur hated that he could not explain his father's decisions, but he hated even more that he agreed with the Natives for being angry.

"So you are setting aside differences with the other tribes in preparation for war," Arthur guessed.

"Hence the marriage I do not want to Elk Hunter's barbarian son."

"Historically there is no better way to cement an alliance than ..."

Her glare made him pause. He could almost hear Marshall chiding him for not being diplomatic enough.

"Firstborn curse," he finished. "My apologies, if the arrangement is not to your liking."

"It is not," she said. She released a deep breath, and tension left her tall frame. "I prefer my situation to yours. I know where I stand in all this."

Arthur smiled faintly.

"You have a respected reputation among my people and many others. For this reason, and because I am not yet ready to face your father, I will grant your request to treat your friends as guests rather than prisoners. Leave my village before I ransom you," she ordered quietly. "I'll give you til noon then send my youngest trackers after you." She stuffed the canteens and more weapons into the satchel before slinging on the satchel with agitated movements.

"Thank you," Arthur murmured and picked up the stack of thin strips of paper.

She did not reply but slammed open the door and walked out.

Arthur sat next to a light and began to read. True to his father's ways, the messages were each one sentence long and abrupt.

"Hanover."

He looked up at Chases Deer's voice.

She leaned through the doorway. "We do not want war," she told him. "But we will stop your father, or anyone, from hurting our people, by any means necessary."

"I understand," he responded. "I hope to stop whatever it is we all sense coming before it happens."

"I hope you can." She ducked outside once more.

"I do, too," Arthur whispered. Chases Deer could not know what he had seen in a vision, that nothing would stop the destruction his father would inflict, if Arthur did not act.

He started to read the earliest messages – dated two weeks ago, before Tiana's journey to the forest. Edwin Hanover had demanded the return of his heir multiple times. He offered no incentives for his allies to comply, only sent stark threats.

USE all your resources to see that my heir is returned, or I will use all of mine to punish you for failing me.

EACH MESSAGE BECAME MORE difficult to read, not because Arthur was surprised but because he began to sense something in his father he had never noticed before: desperation. It left him uncomfortable. Edwin Hanover was never desperate, because he knew what power and influence he possessed at his fingertips. Arrogance was a truer representation of him.

Why would his father be desperate about anything?

Arthur skimmed several more messages before coming to one that jarred him out of his train of thought.

NEGOTIATE the return of my daughter, and I will offer my son in marriage to your valiant daughter to celebrate our alliance.

ARTHUR UTTERED a low curse in surprise.

He re-read the politer note and checked the date then compared the handwriting to that of the other missives.

His father, who had refused to allow Arthur to attend routine council meetings in case an assassin caught them both in the same place, was offering him up to the Newe in exchange for Tiana.

Arthur read through the messages from the past few days with a sense of disbelief, if not outright confusion. Edwin had sent out two-dozen messages in three days, as opposed to the six messages sent out over the course of the two weeks preceding Tiana's escape from the city.

Every one of the dozen was about Tiana. None of them mentioned him, except to repeat the first concession of a marriage between the city and Natives to cement a truce.

"What is going on?" Arthur muttered aloud.

Why was Edwin willing to sacrifice his heir in exchange for the unwanted daughter who would not have survived her childhood, if not for Arthur?

"Hanover," someone called from outside the cabin.

Arthur remained in place for a moment, contemplating what was before him with little comprehension. Nothing made sense anymore. Not the skinwalker and his wolf, not Arthur's growing respect for a Cruise, not Tiana's emerging powers, not Edwin Hanover. Arthur had the sense he had stepped into a new reality, one he was unprepared to deal with.

Finally, Arthur plucked the first message about Tiana free from the pile, replaced the rest of the messages, and rose. He strode to the door. One of the adolescent warriors in training held the reins to a gray horse.

"She did not jest about giving me her best horse," he said with a nod of appreciation. The stallion was one of the prized horses from Chases Deer's father's infamous band of rare Arabians. No finer animals were found for two thousand miles, and no other horse matched the stamina of his horses. The horse was saddled, bridled and bearing saddlebags with canteens dripping with water clipped to them.

The youth held out a handgun, two knives, and a pouch whose clicking sounds from within were those of flint.

"Much obliged," Arthur said and accepted the offerings. "Assure your warrior princess I will return when it benefits us both." *And not to marry her*. Although, this part he kept quiet. His heart belonged to the man sleeping in the clinic. He had managed to outmaneuver his father's attempts to marry him off for several years.

With the sun soon to break the horizon, Arthur dared not linger much longer. As unsettled as he was about abandoning Warner and Marshall to the kindness of allies who were quietly choosing a different side, he could not quell the urgency in his blood warning him something much worse awaited them all, if he did not reach the city before the scene from his vision unfolded and condemned everyone.

He mounted. The gray stallion pranced impatiently beneath him and tossed its head, eager to move.

Arthur did not dissuade him. They were both anxious.

With a nod at the youth, and one last glance in the direction of the clinic, he released his hold on the horse's head and urged him forward, towards the plains separating the village from the city.

Arthur reached the edge of the forest by noon. The roads through Native land coalesced into one solitary path leading towards the city. It was a matter of defense for the city, and an agreement made with the neighboring tribes, that only one road would be maintained in each cardinal direction.

Taking the road made Arthur a target.

Going around it extended his trip.

On any other horse, he would have chosen the slow route so he could hide if the Natives tracking him caught up. But on the fastest horse north of the city, Arthur brazenly chose to ride exposed and fast, straight for Lost Vegas.

SIX

HIS BACK to her and eyes on the forest across the clearing, Diving Eagle tossed an apple in the air above his head. Tiana followed it with her eyes from her position seated at the base of a large tree. Rocky was moving through what he called fighting forms – smooth, controlled, slow blocks and strikes. He was sweating despite the cool mid-morning.

After a day of waiting in this spot for the neighboring Newe tribe to grant them permission to enter their territory, Tiana was bored enough to be antsy. Diving Eagle's rhythmic tossing of the apple provided her some distraction, though nothing seemed to take the edge off she had felt since she faced the skinwalker the first time.

Was his proximity the reason she was barely able to sit still? That the forest felt too small?

She absently ordered the apple to stay in the air without expecting it to obey.

But it did.

Tiana sat forward. She had never considered using her magic to occupy herself, not after a lifetime of being punished for failing to control it. Out here, with a man who disapproved of everything she did no matter what, and Rocky, who was not fazed by anything, she felt somewhat safe experimenting with it.

She tilted her head and ordered the apple to move in midair until it was over Diving Eagle's head. Then she let it fall again.

He was tense enough to jerk when the fruit hit his head. The Native warrior leaned forward to swipe the apple off the ground. He tossed it up again.

She shifted it midair and dropped it.

This time, he stared down at the apple on the ground, then glanced at his hand, before he plucked the fruit up again.

Tiana grinned.

He tossed it once more.

She did it again and dropped the apple on his head.

He turned to face her.

Tiana ducked her gaze but did not hide her smile before he saw it. She waited for him to reprimand her.

"You have some control over it?" he asked instead.

"I seem to," she replied.

He stepped back and grabbed the apple. "Do it again." He tossed it up over his head.

She paused it in midair.

Diving Eagle studied it. "Send it higher."

She obeyed.

"Send it across the field and back."

Tiana did.

He shook his head. "It requires no effort for you to do this?"

"Not this," she replied. "Facing the skinwalker drained me."

"But ..."

She gazed at him blankly.

"You have additional insight."

She did. Not certain how he knew she had not completed her sentence, she nodded. "He ... drained me. Or tried. What I experienced was not natural. When I was close to him, I felt recharged, until he starting pulling my ability from me."

"What part of that was your uncontrolled emotion?"

Tiana's cheeks flushed hot. The way he asked the question left her no doubt about what this careful man thought of *uncontrolled emotion*. "Most of it maybe," she mumbled.

He held out his hand, and she dropped the apple into it. "The more you practice, the better you will manage it when you are not in control," he advised. "You can be more than a weapon who throws skinwalkers into the sky."

Her brow furrowed. She had never considered *how* to use her abilities.

"I imagine you could build a village with your mind in a day," he continued. "Or herd enough buffalo for a tribe to live off of for the winter."

"There are practical uses for your talents," Rocky added, settling onto the ground beside her. "What exactly is the extent of your gift?"

Both of them gazed at her, waiting with an edge she was unable to interpret, but which left the hair on the back of her neck standing on end.

Were two of the bravest people she had ever met ... afraid? Of *her*?

How was that possible?

"I do not know," she admitted.

"We know you have crushed and thrown a skinwalker so far into the air, he landed five miles away," Rocky said. "And Aveline said you killed your stepmother by smashing her head."

Tiana's hands twisted in her lap. There was no judgment in his tone, and Diving Eagle appeared interested.

"You can levitate things with your mind and control them in the air," Rocky continued. "What else?"

"I ... well, I do not know how, but I made the Ghouls leave us alone once," she said. "And I have visions of the future. Bad ones.

This is how I recognized the skinwalker when I had never seen him before." She paused, thoughts on the latest vision, where the skinwalker had tried to speak to her rather than attack her. Tiana shook her head. "I also hear thoughts sometimes. Not often, though."

Her words were met with a long silence.

"You all have a word for this?" Rocky joked uneasily to Diving Eagle.

"No."

"My father calls them deformities," she said. "My brother has them as well."

"Does your father?" Rocky asked.

"Yes," Diving Eagle replied.

"No," she said simultaneously.

"I have a feeling he does," Rocky said. "It would explain how no one will oppose him after burning half the population of the city."

"I would prefer never to find out why he does what he does," she said softly. "I intend to never see him again."

"I wish you luck. It's rare when someone can escape his past." The wise words were quiet.

She glanced up at him, realizing she knew nothing of his story, either. She knew little of the men with her, especially how they thought or who they really were.

"Out of curiosity, how often do you read minds?" Rocky asked.

"Rarely," she replied. "Before last night, it had been weeks. I hear only a sentence or two."

"Last night?" Diving Eagle prodded. "Was this why you fled the council?"

"No. I read your mind."

He stared at her. Hard.

Rocky laughed. "A word of advice, Tiana. Don't tell people you can read their minds," he said. "Unless they're friends. Aveline and I wouldn't care, but some people might."

"Agreed," Diving Eagle and shifted to see the forest across the clearing once more.

Tiana sensed she had offended him. Rocky's wink and amused smile, however, left her feeling less concerned. If the assassin was not worried, she would not be, either.

The three settled into quiet again. Diving Eagle replaced the apple in his bag and walked a few feet into the clearing.

Rocky removed two bone knives and began to polish them.

Tiana rested against the tree trunk and let her head fall back. The pine needles lining the branches above her head brought a smile to her face. Their rich scent and color were magical – and more beautiful than she ever imagined possible when she was trapped in her room in the city.

Her eyes drifted closed, and she drew several deep breaths to help her wired body relax. She listened to the breeze whisper through the trees. The morning was the epitome of spring: cool air, warm sunshine, and filled with the bright songs of birds. An instinct stirred at the far reaches of her mind, almost too faint and far for her to make out.

She opened her eyes and listened hard at what her deformities were trying to tell her. She was able to find someone with her mind when she actively tried. She had never experienced this sense before, though, as if someone was entering her mind unbidden to tell her he or she was present.

"I think someone is coming," she said and stood.

"I see no one," Diving Eagle said, eyes trained across the meadow.

Tiana listened again then faced to the right. "From that direction." She pointed to the east rather than the north.

Diving Eagle glanced from her to the trees. He appeared to think for a split second before starting off in the direction. "Wait here," he ordered them both.

Rocky swiftly returned his weapons to their sheaths at his waist and ankles then stood. "Can you make a tree fall on him?" he asked when Diving Eagle had disappeared into the forest.

Tiana looked at him in surprise.

"Not now," Rocky said quickly. "But in case he ends up betraying you, like I think he will. Can you do that?"

"Probably," she replied.

"You're almost confident. That's an improvement," he said. "Remember – you always have the upper hand with us normal people. You can crush us at any time."

She absorbed the words, uncertain why they struck her as odd. "I would not purposely hurt anyone," she said.

"But you *can*. That's the important part. You should never feel scared of anyone or anything. You can take care of yourself."

"Except when I am not certain of the threat."

"That's what I'm for. To make sure no one gets to you before you crush them."

I do not plan to crush anyone ever, she said to herself. Tiana smiled faintly. She was starting to like Rocky as much as she had Aveline. For assassins, the pair were honest and helpful in a way no one else was.

They waited in comfortable silence.

Twenty minutes later, Diving Eagle reappeared, accompanied by a lean woman his height who was armed with more weapons than he, and four additional Natives trailing them.

Rocky's wariness increased. He shifted to a position ahead of Tiana by inches. Her eyes were on the warrior woman, who moved with the same controlled, efficient movement as the male warriors.

She and Diving Eagle walked abreast – but with enough tension between them, even Tiana picked up that something was not right.

The warrior woman slowed as she approached, her eyes on Tiana. Diving Eagle joined Tiana and Rocky, staying a few feet in front of both.

The warrior woman looked from Tiana to Diving Eagle and spoke a flurry of words in her Native tongue.

"Speak so they can understand," Diving Eagle replied.

"This girl? Has she any muscles at all?" the woman said.

Diving Eagle's quiet rebuke was in his tongue.

"Respectful of what?" the woman retorted. "You demand access to *my* territory and *my* village and offer up a tale about a monster who will slaughter us all in our beds if I do not allow a girl without muscles into my village?"

"I act in your benefit," Diving Eagle replied. "It is out of respect for you and your father that I did not raid your village and take him. I would have raided any other tribe but I chose not to offend yours."

"If you took one step into my village uninvited, my father and his allies would crush you."

"Your father currently favors my tribe, because he understands what we have to offer."

"My father thinks you are a barbarian!" she snapped.

Diving Eagle turned away and sighed.

Tiana and Rocky exchanged a look.

"They are unhappy with one another, are they not?" she ventured.

"I'd say so. Might be time to make something float," Rocky advised.

Tiana had been thinking along the same lines. With Rocky's support, she focused on the angry warrior woman.

The Native lifted off the ground. Tiana concentrated, not wanting to hurt her, and gently lifted the woman into the air until she was a solid twenty feet up.

The Native woman had gone completely still and silent.

"If I were you, I would listen to Diving Eagle," Rocky called up to her. "There is a real threat in your village, and only this girl with no muscles can stop it before it hurts anyone else."

The female warrior erupted into what Tiana imagined were curses in her language. She thrashed in the air.

For once, Diving Eagle was smiling. Rather, half-smiling. Tiana doubted he was capable of a full smile, but the right side of his mouth tilted up as he watched the woman flailing above their heads.

Tiana lowered the woman to the ground. The Native stood very still for a moment and then released her breath. Her eyes settled on Tiana.

"You did that?" she demanded.

Tiana nodded.

After a thoughtful quiet, the warrior woman spun. "You may enter my village. You will be gone by dusk."

Rocky waited until she was a safe distance away before leaving to gather the horses.

"Why do you two hate one another?" Tiana asked Diving Eagle.

"Many reasons," was his curt response.

"Are we safe in her village?"

"Does it matter? You can throw her warriors into the forest."

Tiana said nothing. She had the sense those around her gave her more credit than she deserved. Lifting one woman into the air, and controlling her abilities when she was emotionally upset, were two separate skills. If someone attacked her, she was more likely to cry and run than fight.

They mounted their mules and trailed the warrior woman into a familiar village. Tiana cheered up when she recognized the place she had been before recently, on her way to find Arthur. They passed the tallest, oldest tree in the forest, whose lights were dark this day, and continued to the medical clinic at the center of the village.

Tiana dismounted before anyone else, eager to see if Warner had healed.

"Tiana!" Rocky called as she entered the wooden clinic unescorted.

She allowed her eyes to adjust for a split second. The beds were empty, and she frowned, stepping deeper into the clinic. In one of the rooms off the main bay, she saw movement through a half open door and drew nearer.

A healer was changing the bandages on an unconscious Warner. He straightened when she pushed the door open.

"You return," he observed. "Your brother is no better."

She went to stand beside Warner. The black wound looked the

same as the last time she had seen it. "He is not healing at all?" she asked, disturbed.

"His condition worsens."

Tiana knelt beside the low bed and rested a hand on Warner's warm skin. Her gifts were too vast for her to understand their limits. Was it possible for her to heal someone, too?

She concentrated and pushed the agitated magic towards Warner. His body glowed briefly before the energy sank into him. She kept her eyes pinned on the wound for signs it was healing.

It did not change.

She tried again, ignoring the presence of Rocky in the doorway.

No change.

Tiana dropped her arm. "I have limits," she reported to Rocky. "I cannot heal."

"No one is perfect," he said. "Who is this?"

"Warner. He traveled with me from the city."

Voices from the bay drew both of their attention. Tiana left Warner to join Rocky in the doorway.

Diving Eagle and the warrior woman were quietly arguing. The Native woman gesticulated towards a bed with rumpled bedding.

"Was someone else here?" Rocky asked the healer.

"A man with wounds that should have killed him," the healer said. "His body was crushed. He barely breathing when they brought him in two evenings ago. This morning, he stood up and said he was well and walked out. I told him he could not leave the village. He said he would go where he pleased and vanished before my eyes. I have never seen anything like it."

Tiana's breath caught in her throat. She and Rocky looked at one another.

"That's not good," Rocky said for both of them.

"His companion has been placed under guard until the ransom promised by Arthur Hanover is paid," the healer added.

"Arthur was here?" Tiana asked.

"For the night. He left yesterday morning. His companions, and your brother, are being held for ransom."

"Brother?" Rocky asked with a glance at Warner. "You have two?"

"I have one," Tiana clarified. "But we thought it best not to tell people who I was when I traveled, because everyone hates my father. Warner is a friend to Arthur."

"You're a Hanover," the healer said.

She nodded.

"Chases Deer knows where your brother went." The healer nodded towards the Native woman.

"She's a real warrior?" Rocky asked.

"The swiftest for a thousand miles. She will lead our people when her father dies, which many believe will be soon, because of his age," the healer answered.

"Amazing." Rocky's eyes glowed.

Tiana lifted an eyebrow at him.

"Not that her father will die," Rocky said quickly. "But a warrior princess. Aveline is the only female assassin in the city. She would love to hear this."

Tiana was not as certain. Chases Deer seemed much more confrontational than Aveline had ever been. She waited until there was a lull in the conversation between Diving Eagle and Chases Deer.

"If I may interrupt," she said, moving closer to the two. "The healer said my brother left yesterday morning. Do you know where he went?"

Chases Deer turned her intense gaze on Tiana. "Brother," she repeated.

"Arthur."

"You brought a Hanover into my village," Chases Deer said icily to Diving Eagle. "*The* Hanover everyone is looking for." She pushed past him and glanced at Tiana. "Your brother went to the city to stop your father from creating war with the Natives. You all will remain here until I have had a chance to speak to my father." She swept out of the clinic.

Only when she was gone did Diving Eagle roll his shoulders back and relax.

"You should have raided her village," Rocky said wisely.

"Agreed," the warrior seconded.

"I like her," Tiana said. Chases Deer did not fear Diving Eagle the way Tiana did. In fact, Tiana guessed the Native warrior feared no one for any reason.

I want to be like her. But she doubted she ever would, not when she feared herself as well as the rest of the world.

"We are stuck here for now?" Rocky asked their companion.

"It would seem so." Diving Eagle faced Tiana. "Can you sense the skinwalker?"

She tilted her head, listening and feeling for any kind of anomaly that might indicate the skinwalker was close. He had a definite impact on her; if he were nearby, she should know.

She left the confinement of the building and stood in the open space in front of it. Tiana closed her eyes. A tiny whirlwind of energy tossed her hair around her shoulders and lifted the loose layers of clothing she wore.

A whisper of an instinct came from one direction. She opened her eyes. Her clothing and hair settled once more.

"Maybe ..." she said and pointed to the west. It was too faint to determine with certainty, as if he were trying to hide himself from her. She turned to find Rocky and Diving Eagle regarding her with different levels of wariness on their features. Rocky managed to smile. Uncertain what had disturbed them, Tiana cleared her throat.

"The healer said your brother traveled with a companion." Rocky was the first to speak.

"Marshall," Diving Eagle supplied. "They both disappeared from our captivity."

"Marshall," Tiana repeated, recalling Marshall's sister Matilda, whom Tiana had accidentally killed. Little had she known Matilda would be the first of many Cruise deaths.

"Chases Deer said the spirit wolf is with him. The wolf is the skinwalker's companion. Perhaps she can take us to him."

Tiana was quiet. She did not want to face Marshall, a stranger she had met on only one other occasional before finding him and her brother chained in cages in Diving Eagle's village.

"Can you find Marshall?" Rocky asked her.

She shook her head. She did not wish to try.

"I may know where he is," Diving Eagle said and struck off in the direction of the large tree.

"You've been imprisoned here before?" Rocky and fell into step beside him.

"More than once."

Rocky laughed.

Tiana trailed, spirits dampened when she thought of Marshall and his family. He would hate her – for good reason. Disheartened to face another victim of her father's madness, she kept her thoughts to herself as she followed them through the village and to a small cabin guarded by two Natives.

They were permitted to pass through and entered. Tiana lingered in the doorway, afraid of Marshall's reaction. The wolf with marbled fur curled up on a blanket in the living area drew her attention. The last time she had seen it, the wolf was black.

"Marshall?" Rocky called.

"In here," came a voice from one of the rooms off the main living area.

The two men went towards Marshall, but Tiana crossed to the wolf instead. She knelt.

The great wolf lifted its head to peer at her with golden eyes.

Tiana reached out to it and ran her fingers through its hair. "What happened to you?" she whispered.

An image of six puppies flashed across her mind.

"Ah. Are they healthy?"

Yes.

"But you are not." Tiana touched the white fur. It was unnaturally cold compared to the black fur.

Dying.

Her fingers stilled. "I am so sorry. Why?"

My time.

"It is not because of a Hanover?" Tiana joked.

Hanover kind.

"You are the only one who thinks so."

Hanover good. Help others.

"I do not. My brother might but ... I have been pretty useless," Tiana said. "Thank you, though, for the kind words."

"This is what I was telling you." Marshall's voice jarred her.

Tiana twisted, terrified to see him with a weapon ready to strike her down in revenge for murdering his sister. He stood several feet away, arms crossed, Rocky and Diving Eagle beside her.

He does not know.

Tiana glanced at the wolf.

Marshall good. Safe. Arthur scared to hurt him.

Tiana almost sighed. She had never heard of a *good* Cruise, but she knew nothing of the family outside of her experience with Matilda and what Arthur had shared with her.

"The Hanover's have this disconcerting ability to speak to magic wolves," Marshall said. "Do you not?"

It took Tiana a second to register his question. She was trying too hard not to imagine what it would be like if she lost her brother and everyone else she cared about.

Marshall did not know.

Should she tell him?

Yes, said the wolf.

"Yes," Tiana answered Marshall. "I can. She says she is dying."

"Does she speak of her master? The skinwalker?"

Tiana returned her attention to the wolf.

The image in her mind was a blur of forest and sky.

"I do not understand," she said.

You find him soon.

"She says we will find him soon," Tiana told the others.

They were quiet.

The wolf rested her head on her paws and closed her eyes. Tiana rubbed her ears, saddened by the idea of the animal dying. "Where are her puppies?" she asked.

"In my room," Marshall answered.

Truth. The wolf said quietly into Tiana's mind.

Tiana drew a deep breath. She stood and faced them. "Marshall, I need to speak to you."

"Speak," he replied curtly.

"Alone." She gave Rocky a look.

He nodded and stepped aside.

"Very well," Marshall looked between her and Rocky. "Come meet the puppies and we can talk."

She trailed him into his room and closed the door behind her. On his bed were six small puppies sleeping and surrounded by a blanket wall to prevent them from wandering off the bed.

"Supposedly, one of them is magic," Marshall said and knelt beside the narrow bed. "Your brother abandoned me here to the Natives."

"I am certain he had his reasons," she murmured.

"As am I. But he could have shared them with me. We have spent the last few weeks together in a wild chase to save *you* from a skin-walker whose life you almost took."

Tiana listened. She leaned over to peer at the puppies and smiled.

"I am ready to leave the forest behind and feast at your father's table again," Marshall added.

Her gaze rose, and she straightened. "That cannot happen, Marshall."

"Why not? I helped save your father's two stray dog children," he replied with no heat. "I feel I've earned my place at my father's side at the head table. Arthur and I put aside our differences. I would consider us friends."

Tiana's mouth felt dry. She wet her lips and drew a breath. How would Aveline broach the news to someone? Her assassin friend, much more experienced in the world, had always been direct with her.

"Marshall, your family is dead," Tiana said. "All of them."

He stared at her.

Tiana took a step back towards the door. "Arthur did not know," she added, wanting to spare her brother the dishonor of lying to a friend, Cruise or otherwise. "My father burned everyone."

Disbelief crossed Marshall's features. His mouth dropped open as he gazed at her. His cheeks flushed red. After a moment of shock, a strange sound emanated from his mouth, one that sounded half like a scream, half like a shout.

And then his hands were around her neck, and he was slamming her into the floor. Black edged Tiana's mind. She did not fight him and closed her eyes, preparing for a beating the likes of which his sister used to give her routinely.

The door slammed open. Marshall, still screaming, was hauled off her. Someone snatched her arm and yanked her up and out of the room, through the cabin and outside.

The two guards were peering into the cabin at the otherworldly shriek originating from within.

Tiana shook her head to clear it and steadied herself against Diving Eagle's warrior body. She touched the tender back of her skull with a wince. The skin around her neck burned and promised to bruise.

"What happened?" the Native demanded.

"My father's reach extends even here," she said hoarsely. She wiped away tears of pain and turned away from the cabin. "My father murdered Marshall's family. Every last person in the city who had a drop of Cruise blood in them was burnt. Marshall did not know, but I thought he should."

Diving Eagle released her, eyes pinned to her features as she spoke the difficult words. "Why would the Hanover do that?" he asked.

"Because he is mad," she replied. "Because he is the monster you believe him to be."

"You could have hurt Marshall. Ended his family line the moment he touched you."

"I am not my father," she said quietly, vehemently. "I have told you this many times. Arthur and I are different." She stepped away from him.

Diving Eagle was silent.

Tiana did not dare look up for fear of his judgment.

"You're a selfish coward, Tiana Hanover," he said finally. "You bear immeasurable power and think only to escape him when you alone may be able to stop him from destroying anyone else." Without another word, Diving Eagle strode into the cabin and slammed the door closed.

Marshall's scream was instantly quieted.

Tiana looked up, startled by the rebuke but more so by the idea anyone thought *she* could do anything to oppose her father.

The image of throwing the skinwalker into the air returned to her thoughts.

What if he is right? She thought. What if she had spent her life feeling helpless and vulnerable and cowering away from anyone who spoke – but she and her hated deformities were strong enough to overcome her father?

She had not always understood her deformities and feared those monitoring her too much to test her limits. Whether she always had the level of ability needed to kill, or it was new, she could not know with certainty.

Was the Native right? Was she strong enough to protect herself now?

Rocky seemed to think so.

What is wrong with me? She thought, distressed. How could she possess an ability and fear using it to the point she cowered away from ... well, everything?

The faint presence of the skinwalker stirred at the edges of her mind. She turned to face the direction in which he was located. A new thought entered her mind. With a last glance towards the cabin, Tiana began to walk towards the forest.

SEVEN

THE STALLION BRED for endurance and speed lived up to its reputation. Twenty-eight hours after leaving the village, Arthur barreled through the city, past the smoky area where his father burned dissidents, and towards the pyramid at the far side. Cries from the Shield announcing the movement of a Hanover through the city followed him. He did not bother to stop and speak to any of the Shield members.

He had slept fitfully for a few hours atop the horse and was plagued by the same vision of his father watching the city fold in on itself and die. The images stuck in his mind, and Arthur had discarded the saddlebags and saddle – even his weapons – in order to relieve any excess weight so the horse could travel faster.

Half-crazed, praying his father had not had the chance to act out yet, Arthur ignored everyone and everything, breezing past the soldiers who greeted him in surprise, the outer city residents who cried out in joy, even George, who appeared startled as Arthur galloped past him.

Arthur slid off the horse's back once he reached the stables behind the pyramid. A groom rushed out to take the horse, and

Arthur patted the sweating animal before hurrying towards the entrance to find his father. From the corner of his eye, he saw George running after him and waving his arms to attract his attention.

Arthur ignored him. Nothing else mattered than ensuring his father was still present in the city and never left.

He reached the personal residences of the Hanover's at the top of the pyramid.

"Father!" Arthur shouted and strode past the guards stationed at the door leading into the apartments.

It was just past dawn, early enough in the day that his father should still be present in his quarters.

Arthur hurried down the hallway and stopped in front of his father's door. He pounded on the door.

"Father!"

Seconds later, a slave opened the door. Arthur pushed his way in, eyes wildly seeking his father's familiar form in the living area of the personal quarters of the Hanover ruler of Lost Vegas.

"Arthur," Edwin said and lowered his teacup. He sat near the window, reading the Shield's morning reports, appearing relaxed and rested.

Arthur bent over at the waist, sweating, dirty from the muddy path to the city, and panting.

"I did not believe I would ever see you again." Edwin rose and approached. He kept his distance with his hands clasped behind his back.

When he caught his breath, Arthur rose. "I negotiated my release with the promise of wealth," he reported.

"Your sister?"

"She is being held by our enemies," he said.

"And you return without her." The disapproval was clear on Edwin's face.

Arthur hesitated, uncertain how to respond. His father had rarely ever asked about Tiana let alone cared for her circumstances or even her health. Arthur had tried to convince himself the message he carried in his pocket – sent by his father to Chases Deer's father – was somehow misread, or perhaps, was an attempt for Edwin to manipulate someone into doing his bidding by using Tiana.

"You will have to return and negotiate her release. After you have rested." Edwin turned away and walked back to his chair. "And bathed."

While there was never affection in their relationship, Arthur was accustomed to some small display of warmth or at least, pride.

His father sat, picked up the report, and began to read again.

Arthur stood awkwardly after the dismissal. What had changed? Why was he, his father's heir, being rejected?

"I rode night and day until I reached the city," Arthur heard himself saying. "Are you not pleased to see me?"

"I will be pleased when you bring your sister home."

"You have hardly ever asked about her welfare at any point in my life," Arthur said. "I have been gone for weeks, Father."

"I did notice both your absences, if that is what concerns you," Edwin said with a glance.

Arthur waited.

When his father made no other response, a flicker of sadness settled deep inside him.

Is this how Tiana feels? The fleeting thought was replaced by another.

"Are you not interested in what I have been through?" he asked. "In the war brewing outside the city? The alliances among the Natives are shifting, and not in our favor."

"It would not be the first time in the history of our family that we faced such a situation," his father replied. "They know they have no chance to take the city. Do not concern yourself with such matters, Arthur. Your usefulness to me is your ability to bring back your sister."

Had Arthur heard his father right?

"The Cruises," Arthur tried a third subject. "Is it true what I heard? They are dead?"

"Traitors to the city and our family," his father said. "My own Cruise wife tried to murder my daughter, and did Marshall Cruise not try to murder you?"

"Yes, but –"

"Has your adventure outside the city made you soft? How can you forgive anyone who hurts our family?"

Arthur said nothing. His exhausted mind was filled with emotions and thoughts he had never considered before. The sense of having entered a parallel world, one that looked like his but was starkly different, returned. His father had always awed him in his calm handling of every situation he dealt with. Before this, never had Arthur considered the idea his father was incapable of feeling. He thought Edwin was a master at dealing with his emotions.

"You want me to bring back Tiana," Arthur said.

"Immediately."

"Father, I ..." Arthur drifted off.

He had intended to warn his father about the vision. But his cold reception, and the experiences and insight he had collected outside the city, left his intuition whispering he should keep the vision to himself. For now.

"... I will go immediately when I am rested," Arthur finished.

"The sooner, the happier I will be with you."

"Very well."

Arthur turned away and left his father's quarters.

Deep in thought, he stood in the cul de sac where the bedrooms of all the family members were located.

He was accustomed to returning from the Winter Hunt to a parade and a feast, with his father speaking warm, glowing words about him in front of everyone in the outer city. Edwin Hanover had never been this cold towards his heir.

What did the newfound chill between them mean? How could his father claim Arthur's only use to him was to find the forgotten sister who only survived because Arthur ensured she did?

The vision of Tiana being chased by their father entered his mind again.

Whatever had changed with his father, it was potentially dangerous for more than Tiana.

"Sir?" George spoke and cleared his throat. "Your bath is being prepared, and food has already been delivered to your quarters."

Arthur blinked. How long had he been standing in the hall?

His eyes settled on his loyal slave, who had been the only person Arthur entrusted to check in on his sister for over ten years. Arthur motioned for his slave to follow him and entered his quarters. The scent of roast meat and vegetables and fresh bread struck him hard. Arthur's stomach roared to life. He had discarded his food the day before in his attempt to purge extra weight from the horse.

Arthur crossed to the table where another slave had just finished unloading a tray of food. He sat and began to eat, almost sighing at the flavors he had missed for several weeks. He wolfed down his food and waited for everyone but George to leave.

When his stomach was full, Arthur leaned back. "George," he started. "Something is wrong here."

George was quiet.

"Do you sense it as well?"

"I do," George confirmed. "Aside from your father ordering ten times the amount of people to be burnt each day, he all but declared you dead and Tiana his heir."

While not expecting this news, neither was Arthur completely caught off guard by it either. It explained the sudden change in his father's messages to Chases Deer. "Has he spoken to a clairvoyant?"

"I would not know, sir."

"From where does this change of policy – and heart – come?"

"No one knows. It was sudden. You missed his proclamation by no more than two days."

Arthur shook his head and stood. "I can explain nothing anymore," he said, mind racing. His father's rejection solidified resolve that had been building since he last spoke to Marshall. "I need for you to arrange a private meeting. In the inner city."

George raised an eyebrow. "You know no one approves when you visit the inner city."

"No one will know this time. I will take no Shield members with me," Arthur said. "Only you, I and this person are to know. Do I make myself clear?"

"Yes, sir."

Arthur provided the name Marshall had given him and only those details George would have to convey to convince the high-ranking member of the outer city to meet him. Once his slave had left, Arthur went to the bathroom for a much-needed bath and to think.

Several hours later, after resting, Arthur sneaked out of the pyramid in a slave's cloak with its hood up and walked through the outer city. Spring rendered the streets busier than they had been, and he passed through two small markets tailored to the pleasures of the upper class before crossing the bridge into the fish market and walking into the inner city.

The late afternoon was pleasantly warm, though mud still mired the streets. Arthur took a roundabout path to ensure no one followed him, his senses trained on the activity of the streets belonging to the poorer classes. Fatigue from his time outside the city lingered, and his tired mind and body wanted nothing more than to sleep until he was recovered.

But sleep was a temptation he dared not allow to lure him away from his visions. The political landscape had been dramatically altered by his father in the short time Arthur was away, to the point Arthur was not certain if he could trust anyone in the pyramid or outer city at all. Tiana had been tolerated but not valued by Edwin, and Arthur did not want to press the limits of where he stood with his father any more than necessary before he had some feel for all that had happened and what approach he could take.

He reached the rendezvous point – a market in a barn where

illegal merchandise was bought and sold – and sank into the shadows to wait and watch for the man he sought. After an hour, he began to think either Marshall's ally was spooked after the mass burnings of the Hanover's political rivals, or that no one would trust any Hanover after all that had occurred.

His body grew stiff from the lack of movement, and he paced a few times around the small market. On his third trip through, he spotted the white hair and well-tailored cloak announcing the arrival of the man he sought.

As instructed, Gavin Ingram had left his personal guard outside. He stood out among the thieves and criminals in rags, and Arthur made a mental note not to meet somewhere quite so public, when his potential ally did not know how to dress to fit in.

Arthur tugged his hood down and approached the clueless Ingram.

"Follow me," he directed quietly.

Ingram jerked away.

Arthur led him out of the market and to a neighboring tavern populated by the same clientele as the market. No one looked up when they entered, and no one would ask questions.

Arthur sat on a bench at a table with enough room for Ingram to sit beside him.

Ingram did so. The wealth of his dress drew the attention of more than one criminal.

"You are not likely to leave here with your cloak and wallet," Arthur said with a half smile. He kept the hood to his cloak up. His father had mastered the art of finding those planning to kill him through a combination of visions, clairvoyants, and spies. Arthur would take the smallest risk possible, given he was sitting with one of his father's dissidents.

"This place is beyond unsavory," Ingram replied. "But I understand why you chose it. Your father would not think to put a spy here."

"You would know." Arthur lifted his hand to order food and drink in an attempt to fit in with the locals. "Does he still entrust you with the doings of his spies?"

Ingram waited until the server had left before responding. "He has become very reclusive. More so than usual. But it is his prerogative, and I do not question the man who keeps our city safe."

Arthur chose to ignore the claim to loyalty. "I imagine he changed after my sister disappeared."

"Two days after," Ingram admitted in a low voice. "Also his prerogative. Why have you asked me to meet you here, Arthur? Why not in your father's council room, where we normally talk?"

"Do you have to ask?" Arthur asked with some amusement.

From the expression on Ingram's features, he was suspicious.

"We have a mutual friend," Arthur began carefully. "Marshall Cruise."

"Cruise?" Ingram echoed. "Traitors, all of them. Condemned to burn for their crimes against the Hanover family." The words were spoken in a rush.

"Marshall is alive," Arthur continued. "He is being held hostage by our former allies beyond the city. He is safe, if you are concerned."

Ingram wore the purposely-blank expression he always did when Arthur had seen Edwin address him during dinners and public events.

"He will not be safe for long, if my father discovers he is alive," Arthur added. "Marshall and I discussed the future of the city, and I understand your ... group has big plans for it and for me."

Ingram glanced around.

"I know you intended to speak to me about this upon my return from the Hunt. Marshall confessed he was supposed to evaluate me and, if I were the person you all think I am, he would approve the decision for you to approach me," Arthur said.

Ingram was silent. Arthur assessed he was trying to decide if this were a trap or not.

"My father will destroy the city and everything around it for many miles," Arthur whispered. "I cannot stop him, if I do not have allies."

"How do you know this?" The question was careful enough that Arthur suspected more than Marshall knew the Hanover's were deformed.

"I have had a vision," Arthur said and drew a deep breath. "A very bad one. One that would unite me with your cause, even though I care for my father and my family's legacy. I cannot rule a city that does not exist, now can I?"

They fell into an uncomfortable quiet as the server brought each of them a plate of food. Ingram scowled at the dirty plate and fatty meat, but Arthur dug in.

"What exactly have you seen?" Ingram asked and poked at the undercooked root vegetables on his plate.

"It is as much what I have seen as what I know," Arthur explained. He quickly shared his insight into the brewing alliances among the Natives as well as the vision. He spoke of everything he had learned or foreseen – except for the visions about Tiana. Unable to explain his sister's presence in his vision, he had yet to decide how much to tell anyone about her deformities.

Ingram listened, his food ignored.

"I owe Marshall my life twice over," Arthur finished. "At first, I did not care to hear anything he said. But the more I saw of the world outside our city, and the longer I listened to Marshall, the deeper I understood the danger my father poses."

For a moment, the head of the underground opposition party sat in contemplative silence. He was too much the politician to reveal what he thought or felt in his expression, but Arthur guessed he was, in part, surprised.

"It is believed, among those few of us who have protected the knowledge of your family's capabilities, that your sister has inherited your father's unique traits," Ingram said at last. "And this is why he replaced you as heir."

"I have my own unique traits," Arthur replied.

"You do not display the level of deformity your father and his predecessors did."

"My father trained me, but always told me I would learn the true secrets to ruling only when I assumed his position."

"My theory is that he was waiting for your full abilities to manifest. They did not. But perhaps, Tiana's did."

It was Arthur's turn to be perplexed. "To what abilities do you refer?" he asked. "I have revealed my own deformities. They are not undeserving!"

"They are not," Ingram agreed quickly. "They will protect the city. But your father wields a different kind of deformity. The ability to move things with his mind, to *change* the composition of anything with a thought, to control the future he foresees, to replace the thoughts of others with his own. We do not know his limits, because he is very strategic in how he uses these gifts. He can alter the fabric of our universe itself."

Arthur could not recall ever witnessing his father use this kind of unnatural power at all. When he demonstrated to Arthur how to use his own abilities, Edwin had only used what power Arthur had. Arthur had no reason to believe his father possessed any other abilities than what he had displayed in private.

For the second time since returning home, Arthur had the sense he had never really known his father, or the depths of the secrets the Hanover leader maintained.

"Your father, and your forefathers, wielded absolute power, Arthur."

"And you think Tiana does now?" Arthur asked doubtfully.

"What you and I think is irrelevant. Your father appears to believe she is his heir."

Arthur wiped his mouth and dropped his fork, no longer hungry. "How did you plan to oppose my father? A man allegedly possessing absolute power?"

"We had intended to pit you against him by murdering your sister before her eighteenth birthday, while you were on the Hunt, and sending word to you that your father was responsible," Ingram admitted.

Arthur's mouth dropped open.

"Perhaps this is better."

"Better?" Arthur managed. "How so?"

"To replace one man possessing absolute power with another would condemn us to four more centuries of mad rule. You do not possess these deformities. You truly can become a different kind of leader," Ingram answered. "You might even save the city from this war you believe is coming."

Arthur's protective instinct stirred once more. Ingram did not address what he wished to do with Tiana, assuming she possessed these abilities.

"I must speak to the others," Ingram said. "How may I contact you?"

"Through my slave, George. I trust him with my life," Arthur said. "My father wishes me to return to the Natives soon to negotiate Tiana's release."

"I will contact you within the next two days. You must not leave here before you hear from me, Arthur," Ingram said. "In the meantime, do as your father says. Keep his trust and if you are in danger, flee and send me word."

"Danger?" Arthur smiled. "Your concern is misplaced. He is my father. I do not fear him and his power."

"Have you never wondered why there are no cousins of Hanover blood, even though every leader bears two children at least?" Ingram asked.

Arthur's smile faded. He had cousins – but they were from his mother's and grandmother's kin, and not directly related to the Hanover's. He was about to reply that his family had a history of young deaths but abruptly realized that four centuries of siblings who died suddenly at young ages did not paint a very healthy picture of the intra-family politics of the Hanover's.

He had never thought to ask his father anything other about his uncle than his name and when and why he died. Edwin's brother had been poisoned, and Arthur assumed it was by the enemies of the Hanover's, and this was why his father was adamant about security.

What if the Hanover's had a much darker history to the deaths of family members?

Ingram rose. "Stay safe, Arthur," he said before walking away.

"Thanks," Arthur murmured.

He returned his focus to his food. Nibbling on another piece of stringy meat, Arthur then pushed his plate away and finished his ale.

The meeting with Ingram had revealed more than he thought possible. Arthur's visions of Tiana's death had been accurate. Now that he knew the source of them, he could not help feeling uneasy about trusting Marshall's allies, even if they were the only people in the city willing to plot against his father. If they had planned to murder Tiana once, would they do it again, now that they suspected she was intended to replace the Hanover leader?

How could anyone – including his father – ever believe her capable of becoming the kind of Hanover who repressed and burned her people at the stake?

Or did the power corrupt every leader once it manifested? Would his sweet sister become like every other Hanover leader? Was this why she had crushed and flung the skinwalker five miles away?

No. Arthur would not allow this thought to take root. Tiana was not the typical Hanover – and neither was he. Everything he had done the past few weeks had been to protect her. If anything, possessing a deformity this great would allow her to learn to protect herself.

Maybe, she could help him depose their father and create balance and stability in a region that had never known either.

Maybe she can heal Warner, he thought. Whenever he let himself think about his lover, his insides twisted, and his heart felt as if it were gripped in the vise of his chest.

He could not, would not, allow his despair over anyone's fate to prevent him from acting. His father had trained him since he could walk how to be an effective leader. The first rule was never to allow emotional entanglement to interfere with what needed to be done.

Arthur would find a way to save Warner. And Tiana. And Marshall. But he needed help, and he needed a mind clear of the fatigue weighing him down.

Arthur left the tavern and made his way through the city once more. By nightfall, he reached his quarters and locked the door then dragged furniture in front of the door in case Ingram was right, and Edwin Hanover planned on murdering his own son.

EIGHT

THE NEXT MORNING, Aveline arrived to the city exhausted and anxious. Her first deep breath in the smoky city reeked of too many humans crammed into a small space – and it was the most comforting breath she had ever taken. She was tired of horses, of grass, of the forest. Lost Vegas was her home, and the moment she set foot in the city, tension released from between her shoulder blades.

As little as she cared for horses, or the bruises riding them left on her behind, she understood the usefulness of their speed and remained atop hers until she reached a familiar part of the city.

Aveline slid off the horse with a hiss and a groan in the ward known to house the Guild. She had been debating what to do for two long days during her journey back to the city. Long before fatigue fogged her mind, she had made the decision to go first to the Guild and reveal the fact she was alive, before pleading with her late father's former friends to help her find Karl.

Her time was short, and her plan to ambush Tiana's father relied on her conducting reconnaissance tonight. It was Sunday, and she had to know if Tiana was correct about her father being in the hidden passages. With no guarantees she could enter the privileged

Hanover's apartments, she would need time to test the limits of what she could do before she began to explore the top floor of the pyramid to find other hidden entrances to the passageways where Tiana used to hide and spy on her family.

Aveline straightened and looked around. The horse would fetch money or provide her a means to leave the city and check on Tiana. After a debate about where she could fit an entire horse comfortably, she began walking through alleys towards the streets of the city's oldest market.

Aveline walked until she reached a quiet part of the inner city where one of Rocky's hiding places was located. The abandoned building served as a refuge for several criminals. She entered the shed behind it, whose door was marked in the lower corner by two crossed knives – the sign of the Guild – which Rocky had carved. While criminals were as likely to prey on other criminals as not, most were wise enough to leave assassins alone.

Entering, she saw that none of Rocky's clothing or sparse furniture had been disturbed. No one had bothered the discreetly marked hideout.

The shed was barely big enough for the horse. Aveline pulled off its saddle and bridle before maneuvering around it to leave the shed. She closed the door behind her. Her nose wrinkled at the combined scent of refuse and smoke.

The Hanover leader was burning more people than usual. The smoke rendered the grassland around the city cloudy and settled over the inner city in a thick fog. The sun was a glowing disk in the smoky sky.

Unsettled by the smoke, and by the thought of facing Tiana's insane father, Aveline left the shed at a jog with the intention of going to the Guild members and throwing herself on their mercy for help finding Karl.

If something went wrong this week, if Tiana's father used the deformities the Natives claimed he possessed to kill her, she wanted to die knowing she had found Karl or that the Guild would find him on her behalf.

Aveline's hands shook. She rubbed them on the leather material of her thighs, being careful not to rip her pants with the bear claw of her left hand. She wanted to write off her shakiness as exhaustion, but she could not take her mind off of what she had to do this night. She did not fear taking a life. She did not fear for her own life, either. But what caused her hands to shake and her heart to race? What filled her with urgency and wired energy when she had not slept in two days and was too tired to think straight?

Aveline self-consciously draped the edge of her cloak over her forearm and hand to hide it. She continued walking, only half aware of where her feet took her. When she realized where she was headed, she slowed.

She had intended to visit Guild Main and instead, was two wards away, near the home she had shared with her father.

Aveline glanced towards the sky and wondered if her father were watching her now and if so, what he thought about her case of distraught nerves on the week of her first official assassination.

She debated turning away from this direction and going to Guild Main. A thought stopped her, and she shook her head before continuing.

She wanted to visit her favorite place in the city one last time, before she spent the week researching how to murder Tiana's father. If she failed ... she would never be here again.

She continued through the fog until she reached the corner of the block where her father's house once stood.

The blackened shells of home and buildings met her gaze. Her breath caught, and she stared down the block where many of the high-ranking Guild members used to live or frequent.

The entire ward had been torched. She began to realize the dense smoke in the city did not just emanate from the burnings at its center, but rolled off of other parts of the city as well. It was difficult to see from outside the city, when all the smoke seemed to coalesce at the middle of the city and rose towards the sky in one thick column.

It's unnatural. Smoke doesn't move that way. The errant thought did nothing but muddy the scene before her. An area of the city known to harbor Guild members had been burnt to the ground. There was no way for her to know with certainty that the fire was created any other way than by hand.

Except ...

Aveline closed her eyes to focus her other senses on the destruction in front of her.

When Tiana used her magic, the air around her became charged to the point where Aveline was agitated by the strange energy. Tiana had charged the air around her without using her gifts in the Native village the night before Aveline left, leaving Aveline to conclude she was either growing more sensitive to the magic, or Tiana was becoming stronger.

Aveline felt that same charge in the city around her. Had it always been there? Was she just now feeling it, after her own unique deformity manifested?

Was this strange power the same causing the smoke to behave as it did?

Or ... had it always behaved this way in the city, and she was just now noticing the world around her instead of dwelling in the comfort zone of the place she had always been?

She rubbed the fur on the back of her left hand absently, trying to make sense of the intensity of sensations running through her. She was more tired than she had ever been but felt compelled to run through the city or fight half an army. The charged energy racing through her blood would not abate enough to allow her to rest.

The city had changed since she left it a week prior, or perhaps, she had. She did not know with certainty which it was, but she understood the source of the urgency in her blood overruling her physical exhaustion. She had always been affected by the Hanover power.

Was she now feeling the power of Tiana's father? Was it possible for her to feel him when he was several miles away at the other side of the city?

Was he that strong?

Opening her eyes, Aveline could not decipher which frustrated her more: not knowing why she felt the way she did, or once more witnessing the aftermath of Hanover destruction. The Natives believed Tiana to be her father's heir, because of her demonstration of power in the center of their village.

What if they were right? And Tiana's power would one day rival her father's, to be felt throughout the entire city no matter where he was?

Would it drive Tiana mad, too?

It'll drive me mad if I don't stop it, Aveline thought, agitated.

She closed the distance between her and the remains of her home and stood in front of it. In her mind's eye, she pictured it the way it used to be, and her father alive within it.

She sighed, saddened by the memories and more so by the knowledge something very important had been kept from her.

"You could've warned me," she whispered to him. "You could have mentioned this." She lifted her deformed arm. "Or told me never to leave the city."

Was his spirit listening? Was he capable of regret?

If he were watching, he would want her to act like the daughter of the Devil. He would want her to respect her oaths, to fulfill all her duties with the discipline he had instilled in her. She had long since lost the envelope he left her that she swore to protect.

I messed up once. I don't want to disappoint him again. Leaving Tiana outside the city had not been ideal, but even her father could not find fault with assigning Rocky the protective duty for the Hanover girl. Rocky was her father's own protégée, the youngest assassin ever accepted into the Guild. Aveline had not abandoned her friend and was not about to turn away from the deal she made to save Tiana's life, and Jose's, from the Natives who held her.

Turning away, Aveline began walking towards the center of the city again. She broke into a trot then a run, needing to exert as much of the wired energy permeating the city and her body as possible.

She was out of breath by the time she reached the area where Guild Main should have been. Halting, she breathed in the smell of fire and burning wood, refuse and bodies. She lifted a hand to block the brilliant flames that had all but decimated the buildings crammed into this ward.

At the center of the fire was the hidden headquarters of the assassins. Dozens of people had gathered to watch the buildings burn. Few people spoke, and none of them wore Guild blacks.

Aveline hid her deformed arm and approached the crowd – then stopped abruptly. A new sensation smashed into the base of her skull, a strange pattering. For a moment, the pounding overwhelmed her. She took one step back then two, then turned and bolted down the street, until the beating at her brain was at a tolerable level.

Heartbeats. She had not noticed them in the Natives' village, possibly because she was drugged up on pain medicines. She had encountered no one else on the path returning to the city, and she had avoided the crowds going to watch the public executions on her way to Rocky's hiding spot.

The crowd outside of Guild Main, her destination, erupted into heartbeats that slammed into her mind when she neared. She tested her ability to manage the discordant pattering at her brain. She could venture no nearer than ten feet to the gathered people without staggering from the pain of their heartbeats.

A week outside the city had ruined everything!

Hearing herself panting, Aveline scratched at the fur that covered her chest and neck. She retreated to the shadows of a nearby building while searching the crowd and passersby – whose heartbeats she heard before she saw them – for any familiar faces. She recognized many of the residents and frequent visitors to this part of the city without identifying any of the assassins who had worked with or for her father.

First the section of town where the former Guild leader and all his lieutenants lived and then Guild Main itself. The destruction of two strongholds of the assassin organization could not be coincidental.

Then again, she did not know the extent of damage done to the city by the mad Hanover leader. Judging by the smoke, more of the city was on fire as well. Were his attacks random?

What had changed in the city while she was gone?

Aveline glanced again towards the sky, this time to judge the time. It was early afternoon, shortly after midday. She would need days, if not weeks, to prepare for her assassination. She had only this night to determine if what Tiana said was correct about her father walking through the passages on Sunday nights. The Natives had given Aveline ten days. Two were spent in travel, and two Sundays fell within the timeframe they provided. If Aveline failed to reach the pyramid this night and conduct her reconnaissance, she would not know if she stood any chance at all at murdering the Hanover leader next Sunday.

Her eyes remained on Guild Main. If not for Karl, she would have journeyed to the Freelands with Tiana to ensure her friend made it then returned to the city.

She stalked away from the burning ward, mind racing between her two duties and the diminishing window of time she had to accomplish both. The throbbing collective of unharmonious pattering ease and stopped as she put distance between herself and the crowd. More heartbeats thrummed when she neared more gatherings and passed people. Individually, a person's heartbeat was tolerable. She experimented as she walked to determine how close she could come to others, and groups of people, without feeling as if her brain would explode.

How was she going to slip into the pyramid where Tiana's father and the social elite lived? How could she possibly survive her own deformity long enough to remain in the city for a week?

She wracked her brain to solve this problem as she sought out two more areas of the city where Guild members were known to hide out. Every area she went to was on fire or already embers, and she began to accept that the Guild's secret locations had not been accidentally destroyed, but targeted, which put her in a more difficult situation.

Their training, she knew from her father, would influence the assassins to scatter until the leadership determined it was safe to meet again.

She would not find a gathering of assassins, or the council that ran the underground organization, but what if she found *one* Guild member? Someone who could fill her in on what was going on and maybe provide insight into where Karl had gone?

After walking aimlessly for a few minutes, she found herself turning towards the center of the city. Her father's most loyal ally had always been Karl. Karl's brother, also an assassin, had lived close to the burn yard. Rocky had suggested finding Wilhelm. Aveline suspected he would be the last assassin to turn on Karl but could think of nowhere else to try.

Hoping not to find his home burnt to the ground, Aveline treaded behind a small group people headed towards the center of the city. When their ranks swelled to a dozen, she fell back and touched her temple. Spotting the jammed streets ahead, Aveline broke away as close to her destination as she dared go. She made her way down a quiet street lined with brick buildings, each of which housed two hundred people or more. The pattering of heartbeats was quiet but present. She listened to the instinct that warned her a few seconds before the intensity of the sensations increased and slowed or quickened her step in order to avoid coming too close to anyone.

She had visited Karl many times when she was young and knew his brother to be located in the same building.

Alert and wary, Aveline entered the building and headed towards the fifth floor, where Karl had lived before he took up residency in the street where she grew up.

The beating at her brain grew louder, and she focused on sucking in deep, steadying breaths.

Open bays and private rooms alike lined the hallway. Aveline walked slowly through the dilapidated building and peered into rooms as she went. The bays were mainly empty. She sensed no more than five heartbeats in any one bay, with many of the individual rooms empty.

Passing a large bay, she paused to peer at the faces of the few men and women who had turned the open spaces into their homes before continuing on.

The sign of two crossed knives caught her attention, and she paused in front of a closed door leading to a private room. The small marking was faded and worn.

Aveline knocked.

No one answered.

A faint heartbeat came from within.

She counted to five then pulled a knife free and jammed it between the door and the lock. Aveline wriggled it until the door-jamb splintered. Keeping hold of the knife, she pushed the door open and eased in.

The ill-kept abode was well lit, though too cluttered for her to push the door open completely. Aveline squeezed into the living area and closed the door behind her. Was the state of the apartment a defensive mechanism? To trip anyone who tried to enter?

Her nose wrinkled as the scent of human waste reached her. Outside of the outer city, no one had indoor plumbing. Alleys were for dumping waste and refuse, but it smelled as if someone had missed the open window or not bothered trying.

"Wilhelm?" she called. "I know you're here."

Aveline searched the floor visibly for booby traps before taking several steps deeper into the quiet apartment. As she neared the single door in the apartment, from which the heartbeat came, she heard a strange sound. Part rattle, part exhale. Both sound and stench came from the room off the living area.

She gripped her knife and untangled her bear claw from the cloak, in case she had to fight.

With a deep breath, she entered the darker space of the bedroom and paused in the doorway.

Compared to the rest of the apartment, the bedroom was relatively orderly. Buckets of excrement and urine lined one wall, a bed the other, and piles of clothing and weapons were stacked neatly along the third.

Guild Blacks.

Her eyes went from the familiar clothing to the form on the bed. Pale, sweating and staring at her was a familiar pair of eyes. Wilhelm was younger than his brother by about fifteen years, but their features were similar enough for anger to light in her blood.

Karl's brother shifted onto his side as she stood in the doorway of his bedroom, but he did not reach for the weapons beside the bed. He rested an arm protectively over his abdomen.

He spoke first. "Are you here to take me to the spirit world?"

"No." Aveline lowered her weapons. Whatever was wrong with him, he was no threat. Feet from him, his heartbeat was faint and irregular, on its last leg, if she had to guess.

"I thought you were dead."

"Not yet."

"Shame. I'm ready to go." He eased himself onto his back once more with a groan.

"You are ill or injured?" she asked cautiously. She was not about to contract a terrible disease during the few days she had to plan the Hanover leader's assassination.

"Injured. Had a run in with the Shield several days ago. They left me for dead."

"You're not far from it," she assessed.

"Tell that to my spirit. It refuses to leave this crippled body!" His words came out with a rattle. He spat up blood, spit it into the nearest bucket, and then relaxed onto the bed once more.

"If you speak truthfully to me, I will fetch a healer," Aveline said and replaced her knife in its sheath.

"I am beyond a healer's ability to help," he said. "Can't you smell my leg from there?" He stretched to tug up one pants leg to reveal the black streaks originating from a deep slash that ran down his calf. The lower limb was consumed by gangrene and rotting.

"Remove the leg, and you might live," she said.

"Except for the blood in my lungs."

Aveline shifted her weight between her feet. Did she owe him anything? He was a member of the Guild.

But I'm not, she reminded herself. If his brother were present, he would tell her the same. She hardened. Tiana's softness was wearing off on her, if she were considering helping Karl's brother.

"I went to Guild Main to find your brother," she said.

"The Guild is gone."

"I know. I saw it burning."

"No, I mean, the Guild members are gone. We received the order to leave the city. The Hanover leader caught wind of an assassination plot and sent his Shield to track us all down and murder us," Wilhelm explained. "Hence my wounds."

"It was not the first time our people had been hired to assassinate them," she stated. "Why act now to take out the Guild?"

"Have you been in hiding?" Wilhelm's blue gaze settled on her.

"Assume I have," she said.

"The city has been in chaos for over a week. Water shortages, missing Hanover children, riots and mass burnings. It's been madness, with the Hanover leader at the center of it all," Wilhelm explained. "The Guild, every last member, was hired to ambush the Hanover leader and failed, and he retaliated."

"Who could afford to hire everyone?" she asked.

He shrugged. "It was handled by the leadership. What does it matter? We failed. Those who tried were burnt, murdered or disappeared. The rest of us were ordered to scatter once the Shield began hunting us. I can't move. I was assigned to get the message every Guild member passing through to leave the city."

"You remain loyal to the Guild?" she asked skeptically.

"Of course."

"Even after your brother left."

Wilhelm sighed.

"Why remain?"

"My brother and I are different people," he said curtly. "I owe the Guild my life, and so does he. He always resented your father for taking the leadership role. Karl was in line to become the leader, until the Devil's Massacre, after which your father brought in a benefactor who paid off the leadership council. He was voted in unanimously. Karl resented him for it."

"Karl was my father's friend. He helped raise me," Aveline said, unable to reconcile the man who helped raise her with the one Wilhelm described.

"Karl is complicated, but he never got over being passed up for the position," Wilhelm said. "I suspect the Hanover leader used Karl's knowledge to find us all."

"Karl betrayed everyone," she murmured.

"Or he was forced to reveal his secrets in the Hanover dungeon."

"He defected after my father's death and tried to turn me against the Guild," she retorted. "If this is his doing, he did it to curry favor with his new masters in the Trench!"

Wilhelm coughed again before answering. "Karl petitioned the Guild leadership to make him the leader the night your father died. The Guild rejected him the next morning," he reported. "They promised him the position if he helped the Guild eliminate your father. Then they betrayed him."

Aveline went still. "Say that again."

"Your father was becoming a liability to the Guild. He became reclusive and secretive and controlling. He eliminated all the bene-factors supporting the Guild, except for one, whose name he would not reveal. Everyone accepted his decision, until the money stopped flowing. Your father went into debt. The Guild did as well. It scared the other senior assassins."

She listened, not wanting to believe her father had been anything other than the strong, powerful leader of the criminal underworld she knew him to be.

"The Guild leaders went to Karl, who they thought knew who this secret benefactor was. They manipulated him for a second time." Anger entered Wilhelm's voice. "No one can forget the Devil's Massacre, and no one would oppose a man with your father's reputation. Poison was the method of choice, and Karl became your father's executioner."

Aveline had always thought her father's sudden death strange. He was healthy and strong. To die of a small cold? It had not made sense at the time, and now she understood why.

"Karl betrayed my father, then the Guild betrayed him," she said. "There is some justice in that." It did not help her feel any better. Acutely aware of the fur creeping up her arm, in response to her emotions, she struggled to contain the anger boiling deep within her. "Where is he now?"

"I've had much more pressing concerns," Wilhelm said and motioned to his leg. "I haven't seen my brother in weeks, since he walked out of Guild Main after they rejected him for the leadership position."

She half-heard his answer. Instead, Aveline was reviewing her interactions with Karl throughout her life, wondering if the answer had been in front of her all along. Had she been as naïve as Tiana to trust the man who seemed like an uncle? Had her father known Karl resented him enough to betray him completely one day?

How could anyone believe her father to be worthy of an assassination? The most celebrated assassin in the city's history? Surely he had an explanation for what he was doing!

Her harrowing experience after her father's death, when she was pursued by debt collectors and sold to a brothel, coupled with the skinwalker secret, left her doubting the father she used to worship.

"Why did the Guild lose faith in my father?" she demanded. "Everyone admired and respected him! If he made these decisions, he had a reason. Why didn't they just trust him?"

"You are naïve if you believe him above making a bad decision," Wilhelm replied.

Aveline's cheeks burned hot with embarrassment. Had she been blind to what her father was doing? Or had everyone else lost faith in a man who kept a secret he could not entrust with anyone else?

Raw pain trickled through her, last felt when she stood over her father's dead body.

Why had her father placed her life in danger? Why had he never shared the secrets of what she really was? Why had he lied about her mother's death? What was in the envelope he made her swear she would protect?

Why had he kept so much of the truth from her?

Had she ever really known her father at all?

There is a reason for all of this, a tiny instinct reassured her. There had to be. Perhaps there were topics he could not share with his daughter. Did he fear her judgment? Fear the truth would place her in more danger?

She blinked and noticed the tears in her eyes. Aveline wiped them away, not wanting to appear weak in front of Karl's brother, a full-fledged assassin.

"It's irrelevant at this point." Wilhelm coughed up more blood. "He's dead, the Guild is gone for now, and the Hanover leader is burning the city to the ground. All we need now is for the Natives to sweep through and murder every last one of us."

His words held more truth than he knew. Regaining her composure, Aveline flexed her bear claw. "You think Karl is involved with the Hanover leader."

"Or imprisoned."

She rolled her eyes. "Fine. Or imprisoned. Either way, you believe them to be connected."

"I do. The strikes on the Guild's members began a week ago. The Shield went from not knowing our identities to tracking and attacking us in a day's time. It's not coincidence."

"No," she agreed. "It's not." Her thoughts grew darker as she thought of Karl and the extent he went to in order to punish those people who had not wanted to promote him.

Then again, should she care about the Guild, when its members had participated in her father's murder? They had always been her extended family. She accompanied them to training and spent hours upon hours in her father's office at Guild Main. Many of the assassins played with her when she was younger, and many more gave her tips on how to fight and kill.

"Speaking of Natives ... what are you wearing?" Wilhelm studied her clothing quizzically.

Aveline did not respond.

"Take my blacks," he said and pointed to the clothing in the corner. "You won't be mistaken for a Native and burned."

Her eyes lingered on the clothing. Her whole life, she had dreamt of the day she would wear them, after a ceremony presided over by her father, and upon gaining the distinction of becoming the only official female assassin in the Guild.

After hearing Wilhelm's explanation behind her father's death, she found herself gutted at the thought of wearing the clothing belonging to those who betrayed her father.

Aveline glanced down at her Native clothing. "My mother was a Native," she said. "I'm not sure I know who my father was anymore."

A pattering of heartbeats sent pain ricocheting in her head.

Aveline left the bedroom to peer out the window.

Dozens of people were passing the building. She touched her temple. Spots appeared in front of her eyes. She left the window but could not escape what the presence of people did to her.

"Do you have pain medicines?" she asked.

Wilhelm snorted. "If I did, I would not be miserable and confined to my room."

"I have to go."

"Wait!" he cried as she turned to the door.

She did.

"Will you ease my passing?" he asked. "A favor from one assassin to another?"

Aveline considered it. She held no warm regard for any member of Karl's family, and his death would not cost her a moment of thought. However, he was Karl's only living relative. If she did not find the traitor, she might need to speak to Wilhelm again or to use him somehow to lure Karl out of hiding.

"I'll return," she said. She then hurried through the trashed living area to the hallway.

More heartbeats smashed into her skull. She ran through the apartment building without seeing where exactly she went. Exiting into the street, Aveline sprinted away from the crowds, down an alley, and ran. She ran until the pain subsided, and she became aware of her mind once more.

She slowed and stopped, breathing hard. "Burn ...me!" she cursed and gripped her head with one human hand, one bear claw.

What was the extent of her deformity? Why was it affecting her mind? She clenched and released her bear paw and stared at it. What did hearing heartbeats have to do with being a skinwalker, or half-skinwalker? Were the two talents connected?

Aveline stood in silence for a long moment. This time, her thoughts turned in a direction she had not wanted to think about.

Tiana, Diving Eagle, Rocky ... even Jose ... had suggested she spent some time talking about her family past, and what she was, with the skinwalker Tiana had tried to kill. Aveline had shunned the Native side of her for her entire life, content to be her father's daughter without ever knowing anything about her mother.

But what if she needed to know something about her mother in order to survive what was happening to her?

She lowered her deformed arm and straightened with another look at the sky.

What did it matter who her mother was, when Aveline had no guarantee she would survive the week? The afternoon was creeping on.

Struggling with what she had learned, Aveline made the decision to focus first on this evening and verifying the Hanover leader's vulnerability. She would then have a week to gather the weapons and supplies she would need, find Karl and verify Wilhelm's account.

She began walking again towards the pyramid in the outer city. Assassins were trained to do one run through minimum to work out the details and account for obstacles or environmental factors which could not be planned for from a distance. If she did a dry run this night, and spent the week looking for Karl as well as finding out what she could about skinwalkers, perhaps she would be in a better position the following Sunday to execute Tiana's father.

Would the charged energy of the city allow her mind and body to find enough peace to sleep?

Better add painkillers to my supply list, she thought.

Fur crept up her shoulder and across her chest. This question, above the others, caused her the most distress. Lost Vegas was her home, no matter how much of it was burning or who controlled the city. Would she have to drug herself for the rest of her life to stay in the city she loved?

NINE

TIANA FOLLOWED the instinct guiding her towards the skin-walker until nightfall. The early spring temperature dropped without the sun to warm the air, and she was soon shaking from cold. She hugged herself and continued onward, pausing occasionally to listen to the sounds of brush and branches rustling. The forest was as alive at night as it had been during the day. She lifted her eyes more than once to catch glimpses of the stars between pine needles. When she reached a small clearing, she stopped in the center and released a puff of air, watching it climb towards the stars.

The cold night was cloudless and moonless, a beautiful canvas of black sparkling with stars. She found herself fascinated by the combination of light and dark and how the two complemented each other. Neither stars nor sky overwhelmed the other; they lived in harmony.

The same could not be said for any part of her life.

I miss Arthur. And Aveline, she thought. The absence of her only two advocates in the world was acutely felt on a night like this. She tried not to imagine Aveline in her father's prison or being burnt at the stake, tried not to imagine Arthur falling back into line and overseeing the burning of any more families.

Two nights ago, she had experienced one vision of her brother in the city. Since then, no other visions of either of them had ventured into her mind, leaving her fearful for both. Chases Deer seemed to think Arthur was returning to confront their father, which placed him in more danger than Tiana was lost in the woods. And Aveline ... Tiana could not bear to think of what happened to her friend, if Aveline failed in her attempt to murder Edwin Hanover.

The only two people she cared about in the world were in the city, and she was out here, relatively safe in the forest.

Whenever she thought of her father, she wanted to cry or run or hide. She did not have the strength to oppose him. She was not Arthur, who was strong and fair and compassionate. She was not Diving Eagle, who seemed as if nothing could scare him, not even Ghouls.

Did Aveline and Arthur think she was a coward? Aveline had been trying to toughen her up since they met. Arthur would never reveal his true feelings, but he hired Aveline to protect her.

If they did not believe her to be a coward, they at least both seemed to find her weak.

The worst part: she was weak in a way no one around her was – in her heart. How did she fix herself? Was it even possible?

The distant scream of a Ghoul interrupted her melancholy thoughts.

Tiana sighed and dropped her gaze to the forest. Ghouls were terrifying – but she had already faced them once and survived. Still, she had no desire to test her deformities again and began walking quickly in the direction of the skinwalker once more.

The sense at her mind told her his direction without offering any insight into the distance separating them. She grappled with this, uncertain how far she was willing to go to find him and prove to herself, if not the others, she was not a completely useless coward. Hungry and thirsty, she did not know how long her body would last her or what she planned to do when she found him or how to find food ...

"Diving Eagle would not think of such things," she lectured herself in a whisper. "He would do what was necessary."

Resolute, Tiana glanced around without knowing where she was exactly or how far the forest stretched. According to the map she made, north of Lost Vegas and past the forest, grasslands sprang up and filled the distance between the forest and mountains. She had never known exact distances, though, only recorded what she had overheard from others.

Did it matter?

She shook her head, tired of being conflicted and scared.

Tiana entered the forest and picked her way through the low branches and bushes, continuing towards the faint presence of the skinwalker.

Sometime later, long after she had lost track of where the meadow was, the flickering pulse of energy representing the skin-walker in her mind shifted.

Tiana blinked out of her thoughts and became aware of her surroundings once more. Shivering from the cold, she stopped to eval-uate what had happened. Had she been too upset to pay attention to his movement? Why did he seem to be back the way she had come?

She looked around, perplexed. Without the sense of a Native or Arthur, who hunted in the forest, she had no way to know if anyone had been through here lately or if anyone was hidden in the trees or brush.

The Ghouls were active this night; their cries had remained distant but consistent, and she tilted her head. Were they tracking someone or were there a lot of the creatures in the forest this night?

Distracted by the cries that sounded closer than before, Tiana did not notice the tug at her energy, or the presence of anyone else, until a branch cracked beneath someone's foot behind her.

She started to turn.

A large hand snatched her by the back of her neck, holding her in place. Her deformities reared to life with her fear, prepared to strike out – only to be drained from her.

She froze, recognizing the sensation from her first meeting with the skinwalker.

The smooth, sharp edge of a curved blade slid around her neck. It pricked her skin, and pain fluttered through her.

... can't kill you but when I am done with you, you will wish I had ...

Tiana swallowed hard at the skinwalker's thought. She wanted to cave in on herself, to cry and hope he acted quickly, whatever he chose to do to her.

But that was not how Arthur, Aveline, Diving Eagle, Rocky or anyone else she had ever met would react.

It was not how *she* could react if she were to confront her father one day.

Tiana forced back tears.

"I thought we had an understanding after our initial meeting," she whispered. "Whatever you do to me, I can do ten times greater to you."

"You read thoughts," his growl was low.

"At times. I know you cannot kill me. Is it because of what I am?"

The blade cut deeper.

Though her eyes watered, Tiana refused to cry or move away from the pain. She had spent the better part of her life in pain. There was only one truth about pain worth knowing: it always ended.

"Not always," the skinwalker replied to her thought.

... promise to your brother ...

Tiana had never loved Arthur enough for all he did for her. Her heart swelled with affection for the man who placed himself in danger for her sake.

"We are at an impasse." Her voice trembled, and she cleared her throat. "You cannot kill me, but the moment you release me, I will make *you* wish you had."

"You do not wish me dead, spirit. Why have you followed me?" he replied.

The question was harder for her to explain than she planned.

Did she tell him it was a matter of pride? Of proving herself to others? Of not feeling vulnerable anymore by facing someone strong enough to murder entire villages?

Or ... was it because some part of her hoped he *could* kill her and spared everyone else the pain of tolerating her?

"Stupid girl," the skinwalker said.

She flushed, hating that he could read her mind and considered her as weak as the others did, even after experiencing her abilities firsthand.

"Alone, your advantage disappears. I know what ... who ... motivates you," the skinwalker added.

"Unfortunately for you, she is not alone."

Tiana's heart raced at the quiet, calm claim of Diving Eagle, from somewhere behind the skinwalker.

The silence grew tense, thick, and she held her breath, waiting to see what the skinwalker would do. Diving Eagle was no match for him, but the skinwalker was no match for *her*.

After a long pause, the skinwalker lowered the blade from her neck and released her. At once, her energy flooded back into her.

Tiana stepped away from the tall Native, whose tense frame and agitated magic gave her some indication he was close to snapping, even if he knew the danger in it.

Diving Eagle stood a short distance behind him, the muzzle of a handgun pressed to the skinwalker's head.

"I knew you were lying to me," Chases Deer stepped from the night, her weapon aimed at Diving Eagle. She uttered something to him in her tongue.

Diving Eagle retorted quietly without lowering his weapon or moving.

"You're fast, but you're not careful," Rocky responded and appeared behind her, a knife at her back.

The cry of Ghouls was closer, and Tiana realized the creatures had been tracking the men and woman following her. Dismayed, she wondered if Diving Eagle had followed because he doubted her ability to do even this.

The skinwalker gave a low, smoky laugh.

Tiana was not certain what to do. The three Natives and Rocky were unmoving, each of them waiting for someone else to strike or back down, while none of them appeared willing to do either.

"The Ghouls are coming," she said.

"Two of us here will survive them," the skinwalker seconded. "One of us here cares if the rest of you live."

Were the words meant for her or the others? Tiana did not know, but she was not going to allow the obstinacy of the others to place them all in harm's way. She drew a deep breath and focused on all the weapons. Sweeping her hand upward, she snatched the weapons with her mind and sent them hovering into the air above their heads.

The skinwalker started away.

She blocked him, too. "You, stay," she said. "I found him for you." She addressed this to Diving Eagle. "But we must go now, before the Ghouls reach us. I cannot control my power enough to guarantee your safety, and the skinwalker will not defend you."

The Ghouls began to shriek. They had found their prey and were closing in. It was the instinct of a protector that made Tiana's blood fill with charged energy without her active summoning of her abilities. The colors of the world began to reverse as her body prepared itself for battle.

She grappled with the magic. She did not want Diving Eagle to see her lose control again, not when he already thought her a weak, selfish coward.

"I'm with you," Rocky said and approached. "Those two have some serious issues with each other." If he noticed Tiana's hair flying around, he said nothing.

"We are both survivors," Diving Eagle said.

"Agreed," Chases Deer's face was upturned towards the weapons. "I will deal with your lies later."

Assured the common threat deterred their tensions with one

another, Tiana lowered the weapons without releasing her mental hold on the skinwalker. She focused instead on the power creeping through her body, preparing her. She knew without looking where the Ghouls were, and that the window of escape was already gone.

"This is your territory," Diving Eagle said to Chases Deer. "Take us somewhere safe."

No sooner had she tucked the weapon in its holster than Chases Deer moved into the forest, away from the sound of the hunting Ghouls. Diving Eagle motioned to Tiana and Rocky.

"Too late," Tiana whispered.

The Ghouls, all ten in the hunting party, materialized out of the night and forest, glowing like specters. The first time she encountered them, Tiana had been too scared to notice their flowing robes or the gaping holes of their eyes. She had been controlled by emotion and adrenaline and reacted out of pure terror.

She felt the magic swell within her – but it didn't explode or overwhelm her as it had before with the Ghouls or skinwalker. She had not thought herself able to control it either of the two instances where it emerged from deep within her.

This was different. The colors of the world reversed, and Tiana remained aware. Seeing. Sensing. In control. She marveled at the sensations of being part of her body but also separate, as if the threats were not real, and she was in no real danger. Aware of the creatures staring her down, she felt Rocky tug on her arm.

"Go," she told him. "All of you."

"Aveline would murder me if I ..." he objected.

She faced him, and he fell silent. His weapons lowered, and an odd expression crossed his features. She did not have time to determine what exactly it was.

"Rocky!" Diving Eagle called from deeper in the forest. "Hanover!"

Rocky stepped back from her. "I'll let them know you'll be along soon," he said.

Tiana returned her attention to the Ghouls awaiting her. She did not know exactly what to do with them or how to fend them off or even what she was capable of.

She heard whispers behind her but paid them no attention, instead trying to figure out what to do with the power whirling within her.

"Control," Diving Eagle called, his voice steady despite the danger. "Imagine them to be your father."

The words triggered her power in a way she did not expect. Tiana felt it roll outward, towards the Ghouls. It swallowed them. Several of them managed to shriek again before all of them, and every tree within fifty feet of them, exploded into tiny pieces, shooting straight up into the air and raining down not as flesh and blood, but as pine needles and pinecones. The needles and cones dropped into piles where the Ghouls and trees had stood.

The explosion was silent, as was the magic.

Tiana released her breath and gazed at the piles, puzzled as to how the creatures came to be plant particles. The colors of the world rippled into their natural hues once more. With the disappearance of the threat, her magic faded. Exhaustion, both emotional and physical, replaced the wired energy of magic in her blood.

"We know how she feels about her father," Rocky joked, though there was tension in her voice.

"We know more than that."

Tiana turned at Diving Eagle's cautious tone.

She had maintained control – and he had still found some part of her to be disappointed in.

She lowered her gaze and wilted before starting into the forest. "We should go."

The skinwalker was smiling coldly, the only person who seemed remotely pleased by the display. Chases Deer's mouth was open in shock.

Tiana hugged herself and walked without knowing where she went. She had taken a full twenty steps in a random direction when the others began to move again.

"This way," Chases Deer called.

Tiana altered her route without looking up. Rocky fell in beside her, while Diving Eagle trailed the woman warrior ahead of him. The skinwalker made up the middle of the procession.

Chases Deer moved swiftly through the forest, navigating unseen hurdles that tripped Tiana more than once. The cries of the Ghouls no longer followed them, and Tiana focused on not sprawling on the ground from the rocks, roots, branches and bushes in her path.

Soon, her lungs and thighs were burning from the effort of releasing her magic and navigating the forest all night, and she began to lag behind the Natives. Rocky took her hand and moved ahead of her, tugging her after him in an effort to keep their pace up.

The two Natives halted suddenly. The skinwalker drew abreast of them. Tiana bent over to catch her breath before realizing Rocky had joined them. All four were standing over something, looking down in silence. Rocky squatted.

Tiana stood, embarrassed to be the only one out of breath – another of her weaknesses, if Diving Eagle were tracking them – and joined them.

When she saw what held their collective interest, she gasped and squeezed her eyes closed.

"He's an assassin," Rocky said. "Or was."

Do not be a coward, Tiana. Tiana ordered herself and forced her eyes open. Tears sprang into them, and she covered her mouth with a hand to quiet any sound of horror she might make.

The carcass of a man had been devoured from the waist up, leaving only a bloodied skeleton. His lower body appeared to be intact and was clad in black.

"What did this?" Tiana whispered hoarsely.

"Ghouls," Diving Eagle replied.

She swallowed hard and she began to wonder how she had been calm facing creatures that could do something like this.

"What was an assassin doing out here?" Rocky murmured and poked around at the clothing of the corpse's lower body.

"Meeting me," the skinwalker said.

"You?" Rocky echoed and peered up at the Native. "For what purpose?"

The skinwalker looked directly at Tiana.

"When we are safe, we will talk," Diving Eagle said. "The corpse will draw more Ghouls and other animals. We need to go."

Chases Deer moved away, as did the skinwalker and Rocky.

Tiana remained, staring down at what remained of the man. "Should we not burn him?" she asked, her throat almost too tight to speak. "He is ... was a person."

"Any other time or place, yes," Rocky said. He returned to her side and tilted her chin up to meet his gaze. "Not tonight, Tiana." His look was warm.

She nodded and did not resist when he took her forearm and led her around the body.

Tiana let the tears flow down her face silently. She had only seen one dead body before – Matilda's. The image of what she had done to her stepmother was burnt into her mind. While she had not hurt the dead assassin, neither had she protected him from the Ghouls.

Weak. Coward. Broken. She could not stop thinking about how useless she was.

Soon, her attention shifted to keeping up with the others, and she channeled what energy she had left into running.

When Chases Deer finally stopped, it was at the edge of the forest, in what appeared to be an abandoned village, half of whose cabins showed signs of severe fire damage.

Tiana's eyes fell to the land beyond the village – and her heart stood still. Panting, she tugged away from Rocky and walked the twenty feet of remaining forest.

The grasslands glowed with stardust and rippled like water beneath the soft breeze. They stretched to the mountains whose purple blue shapes she had seen far in the distance, during the annual summer address her father made in front of the outer city.

The mountains were much closer, their towering forms creating a jagged skyline.

Mesmerized by the grasslands and mountains, as well as the knowledge the Freelands were somewhere beyond those very peaks, Tiana paid no attention to the others speaking but focused on the energy of the cold breeze sweeping over her. Aware of their positions relative to her, she was also aware of the skinwalker standing behind her a short distance.

"Why did you meet with the assassin?" she asked him.

"I do not share my doings with spirits."

"I am not a spirit," she said and faced him.

"You are not of this earth."

"Well, what are you?"

His sharply formed features cast savage shadows across his face. "A creature of this world."

Familiar anger and fear trickled through her. She could not think of him without experiencing the vision that had driven her to attack him before.

But it had changed. Inexplicably so.

She started to turn away when she spotted the three who tracked her standing near a familiar cabin.

Tiana shivered. "We have been here before."

"I have not," the skinwalker replied.

"Yes, you have. Rather, you and I *will* be here. Right there." She pointed.

"You have foresight like your brother."

"What do you know of his deformity?"

"Deformity," the skinwalker repeated with a snort.

Tiana waited.

He said nothing more.

She studied him. Tall and lean, with one leg clad in black, the skinwalker's dark eyes were lifeless, his features incapable of warmth or compassion. She had seen shadows of his other forms and heard the Natives speak of his indiscriminate, mass slaughter, of his black magic.

And even he did not know what she was.

"Where is your friend?" the skinwalker asked. "The half-breed."

"Her name is Aveline," Tiana replied. "She was sent to the city."

"Has she changed fully?"

She shook her head. "Almost but no."

"If her body tries again, without my blood, it might kill her, or she may be trapped as a beast."

"You murder everyone but you somehow manage to care about your wolf and her," Tiana stated. She touched the bracelet she wore, the one belonging to Aveline that matched the necklace the skinwalker wore. The mark was specific to the skinwalkers. "Because she is from your tribe?"

He rolled his eyes.

"I may not understand human nature much, but you saved her life when you did not have to," she asserted. "I know you care."

"She is one of my kind, and I am ... or was ... the last. My tribe was small. She is likely a cousin or niece. If I do not help her, she will die, and there will be no one left to follow my legacy."

"A legacy of murder?" Tiana regarded him skeptically. As soon as she said it, she had the feeling Aveline would approve of learning this about the family of her mother. Her protector had always intended to become an assassin. Perhaps both Aveline's father and mother were both assassins.

The skinwalker did not answer.

Her gaze slid to the faint ghost materializing beside him: a Native child with large eyes and a slashed chest. She had seen him in the vision, flanking the skinwalker.

"What was your vision?" the skinwalker asked.

"It was too short for me to know with certainty. But we will be here, and you will ask me to help you."

"Your deformities could be useful, though I cannot imagine an opponent I cannot face on my own."

"I can," she said, thinking of her father.

"Someone you cannot defeat?" He appeared interested.

"I have never tried," she admitted.

"Coward," the child beside him whispered in an airy voice.

Tiana blushed.

"Ignore him. He is vengeful," the skinwalker said dismissively. "He knows the fears of those who can see him and leads them to their deaths."

Tiana shook her head. She knew nothing of spirits, let alone vengeful ones. That skinwalkers existed was enough to scare her.

"He's right." She released her breath.

"You nearly murdered me, a feat no one has managed in a hundred years. You should control those around you and rule them all. How can you fear anyone?"

"You, too," she muttered and crossed her arms. "My father is powerful and I ..." She trailed off without knowing how to finish.

"You are eighteen?"

Startled, Tiana glanced at the sky. If it was past midnight, then she was officially eighteen and had survived to her birthday. "Yes."

"Skinwalkers manifest their abilities around this age. You may as well. If you did not have the power to face him before, you do now."

"It is more complicated than that," she said.

"Because he knows better how to use his abilities."

"You assume he has them."

"You and your brother both do. They are passed down. I know nothing of your city, except the legend of the Hanover's, who have ruled un-challenged for four centuries," he replied.

It was harder to deny what everyone else assumed was true about him. Tiana wanted to think her father was not deformed. It was much harder to think he was – and lied to her and imprisoned her throughout her life because of her deformities.

"Do you sleep?"

She blinked at the odd question. "Of course."

The skinwalker smiled coldly. "I do not. Can you keep me here, and your companions safe, when your eyes are closed?"

Tiana had not thought about the measures required to imprison the skinwalker until Diving Eagle's father decided to use him.

"She will not have to," Diving Eagle said as he approached. "I know you have some respect for trade. I want to hire you, Black Wolf."

The skinwalker faced the newcomer and studied him briefly. "You cannot afford me."

"You were eager to deal with me when I held the Hanover heir."

"And why did that negotiation fall through?" the skinwalker asked. "Because you attacked me in your village, perhaps? Or lost your prized possession."

"You had no intention of ever delivering on your promises," was the cold reply. "Your wolf stole our prized possession, and you would have slaughtered us, if not for the Hanover girl."

"That was the plan." Black Wolf smiled. "Saved by your enemy. I am certain you will repay her with a quick death."

Tiana listened to the exchange, wary of the skinwalker, in case he decided to attack either of them. When Diving Eagle did not immediately correct the creature, she shifted her focus to the Native.

"They will set me free," she said, prodding the Native.

"Will they?" the skinwalker challenged.

"Diving Eagle, your father said I would be free to leave."

His jaw ticked, and he looked at her finally. "That was not the original plan."

She stared at him.

The skinwalker chuckled.

Tiana was uncertain when – if ever – she had experienced the sense of betrayal sliding through her. It was not what she felt when she thought of her father.

This was different. Worse.

She had trusted someone, other than Arthur, for the second time in her life. Was her judgment as weak as her heart?

Was there no part of her free from deformity?

"I will leave you two to discuss your business," she said and started away.

"You do not need a master, spirit," the skinwalker said. "You can control them all."

Tiana ignored him. Part of her wanted to walk away without caring if the skinwalker slaughtered everyone once she was gone.

But another part of her – perhaps the deformed and weak pieces of her – could not bear the idea of anyone else being hurt. She left the immediate area but did not go too far to help, if the skinwalker acted out.

Cold and tired, Tiana sank down against a tree facing the grass-lands. The soothing rustle of grass and pine needles comforted her some, though nothing could take away the pain she experienced knowing she had been betrayed.

Aveline and Rocky were both right not to trust the Natives who were eager to work with her. Like her father, they did not value her at all. No one cared for her, except for Arthur and Aveline, even though she cared what happened to others.

She wrapped her arms around her legs and rested her chin on her knees, shaking from cold but unwilling to be around anyone else at the moment.

Her eyes closed, and she began to doze, fatigued after the long night.

"You have to understand you are the enemy of my people," Diving Eagle said, interrupting her solitude sometime later.

She sighed, wishing she could be somewhere else at the moment.

He draped a cloak lined with fur over her shoulders.

"I am not like you. Any of you." Tiana tugged it around her, grateful for the warmth after her cold trek into the forest. "I do not care for a war I know nothing about, and I do not resent anyone or wish you ill."

"This is not the way of the rest of the world."

"I do not care," she said softly. "I have lived my life enslaved to others and wish only to be free of it all."

He was quiet.

"Have you been truthful with me about anything?" she ventured.

"Not about anything that mattered."

Tiana shook her head. "I suppose it is easy to lie to someone who does not know better, who trusts you at your word."

"It's not." His response was softer, without its normal edge. "We did not make this decision lightly."

"Perhaps it is my fate to be betrayed by those I trust."

"And you accept that?"

"That those who should protect me instead lie to me and plan to murder me?" she replied. "You are not the first. Why do you think I fear my father so much? I would not have seen this day if I stayed in the city."

"Perhaps you should place your faith in yourself rather than others."

She twisted to see him, frowning. "Why advise me at all? You plan to murder me." Anger fueled the words she would not otherwise dare speak to anyone.

"I said it was our original plan," he replied, meeting her gaze. "It was the council's preferred plan as well."

She waited, not quite grasping what he was saying and afraid to trust him, even if she assumed she knew.

"I cannot imagine any version of events where you live," Diving Eagle continued. "Your enemies ... your father's enemies ... will ensure you do not, and your innocence of how this world works, of how deeply this hatred of your family is buried in the breasts of men like me, will prevent you from knowing the danger until it is too late to stop it."

Coldness seeped deep into her, chilling her again, despite the heavy cloak. Aveline had tried to warn her of the danger of her inexperience.

"I cannot believe that men are so disillusioned by hate not to see what is in front of them," she said.

"And that is why you will die."

She felt the truth of this to her spirit. It was not in her to see the intentions of someone beyond their words or to believe everyone she met wanted her dead.

"My father has left the decision up to me," Diving Eagle said.

"I understand," she whispered, not because she did, but because the discussion was hurting her on levels she did not understand. It was worse than how she felt when he called her a coward.

She was ready to be alone with her thoughts, away from Diving Eagle's intent look.

"I do not wish you dead, Tiana."

It was the first time he had used her name. She frowned. "Are you lying to me again?" she asked.

"I will do everything in my power to ensure you live, unless your life conflicts with the lives of my people."

"Out of respect for your father?"

"Partially. If I am to become a great leader like he is, I need to understand the danger of allowing my pride to interfere with the truth. My father encouraged me to remain open when it came to you, to see the truth of who you are. I did not believe him at first." He paused.

Sensing there was more, she waited.

"His health has been failing for some time. I do not believe he will see the end of this war. Either that or ..." He frowned as he studied her. "... or you have triggered my gift. I am beginning to understand his words in a way I had not before." As he spoke, he rose and stretched his legs. "I will let you choose your fate, Tiana. I believe the skinwalker to be willing to work with us. You can leave, tonight, for the Freelands and never return. I will tell the council you died. Or, you can help my father and me lead a war against your father. I will not tolerate traveling with a coward. Those are your only choices."

Tiana's heart beat slow and hard against the cage of her chest. Before she knew how to respond, Diving Eagle began to walk away.

"Chases Deer is hunting for our next meal. Do not venture far," he said over his shoulder. "I will expect your decision by dawn."

She watched him, speechless, and then faced the grasslands again.

Diving Eagle was giving her a choice. Not only had she never expected him to offer her this, but the idea she alone could choose what happened next in her life left her feeling overwhelmed.

And ... conflicted.

How long had she dreamt of going to the Freelands? Her entire waking life!

But now? When her father could hurt her brother and Aveline any day, or the Natives could destroy the city?

Rocky dropped into a cross-legged sit on the ground beside her.

"I feel like I've missed everything my whole life," she voiced sadly. "I struggle to understand anyone, but Diving Eagle?" She shook her head. "How can he hate me so much? I do not even know him."

"He likes you."

"If this is true, I have misunderstood every interaction I have ever had with him!" she said.

"He is not an easy man to understand," Rocky agreed. "But he followed you out here of his own choice and put a weapon to the head of a skinwalker that could crush him faster than you would because he thought you were in danger."

"He followed me because he wanted the skinwalker to use against my father."

"Maybe." Rocky smiled.

He read people better than she ever would. Even so, she did not believe Diving Eagle was capable of liking her. If he decided not to kill her, it was likely because he no longer hated her. But the chasm between no longer hating someone and liking them seemed vast for a man who declared her to be his blood enemy.

Tiana doubted she would ever understand anyone.

"You look scared," Rocky observed. "What's on your mind?"

Everything. She thought. Nothing she could explain in a way that made sense. She felt no elation or excitement when she thought of the Freelands. While she wanted to go, the timing was off. Either she walked away from her brother and friend as war was about to ignite the region, or she stayed with no promise of surviving to see another opportunity to be free.

"Apparently he and the skinwalker came to an arrangement," Rocky added when she did not speak.

Tiana roused herself from her complicated thoughts. "They want him to murder my father, if Aveline fails."

"It's a suicide mission."

"What do you mean?"

"I mean, the Guild has tried to take out your father no less than a dozen times the past ten years. Aveline has the training, but your father somehow always knows. I don't know what he does to those assassins, but they're never seen again."

Tiana's pulse quickened. "You think she is in danger."

"I think anyone who challenges your father is in more danger than they can imagine."

"Then why did she go?" she asked anxiously.

"Because Diving Eagle threatened to kill you, me, and Jose if she didn't."

"I know but ... why did you let her go alone?" she asked, not caring about the emotion in her voice when Diving Eagle was not around to judge her for it. "Are you not her friend?"

"We were raised together. We may not share the same blood, but she is my little sister," Rocky said. A shadow crossed his features but was just as quickly gone. "I tried to talk to her about it but had the sense she already made up her mind. She would not risk your life for any reason, and not just because you are her sworn duty to protect, but because she cares for you. I believe she thinks that she can protect you if she eliminates the source of danger to you. While I did not agree with her decision, I understood and respected it. Aveline can handle herself."

Tiana could not think of Aveline and Arthur in danger without panic stirring inside her.

"And ... I'm taking the risk that you won't let her die in the city, and certainly not at the hands of your father," Rocky said.

"You think too highly of me," Tiana whispered.

"You saved her life and the lives of everyone in Diving Eagle's village."

By accident, and in such a poor fashion, Tiana was embarrassed an assassin knew anything about the incident.

"Ultimately, this is your life and your decision. You can leave any time you like," Rocky said more quietly. "Preferably with me. I tend to think you will be safer in the Freelands than anywhere around here and am happy to escort you there, if you so choose."

She searched his features before shaking her head. Her eyes found the skinwalker, who sat at the fire Chases Deer had started. "My whole life, I have wanted to be free. But not if it means I lose the only people I care about. That would make me no better than my father, who sacrifices entire families for his purposes. My deformities ..." she lifted her hands, and the branches of the tree above them pointed towards the sky. "... how can they be good? I am not strong like you. The thought of facing my father makes me want to weep! How will that help anyone?"

"Everyone fears something, Tiana. I don't understand the nature of your abilities, but I think, and Aveline agrees, that you don't have to become like your father. You can do good things with your deformities."

Then why was no Hanover leader in the city's history regarded as sane? Tiana did not feel madness when she used her deformities, but would she know if she did? How did she help others without also putting their lives in danger?

"I do not know what to do," she said.

"When you do, let me know."

She nodded. Her thoughts were heavy with new insight, and she could not help feeling Aveline, if not Arthur, was going to need her help soon and also that she was the last person in a thousand miles who should provide it.

TEN

AVELINE MADE her way through back alleys, avoiding the center of the city, and crossed from the smelly, crowded inner city to the quieter, well kept outer city. Fewer people populated the outer city. Wealthy residents and their servants looked twice at her when she passed, though she waited until the last street before the pyramid to move out of the public street and into the narrower alley. Sweating from her quick pace, she rested briefly while watching the slaves and elite passing the mouth of the alley.

She listened to the heartbeats to identify any slave alone and moving at a pace that would make him or her easy prey. She had expected the charged energy to grow stronger when she approached the pyramid, but it remained steady. The Hanover magic was equally spread for miles. She did not recall sensing it outside the city, which meant either the city limited its affect, or the Hanover leader did.

Aveline identified one ideal slave by his heartbeat – until he crossed the mouth of the alley. The slave was close to seven feet tall and overweight. His clothing would never fit her well enough for her to look as if she belonged in the pyramid.

She retreated into the shadows of the alley once more and

listened for another chance. As she did so, she could not help thinking the odd skinwalker abilities were going to be useful in her line of work. She could hear people, track them, without seeing them. She even knew what direction they were located, and how fast they were moving by their heartbeats. No dark room would ever challenge her again now that she was able to sense people no matter what the environment did.

A second candidate registered in her newfound ability. Aveline went to the edge of the street and spotted the woman ten or so years older than her and just her size. She left the alley and trailed, waiting until the unsuspecting slave entered an area with few other people.

Moments later, Aveline was walking down the street once more, this time clothed in the slave's robes belonging to the unconscious woman she left in an alley. A slave entering the pyramid was nothing to concern the Shield members posted around the large building.

The nearer she went to the pyramid, the more the pounding in her skull increased. Aveline lost precious time circling the pyramid to find the least busy slave entrance. If she could reach the top of the pyramid, which was sparsely populated, she would be able to tolerate the pattering of heartbeats in her mind.

Reaching that point, though, left her grinding her teeth.

It was dusk. By the time she went to the top of the pyramid, and found Tiana's passageways, it would be well past dark. She did not know how much time she would have to explore the hidden corridors and plot the right place to ambush Tiana's father next week. Feeling rushed again, Aveline recalled what her father had taught her about creating the perfect conditions for an assassination.

He would advise her to prepare and train and practice every detail of the mission.

I do not have time for that, she thought in frustration. She would have to walk in, assess everything from the layout of the corridors to hiding places, the responsiveness of the guards, the Hanover leader's schedule, ideal places to stash her weapons, an escape plan ...

The more she thought about all she had to do, the less hope she had at succeeding.

"One thing at a time," she told herself at last. She would now know how futile her efforts would be, until she determined the layout of the corridors and whether or not she would be able to hide within them. Every other part of her plan would hinge upon those passageways existing, being accessible, and Tiana's information being accurate. The most critical part of her plan was to survey the assassination location under the exact circumstances she would be in next Sunday, when it was time to execute the plan.

Aveline concentrated on using her ability to track heartbeats to find a way into the pyramid. She ignored the Shield members, who likewise paid no attention to a lowly slave.

The slave entrances were all busy. Disappointed, she chose the one nearest the private elevator leading to the top of the massive structure and braced herself to experience the pain of being around too many people. By the time she was ten feet in, her head was killing her. Aveline pushed herself onward. Rather than go straight up, she descended to the less traveled halls beneath the pyramid and stopped in a quiet hallway to breathe. The pounding lessened enough for her to refocus on where she was before she began to make her way through the hallways she had explored when bored.

She went to the laundry area and entered the steamy, hot bay where dozens of slaves labored over cleaning the clothing and linens of the elite. Wincing at the pain, Aveline took a more direct line to her destination than she would have normally. She pawed through several bins of dirty slave laundry before a flash of green caught her attention. Yanking the sash out that marked her as being a slave to the Hanover's, she exited the busy laundry room quickly.

After another break to ground her senses again, she ventured from the maze under the pyramid onto the main floor. The moment she set foot on the main floor, the hammering at her mind began. She staggered and leaned against the wall, waiting for a group of elite kids to pass. When they had, Aveline trailed them at a distance towards the servants' elevator.

She glanced towards the Hanover's private lift as she passed it.

The Hanover leader was exiting his elevator, escorted by three Shield guards. He headed towards the center of the pyramid.

My luck is turning, Aveline thought. She took note of the time and gauged she had an hour, maybe two, before he would venture into the corridors, if Tiana were correct about him being there around midnight.

The kids peeled off from ahead of her, also heading towards the center of the pyramid. Aveline all but ran towards the private elevator that would take her to the Hanover's private residences. She stepped in with another slave in green who eyed her before returning his attention to the linens he carried.

They left the ground floor, and Aveline breathed a sigh as the heartbeats of those people crowding the bottom of the pyramid faded. She sensed the two guards awaiting them long before the elevator stopped.

"You need help?" she asked the slave beside her.

"No, I —"

She grabbed half the stack of linens before he could finish. The slave glared at her. Aveline did not have the chance to assure him she was not trying to edge him out of his job before the doors opened.

The two guards outside the Hanover apartments regarded both of them closely before waving them past. Aveline released her breath, grateful they remembered her and that Tiana's father had not thought to put out an alert for the guardian of his daughter. He most likely assumed she would be with Tiana in the forest.

Aveline handed the linens back to the other slave, who grumbled a curse at her, before entering the utility room where extra linens and other service items were kept.

Aveline headed towards Tiana's old room, listening carefully for the heartbeat of anyone present. She heard no one and relaxed.

The door to Tiana's old room was nailed shut.

Aveline studied it then her bear claw and rested it on the door. Her deformed hand was much larger than her normal one, and she hoped, stronger. She used the long nails to slide between the door and the frame, drew a deep breath, and wrenched the door open.

Nails popped out of place and landed with the tinkling sounds of metal on marble behind her.

Impressed by her own hand's strength, Aveline collected the nails before she opened the door and entered Tiana's quiet room.

It was even smaller than she recalled. She gazed around in distaste, remembering the weeks she spent there as well as the incident with Tiana and Matilda. The room had been scrubbed clean of even the smallest sign of blood from the incident. With the window boarded up again, it was dark, and Aveline turned on the light to the bathroom.

She went to the closet and opened the door.

Frowning, she looked over the wall where the entrance to the passageways had been. Wood boards over fresh concrete blocked off the passageway, and Aveline debated what to do. The passage had run around the cul de sac of the apartments, to Matilda's former room and Arthur's. She had explored its length once and did not recall any other entrance into the crawlspace.

Aveline touched the new wall. Breaking through it, or attempting to, could very well take a week and tools she had no idea how to sneak up to the Hanover's apartments. The sound of destroying the wall alone would guarantee her discovery or capture.

A heartbeat reached her.

She left the closet and turned off the light, listening and waiting as it approached. It paused in the hallway outside the door before continuing into what she judged to be Tiana's new room.

Aveline peeked out into the hall and saw Tiana's door open. Satisfied it was a slave and not a guard, she closed the door and waited for the person to leave. A few minutes later, the person exited and retreated down the corridor leading to the personal quarters of the Hanover's.

After another moment of debate, Aveline left Tiana's old room and stood in the center of the hall. She had never been in Arthur's room or in the Hanover leader's quarters. Tiana's passageways had run from her closet to Arthur's room on one side and Matilda's on the other. She said she heard her father move around beyond the corridor. Given the layout, it was logical to assume, if there were a second entrance into the hidden passage, it would be through the Hanover leader's quarters.

Aveline went to his door and tried the knob. She was not surprised to find it locked. Unlike Tiana's door, she would need a gentler approach than prying this one open with her bear claw. She pulled the lock pick kit, which had been part of the fancy weapons Arthur gave her. Within seconds, she had the door unlocked and pushed the door open.

Aveline stepped into the Hanover leader's quarters, tense and ready to confront anyone lingering inside, even knowing no one was. She did not know what to expect of his quarters, but it was not to find the immaculate rooms to be normal. The décor was masculine and far more subdued than Matilda's gilded chambers had been. The windows were opened, and the room smelled of a combination or roses and citrus cleaner.

Uncomfortable knowing whose room it was, Aveline gave it a cursory search before going to the wall where she suspected a passageway entrance would be. The Hanover leader's quarters were smaller than Matilda's with three separate rooms off the main living area and two bathrooms. The apartment floors were all padded with expensive rugs and the walls bedecked with drapes and antiquated paintings Aveline guessed were from the Old World.

In order for Tiana to hear someone on the other side of the wall, she would have had to have been parallel to Arthur's room, which put the passageway at the end of the apartment away from the bedroom.

Unlike the other rooms, there was no window to provide light in the small area. Aveline turned on a light in the hallway and pushed the door open fully. She entered. The room had been turned into a museum or treasure room by the walls packed with paintings, domed glass over jewels and ancient books, and other trinkets and objects cluttering every inch of surface space available.

Ignoring everything, she concentrated on the wall neighboring Arthur's quarters. She went to use two hands to explore, but her bear paw was too large to do what the fingertips on her other hand could. She traced the space between paintings with her fingers, searching for any sign of a hidden passageway: cracks in the wall, breezes where there should not be any, or anything else to give away the entrance.

Close to the corner of the wall this room shared with Arthur's quarters, her fingers slid between two paintings – and kept going. She pushed farther, waiting to meet the wall but did not feel it.

Aveline wiggled her fingers to determine how much room she had then carefully slid her bear claws into the space.

"Don't fall," she told the paintings on either side. She wrapped her fingers and claws around the door behind the art displays and pulled.

It did not give. She shifted her hips to give her more leverage and tried again.

The door leading to the hidden corridor slid open to reveal darkness.

Thrilled to know Tiana was right, Aveline stepped through the entrance. A faint pattering against her skull reached her the moment she did. She pulled the door closed behind her, wary of being discovered by a slave. Confident the Hanover leader would not be returning until later, she stood still, waiting to see if any light source would become apparent.

None was, and she stretched her hands out straight in front of her, walking forward until she found the wall of the passage. She turned left, away from the direction where Tiana's hidden corridor lay, and began to move slowly down the hall. Her hands trailed on either side of the passage. Without knowing what kind of flooring was installed, or if there were obstacles, she placed her feet carefully, one directly in front of the other.

She counted twenty feet before her toe hit something solid on its way down. Aveline used her foot to feel around before settling it on a stair. The heartbeat was becoming stronger, not fainter, and she paused on the bottom stair to read the senses she was not comfortable with yet. It was possible someone was in the Hanover leader's room, whose wall she walked inside. But it felt like the heartbeat came from ahead of her, not the side or behind.

It was not Tiana's father ahead of her; this much she knew. She did not fear meeting anyone else and planned on leaving before she stumbled upon a slave or anyone else.

Her pulse quickened, and she drew a knife, just in case she needed to threaten a slave. She took another step, then another and another. The stairwell was the same width of the passage – narrow enough for fingers to touch both walls when she held out her hands – and spiraled as it led her upward, into the steeple of the pyramid.

Someone was definitely ahead of her. Aveline continued, her senses listening for any sound the person had begun retreating down the stairs towards her. The devil's blood inside her stirred with its eagerness for confrontation, and fur crept across her body.

The heartbeat remained where it was. Aveline crept forward, pausing at intervals to ensure the person had not moved, and she had time to escape if someone did.

The spiraling stairwell was dark and silent, aside from the brush of her boots against stone, until the curling of its ascent stopped. Light – candle or torchlight by its warmth – edged a door at the top of a straightaway directly ahead.

It was then she noticed the second heartbeat. It came from behind her – and was closing fast. She had been too focused on her destination, and the person ahead, to pay attention to what followed. The heartbeat that trailed her was strong and steady, and it struck her that the heart ahead of her seemed ... weak, fluttering in comparison. Arrhythmic. It had not moved at all since she first sensed it.

Whoever was ahead of her was not ... normal. She had not

noticed the difference until she contrasted it with the normal heart-beat of the person climbing the stairwell behind her.

A shiver worked its way down her spine.

Uncertainty fluttered through her. She had not thought about *why* the passages exited or why Tiana's father sneaked away from his guards and family weekly to enter them.

Who – or what – was secreted away at the top of the pyramid?

The unnerving sense of her bicep expanding in response to her emotions reminded her how important it was for her to remain in control. Aveline stretched and steadied her breathing, aware of the progress of whoever followed her. His heart remained slow, his step unhurried, as if he did not yet know she was present.

She searched the area around her before realizing that she faced only two options: straight ahead or back the way she came.

Aveline began to climb again on her tiptoes. With luck, the door ahead of her hid an apartment much like the others with multiple rooms. She would have a chance to hide before the person following discovered her.

What about whatever is ahead of me? She gripped her knife harder, unable to make sense of the unusual heartbeat awaiting her.

By the time she reached the door, every inch of the skin on her neck was engulfed with fur, and it had spread down her chest to her stomach. With another deep breath, Aveline opened the door a crack and peered through it.

Only one room appeared visible. A fire burned in a hearth oppo-site the door, and she smelled herbs. No one was present in her restricted view.

She pushed the door open more fully, eyes roving the area and knife ready to strike. This room was well lived in and consisted of two chairs, a small table, rugs, the hearth, and two wardrobes. A second room, which had been beyond her initial ability to see, branched off of the small space. Sweat popped out on her forehead and body. The air was heavy and hot, similar to the laundry rooms beneath the pyramid. But it was not just this that left her skin crawling and her devil's blood agitated.

Charged energy. She felt like she was standing beside Tiana the day the Hanover girl killed Matilda. The sensation was thick enough, Aveline found herself shaking out her arms, as if she could push off the energy bombarding her.

The heartbeat behind her grew nearer.

Aveline closed the door behind her and looked for a place to hide.

Someone stirred from the other room. The heartbeat remained faint, fluttering, its rhythm unlike anyone else's she had heard.

Did it belong to an animal? If so, why had she not noticed her horse's heartbeat? Or the hearts of the rats infesting the inner city? She could think of no other explanation for what it was, or what else the Hanover leader hid in the attic of the pyramid.

After meeting the mad, if enigmatic Hanover leader, she did not think he would be hiding an animal up here. Whatever it was, he hid it here for a purpose.

Aveline inched forward rather than retreating to hide in a wardrobe, agitated by the energy and perplexed by what her newly awakened senses were picking up.

She reached the doorway of the second room and froze. Her mouth dropped open. How long she stood there, she did not know, until someone spoke from behind her.

"Little assassin. We meet again," Tiana's father said.

Before she could react to the words, Tiana's father had touched her. Lightly. On her arm.

Hot energy shot through her, stirring and feeding her devil's blood. Aveline staggered and dropped to her knees. Pain and power roiled and swelled within her. It was stronger than her, fed by Tiana's father – and familiar.

As she writhed on the floor, Aveline recalled when she had first experienced it, the day she arrived to the Native's village. The day she could not remember.

"Why is my daughter's protector here without her?" the Hanover leader mused. He stood above her, relaxed, with his arms folded across his chest. "You are both eighteen this night. Congratulations. You made it."

Aveline fought to control the instinct to transform, triggered by the Hanover magic. She convulsed, bewildered by the sensitive senses of an animal that were overtaking hers.

"I cannot have you talking about what you found." Tiana's father said with a glance into the room. "But I cannot kill you, either." He leaned down and touched Aveline again. "It is said killing a skin-walker brings years of bad luck upon someone." His amused smile chilled her to her core. His charged energy shot straight through her again. Her devil's blood roared to life, destroying her attempts to control it.

"Find my daughter. Return her to me," he ordered quietly. "Quickly."

Aveline's clothing ripped. Fur raced across her body, while her muscles bulged and expanded to several times their normal sizes. The necklace bit into her neck without snapping. The transformation was agony. Her body tore itself apart slowly only to begin rebuilding seconds later. Her scream turned into a roar, and her hot tears dripped down the long muzzle that replaced her nose.

She screamed until her throat was raw.

The Hanover leader's words pummeled her brain, searing themselves into her mind. The compulsion to obey was as strong as the instinct to attack him. For several moments, as she transformed, the conflicting urges warred within her – his will against hers. Finally, her body ceased bucking and changing and went still. The image of Tiana was forefront in her mind, and the desire to fight fell away.

Aveline hauled herself to her feet. Her animal senses and human senses clashed, rendered her surroundings a blur of color, smells and sounds she could not fully make out.

"Go. Now," Tiana's father commanded her.

A whisper crossed her mind, a memory, a reason why she should resist.

It was swallowed up by animal instinct and the compulsion to obey, fueled by the Hanover magic corrupting her devil's blood. Aveline turned and barreled away, out of the room, and into the dark stairwell.

"Run, assassin!" the Hanover leader shouted after her.

ELEVEN

THE NIGHT BEFORE, Arthur's dreams had consisted of the vision of his father destroying the city. Over and over, until he could feel the ground beneath his feet tremble each time the city collapsed.

Unable to face another night of visions, he prowled the city streets as he and Warner used to do when bored. The weight of the city's impending doom was made heavier by the knowledge he had been all but ordered by his father to leave in the morning.

In a few hours, when dawn broke, Arthur was expected to be sitting atop the horse he road into the city, ready to obey his father's command, and find his sister.

But if he left ... there would be no city to return to. His visions left him no doubt as to the fate of everything around him.

If he stayed, he would have to defy his father.

No one who ever openly opposed his father had survived the day.

Ingram had not contacted him again, and his hope of finding support in Marshall's allies had faded with the sunset this day.

Dressed in black, and wearing a mask, Arthur crouched on top of a building to peer at the damage done to part of the city by his father. No one could explain what his father was doing, or why he set parts of certain buildings on fire and not the entire ward. His father's council had rebuffed Arthur's attempts at conversation. It was not entirely because of Arthur assuming Tiana's position as the rejected Hanover child.

It was fear. He had seen it in their eyes. The meetings and gatherings inside the pyramid held the same dead air surrounding the burnt, collapsed buildings of the city. No one would so much as whisper insight into what his father was doing or planning.

I cannot leave the city until I am certain it is safe, Arthur thought again and rose. As his father's original heir, he had the importance of preserving the city drilled into him from a young age. His father had burnt many a person in his time leading the city, but he had never attacked the city itself.

What made him turn on it? The mercurial Hanover leader was becoming the largest threat facing the city four hundred years of predecessors had strived to protect.

Arthur could not ignore what his visions were telling him. His father would decimate everything.

Arthur paced restlessly before nimbly scaling down the building to stand in the quiet street whose lampposts had been likewise destroyed.

How did he stop Edwin without allies among the powerful? It was not as simple as facing one man – but one man whose deformities granted him an unknown amount of unnatural power in addition to all the people who would back him out of fear.

"How does one man save a city?" Arthur whispered to the ashes he faced. He could not ever recall being helpless. His whole life, he had been the Hanover heir and commanded respect, power and loyalty by virtue of his birth.

Alone, he began to understand the enormity of a task leading the city truly was. It took a different kind of power than being born in the right household. It took courage and compassion and allies. His father, mad as he was, deserved admiration for managing and protecting a city that would have perished long ago, even if his draconian measures lacked consideration for the life of his people.

Did his father's lack of compassion make it easier to lead? If he were not concerned about preserving life but the city as a whole, no matter how many people had to die?

Arthur did not know the right answer, just as he struggled to find any solution to curtailing the danger the city faced.

Over and over, he drew the same conclusion. He could not leave. The visions were too strong, lingering long after they should have, for him to dare leave his father alone with the city.

But what difference would it make if Arthur remained and could not stop his father?

Tired of arguing with himself over the impossible problem, Arthur turned away from the destruction and started towards the other side of the city and his home. The only good he saw in his situation was that his lover, sister and Marshall were safe outside the city. If he could not stop his father, or ended up imprisoned or dead, those he cared about would have a better chance of surviving on their own among Natives that resented them than facing Edwin Hanover and his strange power.

The rest of Lost Vegas would suffer, though.

Arthur sighed.

By the time he reached his home, it was close to midnight. He removed his mask before emerging from the shadows of the street leading to the great pyramid and tucked it in a pocket. The Shield members greeted him quietly, but none of the elite residents of the outer city would look him in the eye when he passed them. Before Arthur headed towards the elevator that would take him to his apartment, his faithful slave, George, moved to intercept him.

"Sir, there is a matter requiring your attention," George said brusquely.

"From the friend I had you visit yesterday?"

George nodded.

"What does he say?" Arthur asked eagerly.

George hesitated. "Will you follow me, sir?" he asked.

Arthur nodded.

The slave led him out of the pyramid and into the night. He paused in the shadows of a stack of crates containing food that were being unloaded from several carts.

The normally unflappable slave lifted a black piece of cloth, his cheeks red. "Forgive me, sir. I did not want to agree, but they insisted."

"Paranoid, are they not?" Arthur took the hood with a smile, hoping to reassure his slave. "I will do what I must," he said and slid it over his head. "Lead on, George."

"Wait here."

Arthur obeyed. George left his side. Moments later, a horse nuzzled Arthur's arm. He touched its face briefly before someone spoke.

"Mount, please," Ingram directed quietly.

Arthur obeyed.

Ingram took his reins and led him away from the pyramid. The sounds of movement gradually disappeared. Arthur listened and timed their travels. They made two turns, crossed the paths of few people, and generally rode straight away from the pyramid. He was able to identify the moment they left the city by the change in the sounds of the horses' hooves on the ground. The city bore cobblestone and dirt streets; the roads leading out of Lost Vegas were a mix of stone, gravel and dirt.

When he assessed they were safe, he addressed the conspirator. "I expected to hear from you sooner," Arthur said.

"We had to verify parts of your story," Ingram replied. "We are cautious."

"As well you should be," he agreed. "Should I take this journey outside the city as a sign you have decided in my favor? Or are we headed to my execution?"

After a pause, Ingram spoke again, this time from beside Arthur instead of in front. "Your account of what occurs beyond our city appears to be truthful. We are unable to verify whether or not Marshall lives, but our leader has chosen to act after the events of the past week."

"Leader. Are you not the third most powerful man in Lost Vegas?" Arthur mused. "Who would a man like you answer to?"

Ingram did not answer.

"When will I meet your co-conspirators?" Arthur prodded.

"You will meet one now." An amused note was in Ingram's voice. "Though I doubt you will thank me for it."

Arthur did not know how to take the statement. "I am supposed to leave tomorrow morning. Has your leader taken this into account?" he asked. "I cannot oppose my father's command."

"We are aware. Through our other channels, we learned your father intends to send four of his personal Shield guards with you tomorrow morning. They have one order, and it is not to escort you to the forest."

Arthur understood the possibility of his father turning on him, but the words still fell like blows. He shifted atop the horse, struggling with his emotions. From cherished heir to ignored nobody, he had plummeted in worth in his father's eyes in a matter of days. Knowing his father's cruelty, should he experience the sense of loss yawning open at his core? Should he yearn for his father's acceptance?

"I am sorry, Tiana," he murmured under his breath. He had never understood her pain in being rejected, or why she always asked him about their father each time they spoke. He shook his head. "I do not intend to die tomorrow."

"We agree. But we think your father needs to believe you are dead, in order for you to help us," Ingram said. "Ride out as planned tomorrow morning. There is but one route towards the north. We will arrange for your group to come under attack by Native allies before the Shield members can execute their orders. You will be dead in name, with your father's guards as witnesses."

Arthur listened.

"You will then secretly return to the city afterwards and work with us to overthrow your father."

While effective, it was not the greatest plan Arthur had ever heard. His instincts bespoke of no danger from Ingram and blared with danger whenever he thought of his father. Ingram, and his co-conspirators, had everything to fear from the failure of their plan, including the loss of their families. They were taking a risk in trusting Arthur, let alone saving him.

Arthur's vision played through his mind. "I have no choice," he said. "The city is doomed. I cannot leave it in the hands of my father. Of this, I am certain. My visions kept me awake all night."

"The same you shared with me?"

"Yes. Absolute destruction."

"What of your sister?"

"What of her?" Arthur kept his tone neutral.

"Have you seen her in this vision?"

"No."

Ingram was quiet again. He slowed his horse and then stopped both of their mounts. "Your sister is believed to be cooperating with the Natives. Are you aware of this?"

Arthur shook his head but was not surprised by the news. He could not imagine what the Natives wanted from Tiana, unless she was as powerful as Ingram seemed to think she was. In that case, everyone could find a use for her, and she was too naïve to know her own danger.

Not for the first time, he silently thanked Aveline for being present to help his sister.

Ingram's original plan – to pit father and son against one another in the hopes Arthur won – returned to Arthur's thoughts. Was there a chance Tiana was the key, since she was believed to have inherited his father's much speculated about powers? Was that why Arthur's initial visions had been of his sister in danger? Why his father was chasing Tiana through a field in the latest version? Why the Natives wanted her help?

He did not trust Ingram enough yet to voice his thoughts.

Ingram dismounted. "Come down," he told Arthur.

Arthur obeyed and waited. He heard the nickering of other horses and assessed they were no longer alone.

Ingram removed the hood, and Arthur blinked to focus in the night. Ingram stepped aside to reveal a man whose features were familiar but whose face was not. Half a dozen other men, wearing all black to include hoods to hide their faces, stood behind horses behind the stranger. Arthur studied the man, uncertain why he felt he should know him. His hair was the same shade of blond-red as Arthur's, his blue eyes as well. He was older, in his fifties, seasoned by the sun with leathery skin, tall and sporting a fighter's build.

Ingram had brought Arthur outside the city and behind a nearby hill. They were invisible from the road and city yet close enough for the Native scouts watching the city to remain at a distance.

"Arthur, I would like you to meet Simon Hanover," Ingram said quietly.

"Hanover," Arthur repeated. He studied the stranger, suddenly understanding why he appeared familiar. Simon bore the same features as Arthur – and Edwin. "Uncle Simon Hanover who died from poisoning shortly after I was born?"

"That was the rumor," Simon replied. "As a general rule, a Hanover will not kill another Hanover. But we will hire someone else to do it for us. Every once in a while, an assassin fails. Or is paid off."

Arthur was speechless, disbelieving.

"We do not have much time," Simon said and closed the distance between them. He motioned Ingram to step back, and spoke in a low voice for Arthur alone to hear. "It seems the Cruises were right. I spent years tracking a skinwalker to kidnap you, and all I had to do was ask for a meeting." His smile was fleeting. "I wanted to look you in the eye so I knew you were serious about betraying your father."

Arthur shifted. "You hired the skinwalker," he said, recalling Black Wolf's claim.

"I did. I ordered an assassination on your sister as well."

"And you are plotting to murder my father." Arthur did not know what to think. A man who should not exist was leading a silent rebellion against his father.

"I am. Do you agree to help us?"

Arthur heard the dangerous note in his uncle's voice, the one that told him Simon Hanover was not beyond murdering his own kin. "My goal is to save the city," he replied slowly. "Whatever form that takes, I will support. But it is my city, and I will not let it suffer any longer. If you intend to replace my father, then I will not hesitate to dispose of you as well."

Simon held his gaze. The two stared each other down, while Ingram shifted away, lest they resorted to violence.

"Arthur," Simon said. "I do not want the city. I want to stop the madness that runs in our family. I have heard from many people you will make a strong leader."

"Then why did you bring me here? Why not approach me in the city?"

"Because I cannot enter the city. Your father's power prevents me."

"He knows you are alive?"

"Initially, he believed me to be dead. I survived on my own, outside the city, for several years, before he figured out I was alive. I made friends of the Natives and have been hiding among them. A failed assassination attempt alerted my brother. I have not been able to move as freely since then."

Arthur glanced at Ingram. "What do you want, if not the city itself?"

"I told you."

Arthur raised his eyebrows. "No one goes to this extent, and risks the lives of so many people, to walk away benevolently when it is over. There must be a reward in it for you."

"Spoken like a true Hanover," Simon said with a smile that did not reach his eyes. "We will discuss more later. For now, we will work together towards our common goal."

Arthur recognized deception when he saw it. "What of my sister?" he asked quietly. "What is your plan for her?"

"That will depend upon your sister and the actions she takes. If she behaves like a Hanover, she will be treated like a Hanover."

Although Tiana had never once behaved like a true Hanover, Arthur could not stop the churning in his stomach. The man before him was as dangerous as Edwin.

"Do you share my father's abilities?" he ventured.

"I do not. I share yours, or deformities similar to yours in their extent," Simon answered. "We are the lesser sons, the Hanover's that do not normally survive."

Arthur sensed this was the truth.

"Go. Before your father notices your absence, or Ingram's." His uncle moved away towards the horse awaiting him. "You do not trust me, Arthur, and I do not blame you. You will tomorrow morning, after you see how we work. The Natives will help us stage your death."

Or they will kill me, Arthur added silently.

No part of him trusted his uncle completely. What choice did he have? This plan was the only one that might allow him to live long enough to save the city and reunite with Tiana. For now, it would have to be enough that he shared a goal with Simon, and that Simon hated his brother enough to try to depose him.

Arthur would take the political high road and play along, until Simon showed his true hand.

Unsettled by all he had learned, suspecting his sister was in great danger from Simon and Edwin, Arthur mounted his horse and rode with Ingram back to the city. His thoughts reeling and instincts fluttering between alarm and acceptance, he said nothing to his companion as they sneaked along secondary streets towards the pyramid.

"Is Marshall really safe with the Natives?" Ingram asked when they reached the stables.

"Are the Natives not your allies?" Arthur retorted.

"They are your uncle's allies. I have little experience dealing with them. Marshall risked his life to sway you. I would like to know not all the Cruises have been sacrificed."

Whenever Arthur thought of Marshall, he was torn between guilt and regret. Marshall had lost everything in his pursuit of Arthur, and Arthur had nothing to offer in return but the reality of what his father had done to the Cruises. Why had Arthur not listened to him sooner? How had he ever chosen to ignore the horrors his father unleashed upon everyone in the city?

"He is safe. The Natives are awaiting the ransom I promised for him," Arthur confirmed. "Whose plan was it to murder my sister?"

Ingram was quiet for a moment. "Simon's."

"And whose was it to try to recruit me?"

"Marshall's."

Arthur felt sick to his stomach. Marshall's compassion, and devotion to non-violent politics, ran deeper than Arthur had ever suspected.

Nothing I can ever do will make things right for him, he thought.

"We are finishing the planning for tomorrow and will send word in the morning before you leave," Ingram said.

Arthur nodded. Distraught, certain he could not sleep after tonight's revelations, he turned away from his home with the intention of roaming the city again.

A scream froze him in place. It came from inside the pyramid and pierced the night to float for blocks in each direction. An involuntary shiver ran through Arthur. He turned around to gaze up at the pyramid.

It was not a human scream. Neither was it an animal's roar.

It was something in between – and familiar.

Skinwalker. His instincts answered before he could search them for what it was. He and Marshall both had heard that horrible sound on more than one occasion when they were trailing the skinwalker through the forest.

"Find shelter," he said to Ingram and bolted towards the pyramid.

Confused members of the elite were milling in the entrances and ground floor. The Shield had yet to react – and why would they? Arthur alone understood the danger and source of the sound.

He paused when he reached the cavernous interior and let his senses adjust to the noise ricocheting off the walls. The scream bounced around him, until the inner pyramid was filled with a deafening roar. With some effort, and the assistance of his deformities, he determined its source: the apartment at the very top.

Unable to explain how a skinwalker could possibly be in his home, Arthur nonetheless sprinted to the elevator reserved exclusively for the Hanover's and rode it with great impatience to the top.

Before he reached the family's private residences, the sound suddenly stopped.

He sprang out of the lift as soon as the doors opened, past the baffled guards, and down the hallway.

Arthur drew his weapons, already knowing they were useless against the creature he had seen destroy villages, and slowed his pace.

"Father?" he called.

"Sir, the Shield –" one of the guards shouted after him. The man trailed him towards the other end of the apartment.

"Go." Arthur turned and snatched his tunic. He hauled the guard close. "Keep everyone away! Do you understand?"

The guard nodded hastily and stepped back. Arthur waited for him to leave the hallway before focusing again on what was before him.

With any luck, the skinwalker would not be willing to murder him, until he had fulfilled his end of their deal.

Questions poured through Arthur's mind as he moved towards the faint flicker in his mind indicating where the creature was. How had Black Wolf made it this far without being seen? How had he accessed the most secure residence in the building?

How had he done anything without leaving a telltale path of slaughter behind him?

Arthur drew a deep breath to steady himself as he tiptoed down the hallway. His father was present in his quarters, though Arthur's magic was unable to tell what condition his father was in. He was torn between two conflicting thoughts: hoping the threat to the city was dead and praying his father was alive. Anger fluttered through him.

Arthur pushed his feelings aside to focus on his current objective.

Oddly enough, his magic indicated that the skinwalker was in Matilda's room, which Tiana had told him transitioned to her after Matilda's death. Arthur passed his room and his father's then paused in front of Tiana's.

He opened the door and entered, bracing himself for an attack.

"I know you are here," he whispered to the dark room beyond the door. Easing the door closed, he breathed deeply, took a step, and then stopped to listen.

A growl resounded from deep within Tiana's quarters.

"We have a deal, friend," Arthur reminded the skinwalker.

Was it capable of comprehending a person when in its beast forms? Arthur had not thought to ask this or any of the other questions suddenly entering its mind.

He took another step.

The growl grew louder.

He stopped.

"Do you remember me?" he asked. "Remember our common friend? The sweet creature who protects you? Who helps me?"

The growl subsided without disappearing.

"You do know who I am," he said.

His mind told him where the creature was. The fact the skinwalker wasn't attacking was the best sign Arthur could imagine.

"I am placing my weapons down," he said. "Then we can talk." He lowered his knives, heart pounding loudly in his ears. "See? They are down." He pushed them towards the skinwalker with a foot. "You are in no danger." He dropped his hands to his sides.

The growling stopped.

Arthur licked his lips anxiously. Either the beast was preparing to pounce or was calming down. "Come on out of there," he said and stepped closer to the closet in which the beast hid.

Silence filled the room. Outside the door, he heard the clatter of Shield guards gathering.

Arthur retreated and locked the door before returning to his place near the closet door.

"Those men outside the door will overreact when they see you," he warned the skinwalker. "While I'm well aware you can take care of yourself and murder everyone for miles around, I also know this floor can be locked down completely. You will not be able to escape the building, no matter how many Shield members you kill. You will have no choice but to leap out the window. Even you cannot survive that fall, my friend." He inched closer. His stomach turned over and over, and his instincts – reading the intentions of the creature – were torn between warning him away and telling him it was safe. "I can help you. Come out, and we will leave here together."

Arthur held his breath. The stillness of the creature was as telling as its growl. He waited despite knowing how likely it was for the Shield to break down the door soon. He was no longer the heir to his father, but he was still his father's son and one of the only two Hanover's currently located in the city.

Come on, he urged the creature mentally.

The beast stepped one foot out of the closet without making a sound. Its fur was the color of night, its eyes glowing the shade of the moon.

Arthur noted the eye color but did not have the chance to dwell on why it had changed from the last time he saw the beast.

The skinwalker took another step out of the closet then a third and fourth. It stood, the hair on the back of its neck standing on end, and its body crouched as if to attack. It had not chosen the form of a bear this time but of a great black panther.

"I have not seen you in this form before," Arthur said. "You seem ..." *smaller.*

The words died in his throat. Moonlight from Tiana's windows reflected off a medallion around the beast's neck, and the reason behind the noticeable changes in the beast suddenly made sense to Arthur. During the time they shared together in the Diné village, Tiana had shown him her medallion and explained how her guardian possessed an identical one that lit up when they were close.

Arthur's eyes widened, and he stared at it ... at *her* ... in quiet disbelief.

"Aveline," he breathed finally. To some part of him, buried deep enough it was intertwined with his instincts, he was expecting this. The daughter of the Devil had always been special in the same way Tiana was: in her blood. Arthur knew from the moment she appeared in a vision to him, even before he sent out search parties to find the elusive assassin-in-training who was destined to become his sister's guardian. "What are you doing here?"

The skinwalker's mouth opened, and she made a quiet, plaintive sound. Arthur tilted his head, hoping to hear her words, as he often did with Black Wolf's spirit guide. No words or images formed in his mind.

"Can you not turn human? I will understand you better," he said.

She shook her head.

"You cannot turn human?" he prodded.

Another shake.

Before Arthur could respond, one of the Shield members pounded on the door.

"Go back in there and hide," he ordered her quietly. "We can sort all this out later. I need to protect you first."

Aveline obeyed and slinked back into the closet.

Arthur went to the door and yanked it open. "Whatever it is, it is not present here," he told the phalanx of Shield members jammed into the hallways. "Has anyone checked on my father?"

"We evacuated him," one of them reported. "We will do the same for you."

"Gentlemen, I am one of you," he said and smiled. "Who better to show you the hiding places no one other than my family knows?"

He walked into the hall and closed the door behind him. "No one is to enter the sacred personal space of Tiana, the Hanover heir, unless he is accompanied by my father or me."

No one objected to his firm tone, and Arthur pointed to his father's quarters with one hand and his with another. "Search those two rooms and report to me your findings."

Five Shield men piled into each room, and another two into the cramped space of the room where Tiana once resided.

Arthur remained close to the door to Tiana's quarters. As if suspecting the danger her movement or sound could place her, Aveline did not stir from within the dark space.

Arthur managed to subdue the flurry of thoughts running through him. His situation had become more complicated than before. If Aveline were unable to turn into a human, and Arthur had an appointment to fake his own death in the morning, how was he supposed to sneak a panther out of the pyramid beneath dozens of watchful Shield eyes?

Lost Vegas Series
Aveline
Tiana
Arthur
Black Wolf

BLACK WOLF

TWELVE

THE PRESENCE of his wolf drifted out of the skinwalker with the same gentleness the creature had always used to guide him. One moment, the subtle, warm energy hummed within him. The next, it was gone, replaced by a void that felt cold. Empty. Alone.

The skinwalker sat up, focusing hard on the spirit wolf. No whisper of her energy remained. No image of her appeared in his mind.

He bowed his head and wished her safe passage back to her realm, and then stood. The spring night was cool without being cold. The air smelled of the rainclouds blown in by a stiff breeze. The weather was unpredictable this time of year, though warmer than he was accustomed to.

The skinwalker slept apart from the others, who had all sought shelter from the elements in one of the burnt out buildings remaining of the village that once stood in the shade of pine trees, beside the great expanse of grasslands covering the distance between this forest and distant mountains. He had created his own shelter out of the poncho and fur cloak in his possession.

Black Wolf left his shelter, impervious to the chill in the wind, and strode to the place where the trees met the prairie. He stood, senses outstretched and thoughts drifting among his options.

They were few now that she was gone. Neither of them would ever see his homeland again. This much he knew without a doubt.

He stood silent, unmoving. For the first time since he was a child, he did not entirely know what to do. His guide had found him when he was five and had been a constant source of wisdom.

He felt the magic of the pale-faced girl brush the back of her neck before she spoke, and twisted his head to see her from the corner of his eye.

"I hope you do not intend to run," she said. Her voice was firm with him alone. Around the others, from whom she had no need to fear anything, she cowered and spoke tentatively.

Black Wolf faced the prairie again, a half-smile on his face. The pale girl afraid of her shadow was a predator who responded to another predator in her territory. While he had learned the arts of both offense and defense at a young age, the Hanover girl knew only defense.

She's a half-predator. His smile faded. His wolf would have appreciated his humor.

But she was gone, and he was alone in the world.

"Your fingers are tiny," he said and turned to confront the Hanover girl full on. "You will do something for me."

Her guarded expression grew suspicious, and she folded her arms across her chest. Unless he attacked her companions, she was harmless. Ignoring the swirl of power around her, Black Wolf retreated to his shelter for a knife and then sat on a stump nearby.

The waif followed.

"One hundred braids," he said.

There was a pause.

"You want me to braid your hair?" the Hanover girl asked with no small amount of confusion in her voice.

"Yes."

"Why?"

"My wolf has died. I will burn my hair with her body." He felt the shift without seeing the woman behind him.

"I am sorry she died," the Hanover girl whispered.

Black Wolf said nothing. Seconds later, her light touch was on his hair. She released the leather tie that kept his hair length at mid-back rather than its full length past his ankles.

"Why do Natives grow their hair so long?" she asked absently and shook out his hair.

"It is an extension of our spirits. Hair is sacred."

The Hanover girl asked nothing more, and the power around her gradually relaxed and became stable again. He had never met someone with her unique sort of magic. After a lifetime exploring his own capabilities and the world, he was not surprised she existed, only that she had no idea how to wield the immense deformities she possessed.

She started on the left side of his head, and he on his right.

The skinwalker glanced towards the shadows. He had placed the knife three feet from where he sat, aware of the assassin lingering in the darkness, charged with guarding the Hanover girl. One day, he hoped to test her abilities, but not while she was guarded, and not when she was fully rested. Whether an enemy possessed physical strength or magical, it was never wise to incur the wrath of someone at full strength but to wait until the circumstances favored him.

"Your wolf was very kind to me," the Hanover girl said.

No one could understand the depth of his relationship with a companion he had traveled with for a hundred years. Those who could speak to his guide had been very few – the Hanover's, an ancient skinwalker Black Wolf met on his journeys, two shamans, and a random stranger who had fled screaming when the wolf spoke to him some forty years ago. The skinwalker remembered everyone who spoke to his spirit wolf, even though he dismissed the faces and identities of all the lives he had taken and deals he had made, once he received his payment.

Those who spoke to her were special. Those she chose to spoke to were even rarer. There was something about the Hanover siblings his wolf had liked upon meeting them. For his part, Black Wolf had not wanted to understand initially. The brother and sister had caused him more trouble than anyone else he could recall. On the surface, and in their thoughts, the two were too simple to interest him. The girl's thoughts were always pure, naïve, the boy's proud and kind.

They were boring.

Except ... they were also complicated. Predators who chose to dote over prey rather than realize the extent of their abilities. The combination of purity and magic, of kindness and strength, of absolute power and selflessness, was rare enough in the world that Black Wolf reluctantly understood his spirit guide's fascination with the siblings. Even he was forced to acknowledge they had been drawn into something unique.

With four hands braiding, the job went quickly. He gathered a handful of hair into one hand.

"Take the knife and cut them at the base," he said.

Tiana hefted the knife. "I cannot guarantee I will not cut you," she replied.

"I have seen the scars on your arms. You know how much force it takes to penetrate skin. Use less."

Her breath caught in what he assumed was embarrassment, and she tugged her sleeves down to her wrists. The Hanover girl returned to her position at his side and began to carefully cut the clumps he created from his scalp.

The touch of cool air against his skull was unwelcome. It felt as if the wind slid through his skin to join with the void that had formed earlier inside him.

The Hanover girl was slow in her duty, and dawn lifted the night from the forest. An odd silence fell when she had finished. He sensed no threat and twisted to see what she was doing.

The Hanover girl was studying the braids in equal parts curiosity and understanding. He glanced at the hair he had grown over many decades and noted the stripes of white that had not been present before his guide died.

"You are dying, too," she said.

"So I am."

"Are you afraid?"

"No."

She met his gaze with her Ghoulish eyes. "But you are," he assessed. "You cut yourself and fear death."

"I know what to expect from pain," she replied with the honesty that was unique to her.

He shook his head. "What you fear is not death. No man fears eternal peace. He fears dying at a time not of his choosing, before he has accomplished all he wishes to."

"Is this what they tell you before you murder them?" she asked, a flicker of wariness entering her gaze.

"It is what they tell me when they cross over."

Her eyes dropped to the space beside him, and he sensed one of the spirits was visible. Her expression became shuttered.

"You are grateful I will die soon," he said with a faint smile.

Her cheeks blazed red, and she looked down. "In truth, I was not thinking of you." The Hanover girl set the braids gently across his lap and stepped back. "It is not right to wish anyone dead."

"To wish and to kill are different," he replied. "You murdered Ghouls. Sentient, intelligent creatures who resemble us and act differently."

"Self-defense is different," she said, though she was frowning. "I think."

Black Wolf did not have enough time left in the world to mold her into the predator she was capable of becoming. He gathered the braids and stood but left the knife as a truce offering to the assassin whose energy he felt each time Rocky poised for action.

Voices came from the direction of the burnt out cabin where the two western Natives accompanying their party had slept.

"They never stop arguing," the Hanover girl said, looking in the same direction.

Black Wolf half-listened to the Natives with his keener-than-human senses as he placed the braids of his hair into a satchel.

"Do you know why they are arguing?" the Hanover girl called after him.

"Over you. Over me. The route we took. The route they want to take to return. Whose father will be charged with leading the first assault on the city. How many more trained warriors each one of them has. Whose tribe has first rights to trade agreements when the Hanover's are gone." Black Wolf shrugged. "Meaningless chatter."

"Meaningless?" the Hanover girl exclaimed. "This seems important to me!"

"None of those things matter."

She shook her head, clearly not understanding. He debated leaving her small mind to figure it out for herself. Acutely aware of his waning existence on this plane, he decided to enlighten her rather than wait.

"If you or I choose to enter the assault, it will not matter how many warriors exist in the world. It will only matter whose side one of us is on," he explained.

Realization crossed her face. "I am not like you. Or my father," she said. "I will fight no war."

"If I hit you, you will let me. If I hit him," he pointed into the trees, "you will crush me."

Her quizzical gaze went to the area where the assassin had been hiding for hours. Rocky emerged from the brush when Black Wolf pointed.

"If the man you fear threatens those you care about, you will take the war to him. It is only a matter of time before he hurts the person who will compel you into war." Black Wolf said. He saw the truth in her eyes before she ducked her head once more and mumbled her disagreement. "Gather your things. We are leaving now." He packed up his shelter swiftly before striding towards the two Natives brooding after their latest disagreement. "We must go," he told them.

They both looked at him. The resentment in Diving Eagle's eyes had been present since the Hanover girl prevented Black Wolf from murdering everyone in the village. The female warrior, however, was unconvinced of the danger, or she would not be arguing with her new ally about the threat both skinwalker and Hanover posed.

"Now," Black Wolf added.

"Prisoners do not give orders," Chases Deer snapped.

Diving Eagle, however, nodded. "We're leaving now." Rather than remain and argue, he snatched his possessions and left the area.

Chases Deer remained defiant.

Black Wolf lingered, unaccustomed to backing down when challenged. As if sensing his magic shift, the Hanover girl's shield tightened its grip around him.

"There may come a day when you are not so fortunate," he growled to Chases Deer before turning away.

The waif, flanked by the assassin, was watching him closely from a distance. The assassin's casual stance and smile were more deceptive than Black Wolf had ever been about anything in his life. The Hanover understood Black Wolf's threat and was willing to oppose him – but she had no comprehension of how dangerous her other companions were. Black Wolf posed no danger to her.

The assassin did.

Diving Eagle did.

Chases Deer did.

And yet the Hanover only had eyes for Black Wolf.

This, too, made him smile and would have amused his deceased spirit guide, whose otherworldly magic had given her unparalleled insight into people and their motivations.

The Hanover girl frowned. She did not relax again until Black Wolf had put some distance between Chases Deer and himself. Diving Eagle motioned to the Hanover girl without speaking. She lowered her eyes to the ground and approached him, without the assassin.

Black Wolf watched. Diving Eagle spoke roughly no matter whom he addressed, but his tone took on a softer note with the Hanover. Their exchange was short, and she responded with two nods, before the Native moved away.

Black Wolf did not know what had passed between them, but the Hanover girl flung her head back to stare at the sky when Diving Eagle was gone and did not move, as if deep in thought. The assassin approached and nudged her after a moment, and she went, following Diving Eagle, who had stalked into the forest.

The skinwalker followed them both. The dynamics around him had shifted subtly but noticeably in the short time he had spent with the four. By the time they reached their destination, he hoped to understand the motivations of those around him better, without the aid of his guide, who had always acted to protect him.

When it became clear Diving Eagle meant to leave her if she did not comply, Chases Deer trotted after them to make up the last member of the procession.

The two snapped at one another often as they walked, he in his language, she in hers, and both ignoring the three people separating them. Black Wolf listened for details he could use later or information that would flesh out the motivations of the two. He had thought their dislike of one another superficial at first, two people with competitive natures who would gradually learn to work together. But after spending time with them, Black Wolf suspected they just could not stand one another. Whether it was a shared history, clashing personalities, the tension created by the shifting alliances, or a combination, they genuinely despised one another.

After three hours of trekking through the forest, the silence between the two seemed ready to last.

"I never hear our names mentioned among the many discussions between Diving Eagle and Chases Deer," Rocky observed. "What do you all call us, if not by name?"

Neither of the Natives spoke, and Black Wolf knew why. "The Diné refer to the Hanover girl as *daughter of my enemy* or *enemy blood* or *the not yet dead*. When one of them is particularly upset, it is much more interesting. They have created an entire language around cursing the Hanover's," he replied. "Chases Deer refers to her as the girl with no muscles. Both of them call you the smiling assassin."

"Sounds like I got the better end of that deal," the assassin replied.

"They have had hundreds of years to invent names for my family," the Hanover girl said. "I imagine there are many, none of them pleasant."

"One is," Black Wolf replied.

Diving Eagle gave him a sharp look over his shoulder.

The Hanover did not ask, as if suspecting the sliding scale of insulting names could never be pleasant. Black Wolf kept this tiny secret, and Diving Eagle's warning look, for use later. When trading or dealing with someone new, he always waited to name his price until he had time to study the person more. Diving Eagle had two weaknesses – his people and position as the next chief. Was it possible there could be a third weakness?

Black Wolf was not yet certain.

With time, he always uncovered the greatest weakness.

The group was quiet. Since he was leading them through the forest, Diving Eagle chose the path. After the last argument between the two western Natives, Black Wolf understood their destination to be Chases Deer's village.

Black Wolf had planned to return for his wolf's body and her pups anyway, before deciding his next move. He would make no more agreements now that his wolf was gone, and he had already decided to dismiss those he was not likely to fulfill. His time was short; he felt the truth of this to his soul. The only agreement that mattered: the one he made with Diving Eagle, a deal he suspected would put him on track to meet his death.

"The half-breed is in the city?" he asked, focusing on the back of the Hanover's head.

"Her name is Aveline, and yes," was the quiet response.

"Your brother as well?"

"Yes."

The man who hired Black Wolf to find the Hanover heir was located near Lost Vegas. And Diving Eagle indicated the target Black Wolf was supposed to kill was inside the city.

All roads led to the city Black Wolf had thus far avoided. If his spirit wolf was watching, was she amused or concerned? For in very few instances in life was it possible for all roads to cross at one place or moment in the future. In fact, he could not recall the last time this was true, other than the circumstances surrounding how his spirit guide had originally found him.

Once, when his life was just beginning.

A second time, when his life was about to end.

He could appreciate the symmetry of these two periods of his life and knew his spirit wolf would, too.

THEY TOOK A BREAK AT MIDMORNING, another at noon where Chases Deer shared more meat from her kill the previous night, a third mid-afternoon, and a fourth at dusk. The two Natives spoke twice to discuss the distance remaining, but Black Wolf did not need to be familiar with the forest to know how far he was from the wolf's pups. Their energies were tiny whispers in his mind, and he gauged less than two hours of walking remained.

The two western Natives were arguing quietly again, this time about the Hanover girl, who looked ready to collapse after the long day on her feet. Diving Eagle wanted to rest longer then finish the journey. Chases Deer believed the girl could rest when they arrived. With Rocky casually standing guard, the Hanover girl sat on a log, hunched over and gripping her head.

"Are they arguing about us?" Rocky asked Black Wolf, eyes on the two Natives.

"Always," Black Wolf replied.

"She's dehydrated. Tell them she needs a little recovery time." His eyes were on Chases Deer. In fact, they rarely left the warrior woman, and Black Wolf assessed the smiling assassin was attracted, or fascinated, by her.

Black Wolf walked away and relayed the message to the two Natives who glared at him when he approached. Diving Eagle handed over a canteen while Chases Deer rolled her eyes and moved away.

Returning to the assassin, Black Wolf started to toss the canteen and then paused. He tilted his head, assessing the Hanover girl's still body. He had not ventured this close a moment ago, but this time, he felt it, the charging of her magic, the build up in the air around her. She had not moved from her position since they stopped, five minutes before.

"Step away," he told Rocky.

"No," the assassin said with a quick smile.

"Your choice. But if you want her not to burn you where you stand, you will move away," he said. "She's not conscious. She can't control what's happening."

Rocky glanced towards the Hanover girl and then back. Frowning, he shifted closer, only to stop a foot from her. His hair stood on end, and his clothing inflated and ballooned around his form, as if filled with her loose energy.

He stepped back.

"What is wrong?" Diving Eagle asked, approaching.

Black Wolf did not bother to respond. None of them really understood what magic was, or the Hanover's inconsistent control of it, and never could. He stripped his weapons off his body instead and set them on the ground then lifted his hands to show he meant no harm.

As if they could stop me if I wanted them dead. At the moment, the Hanover girl was disabled, and they were at his mercy.

None of them knew that, either, or that, for the time being, his purpose and theirs were in alignment.

"You may want to find cover," he said.

Rocky had taken another few steps away, until his clothing deflated. His hair remained standing on end. When Black Wolf drew abreast of him, he began to absorb her energy, the single most effective defense against the girl that he had discovered by accident when she attacked him the first time. With little to no conscious control over her abilities, the Hanover girl did not know how to defend against the depletion of her power.

The assassin started to follow him. Black Wolf did not have to stop him; Tiana's magic rolled off her in waves and stopped her guardian in his tracks.

"Rocky," Diving Eagle called. "Do as he says."

With reluctance, the assassin retreated towards the other two, who were kneeling behind a large rock.

Black Wolf let Tiana's power fill the void within him. It energized him and sent his limbs changing forms. He made no move to control his body's transformations and focused on the girl who had fallen unconscious. Unwilling to touch her until he knew with certainty what her condition was, Black Wolf crouched in front of her.

Her eyes were open, unseeing, and white instead of black. Her magic swirled around her before it was vacuumed into him. He could not recall ever feeling this level of magic before. It prickled his skin and swam inside him, safe within the confines of the body he had spent a century training to contain magic. It took practice and patience not to push back at the power pushing at him. If he tensed, the power erupted. If he remained flexible, the magic likewise responded to his signal and remained fluid.

Not sure what kind of trance the girl was in, Black Wolf stretched out a hand and rested it on her forearm. No sooner did he feel the warmth of her skin through her clothing than power smashed through him and threw him back ten feet. He landed hard on his back. Before he could rise, a vision erupted into his mind.

THE ABYSS. Smoke. Thousands of spirits screaming and fleeing the two figures in the center. The scene was too chaotic for him to understand where it was or even if it was on this earth. The spirits had no faces, the world little recognizable form.

Tiana and a man he did not recognize were trapped in a silent, motionless confrontation, Tiana on land, the man hovering over the abyss, while magic tore the world around them apart. Black Wolf felt every sensation of being present with intensity he rarely experienced for anything. The world disintegrated beneath his feet, while smoke clogged his lungs and his spirit felt as if it were being ripped from his body. He was falling and soaring, panting and breathless, stuck and being torn apart.

The vision flickered and changed and this time, the world and the people in it remained in solid form, appearing the way they were supposed to. The abyss formed and closed then vanished completely. Spirits emerged from the black hole in that short moment and raced around without hurting him this time.

The Hanover girl and the stranger were visible – then gone as abruptly as the abyss. But someone else remained. A hunched, shadowy figure swallowed too quickly by the vision for him to make out any identifiable features.

But the magic possessed by the form ... he knew this magic as well as he knew his own.

WHEN HIS EYES SNAPPED OPEN, it was not only the vision that lingered but also the faint pulse of power, this creature's presence in his mind, coming from the south.

Black Wolf sat up and stared around him, orienting himself. He lay beside a fire. It was past dark, and his sense told him four people were nearby.

"He's awake!" the assassin called to the others.

Ignoring everyone, Black Wolf climbed to his feet and looked up and around until he identified the highest tree nearby. He crossed to it, stripped out of his clothing, drew a deep breath, and transformed instantly into the form of an animal with the claws he needed to climb.

The onslaught of night on his senses could not override the pulse or images in his mind. His guide had experienced visions at intervals, to include the one that eventually brought them west. Despite his list of abilities, Black Wolf had never had his own vision. He had never considered himself fortunate for this before now. How had his guide born such horrific experiences with grace? He felt as if his spirit had been ripped from his body for those short moments, wrung out, and replaced with half its energy drained.

He scaled the tree and reached the top. Peering out over the forest's canopy, his eyes went first in the direction of the pups awaiting him, then towards the newfound energy in his mind beckoned him to go.

The smoke above the city was visible. Light reflected off it, giving it an unnatural glow. Unable to identify exactly which side of Lost Vegas compelled him, he at least confirmed what he had suspected earlier this day.

All roads led to Lost Vegas.

Brooding, feeling as if his life was out of his control, he remained in the tree, unable to escape the visions or the crumpled form that had somehow implanted its energy, and location, in his mind through the vision. Too many questions pummeled his brain for him to know where to begin.

How was this person certain to reach him? Why beckon him to the city at all? Most importantly, he recognized kind of the energy, but *whom* did it belong to? He had believed himself to be the last of his kind before traveling toward the city of Lost Vegas. Would he not know if there was another?

Black Wolf remained on his perch, thoughts flickering between the visions and his spirit wolf, whose departure could not have come at a worse time.

When he felt calm enough to handle the annoying humans awaiting him, he clawed his way down the tree and transformed.

The three waiting for him backed away. One of them had drawn her weapons and was poised to attack. None of them stood a chance, but only two of them understand that. Chases Deer's shock turned her paler than the Hanover, whose protective field was back in place around the others even though she was nowhere in sight.

Rocky tossed Black Wolf his clothing. Diving Eagle crouched nearby, displaying no fear but nowhere near relaxed either. Anger burned in his eyes.

Chases Deer was babbling in her tongue, her arm shaking and eyes wild after witnessing what Diving Eagle had been trying to warn her about.

Black Wolf winked at her and pulled on his clothing as he sought out the one person who had not bothered to greet him when he left the tree.

"Hanover!" he shouted.

"Easy," Rocky warned in a tight voice. "No one gets hurt."

"He knows that," said the Hanover from behind them.

Black Wolf whirled, bristling with the remnants of her power as well as his. Her eyes were rimmed with red.

"Who was that?" the skinwalker demanded, ignoring the two Natives moving closer.

The Hanover glanced away then back. "My father."

"What're you talking about?" Rocky asked. "Your father isn't here, is he?" He looked at the Hanover girl with a frown.

Wired, Black Wolf reached up to his head – and grimaced when he felt the baldness where his hair had always been. He did not need the reminder that his only friend was gone, and he would soon follow.

"He is not here," the Hanover said.

She said nothing else.

"What has you both upset?" Rocky prodded.

Black Wolf growled, and the Hanover sighed deeply but remained silent. No part of him wanted to involve the lesser beings around him in the discussion he needed to have with the Hanover, but he had an audience now.

"Why don't we return to the fire and rest?" Diving Eagle said.

Black Wolf nodded and stalked towards the glowing bonfire before anyone else had moved. He sensed the Hanover trail him and her guardian follow her. When he reached the blaze, he heard the two Natives break out into another of their quiet arguments.

Chases Deer was refusing to remain, and Diving Eagle refusing to leave.

Black Wolf sat heavily beside the fire and rubbed his baldhead, irritated by it and suspecting his true emotion stemmed from the vision, the figure he saw last, and not knowing what he was involved in.

The Hanover sat closer to him than she had ventured before, and his glance lingered on her. She had admitted her ability to read minds was sporadic. His was stronger. He had learned young that his telepathic abilities became enhanced with extreme emotion or pain.

With a look at the assassin who remained in the shadows rather than nearing the fire, Black Wolf pulled out the smallest of his knives and tossed it to the Hanover. It landed in the dirt beside her. Her gaze rose from the knife to him, and he motioned for her to take it then drew a line down his forearm.

Chases Deer hastily gathered her belongings, while Diving Eagle told her she was foolish for leaving.

The Hanover ignored them and sliced her arm, confirming the skinwalker's suspicion most of her cuts were self-inflicted. Her eyes drifted closed, and her hunched shoulders dropped as blood appeared.

Who was the other person? He asked her telepathically.

Her eyes opened, and she gazed at him wordlessly.

Pain. He glanced at her arm. *It's a common trigger.*

She covered her arm self-consciously. *I did not know that,* she replied, her voice clear. *But ... it makes sense.*

Who was the other person? He asked again.

I do not know. She shook her head. *I was more concerned about my father destroying everything.*

From where I stood, you were both destroying everything.

The Hanover flinched and was quiet.

In one instance when you faced him, and you both used your power, the abyss swallowed everything, he mused. *In the second, it did not, and the other person was there.*

I saw him ... it ... but I have never seen it before, she replied. *I could not even tell if it was human or a lump of clothing.*

Black Wolf gazed into the fire. He would not have known either, if he had not recognized the energy.

Who was it? She asked, hearing the thought.

Not who. What, he said.

Diving Eagle knelt between them and gripped the Hanover's forearm. He placed a cotton cloth on the wound and elevated it. Rather than melt as she usually did around him, the Hanover was staring at him in surprise, as if she had heard in Diving Eagle's mind what Black Wolf had begun to believe when he heard Diving Eagle muttering about the girl whose heart infected others.

"Enough," her guard dog said from the shadows.

Diving Eagle rose but left the cloth. He paced away to the edge of the circle of light around the fire and planted his hands on his hips.

The Hanover girl was watching him, puzzled.

"Why did you tell her to cut herself?" Rocky asked from his safe place in the darkness.

"It is not your concern," Black Wolf answered.

"Because apparently, it is the only way I can read minds," the Hanover said.

"Ah. So you two want to talk without the normal humans hearing," Rocky said, amused. "For what it's worth, I've got no dog in this fight. I'm here to protect you, Tiana. That's it."

"Maybe I want to protect you, too, Rocky," she said softly. Her gaze was on Black Wolf.

You have no allies, Hanover. Black Wolf warned her with a glance at Rocky. *You should not trust anyone.*

She followed his gaze. She wrapped the cloak given to her by Diving Eagle around her shoulders and then curled up on her side by the fire.

Black Wolf required little sleep. Normally, he would prowl the night until the others were ready to leave again. But tonight, he was unsettled enough to want to stay near the fire, and the one little girl who could fight any monsters he was unable to.

THIRTEEN

HAULING A HUNDRED AND FIFTY POUND, feral cat from the uppermost floor of the pyramid posed many challenges, but the worst was that Aveline seemed to be claustrophobic. Every ten steps Arthur took, he had to pause and pretend to shift his pack while hissing at her to stop thrashing inside the oversized rucksack. The pack could fit with a month's worth of supplies, and no one would look at him twice for carrying it, unless it continued to move. Fortunately, pre-dawn, most of the wealthy were sleeping off their wine or waiting for their slaves to dress them.

Two steps before he managed to make it out of the pyramid, without being noticed by the slaves carrying food to their masters, Arthur's balance was knocked askew. He stumbled backwards and caught himself against a wall.

"Aveline!" he snapped quietly. He was panting and sweating from the long journey from his apartment to the ground floor. "I told you! Be still for five more minutes!"

She gave another of her plaintive cries and pawed at the heavy canvas bag.

"Think your words," he reminded her. He had met only one

other creature that spoke into his mind – the spirit wolf – and guessed speaking telepathically was a learned trait, for it took Aveline effort and time to formulate her responses.

Hot, she said finally.

Arthur rested the pack on the ground and opened the drawstring tie at the top. He peered in. Her glowing eyes glared back at him. "Can you breathe better?" he asked.

She blinked twice for yes.

"We are four feet from the entrance. You need to be still, or no one will believe you're a tent. Understood?" he asked.

Two more blinks.

Arthur drew a deep breath and hauled the pack onto his back once more. She squirmed, and he waited until she had gone still again before continuing out of the pyramid.

He straightened and strode towards the stables, willing her to be quiet long enough for him to get her situated on top of a horse. Arthur breathed in the cool morning air. The heavy rains from the night before had retreated into a steady drizzle. His boots stuck in the mud, and he made his way to the party of six awaiting him.

He slowed, observing the dress of the men who would accompany him. He knew their faces but not their names. They were, as promised by his uncle, the Hanover leader's personal guard. If Arthur had not known the truth behind his father's intention in sending them, he might have been pleased to see the best fighters in the city waiting to escort him.

One of the glanced toward him. He forced a smile and picked up his pace, not about to let any of them know he had any insight into their true purposes this morning.

My father wants me dead. The thought had become no easier to bear despite the long night he spent in contemplation about how little he understood his father. It was humbling to think about his own insignificance to the man who raised him.

"Remember. Do not tip these men off," he whispered to Aveline.

"They are very dangerous. We will fair better with the help of my uncle's men."

Aveline head butted him impatiently through the canvas. Arthur stumbled and caught his balance.

"Need a hand?" one of his escorts asked.

"Too much wine and mud," Arthur replied with a quick smile.

No one took any interest in the pack he was struggling to carry upright. The proud horse gifted to him by Chases Deer was saddled and prancing. He went to it, pausing to lean against it before deciding how best to hoist Aveline onto its back. Smelling the predator, the stallion tossed its head and moved away.

Arthur shushed it and lowered the pack. He rolled his shoulders back, patted the horse, and then hefted Aveline up behind the saddle. Securing her was a different matter. After several minutes of fumbling around, he managed to tie the canvas bag around the saddle and girth.

"Be still," he whispered once more and patted her back. Aveline kicked at him in response, and he looked around quickly to make sure no one noticed.

"Ready?" an escort questioned.

Arthur's pulse began to race. He was leaving the city, his home, for what could be the last time, if his uncle's plan failed, or if his uncle left him to die among his father's men.

"I am," he said. Whether or not he was prepared, Arthur's life was about to change. There was no going back to how things were, to his standing as heir, to the favor of his father.

Arthur mounted the stallion and set out with the men intending to murder him. He rode in the middle of the procession through the muddy streets and towards the edge of the city. Few people were out, and he let his eyes take in every detail he could of his surroundings, in case he never returned. His uncle had been banished; he had to think this was a possibility for him as well.

Mentally, he reviewed where his weapons were placed and the order in which he would reach for them. They neared the edge of the city, and Arthur refocused his attention on what was coming. His eyes sought the first major impediment on their trail, visible beyond the layer of smoke surrounding the city. They would have to go around a hill, behind which they would be hidden from the city for several miles on the road leading to the forest.

That point was where his uncle indicated the staged Native attack would take place, and also where Arthur's father's men planned to slit his throat.

Sweating this time from anticipation, Arthur slid his feet out of the stirrups and shook out his arms. He tested his body to ensure it was ready to move when the right moment came, and he loosened the drawstring covering of Aveline's canvas bag. Unwilling to alert those around him by speaking to her, he listened for any sounds she made that might indicate he had tied her too tightly to the horse. She was quiet, which he took to be a good sign after the arduous journey from the top of the pyramid to the stables.

With three men leading him and three behind, he began to calculate who would attack him first, when mayhem broke out. If the men followed standard training, the person directly behind Arthur – in his blind spot – would be the one who would be assigned to kill him. Unless … the three in front of him were far enough ahead to create an ambush when they rounded the hill and take him by surprise. After a split second of consideration, he decided the danger came from in front of him, not behind him.

None of them carried firearms that Arthur could see or smell, and no one had bows. This meant they were counting on discreet, close combat to execute him. Too far for anyone to hear him scream, they were likely counting on surprise and brute force to counter any attempts he could otherwise make at fighting back.

Efficient planning, as always. He could not help the twisting of his stomach when he realized his own father had carefully plotted his assassination. Did Edwin Hanover spare his son a moment of thought during the plan? Was he capable of regret?

Arthur steeled himself for the battle to come. It was not a time for emotion but for action. He tapped into his unnatural senses to identify where his uncle's men were positioned.

His breath caught.

No one was present ahead of them, around the hill, or within miles.

Had his uncle somehow shielded his men? It was possible, for his uncle possessed unknown deformities, similar to every other Hanover. This idea eased some of Arthur's concern without banishing it completely.

He began to review the discussion with Simon from the night before to identify any sign the man intended to betray him. If he meant to let Arthur die, would he have warned him about Edwin's plan? Would he have met with him at all?

Arthur did not know enough about Simon Hanover to answer the questions popping up in his mind. As his thoughts raced, and he prepared his body to fight, he could not help thinking that, if his uncle was anything like his father, he would not care about sacrificing one life to further his goals.

Had Arthur's life lost all value?

Not to me, he thought. He would not so easily dismiss his fate to become the leader his father was not. He glanced at the men in front of him.

The first one went around the hill.

Ducking his head, he spoke to the panther slung over the back of his horse. "Aveline, do you sense anyone other than those of us on this road?"

There was a pause, then a quiet, *No.*

What if Simon had betrayed him, too?

The second member of his escort went around the hill.

"If I die, find Tiana and protect her," Arthur said and reached for a knife. "Do you understand?" He was among the best fighters in his father's army, thanks to Warner. If his fate this day were to be murdered by his father's men, he would kill as many of them as possible on his way to his death.

Arthur did not wait for Aveline to formulate her answer but spurred his horse onward. The stallion bolted forward, startling the escort directly in front of him. Arthur raced past him, around the hill, and almost smiled when he saw the two men who had dismounted and set up to ambush him.

Leaning closer to the horse's neck, he urged it forward at a dead run, towards the forest. His escorts began shouting at one another, and hoof beats pounded after him.

Burdened by the extra weight of Aveline, with hooves that sucked and stuck in the mud road, Arthur's stallion could not exert the speed it had bringing Arthur home several days before. Arthur gave the horse its head and drew a short sword, preparing to fight the men who were quickly gaining on them.

The first drew abreast of him and stabbed at him with a long knife. Using his seat and legs to guide the horse, Arthur twisted and hacked at the man's arm. The attacker cried out and fell back, clutching his nearly severed forearm, and was just as quickly replaced by another. This one landed a slash across Arthur's bicep and another across the stallion's rump before Arthur managed to lasso the man around the neck and yank him off his horse. He released the rope as soon as the man was down. With too much weight already impeding his stallion, he could not risk adding to it by dragging his escort to his death, no matter how much it was deserved.

With anger burning in his blood, and the calm focus of a seasoned warrior, Arthur hacked a third escort down and sent him tumbling over the back of his horse. Too engaged in the battle to his left, he failed to understand his danger until it was too late. Arthur saw the bulk of a large Shield member hurling toward him seconds before his attacker smashed into him.

Arthur's stallion cried out as they were taken to the ground. Arthur hit hard and rolled away through the mud while his horse's legs kicked helplessly in the air. Aveline was thrashing inside the canvas, destabilizing the horse's attempts to stand.

The remaining two horsemen were wheeling their mounts to

return to the battle, while the burly shield member who unseated Arthur climbed to his feet a yard away. Arthur snatched a knife from the sheath at his ankle and rolled onto his back to avoid the first downward slash from his attacker.

He clambered to his knees and scampered forward, acutely aware of the man poised to smash an axe into his head, but more concerned about Aveline and his horse. Arthur dived for the horse and slashed at the rope binding Aveline to the animal then staggered away when the axe grazed the side of his face.

Aveline was still trapped, though the rope was frayed.

Arthur glanced towards her then at the burly man in his path. He stretched his senses – and felt no one, aside from his enemies.

His uncle, like his father, had betrayed him. But was he really surprised to learn the brothers were more alike than either of them would ever admit?

In a moment of adrenaline and clarity, he could only wonder why he had considered trusting his uncle at all.

Arthur struck first and tackled the large Shield member to the ground. Lean and quick, he avoided the slow strikes of his attacker and managed to wrestle him into a hold. With his enemy's shoulder and head smashed together, and his body firmly gripped between Arthur's legs, he risked releasing one hand of the hold to reach for Aveline once more.

Arthur wriggled forward in the mud until he could reach the frayed rope holding the writhing canvas to the horse struggling to get up. His enemy broke through the half hold and wrenched away.

Arthur slashed desperately at the rope. His knife slid through it. Elated, he staggered through the mud to his feet and yanked the rope free from the saddle.

"Go, Aveline!" he cried and pushed her off the horse.

The stallion squealed unhappily and climbed to its feet while Aveline thrashed inside the canvas.

"It is over, Hanover!" shouted one of the escorts behind him.

Arthur breathed deeply to face the three Shield members waiting to murder him. With a glance at the surroundings, which were vacant of the help he expected, he shook his head ruefully. "You are righter than you know," he said with feeling. "It is over. All of it." There were only three people in the world he could trust, his sister, Warner and Marshall, and all of them were in danger he did not have the ability to save them from, if he did not survive this mess.

Lowering himself into a fighting stance, he beckoned for his attackers to resume.

Two of them started forward, and Arthur prepared to take all three of them with him to his death.

Before the first could strike him, black fur and white fangs streaked in front of Arthur. Aveline smashed into the first man, tore out his throat with a growl and then grabbed the second man's wrist and tore it open, too. She clawed at his chest and face. When the surprised attacker fell back, she slashed open his neck with her talons.

She did not stop at two but tackled the third. Seconds later, after a gurgled scream and many growls, the third man was dead, too.

Aveline spat the man's blood out and turned to face Arthur. Blood marred her face and paws. She shook her head and lifted out of her attack pose.

Arthur lowered his weapons and straightened. He flung mud from his arms and wiped it off his face. "Not bad," he said, impressed by her fast, efficient killing.

Where ... others? She asked him and surveyed their surroundings.

"I have been wondering that myself," he said. Arthur bent to retrieve his knives. "It should not come as a surprise that we have been betrayed by yet another Hanover."

Aveline growled deep in her throat.

Arthur's mind went to Simon. He felt no pain at the thought of this betrayal, only anger. "This may be a good thing," he said, as much to himself as Aveline. "I know where I stand. I know what I need to do – and who my enemies really are."

He gazed towards the city. If he returned, his father would have him killed. But where else did he go? To Chases Deer, who would welcome him only if he came with a wagon filled with money and goods? To the Diné who had tortured him and Marshall? He was a disowned heir without material support and lacking in allies. No one had any reason to help him.

But he was still a Hanover. His name would carry the right amount of weight with the right crowd.

If he could reach the right people.

His uncle had the connections and allies Arthur needed if he hoped to overthrow his father and stabilize the city once his father was gone. Although ... every once in a while, when Arthur thought too long about taking his father's place, he began to wonder if any Hanover should rule the city. Could a benevolent Hanover make up for four centuries of suffering? Would he be given the chance or face assassination attempts from the first day?

Had every leader who preceded him believe he could make a difference as well, only to become another link in the shackles binding the city?

Arthur shook his head. He had one sole purpose since his birth. Without it, he was more lost than Tiana had always been.

"I need your help locating someone," he said, gaze settling on Aveline. "And then we will find Tiana and end this once and for all."

Aveline blinked twice and then asked, *who?*

"My uncle." Arthur turned and walked to his stallion, which stood grazing a dozen feet away.

Aveline growled again.

"Do not think I will believe his lies again," Arthur assured her. "I had hoped one Hanover out there would be different from my father. But maybe ..." *we are all cursed.* He drifted off, focusing on straightening the horse's saddle and bridle and wiping as much mud and grass from both as he could.

His thoughts, however, were not on his uncle, but on Marshall Cruise.

"What I hoped is irrelevant," he said softly. "What is important is that I ensure no one else suffers under the rule of the Hanover's.

Perhaps my uncle did me a favor in betraying me. I no longer have to wonder what his motivations are, or where I stand, or what kind of person he is. I only have to concern myself with murdering him and seizing control of his assets and allies for use in opposing my father."

And saving Tiana.

"Exactly."

Aveline's longing gaze was on the forest in the distance.

"You know I will do anything for my sister," Arthur told her. "I will be in a better position to help her, if I have an army at my back."

Hanover. Aveline's response was tart.

Arthur glanced at her with a smile. "If you did not think you could trust me, you would have let my father's men murder me."

Her growl was softer this time. She tried to say something else, but the words did not quite form. He paused and closed his eyes, concentrating to hear her. An image, almost too faint to make out, formed in his mind. A pile of rags? Why would she show him rags?

"What is this?" he asked, facing Aveline.

The great cat's eyes were closed, as if she, too, were trying to focus.

The image of his father's form flashed in Arthur's mind. A broken scene played out in his thoughts. An unfamiliar, tiny room, firelight, a second door. The rags again, though the image was clear enough for him to see a crumpled form in the middle of them. A blast of energy and then Arthur's father.

We. Need ... that. Aveline said with effort.

"We need what?" Arthur asked.

Face your father. We need ... that. The image of rags remained in Arthur's mind.

"Is that a person?" he asked, frowning.

She sighed, and the image disappeared.

"It is, is it not?" he prodded.

She blinked twice.

Arthur struggled to understand the images and Aveline's insistence. If his father were involved, the crumpled form had to be important. But where was this person, and more importantly, who was it? How had Aveline found him or her?

The great cat was panting from effort.

"First, we murder my uncle and steal his friends," he said with more humor than he though the situation warranted. "Then we find this person. Then Tiana."

Aveline howled.

"You disagree?" he asked.

Two blinks and the image of the rags.

"What makes you think this ... person can help us?"

The series of images this time were of his family's apartments. Aveline showed him the familiar hall outside his quarters, the door to his father's chambers, walking through and his father's trophy room.

And then she entered the wall and walked upwards, to the top of the pyramid.

"Tiana's tunnels," he said and straightened. "I always wondered about them. You are telling me this is where they lead? To a secret attic, and a pile of rags?"

Two blinks.

Arthur's mind began to race in a different direction.

His father hid something – or someone – in the attic of the pyramid. How had no one ever known?

Was this one of the secrets Arthur would have been told upon his succession?

Why his father hid someone in the attic was less of a mystery to him. His father's sole motivation was power. Keeping it, wielding it, passing it on to the next generation of Hanover's. If he took the liberty of hiding someone, then this person either knew something of great value, or was someone of great value, who could directly impact his father's influence over the region.

What if Arthur could find the key to overthrow his father without risking death from the direction of his uncle? Better yet, what if this person could be used to help Arthur barter his uncle's allies out from under him?

"Brilliant," Arthur breathed. "You are right, Aveline. We are going back. I hope your pack is still intact." He crossed to the nearest soldier and tugged off the Shield cloak he wore. "Do me a favor and make sure the other two are dead."

Aveline loped away, towards the unhorsed and wounded men Arthur had struck during his escape.

With a better plan forming, Arthur stripped off his outer layer of clothing to change into a Shield uniform.

FOURTEEN

IF ARTHUR KNEW one thing with certainty, it was that his father would be monitoring him from afar, waiting for the deathblow to be dealt. That gave him and Aveline precious little time to return to the pyramid and discover what was in the attic. And if his father decided to check up on his position ...

"Stop squirming, Aveline!" he hissed to the panther enclosed once more in the backpack. She did not know his father as he did, or the amount of danger they were already in. No matter what happened, Arthur suspected he was not going to leave the pyramid this day once he entered.

Disguised as a Shield member hauling a wealthy person's camping pack, he made it from the stables to the elevator reserved for the Hanover's without alerting anyone. The two guards at the lift glanced his way once and not again when they recognized the insignia of his father's personal guard.

Arthur entered the elevator and set the pack down with a sigh.

"Remember – keep quiet," he warned her. "Once we are on the top floor, we will have a very finite amount of time to find whatever is in the attic. My father is going to know I am here soon, if he does not already."

She wriggled.

Arthur untied the top, in case they had to run, and hefted the bag back onto his back and strapped it in place once more. He drew a knife and hid it within the length sleeve of the stolen over shirt. He waited for the door to open and ducked his head as he stepped off the lift.

The two Shield members moved to stop him.

Arthur debated a split second what to do before lowering the hood and smiling. "I forgot something important this morning," he said.

The men were not the normal guards but another two members of the elite squad protecting his father.

They exchanged a look.

"Gentlemen, you know who I am, and you know I belong here," Arthur said with confidence. "Step aside, or I will report you to my father."

"Apologies, sir," one of them said. He moved, and the other did so reluctantly.

"Thank you," Arthur said and strode past them. He entered the apartment and set Aveline down. Peering out at the two men by the lift, he untied the bag and released the panther.

Aveline shook off the canvas with a glare.

"They will alert my father or call for reinforcement. Take care of them quietly, little assassin, and meet me in the trophy room," Arthur directed her. Without waiting for her response, he jogged down the hallway and through the opulent apartment toward the private quarters. Once there, Arthur ducked into his and retrieved a satchel then stuffed it with items he thought Aveline would need upon her escape: gold and silver coins, bandages, fruit, and anything else within reach. When he finished, he tugged it over his head and bolted to his father's quarters.

Arthur paused to press his ear against the door and ensure the rooms beyond were empty. No sounds stirred from within, and he entered, leaving the door cracked for Aveline.

He moved stealthily through his father's private space until he reached the trophy room. Aveline's vision had been fuzzy about this part, but Arthur quickly assessed the probable location of a tunnel entrance, based on what he knew of his sister's tunnels. He stood in front of the wall of paintings and looked for signs of unusual wear or anything out of place.

The entrance was well hidden, he realized, and stepped back. His eye caught on one of his father's trophies. He snatched it and stuffed it in the bag.

The click of Aveline's claws on the marble floor outside the room drew his attention. She trotted in, her mouth bright red with blood.

"Which one?" he asked.

She went to one painting and nudged it with her muzzle.

Arthur slid his fingers down its side and pulled it away to reveal a stone door. He pushed it open and slid it to the side and then leaned in to peer into the darkness.

Energy radiated outward towards him. The power he sensed was beyond that of his father's magic. He peered into the darkness, uncertain what waited for them on the other side.

Before he could grab a torch, Aveline trotted past him into the dark corridor. Arthur plunged in after her, following the sounds of her clicking paws. She moved fast through the tunnel. He did as well, less concerned about stubbing a toe than being discovered by his father before they could escape with whatever was in the attic.

All went well until his foot slammed into a stair, and he tumbled forward. Arthur caught himself and scrambled up. His pace slowed until he was able to adjust to the winding stairwell. With a hand on the wall, he jogged, following the echoing clicks of Aveline.

Finally, the stairwell evened out – and the warm light outlining a door appeared up another short set of stairs. Aveline reached the top and shoved the door open. With light to guide him, Arthur took the steps two at a time until he reached the door. The tiny apartment at the top of the pyramid was as Aveline had shown him through her mind. The sense of power here was greater, thick enough it was difficult to breathe.

Arthur entered cautiously, uncertain what Aveline had found, or if it was dangerous. He searched the living area visibly before crossing to the small bedroom. Aveline was inside the door, her tail flickering. She opened her mouth and released a complaining groan.

"Think your words," Arthur said automatically.

His eyes fell to the pile of rags. In person, he was able to determine it was not just rags, but someone beneath the worn, holy clothing.

"Hello?" he called, stepping forward. "Are you well?"

Are you dangerous? He added silently.

The form shifted from a lying position into a seated one. Aveline pushed past Arthur and nudged the person.

"Aveline," he said. "Be ..."

The form faced him, and he fell silent.

Of all the questions he had for his uncle, he had not thought to ask how the middle-aged Hanover knew the existence of a skinwalker to be more than a tale. Of all the options the older Hanover had, why did he cross the country to find and hire a skinwalker in the first place?

More importantly, why was there a skinwalker secreted away in the top of the pyramid, where only Edwin Hanover came?

What did his father and uncle know that Arthur did not?

Unable to explain what was before his eyes, or how this one person could be important, Arthur forced himself out of his thoughts. The Native woman's hair was streaked with white. One of her legs held the form of a bear's, while another of her arms was that of a panther. Her eyes were mismatched – one gold, one brown – and her appearance in general unkempt and wild.

Aveline was nuzzling her arm. The woman patted her with her human hand and smiled.

How was this woman going to help him defeat his father or win over his uncle's allies? From where he stood, Arthur could not imagine the answer to this question, either.

"I have a lot of questions, but we need to leave now," he said. "Can you walk?"

The woman regarded him quietly for a moment, glanced at the panther, and then shifted to stand. She took a step. Her limp was pronounced, with her bear leg being several inches shorter than the other.

"Good," Arthur said. Her clothing was too loose and baggy for him to tell if she possessed the strength to hold the satchel he carried or not. "We must go." He faced the panther. "Aveline, if anything happens to me, take this satchel and run to Tiana. There is enough of value in here for you to be heard by Chases Deer or any other Native who might otherwise ignore you. Do you understand?"

Two blinks.

"Scout ahead."

Aveline hesitated and then reluctantly slinked out of the apartment and to the dark stairwell.

"You appear as if you could use a hand," Arthur said as politely as possible. "May I?"

The skinwalker gazed at him briefly before nodding her assent.

Arthur slid an arm around her. She was frail and thin beneath the rags, and he began to wonder if she had the strength to make it out of the pyramid let alone flee the city with the speed he knew to be necessary if they wanted to avoid his father.

"I am Arthur," he said as they left the apartment for the stairwell. "What were you doing here?"

"You are a Hanover?"

"Yes."

"Then you should know."

The woman leaned into him as they left the area lit by the apartment in the attic and began to descend the winding, dark stairwell. When she did not answer, Arthur focused temporarily on making it out of the tunnels without falling. The journey out felt much longer than the way up, and he breathed a sigh when they reached the base of the staircase. The light from his father's room glowed twenty feet down the passage, and Arthur quickened his pace.

Aveline waited for them in the trophy room, pacing and mewling unhappily. Balancing the older woman with one arm, Arthur closed the door to the tunnels and joined Aveline. They left the trophy room and stopped just inside the apartment's entrance.

The energy he felt in the tunnels was completely gone. Arthur had no time to dwell on why the attic radiated magic when the skin-walker beside him barely did.

From outside his father's room, down the corridor, Arthur heard the sound of boots on marble, and the rustle of weapons being drawn. Mind racing between their options, Arthur lifted the satchel from his chest.

"You must carry this," he said to the woman. "No one knows either of you is here. Remain in this apartment, until the others are distracted. Then go to Tiana's quarters and find suitable clothing. At some point, you will have the opportunity to escape. But you must do so quickly. Leave before my father returns. You will have no chance against him."

Aveline's ears twitched.

"When you find your chance, kill anyone you have to in order to escape with her," Arthur said to the panther.

Two blinks.

The skinwalker from the attic managed to stay on her feet when Arthur released her.

"No matter what happens to me, or how my father tries to stop me. Find my sister."

Aveline blinked twice.

Arthur glanced around the apartment. He would need a reason to be in his father's apartment or his presence would arouse immediate suspicion. His gaze fell to the display case of expensive liquor – some of it from the Old World – his father kept. He strode to it and pulled out a bottle with amber liquid.

Chugging a mouthful, he spilled some on his clothing and then returned to the door.

"Do not get caught," he warned Aveline.

Arthur drew a breath and then staggered into the hallway, spilling liquor and grinning. He was about to discover what his father's men were ordered to do with regards to him. If they wished him dead, the dozen men in the corridor could make that happen. But if his father had chosen to murder him outside the city, away from the normal Shield members, Arthur prayed there was a reason for it, and he would not be murdered in his own home this day.

George was present, and Arthur hoped his confidante was safe.

His father's men surrounded him, and Arthur continued to smile. "What ... what's going on?" he asked, purposely slurring his words.

There was a pause, and the leader of his father's personal squad approached. "Are you drunk, sir?"

Arthur laughed too loudly.

"Allow me to take him to his quarters," George said.

"We have orders to take him elsewhere," was the quick response.

"Then let's go!" Arthur said cheerfully. "George, I will need clothes. Mine are soiled!" He motioned to the Shield uniform he wore.

The leader of his father's men motioned two of the men forward. One snatched the alcohol and the other Arthur's arm. Arthur resisted the instinct to react and instead widened his smile.

"Of course, sir," George said and moved out of the path of the Shield members. "I will fetch some at once. Where should I take them?" This he addressed to the Shield leader.

"Prison."

"Tell Ingram I cannot meet him as planned," Arthur said with an exaggerated sigh.

"I will, sir," George replied.

While he could think of much more desirable places to go, Arthur was relieved not to hear he was being taken to the stakes to burn.

George remained in the hallway, pale and frowning, while Arthur happily accompanied the Shield members to the lift. Silently, he willed George to find Aveline and to help her escape before his father figured out the woman in the attic was missing. From there ... Arthur had not yet formed the next stage of his plan.

He accompanied the Shield members down the elevator, through the ground floor, and underground to the prison level. At no point did his escort decrease in number below six, and he found no opening to run, either.

By the time they reached the isolation cells on the far end of the prison, he had accepted that for now, he was trapped here. Arthur entered the cell. His smile slid free only once the door was locked. He looked around at the narrow space and the bed inches off the floor.

"Quite a difference from my usual accommodations," he observed with some amusement.

But he was alive, which he would not be, had his father's plan succeeded this morning. All he had to do was play whatever game his father wanted to play, and bide his time, until either Ingram came to find him, or his father did.

Hands bound, Arthur sat and waited for hours before the sound of the door being unlocked jarred his attention out of his thoughts. Heart pounding hard, he stood, prepared to meet whatever his destiny held for him on the other side of the door.

To his relief, he did not see his father in the doorway but Ingram. The older man passed the Shield member a pouch.

"Five minutes," the soldier said. He turned and walked away.

"It pleases me to see you alive, Arthur," Ingram said.

"Does it?" Arthur observed Ingram coolly. "I was under the impression you had decided to betray me."

"It was not what you think, Arthur," Ingram glanced around him and then stepped into the cell, leaving the door open. "We found out before dawn your father was trying to draw your uncle out of hiding by leaking the information to us."

"If you are saying my father did not intend to murder me, you are lying."

"He planned to murder both of you."

"And letting me die was easier than warning me," Arthur said with a nod. "Great plan."

"Listen, Arthur –"

"No. You listen, Ingram!" Arthur allowed rare anger to enter his tone. "Tell my uncle I learned one of his little secrets about what my father kept in the attic. If my uncle wants to know where this thing is, he will do everything in his power to prove today was an accident!"

"What are you talking about?" Ingram asked, frowning.

"Tell him." Arthur turned his back to his father's advisor. "We are done here, Ingram."

His words were followed by a pause, then the sound of Ingram shuffling out the door. Arthur released the breath he was holding, irritated by the visit. Whether or not Ingram's claim was true, he had learned something about his uncle's plans.

His uncle was willing to sacrifice Arthur to further his own goals, which meant, his uncle probably did not intend to turn over the city to Arthur at all. Simon Hanover could not be trusted, except in his desire to take out the Hanover chief.

But Arthur was not about to become a pawn in someone else's war. He had been raised by a man whose control of the city stemmed from a brilliant combination of strategy and intimidation. He had learned from the best and, even if he were not willing to burn whole families at the stake, he would sacrifice the select few who betrayed him.

He settled onto the floor. Unable to tell the time without a window, he began to doze.

The moment the vision formed in his mind, his light sleep turned deep.

ARTHUR WAS CAUGHT IN A WHIRLWIND, *spinning out of*

control downward into a gaping hole in the ground. He struggled to right himself without success and gasped in air that did not seem to reach his lungs. The sky was dark above, the city below being slowly torn apart and dragged asunder, into the blackness.

The air of the energy was too charged for him to identify whose magic was tugging him apart.

Arthur neared the hole and was sucked in, only to be pulled out by none other than his father.

Angry energy swirled around Edwin Hanover. His touch was cold, his eyes colder.

"Don't worry, son. She's gone. You will continue our line unopposed, as it should be."

THE VISION ENDED. Rather than awaken, he slid into a new premonition, this one calm and quiet.

ARTHUR LOOKED down at himself and then around at his surroundings, recognizing his father's quarters. It was not his father's portrait on the wall judging him, however, but his own.

Arthur stood and crossed to the window to overlook the city he now led, and his breath caught.

Only the wards in the immediate area surrounding the pyramid remained intact. The rest of Lost Vegas had been turned into ash or rubble, with one entire area nothing but a gaping hole.

Protestors jammed the streets while smoke came from the direction of the grasslands surrounding the city.

"What are your orders?" the Shield member behind him asked.

"Burn them," he heard himself answer.

SHOUTING outside his cell awoke him. Arthur snapped awake,

sweating and shaking. The images in his mind shone a light on one of his greatest fears.

What if he possessed enough power to become mad like his father and every other Hanover leader? What had brought the city in his vision to the condition he witnessed? Had he done it? Taken over once his father was gone?

Arthur stirred and took a deep breath, struggling to understand the meaning of the vision. His father had already all but disowned him. But if Tiana died fighting their father, Arthur would become the heir again.

Was that not what he always wanted? All he had ever been trained and molded to do?

He stood in silence, deep in thought, replaying the visions. The first had to have been the result of her sister challenging – and losing to – their father. The second? Had he destroyed the city? What could possibly push him down that path?

Tiana. Warner. His instincts whispered the answers. His father ruled alone. Every Hanover leader ended up alone with his madness.

Black Wolf had claimed premonitions were exactly what they appeared to be, that no attempt at interpretation should be undertaken.

Smoke slid under his door, and someone smashed into it. Arthur stepped back and dropped into a fighting stance.

Gunshots rang out. The hinges of the door exploded. Arthur covered his ears and turned his back to the door. It slammed open, and he faced it again, not about to be caught off guard if someone attacked.

His uncle stood in the doorway, grim and surrounded by smoke. The sounds of fighting came from down the hallway.

"I received your message," Simon Hanover said. "Come on."

"I thought you could not enter the city."

"When have you ever known a Hanover to tell the truth?" His uncle disappeared from Arthur's view.

Arthur followed cautiously but fast. Simon strode down the

corridor between cells with no concern for the chaos behind him. He led Arthur out of the dungeon area and into the subbasement above then kept going. Arthur trotted after him. Simon did not hesitate to turn corners and never slowed to consider where he was or which direction he should go.

Anger fluttered through Arthur as he considered how well his lying uncle knew the route. He shelved his unhappiness for a later discussion rather than make a scene that might get them caught.

Simon led him to the stairwell leading to the main floor of the pyramid.

"We will have to go disguised," he said. "You'll be recognized. Stay close." He started up the stairs.

Arthur caught his arm. "Any chance you will free me first?" he asked. "And what do you mean disguised? I do not have ..."

His uncle turned around, and Arthur stopped. His mouth fell open but no words emerged.

Rather than the red-blonde uncle he recognized, his faithful slave, George, stood before him.

"Stay close. I can change both of our faces as long as you are within three feet of me."

"Are you George or is George you?" Arthur managed.

"We will discuss this later." Simon charged up the stairs without freeing Arthur's hands.

Arthur stood in shock for a moment before taking the steps three at a time to catch up to his uncle. He said nothing more as they entered the main floor of the pyramid. Whatever his uncle did, no one glanced at either of them as they made their way through the crowd.

When they broke free of the pyramid, Arthur released a deep breath and glanced back over his shoulder. No one pursued, and no alarms went up to warn others of the escaped prisoner. His focus returned to Simon.

"I need answers," he said and halted in place.

"We need to hide you."

"Now."

His uncle sighed and turned. The mask of George remained. The two men – one loyal, the other manipulative – could not have been more different. How had his uncle pretended to be George? Because, like every other Hanover, he had a purpose to his manipulation that outweighed the personal cost?

"George is an illusion. The raid to help you escape, also illusion. My deformity allows me to trick people into seeing what I want them to," Simon explained.

"None of that was real? The fighting? Smoke?" Arthur asked, surprised.

"None of it."

"You are George." Arthur could not help feeling disappointed to realize his greatest confidante had been a stranger in a mask. "You left me outside the city to die. If you think I'm going anywhere with you, you're a fool!"

"I am your uncle, who spent two decades protecting you and your sister, to the extent I could, in the only way I could," Simon replied. "I saved Tiana when your father tried to burn her, and I masked the truth about you not being his heir until Tiana's powers emerged. I have been a part of your life since you were born, Arthur. Trust me when I say I had every intention of being there for the raid, but I was prevented from doing so." His uncle eyed two passing Shield soldiers. "I will tell you everything, but we need to hide."

Arthur studied him, hurt by the latest betrayal from a Hanover and stunned by the truth. Without another word, he began walking again and breezed past his uncle, who trailed him.

"Where are we going?" he asked shortly.

"To hide in the city for now." Simon joined him. "Did you really set the skinwalker in the attic free?"

"You knew about her, too?" Arthur swore loudly. "Why did you never tell me the truth about any of this?"

"Because, until a few weeks ago, I believed you to be either too weak, conceited, or blinded to the truth about your father. I asked Marshall to test you and see if you were worth saving."

Arthur said nothing. He understood Simon's position too well. It was the same Marshall Cruise had shared. He did not ask what uncle would have done, had Arthur not passed Marshall's test.

Simon led him into the inner city and to a building close enough to the fish market for the smell to overcome the scent of burning bodies in the neighboring ward. No one looked up or spoke when they entered, leading Arthur to believe they were masked again. Simon led him to a small room on the second floor and closed the door before unlocking Arthur's chains.

Arthur dwelled on all he had learned in the walk from the city and was left feeling like a stranger in his own world. He rubbed his wrists.

"Your rebellion. Do they know you're George?" he asked.

"No. They believe me to be forbidden from entering the city. I do not fully trust my allies, and neither should you. They are selfish men eager to shift the power and do not care who it goes to."

"Were you serious about not wanting to take over the city?"

"My concern has always been ridding Lost Vegas of my brother. Truth be told, I do not think any Hanover should lead the city," Simon replied. "You may have complicated my plan by hiding the skinwalker. Your father will know something is going on. We may not be able to remain beneath his attention for long."

Arthur sat down. "No more games. Tell me what is going on and why you spent twenty years lying to me."

Simon rubbed his jaw. His seasoned features, very unlike the smooth face of George, returned.

"Convince me to trust you," Arthur added. "And I will help you find the skinwalker, whose importance I do not understand at all."

"She holds the key to crippling your father."

"I'm listening."

After a moment of internal debate, his uncle's features softened, and he sat opposite Arthur.

"I came into your service eighteen years ago, when your sister was born. Premonitions run in our family, and I had one of what she would become, if she lived," Simon explained.

"She barely lived."

"The influence of a slave, or a brother, does not go far, as you well know by now. Both of us should have done more."

Arthur lowered his eyes, once again besieged by the vision he had experienced before his uncle rescued him.

"The madness. It runs in all of us, does it not? Even those of us who are not heirs?"

"It does," Simon confirmed. "I used as little as possible, but ... the signs are there. You asked what I wanted, and why I didn't want the city. The answer is simple. Because I, too, will go mad by the time this is over. You may have a decade or more left until you are crippled."

"A decade," Arthur murmured. He had not seen his reflection in a mirror in the vision to know how old he was when he had gone mad. "As for what you wanted?"

"The skinwalker you freed. Their kind are from neither this world nor the next. The Hanover magic comes from elsewhere, and the skinwalker keeps the breach between this world and the next open, which allows your father to rule without challenge."

"The next world. You speak of the spirit realm?"

Simon nodded.

"There has always been mystery surrounding the appearance of the first Hanover," Arthur mused. "You are saying we did not wander into this city during the Age of Darkness, as is widely believed."

"I am saying we did not wander into this city from *this* world. Whatever our ancestor was, that knowledge has been lost. But enough of that creatures remains in each generation to allow the heir the access unimaginable depths of power, at a price."

"Madness."

"If not more. We cannot know with certainty."

Arthur dwelled on the new information. The secrets in his family were shared only from ruler to heir, upon the deathbed of the ruler.

"How do you know all this?" he asked.

Simon drew a breath. "At one point, I discovered the passageway, the benefit of being a slave no one looks twice at. I went to the top to see what was there, and I found that ... creature. In return for answers to my questions, I helped her escape, which turned out to be one of the greatest mistakes of my life." His uncle shook his head. "In any case, your father found her eventually and imprisoned her again. No slave was permitted access to your floor for nearly a year after that. Tiana was born then. I do not know how she survived, or if anyone even fed her. I convinced your father to spare her, but that was all I could do for many months. When I was permitted to see her again, she was tiny, frail, on the verge of death again. I was too terrified to risk leaving either of you alone up there to do anything that might draw your father's ire ever again. I never went back to the attic, but I always knew what was there, and how valuable it was to your father. Until you and your sister were safe, I could do nothing."

Of all the explanations Arthur had expected, this one caught him off guard the most. His instincts gave him no warnings about Simon, even though he did not want to trust his uncle.

"The skinwalker is free," Arthur said. "How do you plan to usurp my father?"

"Nothing short of a full blow insurgency. And ... praying. If the breach begins to close without the skinwalker, your father will eventually run out of power to face us."

"That is your plan?" Arthur asked with a snort.

"We have allies among the Natives who have supplied us with weapons. We can use the skinwalker as a decoy to lure your father from the pyramid. If we can take the pyramid, we might be able close the breach, with the help of your sister, and therefore render Edwin vulnerable." Simon rose. "Come. I'll show you the details."

Arthur remained seated. He doubted the details would make him feel any more confident in Simon's plan, not when he understood the confrontation coming. If his sister challenged their father, as his vision led him to believe she would, all of Simon's planning would not matter. The best Simon could do was distract Edwin long enough for Tiana to strike.

Unable to determine how they were going to succeed against a man with unlimited power, Arthur stood slowly and glanced towards the window, which faced north.

It was possible working with Simon was the only real action he could take to help his sister, even if it proved ineffective at the end. What else was there? He did not even know for certain where Tiana was.

With misgivings popping up in his thoughts, Arthur did not follow his uncle to the door. Of everything he had to worry about, he could not stop seeing the image of himself ordering the protestors outside the pyramid to be burned.

"You do not trust me," Simon said, lingering in the doorway.

"Why would I? You have lied to me my entire life," Arthur retorted. "If you meant to protect us from my father, how did you let my father murder our mother? Tiana's twin? You have deceived us from the beginning."

Simon sighed. "I had hoped never to have this conversation." He pulled his chair out from the table and sat once again. "First, you are Tiana's half-sister. Your mother was the sister to Edwin and me. Inbreeding runs in many of the wealthy family in order to preserve their standing and wealth. The Hanover's hoped to preserve their deformities as well. Edwin and I were the sons of siblings as well. The son of two Hanover's, you were supposed to be the guaranteed heir. It has been this way for generations."

"That makes it worse," he stated. "You let your brother murder your sister."

"Do you not see I have always had to choose between everyone and you children? Between my brother and you, between my sister and you, between my own life and you?" Simon replied with heat. "Can you not appreciate what I have sacrificed to bring you to this very point?"

"I can never appreciate someone who lies to me."

"For your own good!"

"If that is true, then I am old enough for the truth!"

Simon released a slow breath, fighting for control of his temper, and leaned back. "There were ... are three of you," he said. "There have always been three of you. Your father burnt some slave and her daughter at the stake after Tiana's birth, because too many witnesses saw Tiana's eyes at birth. Too many people knew the truth."

Arthur waited, arms crossed.

"Tiana's mother was a Ghoul. It was thought that the Ghouls, who have specific abilities Hanover's had never possessed, would make the Hanover line stronger. If you were to be the heir, and you bred new abilities into the Hanover line by taking Tiana as your wife, you would have expanded the magic. Several generations tried this, but Edwin was the first to breed successfully with a Ghoul who made it to term before he had her murdered after Tiana's birth," Simon explained. "Two slaves saw Tiana after her birth, and they spoke of her Ghoulish eyes to anyone who would listen. In return, your father burnt one of them with her infant child at the stake and claimed it was the deformed child and her mother."

Arthur sought some objection but could not find one, not when he, too, had often wondered about Tiana's eyes. Before meeting a Ghoul weeks before, he was able to write off the strangeness of her appearance as part of her deformity. His confrontation with the Ghouls, where the spirit wolf saved him, left him uncertain how it was possible for Tiana to resemble the inhuman creatures if she were not one.

"You are saying my father slept with a Ghoul," he stated.

"Raped is more accurate, and he was not the first Hanover to try it," Simon said. "Rather than be pleased with Tiana's birth, he abhorred her. Always. I think the experience of taking a Ghoul soured him on Tiana before she was born."

Anger flared within Arthur whenever he thought not only of his sister's treatment at their father's hands, but how he had done little to help her.

"You said there were three," he said. "Who else did my father rape in his attempt to produce the perfect mate for his heir?"

"A skinwalker. Her child was born around the time Tiana was. It is the reason why I helped her escape to the city. When I saw her ..." Simon drifted off. "After I saw what my brother had done to our own sister, and to the creature from the forest, I could not bear the thought of another Hanover child being born to the monster my brother had become."

Arthur's anger vanished. The skinwalker in the pyramid's attic loathed Hanover's. He assumed it was because she was enslaved. How much worse was it that his father had forced her to give birth to a child?

"So you smuggled the pregnant skinwalker out and what? Made a deal with the chief of assassins?" he pressed.

"No. I was wounded in the pursuit. She disappeared, and I left the city. I did not know where she went before I saw the girl you brought to protect Tiana," Simon said. "However, I am all but certain your father knew about Aveline."

Arthur's face flushed with heat. "Aveline. You knew all along who she was."

"I did. What I could not know was what was in her heart, if she had inherited her father's madness or her mother's insanity. It was not until Matilda's death that I understood her nature. She had managed to escape the Hanover and skinwalker curses and posed no danger to Tiana."

Arthur stood and circled the chair. He leaned against it and gripped the back hard, until his knuckles felt ready to pop. He felt his uncle's eyes on him.

"Two sisters. And I have never done anything to protect either," Arthur said at last through clenched teeth.

"You did what you knew to do," Simon replied. "How could you do more? You were raised to be ignorant of the world, of family ties and any duty except that of ruling one day."

"I should have known to do more, or even who Aveline was when I first experienced a vision of her!"

"That you did experience a vision of her, and you brought her to Tiana, had a far greater impact than anything else you have ever done."

"I found Aveline in a whorehouse and threatened to leave her there," Arthur said. "If I had known ..."

"We have all had to make sacrifices and tough choices."

Arthur shook his head. He kept his comments quiet. His uncle could not understand how hard it was to discover how ignorant he had been his entire life. Not to know who Aveline was, not to side with Tiana against their father, not to question his father's madness and fail to do what was just ... Arthur had never considered himself a failure before now, and he had never seriously considered giving up the city to a better leader before this day.

He glanced at his uncle, who claimed to have tried to help him and Tiana. Hanover's were poison in the well. Even their best efforts were wrong or bad or ineffective. As much as he hated to admit it, Arthur began to think he should not lead the city after all. No Hanover should.

"We do not have much time. You freeing the skinwalker will set your father's madness in motion and place both your sisters in danger," Simon said and stood once more.

"On that we agree," Arthur said. "If it were not for their danger, you would be dead, Simon."

"When this is over, you can do as you please with me. But I did my best, Arthur, whatever you think."

Arthur said nothing. He sensed his uncle, too, was experiencing the regret of knowing he had failed, even when he did his best.

FIFTEEN

"THIS IS A MISTAKE," Diving Eagle said as they approached the outermost scouts of the village belonging to Chases Deer.

"Then stay here, and I will go," Black Wolf snapped.

"Me, too," the Hanover girl seconded.

The western Native did not respond. Neither did he stop walking. Rocky brought up the rear of their procession, while the Hanover girl hurried to keep pace with the Diné Native ahead of her.

One scout shouted a challenge without showing himself, though Black Wolf assessed he was in a tree ahead of them.

Diving Eagle stopped walking and responded. Seconds later, the scout beckoned them to follow him into the village.

"No magic, no transforming into forest creatures, no drawing weapons," Diving Eagle told them all firmly. "We fetch your pet and leave." This he addressed to Black Wolf.

No one asked where they went next, and Black Wolf suspected the Hanover girl already knew she was not being kept around as a guest. Each of them had a purpose in the vengeance Diving Eagle was determined to see through.

When they reached the village, Chases Eagle was waiting for

them at the center, half a dozen burly Native warriors at her back. Her gaze was hard and settled on Black Wolf the longest before her attention shifted to Diving Eagle.

Expecting an argument, Black Wolf's attention went past her, to the building where his spirit wolf and her pups were located.

"Come with me," Chases Deer ordered to Diving Eagle. "You, fetch what you came for and return to this very spot." She snapped to Black Wolf. "You two stay here."

Black Wolf did not wait for her to change her mind and strode past the warriors, to the clinic. He entered and paused, allowing his eyes to adjust, before he walked to the bed where his guide's body lay. Sorrow and loneliness trickled through him.

Black Wolf knelt beside the deceased wolf wrapped in a white sheet. His longtime companion, and only friend, would never speak to him again. He began to think he had never appreciated her enough during the hundred years they spent together.

He sat in contemplative silence, replaying the memory of when they had first met over and over in his mind. His guide had taken a frightened and special little boy from a lost tribe and groomed him into the predator he was. Everything he had become, and all he had done, he owed to the spirit wolf who was more of a mother than his own had been.

After a moment alone with the wolf, the mewling sounds coming from a basket on the bed beside the wolf drew his focus from the past to the present. Black Wolf shifted to kneel beside the basket and gazed into it. The pups' eyes and ears were opened. Their clumsy squirming, and developing bodies, would one day be replaced by the grace and beauty their mother had possessed, though he would not be around to see them transform.

He listened hard, uncertain if the pups were old enough to speak yet.

His wolf had told him what to expect, but she had never birthed pups before. One would be a spirit wolf, though which one it was, Black Wolf could not know, if it did not speak up.

He waited to hear a tiny voice in his head before reaching in to pick up two of the pups in one hand. They stilled at his touch, and their energy tickled his palm. Neither spoke. Setting them on the bed, he picked up another two and listened. More energy but no voices. He tried with the last two and concluded the spirit wolf was too young to know his or her role in the world yet.

Black Wolf replaced them in the basket and bowed his head, praying over them briefly and promising their mother he would care for them as long as he was able to, before he gathered the basket and stood. He tucked it under one arm and then carefully lifted the body of their mother under his other arm.

He left the clinic and strode into the common area, where Chases Deer and Diving Eagle argued, while the Hanover girl and assassin looked on. The girl's gaze shifted to him as he approached.

Black Wolf handed the basket to her wordlessly then continued walking, heading towards the forest with the wolf tucked under his arm.

No one stopped him, though he felt everyone watching him. For once, he did not care. The heartbeats of those in the village pattered painfully against his brain, but nothing compared to the empty ache at his core where his spirit wolf had once been connected to him.

He chose a spot he thought his guide would appreciate: a small glen, near a cheerful stream. He gently laid her body on the ground and began to gather wood for her pyre. He used no weapons, and did not change forms, to gather, break and position logs, instead opting to honor his guide one last time by using his human physical strength to create her final resting place.

She had found him as a human, and she had often reminded him that no matter what else he became, he was always a human at heart.

Not that he had a heart. She had been his humanity, and her compassion and wisdom made up for his brute strength and power.

Black Wolf allowed his mind to wander as he concentrated on preparing a pyre worthy of his guide. He cut his hands, bruised his arms, and smashed his toes more than once by dropping logs. He persisted, resisting the urge to transform and make his duties easier. When he finished, most of the day had passed, and he was drenched with sweat.

He dropped onto the ground beside the unmoving body of his guide and rested. Withdrawing the braids from his satchel, he studied the white strands interwoven among the black ones.

He unwrapped the wolf's body, whose marbled fur resembled his hair, then carefully stretched and wrapped the braids around her. When he was finished, he picked her up and rested her on the pyre.

He hesitated. It was harder than he had ever imagined letting go of his companion. When her body was gone, there would be no part of his friend left, no one to advise or guide him, no one to share long days and longer nights with. He gazed at her still form for a long moment, until the chill of dusk brushed his baldhead.

"We will not be separated long," he promised his guide quietly.

Black Wolf knelt and lit the brush at the base of the pyre on fire with his flint and then stepped back. Fire spread quickly across the dried grass and up the logs until it licked at the body of his guide. He resisted the need to protect her, to take her lifeless body away and instead, forced himself back a few more steps.

He stood and watched for hours, while the flames of the pyre stretched towards the night sky and died down into embers with dawn the next morning. He ignored the wind, the chilly night air, the drizzle that began shortly before the sunrise. The skinwalker remained dutifully in place as his friend, and his hair, swirled upward into the sky, returning to the spirit realm.

The cold void inside of him was larger this morning. He began to think it would soon swallow him, that his death would not come from external forces, by from the abyss inside him.

Only when rain extinguished the embers of the fire did Black Wolf move. He gathered up his belongings slowly. Ignoring the cold spring rain, he turned away from the pyre and headed towards the gentle pulse of his pups.

The moment he set foot in the village, Chases Deer's burly men appeared from the forest to flank him. No one interfered, and no one spoke to him. Black Wolf ignored them as he sought his destination and was not surprised to discover his three companions in a cabin surrounded by more warriors. He entered, and his escort remained outside.

Rocky was awake, tending the fire. Diving Eagle paced, and agitation rendered his features tight already. The Hanover girl, and the pups, were behind a closed door. Black Wolf glanced at it, which drew Rocky's attention.

"Your pups are safe. Tiana's sleeping," Rocky said. "She told us about the vision."

Black Wolf's jaw clenched until it hurt. He sat beside the fire and began to pluck food from the platter on the table nearby.

"Do you understand its meaning?" Diving Eagle asked.

"Visions are what they are," Black Wolf replied. "They are not to be interpreted except as they appear."

"Then how can there be two versions of the future?" Rocky asked.

"The future can be changed. For reasons no one is capable of understanding, the future is split," he replied. "It means events are occurring now that will later decide which outcome is realized."

"It's not chance," Diving Eagle said and crossed his arms, frowning. "It can't be."

"It is never chance," Black Wolf agreed. "You could keep the Hanover girl out of the city. That would stop both outcomes."

The silence that met his words confirmed his hunch. Each of the other men had a reason to send the Hanover girl to the city.

Black Wolf was not the only person destined for Lost Vegas. "I need the pups," he said to Rocky, suspecting the assassin would not allow him to enter the Hanover girl's room.

Rocky crossed the living area and disappeared into the bedroom, reappearing a moment later with the basket. He set it down in front of Black Wolf. "I fed them an hour ago." He indicated a bottle of milk on the table.

Black Wolf studied the pups. They were dozing again. He willed any of them to speak, but none did.

Diving Eagle's arms slid to his sides, and his expression grew concerned. He sat near the basket and leaned over.

Black Wolf eyed him, willing to incur the Hanover girl's wrath to protect the pups.

"Are these ..." Diving Eagle stopped. He paused before speaking again. "Can they ... are they special?"

"Very," Black Wolf confirmed. "Too special for you."

"Is this one any different from the others?" Diving Eagle pointed to one of the white pups.

"Why?"

Diving Eagle glanced at him and then leaned back. The look of consternation left his features. Rather than answer, he stood and began pacing once more.

Black Wolf studied him then the wolf he indicated. He picked up the fat puppy whose stomach bore a tiny black star birthmark. The animal was awake and calm. It said nothing to Black Wolf, though its energy tickled his hand.

Did the fact that all of the pups possessed enough energy for him to feel mean anything? His guide had said one of the pups would be like her, but she had never mentioned if it were normal for a spirit wolf to bear more than one pup.

He replaced the pup. The only brindle wolf, which appeared also to be the runt, squirmed. Black Wolf withdrew it and peered at its legs. It was one of two females, and one of its back legs was half the size it should have been. If it survived long enough to grow up, it would not be healthy, and no imperfect creature could be a spirit guide.

"This one will not make it to adulthood," he said and replaced the basket on the cabin floor. Intent on sparing the pup the pain of trying to mature with only three good legs, Black Wolf gripped its tiny head in one hand and its body in the other, preparing to snap its neck for a merciful death.

He felt the Hanover girl's magic graze his baldhead a split second before she smashed him into the wall of the cabin. Black Wolf was frozen in place, the pup in his hands and his body pinned to the wooden wall.

Diving Eagle whirled, and Rocky leapt to his feet.

The Hanover girl was glaring at Black Wolf from across the room. "What are you doing?" she demanded quietly.

He almost laughed. "It is weak and crippled. I plan to spare it the pain of trying to survive," he said simply.

"Because it ... she's deformed?" she snapped. "Because she was born that way, you consider her lesser?"

"Because survival does not favor those who cannot take care of themselves."

Anger was in the girl's eyes – but it was her pain he felt to his core.

You are not the only deformed one here, he told her telepathically.

She glanced towards his blackened leg.

You can spare the wolf the cruel life you and I have experienced.

Neither the western Native nor the assassin seemed to know what to do. The Hanover girl approached and held out her hand.

"She spoke to me. She is mine," she said.

"Fitting," Black Wolf growled. "A deformed guide for a deformed girl."

The Hanover girl's face flared red, this time in embarrassment. She looked down and released her grip on him.

Black Wolf slid to the ground and held out the pup.

She took the brindle wolf and cradled it in her arms before walking away, to the table with the food.

Rocky looked between the two of them. "That's settled," he said.

"Try not to hurt the creature I'm sending after your father," Diving Eagle said.

The Hanover girl was quiet, her back to the room and shoulders hunched. Black Wolf sensed he had managed to upset her for the first time since they encountered one another. He was not sorry to see the Hanover in their midst unsettled.

He sat down once again by the rest of the pups.

Diving Eagle was gazing at the white one with the black star once more.

"Are there deformities in your family as well?" Black Wolf asked.

"We do not call them this," was the quiet but tart response.

"Then you have them."

The western Native did not respond.

"There's none in mine, if anyone cares," Rocky said.

Black Wolf had no love for humans, but he could almost appreciate the assassin and his attempts to keep their party from imploding.

"Is it normal for a spirit wolf to speak to a non-skinwalker?" Rocky asked.

The Hanover girl glanced over at the question.

"Spirit guides adopt who they please," Black Wolf said.

"For what purpose?" Diving Eagle pressed.

"That is for them to tell those they adopt."

Before anyone could ask him more questions about the guides, a knock resounded off the front door.

Features hardening, Diving Eagle crossed to it and yanked it open. Chases Deer stood outside. She motioned him out of the doorway. He moved grudgingly and she stepped inside.

She looked at each one of them, and the basket, before speaking. "I have made my decision," she said to the Native. "You and that *thing*" – she lifted her chin at Black Wolf – "will leave my village immediately. The Hanover stays."

"I cannot allow that," Diving Eagle said firmly. "She and her guardian must come with us."

"This is not your village, and I am not among those people obligated to do as you say," she retorted. "That is my deal. Those two stay, or no one leaves at all!"

Black Wolf glanced at the Hanover girl, whose faint shield around him always became stronger when she sensed his magic flex.

If she let her guard down for one instant when Chases Deer was around ...

"What will it cost us to ransom the Hanover girl from you?" Diving Eagle asked through clenched teeth.

"More than you can afford," Chases Deer replied. "Your tribe is in no position to pay anyone's ransom."

If the pointed response affected him, Diving Eagle gave no indication. Black Wolf recalled how eager the chief's son had been to hand over Arthur Hanover in return for money and guessed the small tribe was hurting to fund the war they wished to lead against the Hanover's.

"You will be treated better here anyway," Chases Deer added, speaking to the Hanover girl. "No cages or torture. I'll be ransoming you back to your father."

Diving Eagle ignored this, too. Black Wolf watched those in the room, entertained by their petty feuding, when everyone knew a much larger storm was more likely to wipe them out.

"Very well," Diving Eagle said at last. "We will accept your terms. Please give us a minute to prepare to leave."

"First intelligent thing you've done in the time I've known you," Chases Deer said. "You have five minutes." She opened the door, started to leave, and then hissed a sigh. "Which one of you is doing that?" She turned and gave Black Wolf and the Hanover girl both searing looks.

"Doing what?" the Hanover girl asked.

"Repeating my name. Over and over."

Black Wolf glanced towards the pups. He sensed the energy one of them was sending out, though it was too weak for him to tell which it was. "It's one of them," he said and lifted the basket. "Your spirit guide."

Chases Deer glared at him.

"Does it say your name over and over?" the Hanover girl asked. She took the basket, her pup in her hand, and went to the suspicious female warrior. "You saw my magic and that of the skinwalker. You must believe me when I say these pups are not ordinary. They possess special gifts. It is where part of the skinwalker's powers come from."

Chases Deer seemed ready to walk out but paused at the Hanover girl's last sentence.

"This wolf will give me magic powers?" she asked.

"It will enhance any natural gifts you already have," Black Wolf responded.

Chases Deer did not deny she possessed any such gift but peered into the basket. She hesitated before choosing a pup. "This is a payment on the ransom your brother owes me," she said to the Hanover girl.

She said nothing else and left, slamming the door behind her.

"I did not expect that," the Hanover girl said and faced Black Wolf. "The pups choose their own companions?"

"They do," he confirmed. "They are here to guide certain people, and they will search for those people until they find them."

Diving Eagle listened closely, eyes on the basket.

Black Wolf took it back and moved towards the door. "We will meet again soon, Hanover."

"I do not like this idea," Diving Eagle growled.

"We'll be fine," Rocky assured the western Native.

"But we cannot stay long," the Hanover said.

"We have a destiny to meet," Black Wolf agreed, earning him the looks of everyone in the room. "Both outcomes are possible. If you plan to ensure the right one occurs, then I suggest you keep the Hanover and me together for now. She cannot manage her power, but I can."

"You won't be here more than a day. My father's influence is needed," Diving Eagle replied. "As you can see, I have none here. When I am home, I will see to it that you are both freed immediately."

"In the meantime, you travel with a monster," Rocky reminded him.

"We have an agreement," was the quick response.

"Because a man who slaughters a village for fun has never broken his word?"

"What choice do I have?" Diving Eagle responded. "I am responsible for cleaning up the mess I made and for ending the feud between the Hanover's and Diné. If that means I keep company with skinwalkers, then so be it."

Black Wolf settled his cloak around his shoulders. His eyes went to the pups once more. The brindle one had claimed the Hanover girl yet all of the pups gave off the same subtle energy indicating there might be more than one guide among them. This idea pleased him as much as the acknowledgement none of them were meant for him disturbed him.

He knelt beside the pups, ignoring Rocky and Diving Eagle as they planned a rendezvous point and time, in case Rocky and his ward were freed.

The Hanover girl crouched beside him. "You have to take them with you," she said for his ears only. "My ... guide says after you find them all homes, you ..." She drifted off.

"I die," he finished.

"Yes."

Black Wolf debated how he could possibly find the remaining pups their homes when his path took him to Lost Vegas and to his death.

Unless all of them would be claimed by the time he finished the last mission he accepted before his wolf returned to her spirit realm. A similar conspiring of spirits and events had led his guide to him all those years ago. Perhaps this was how it worked, with one generation assisting the next, and he was charged with carrying on the sacred tradition on his guide's behalf.

"Good," he said aloud.

The Hanover girl's brow furrowed.

Black Wolf stood, picking up the basket with him. He went to the door and waited for Diving Eagle and Rocky to finish plotting.

Chases Deer knocked on the door. Diving Eagle crossed to it.

"Be careful," the Hanover girl said.

Black Wolf did not have to look her direction to know she spoke to the western Native and not him.

Diving Eagle opened the door and stepped out of the cabin. Black Wolf covered the basket to keep the rain from reaching the four pups and followed.

Chases Deer's uneasy warriors trailed them through the village and towards the southwest. They followed through the rainy, dreary forest, until Diving Eagle reached the tree into whose trunk the Diné tribe's mark had been carved. At that point, the escort fell away, and Diving Eagle's pace quickened.

Black Wolf did not feel the same sense of urgency the chief's son did and trailed behind at his own pace, content to enjoy the last spring rain he was ever likely to experience. The pups were quiet in the basket, soothed by the swaying movement of his walk, and he began to understand his guide's insistence they go west a year ago, long before he was hired to find Arthur Hanover. He had been born into tribe whose unique abilities isolated them from everyone else, and he would die in the midst of the greatest adventure any of his people had ever known, a time and series of events rare enough, they had never, and would never, be repeated again.

The Hanover girl feared death, but Black Wolf relished what was coming. His desire to leave the company of Diving Eagle had vanished when he realized his last agreement was struck with the Diné warrior. This final agreement, too, put him on course to go to Lost Vegas, and the beautiful coincidence could not have left him more eager to follow his fate.

In a state of anticipation, Black Wolf entered the semi-permanent Diné hunting village filled with nothing but warriors and those who hoped to become warriors. No one challenged him, and he made his way slowly to the center, where he had first encountered the Hanover's. The cages where Arthur and his companion had sat remained at the base of the tree where Black Wolf first saw them.

The air of the village was charged, as if everyone who crossed his path understood the significance of both his presence and his destiny.

Black Wolf smiled. If his guide were alive, she would chide him for being too proud about his purpose in the world.

"She abandoned you. You will fail," whispered the vengeful spirit who sought to distract him from his path.

He glanced at the ghost of a child. "Go, before I abandon you the same way," he snapped quietly.

The spirit lingered briefly then blinked out of existence.

Its words, however, fell heavier than Black Wolf wanted. Vengeful spirits had the ability to see the fears in one's soul, and tried to tap into that fear to mislead whomever it was they haunted.

To deny the words was to deny what was inside him. Black Wolf stood in the center of the village, exploring his feelings to find the fear the vengeful spirit had witnessed.

He was afraid. Or perhaps ... uncomfortable. His entire life, his guide had accompanied him on every mission. This was his first, and last, he would commit alone. How did he not fear the outcome, when he had relied on his guide for a hundred years to advise him and help him succeed? Was a hundred years long enough to learn what he needed to in order to be on his own? Why did he feel vulnerable, when he had the best chances of surviving of anyone in the village?

"What's in the basket?"

Black Wolf glanced towards the boy and then back, making sure the youth was real and not there to torment him. "Leave, boy," he snapped.

"I am Red Moon." The lanky youth puffed out his chest. "My father is chief!"

"Ah. I remember you. You are a scout. A tiny one."

"You are the skinwalker who murdered my aunt."

Black Wolf bent to the boy's level and held his gaze. "Do you want to know how many people I have murdered?"

Red Moon hesitated and then nodded.

"Twenty thousand, four hundred and two, all by hand. Do you want to become the twenty thousand, four hundred and third?"

The boy displayed similar anger to his older brother. "You can try, but I know how to fight!" he said and withdrew a small knife.

"Never let someone kill you easily, or you will regret it as a spirit," Black Wolf said and straightened.

"I can kill you easily, skinwalker."

Black Wolf ignored him.

"I asked you a question, and you must answer. My father is the chief," the boy insisted. "What's in the basket?"

"Nothing that concerns you, little boy."

The youth's face flushed. "Something is in there. I can hear it."

"What does it say?"

"Red Moon. Over and over."

Black Wolf rolled his eyes. Leave it to a spirit pup to decide it wanted to be with the proud, skinny child. He knelt and held the basket on one knee then pulled off the coverings protecting the pups from the rain.

Red Moon inched closer and then peered into the basket. He smiled.

"Which one speaks your name?" Black Wolf asked.

The boy pointed at one of the black wolves.

"Then it is yours."

Red Moon looked up to meet his gaze. "Is it a skinwalker?" he asked cautiously.

"It is a spirit wolf, and it has chosen you. If you fail to protect him, or you hurt him, a skinwalker will appear and tear your skin off, then pull off each of your toes and fingers, your limbs, and remove your eyes and organs one by one – all while you are alive," he warned.

The youth grimaced.

"Take him. And remember, his life means more than yours ever will." Black Wolf lifted the pup and handed it to the boy.

Red Moon gazed at the pup. A light was in his eyes, and he

smiled. He replaced his knives and accepted the wolf guide. "I will care for him like a little brother," he said solemnly.

"Then I won't have to hunt you down and murder you."

The boy nodded and shifted away, cradling the pup.

Three down, Black Wolf thought.

"Skinwalker!" Diving Eagle shouted from a tent near the tree line.

Black Wolf watched the youth walk away with the pup before he stood and started forward. He had a feeling he would soon find a home for the fourth pup, if Diving Eagle were not too proud and angry to claim his guide.

From there ... Black Wolf could only imagine the others would find their homes in the city.

"My father would like to speak to you," Diving Eagle said tersely. "He is not well, but he insisted. Do. Not. Upset. Him."

Black Wolf said nothing. Whether or not he taxed an old man was of no concern to him at all.

He entered the sweltering tent alone. The hunched figure of the chief sat beside a blazing fire. Sweating before he reached the seat opposite the chief, Black Wolf set the pups down before he peeled off his cloak and sat in front of the old man.

Dark, sharp eyes studied him.

"What do you want?" Black Wolf asked at the silence. It was too hot in the tent for him. Coupled with the heartbeats of those warriors in the village beating against his brain, he did not feel fully in control.

"To see what manner of creature my son has made an agreement with," came the response.

"One who will never fail to execute his end of the agreement."

"And who never fails to collect a price greater than he deserves," the chief observed. "I see what you are."

Black Wolf shrugged. "I do not hide who I am," he said. "Now, old man, what do you want?"

"To offer you something in place of the price you will exact from my son."

"I never renegotiate after I make an agreement."

"You will." The chief bent over and fished through a satchel at his feet. He pulled out small jars of poultice and ointments before withdrawing a pouch. He handed it to Black Wolf. "Open it."

Black Wolf weighed it in his hand, measured the outline of its contents with his gaze, and judged the contents to be a bracelet. "You cannot bribe me with jewelry," he said.

"This jewelry has been in my family for a while. It saved the life of all my people, when the Hanover's tried to wipe us out," the chief said.

Black Wolf hefted the pouch again without being able to discern anything unusual or special about it. He detected no magic, either, which left him even more convinced the contents were useless to him.

"Several Diné leaders have come and gone since then," the chief continued. "Seven, to be exact. This bracelet, along with a second, and the story behind it was passed from each chief to the next. I understand news of this battle spread to your lands?"

"I recall it vaguely," Black Wolf said. "I recall nonsense about spirit armies."

"You understand the nature of the Hanover's magic, I believe."

"Somewhat," he confirmed, thoughts on the Hanover girl. "How did this stop the Hanover's?" He held up the pouch.

"If there is to be order and balance in the universe, something must exist to counter the Hanover chief's power. This bracelet is one of a pair."

"You claim these bracelets stopped the Hanover?" Black Wolf opened the pouch and dumped the harmless bracelet made of blue stones into his palm.

"Not exactly."

Black Wolf looked up, waiting for more.

"Do you know anything of the mystery surrounding the Hanover's? That the leader never leaves the city, once he assumes power? That there is only one Hanover who survives each generation? Or that this family assumed control, unopposed, and has remained in control, unopposed, for four hundred and fifty years?"

"I have never given them any thought until a few weeks ago," Black Wolf replied with a snort. "You cannot tell me jewelry has anything to do with their power."

"It has everything to do with defeating them."

He met the old man's eyes. "If it is as powerful as you say it is, then why have you not used it to drive out the Hanover's?"

"You are not hearing my point, son," the chief said.

"Are these bracelets magical when combined?" Studying the turquoise bracelet hard to discover its secrets, Black Wolf waited for a better response. "You want me to believe a bracelet or two will take down the Hanover's."

Black Wolf considered the idea. A magic talisman was not out of the realm of possibilities. He had seen many things in his life, to include – twice only – an item that appeared to have magic within it that was usable by whoever possessed it.

"These bracelets stopped a war and saved my people," the chief did.

"How?" Black Wolf demanded, growing impatient.

"I will tell you, only if you agree to free my son from your agreement."

"You said there were two. Where's the other?"

"That, too, will be revealed when I have your word."

Black Wolf found himself wishing once more his guide was present to tell him if this was a trick or not. From what he had witnessed of the Hanover heir's power, and knowing the girl's father possessed the command over his magic that she did not, Black Wolf suspected he would need some sort of help to destroy the Hanover chief.

But these bracelets?

Like the Hanover siblings, the jewelry appeared too simple to be anything other than trinkets. He had been wrong about them.

"The key to victory is in your hand," the chief prodded.

Black Wolf also recalled hearing how crafty the Diné could be, and he had seen firsthand the bravery of warriors like Diving Eagle. Was the chief trying to deceive him? Or did such a magical talisman really exist?

If it did, he would want it to ensure his mission went through as planned.

If not, he would free Diving Eagle from the agreement they made in exchange for a useless trinket. As this had been last official agreement, he was not entirely certain he would even have the chance to reveal his price to Diving Eagle before his death. But oftentimes, power was not about using it, but the potential to use it in order to influence an outcome. With Diving Eagle in his debt, he had an advantage in their relationship.

Was such an advantage worth more than the potential secret the chief claimed he knew?

Perhaps, for this reason, he considered the idea that magical jewelry might help him defeat the Hanover chief.

"I will decide tomorrow," he said and stood.

"No, son, you will decide now, or I will withdraw this offer."

Black Wolf had never met someone harder to read than the old man with sharp eyes and wheezy breathing. He fingered the bracelet in his hand. The beads were cool to the touch. The emblem at his chest – signifying his skinwalker tribe – contained a trace of magic that became exhausted after the first time a skinwalker transformed. If the medallion could help a skinwalker transform the first time, then why could two simple bracelets not help him defeat the Hanover's?

If his spirit wolf were alive, she would know the answer. She had always advised him in situations when he was uncertain which decision to make. He glanced towards the basket of pups, but none of them were communicating with him.

"My son hired you to stop the Hanover chief. You know of their power. I will give you the tool you need to succeed. How can you not be willing to release my son from his side of the agreement in exchange for payment in advance, and the chance you survive your encounter with the Hanover chief?"

Black Wolf had never had a need to consider advanced payment before this, or how to better his own chances of survival. But he had seen the Hanover girl's abilities and had to assume her father was just as strong, with many more years of experience using his power.

"I release your son. Now where is the second bracelet?" he said after some thought. He glanced around the modest furnishings and possessions contained in the chief's tent.

"It is in the safest place it could possibly be."

Black Wolf was quiet. Where would a tool with the ability to stop the Hanover chief be safely kept?

"With the girl," he answered his own question aloud.

"Yes."

"The girl is not in your possession," he pointed out.

"She will not be long missing from my possession," the chief replied. "By morning, she will be returned to us."

"If so, I will be impressed," Black Wolf replied. "Chases Deer knows the value of the girl, and the Hanover will not let me destroy the village to fetch her for you."

"The father of Chases Deer and I have been friends for many years. He does not yet understand what you and I do, that the girl will determine if we win our war. I will risk our friendship, and anything else, to finish what my ancestors started."

"Many men claim they would do whatever it takes, and then balk when they see the price," Black Wolf said dismissively.

"I am not one of those men. I am the Diné who will end this blood feud."

Black Wolf liked the elderly chief more than he thought he should. Few men truly meant what they said when they spoke to him, but this one did, a trait he had passed to his son.

Black Wolf toyed with the bracelet. "The weapon you speak of. This holds no magic. How can it be used to defeat the Hanover's?"

The chief smiled. "A hundred years ago, a woman, a Hanover,

the daughter of the city's chief, stood between the forty survivors of my tribe and her father. She did not have the great power her father did, but she had the heart he did not," he answered. "She helped my grandfather, a man she had never met, escape the Hanover chief, because she feared her father would lose his heart and soul if he wiped out an entire people."

Black Wolf listened.

"She was too late to save him from the Hanover madness. She was not the Hanover heir, and her father slaughtered her where she stood and left her body to rot," the chief finished. "These bracelets were hers. One of my predecessors insisted we keep them, and until recently, it was believed we did so as a reminder of how cruel the Hanover's were to murder their own. But I believe now my predecessor may have had a vision, may have understood that another Hanover woman would someday once again stand against her father to save the lives of others. The weapon I speak of is her heart."

Black Wolf's unique insight into the broken dynamics of the Hanover's stemmed not only from his interactions with the siblings but from being hired by a man bearing the Hanover mark to kidnap another man, also bearing the Hanover mark. He was not surprised to hear of the family's discord. Often, power and family were a lethal combination.

"Whether or not this is true, heart will never overcome power. As long as a Hanover with such power exists, you cannot assume you will ever have peace," he countered. "The Hanover's of this generation may have good intentions but the next may not."

"Which is why I recommend, however you plan to execute the father, you also ensure the daughter never poses another threat," the chief said.

It struck Black Wolf then that he was neck deep in the Hanover family's power struggle, without ever consciously being aware of entering it at all. Moreover, he was charged with winning a war on behalf of a tribe he had not known existed before several weeks ago. And there was no real weapon to speak of.

The chief had bested him. Perhaps, after many decades, it was time someone did. Whether his acceptance of his inevitable death kept him from reacting to the deception, or the loss of his wolf tempered his emotion, Black Wolf could find no real anger inside of him.

"You sent the half-breed into the city to murder the Hanover chief, and now you send me," he mused. "What if we both fail? Who will you send next?"

"Arthur is in the city as well. As long as one of you is there, failure is impossible."

"We are pawns."

"All of you," the chief confirmed. "That bracelet has more power than you understand."

"It's useless. A sentimental tool from a long-dead woman," Black Wolf scoffed. He threw the bracelet to the chief's feet.

"I am sincere when I say this bracelet will determine whether or not you are victorious." The chief stretched a gnarled hand for it. "This bracelet must be returned to the other. They are a set. Together, they represent the heart of the Hanover who saved us. Separated, they are only bracelets."

Growing irritated, Black Wolf snatched the basket full of pups and prepared to leave.

"Son!" the chief called.

The tent flap whipped open, as if Diving Eagle were hovering in case his father was in danger.

Black Wolf tensed, ready to tear them both apart if they tried to imprison him.

"This will bring you luck. You must wear it until the battle is over," the chief said and held out the bracelet.

Diving Eagle glanced at Black Wolf and then strode forward to claim the bracelet. He said nothing, and his father motioned for him to leave again.

When the tent entrance was closed again, the chief returned his attention to the skinwalker.

"You asked me what I would do to destroy the Hanover's and ensure peace. That is your answer."

Black Wolf studied him. Understanding bloomed within him. "You have had a vision."

"I did not need to. I understand human nature in a way you cannot."

"You would risk losing a war, and the lives of your people, on the heart of a Hanover?" Black Wolf asked, curious.

"If I am wrong, I lose my son. But if I am right, I have given you the only knowledge that matters in what is to come."

The Hanover girl had claimed Black Wolf would ask her to help him fight her father. At the time, he was unable to think of a circumstance that would necessitate him needing help at all. The tool the Diné chief had given him was not a tool at all, but a form of insurance, a guarantee the Hanover girl would be where she needed to be in order to finish a war started long ago.

To win, Black Wolf had to position her, and those she cared about, on the board in a place that would benefit him most. The Diné chief understood this and more importantly, knew whom exactly to use to incite her protective nature.

"I meet few minds I admire," Black Wolf said. "No one yet has been willing to use his own son as bait."

The chief's face was unreadable.

"When someone plays a game this risky, there's always a price to pay," Black Wolf added. "You will win, and you will lose."

"I am prepared," was the soft response.

For the first time in his life, Black Wolf believed someone when he claimed he was willing to pay the final price.

All he had to do was wait and play the card at the right moment.

Black Wolf picked up the basket of pups and left the stuffy tent. Only when he was outside did he take a deep breath and pause, gazing up at the drizzly afternoon sky.

He had been manipulated – but he suspected his spirit wolf would have wanted it to be this way. If anything, this was another sign of the direction he was supposed to walk, of the fate awaiting him, and the nature of what was to come. The battle he faced was unlike any he had faced before. Which meant, he had to fight it differently.

Black Wolf's gaze settled on Diving Eagle, who waited a short distance away, his features stony.

Black Wolf approached the solemn chief's son. "Do you want my help retrieving the Hanover girl?" he asked.

"My men can handle it," Diving Eagle replied. "And we do not need to worry about her interfering, if it's not you massacring Chases Deer's village."

"To end this blood feud with the Hanover's, she will have to die." Black Wolf spoke the words and then waited to read Diving Eagle's reaction.

The Native's jaw clenched, but his features did not otherwise betray him. "Then she will finally be free," he said. Without another word, he breezed by Black Wolf and disappeared into his father's tent.

Black Wolf smiled.

Perhaps the chief was taking less of a risk than the skinwalker initially thought.

SIXTEEN

TIANA SNAPPED AWAKE. The brindle pup on the pillow beside her head continued sleeping, but the flicker of a vision in Tiana's mind left her no doubt as to the danger this night. She flung off the blankets and exited the bedroom for the living area. A warm fire blazed in the hearth in front of which Rocky was stretched out and snoring softly.

"Rocky," she said with a glance at the door.

He awoke instantly and sat.

Tiana knelt near him to prevent their guards from hearing. "We must go."

"I know. I'm working on it," Rocky said and ran his hand through his hair.

"Now." Tiana rose and went to the couch. She gathered up his gear and dropped it on the ground beside him. "Hurry!" Not waiting for him to protest, she returned to her bedroom and dressed then gathered up her pup and placed it in a small pouch. The pup grunted and wriggled but stilled once more in sleep once it was nestled in the pouch.

"Tiana, what's wrong?" Rocky asked, leaning in the doorway of the bedroom.

"Diving Eagle is coming," she replied.

"And?"

"He's going to wipe out the entire village if we don't leave now."

"It's called a rescue."

She looked at him. "Everyone will die, Rocky," she said, concerned. "Chases Deer has been kind to us."

"Ah. Chases Deer dies, too?"

She nodded.

"All right. Let's go."

Tiana hid a smile. She had thought Rocky had a soft spot for the warrior woman and was right for once. Her amusement faded when she thought about Warner, who lay unconscious in the clinic, and the prisoner in the cabin beside hers. Marshall might hate her, but he could at least walk away from the village of his own accord.

But Warner?

She tested her ability to levitate the pillow with the pup on top. Her power came more easily each time she summoned it. The invisible hand was steady and did not seem to drain her at all.

"Rocky," she said slowly. "Can you do something for me?"

"Of course," replied the assassin.

"Marshall." She stopped and cleared his throat. "I do not think he will come if I ask him. But we should take him with us."

Rocky's expression softened, and he nodded. "I know you're adverse to pointless violence. Do I take this as a sign you're going to do the heavy lifting to get us out of here?"

"More than you know," she said with a smile. "I cannot bear the idea of more people suffering because of me, which is why we must take Marshall and Warner with us."

"Warner? The man who is dying in the clinic?"

She nodded.

"Bad idea, Tiana," Rocky said firmly. "And not for the reason you think. I'd be happy to carry him out of here, but the problem isn't getting him out. It's how Diving Eagle will react when we do. The clinic here is nicer than any clinic in the inner city, and Chases Deer isn't going to deprive him of care. From what I know, Diving Eagle is not eager to extend the same courtesy."

She listened, disturbed to find he was right. She was not thinking like her brother, a born leader, but like the deformed coward she was trying hard not to be.

"I'll leave the decision up to you, but I recommend the three of us leaving and then we'll figure out what to do about Warner," Rocky said.

"You are right," she said. "I did not think it through. But I do not wish to abandon him either."

"He is safe here and well taken care of. Diving Eagle will do whatever he must to guarantee the result he desires, without regard to anyone's life, even ours. Chases Deer operates differently and believes she'll claim a huge bounty for helping Warner," Rocky said. "Let her believe that until we figure out a different plan."

Tiana sighed. "I understand. Sometimes, it is wise to act with logic rather than feeling."

"Sometimes. But only sometimes," he said kindly with a smile. "Your instincts and concern for others are amazing. Don't let the world make you hard. Stay sweet and strong. Aveline has learned to balance the two, and you will as well."

She smiled, touched by both his faith in her and the gentle words. "I would love to be like her or Chases Deer," she admitted. "I would love to be strong."

"You are," he assured her. "Now, we need to leave before everyone ends up dead. We'll do this your way and slip out without hurting anyone. I recommend we keep this as quiet and isolated as possible. Can you incapacitate the guards in front of our cabin and Marshall's?"

She nodded.

"I can gag and tie them. With luck, we won't encounter any additional resistance."

As he spoke, Tiana left her bedroom for the window beside the front door. She counted three guards in front of each cabin.

"Give me a minute to make gags," Rocky said. He began tearing strips from the spare clothing provided them by Chases Deer. When he was through, he nodded his head to the window.

With no real insight into the extent of her capabilities, Tiana willed the men to be rendered silent and immobile. She felt energy leave her body in response to the commands and waited.

None of the guards moved.

"I think it worked," she said to Rocky.

He withdrew his knives and exited the cabin quietly. When no one charged to confront him, he trotted down the stairs to the ground, paused again, and then strode up to the guards. He replaced his weapons in their sheaths.

Tiana followed him.

The guards' eyes were moving around wildly but they were otherwise statues.

Rocky bound and gagged them all and then dragged them one by one into the cabin before moving on to those guards in front of Marshall's.

"You can stop," he told her over his shoulder, when the last of Marshall's guards was tied.

Tiana willed the magic to release them and glanced into the cabin she had shared with Rocky. The guards were wriggling on the floor. Satisfied she had addressed their situation without hurting anyone, she waited nervously in a chilly drizzle for Rocky to exit Marshall's cabin.

The two emerged after a few minutes. Marshall refused to look her way and trailed Rocky, his eyes on the ground. He appeared pale and gaunt, as if he had not eaten in days. She doubted Chases Deer had forgotten to feed him and guessed he was too sad to eat, a state she understood well after all her time trapped in her room and forsaken by her father.

Tiana did not dare speak. Rocky motioned her forward, and she walked ahead of him, troubled by Marshall's condition and situation. She did not know how to help him or even if he would accept the help of a Hanover, if she could. Part of her believed the Hanover's had done enough to his life, that he would heal only away from her family.

Distressed by the reminder of her father's cruelty, Tiana could not helping thinking of the vision again where she faced her father. How could she possibly confront him? Would it have to come to that? Or could they defuse the situation differently?

As soon as the fear crept into her, she recalled the deal she had made with Diving Eagle. He did not travel with cowards. She did not want to be a coward. She wanted to stop the horrifying suffering her family caused everyone. What form that would take, she did not know, but she hoped she could find it in her to face her father without fear.

Tiana paused behind the cabins and checked her senses. Diving Eagle's presence was faint. She looked in the direction in which he was located. The forest between their parties was thick, and no path was visible.

"Want me to navigate?" Rocky asked, following her gaze.

"Yes."

"Just let me know when we need to change directions," he said. He began walking south of the direction she had indicated, and she spotted the trail ahead of him.

Tiana sneaked a glance at Marshall, who ignored her, and walked hastily behind Rocky. Marshall trailed her without speaking.

Rocky led them through the forest. Only twice did they run the risk of being spotted by a scout, and Tiana distracted them by using her magic to send the scout in the opposite direction her companions wished to go.

She was soon soaked by the drizzle rain. The trail was slippery with mud, and the gentle drone of rain left her feeling more tired than she already felt. Several hours later, dawn began to lighten the gray sky, and their visibility improved enough to avoid the puddles and deepest sections of mud in their paths.

They took a break soon after dawn. Tiana sat on a rock and checked the pup in the pouch. Its eyes opened when the light hit it. She smiled at the puppy. It was warm and dry, unlike the rest of her body.

She fed it from one of the bottles she had packed and then stood.

"How far?" Rocky asked.

Tiana tilted her head and then turned to face the north. "He is right over there," she said. The Native was invisible to her eyes but not to her senses. "Twenty feet away. He just arrived."

Rocky tensed, gaze pinned in the direction of Diving Eagle. "Why isn't he coming closer?"

She smiled.

Rocky shook his head and grinned. He relaxed.

"I know I am important to him but I want him to know my friends are important to me," she explained. "I do not want any of you hurt on my part."

"Hanover's do not possess one conscience among them," Marshall said bitterly.

Tiana bowed her head without answering. She did not think anything she said would help him see she was nothing like her father.

"You're learning," Rocky said. "That's good."

"Until she realizes she doesn't need any of us and murders us all," Marshall replied.

"She's not mad like her father," Rocky replied. "Tiana's a good girl. Come on, before Diving Eagle gets too angry." He motioned them forward, where he could keep an eye on the distrustful Marshall.

Tiana went and Marshall trailed.

"Did you not ever wonder how every Hanover ends up mad?" Marshall asked her quietly. "My father said they did not start out that way at all, that your father was once a good man."

She glanced at him. Coldness slithered through her. She had

often wondered that herself, but about Arthur, before discovering she was her father's rightful heir.

"Your deformities will poison you. Using them will poison you faster," Marshall said.

Tiana's heart was pounding at the confirmation of her dormant fear. How much power did she have to use before it consumed her? Was she close? Would she know if she were?

"Is that true, Marshall?" she whispered.

"Have you ever heard of a sane Hanover leader?"

"No."

"Then I would say it is. You and Arthur were not born mad, but the power does not manifest until later."

"Enough," Rocky said firmly from behind him. "Tiana has one advantage the other Hanover leaders did not."

Marshall snorted derisively.

"What?" Tiana asked.

"Has any Hanover leader ever been a woman?" Rocky asked with a smile.

"Never," Marshall replied.

"Maybe only the men go mad."

They fell into uneasy silence. Tiana was uncertain what to think of the possibility perhaps she would be spared the madness, but Arthur would not have been, had he been born with her deformities.

Diving Eagle melted from the forest, and she stopped in place. Whenever she saw him, she had the urge to fold in on herself but also to step closer to catch a whiff of his scent. The opposing instincts baffled her after the time apart to the point all she did was stare at him. He wore war paint across his features and was dressed for stealth rather than extended travel.

"Free my men, Hanover," he said with his usual bluntness.

She released the invisible wall she had created.

"I had thought you would not use your abilities against us." Diving Eagle's look was penetrating.

"I did not want you to slaughter Chases Deer's village on my behalf," she said in a hushed tone. "They were going to refuse your demand, and you would have ambushed them and left no one alive. If I will not allow the skinwalker to do this, why would I let you?"

"I imagine that's how it starts. Sounds innocent enough, even benevolent, until she burns entire families at the stake," Marshall said.

I will never become like him, she vowed silently but could not help the uncertainty unfurling inside her.

After a moment that grew too long, and caused her face to flush with heat, Diving Eagle turned and gave a few hand signals to the second-in-command nearest him. A shout went up and was passed down the line of warriors, echoing through the forest. She was unable to count the amount of people she sensed but believed he had brought every able-bodied warrior in or near the hunting village, enough to crush Chases Deer's smaller outpost.

Diving Eagle stepped aside and motioned for them to walk down the trail flanked by his tribe's warriors. Tiana did. Diving Eagle relayed orders to two men and then trotted ahead of her, assuming the position of leading them back towards his village.

Relieved to have avoided the massacre she envisioned, Tiana checked her pup and shivered in her soaked cloak. Rocky had taken up his position behind her and Marshall behind him. Tiana was grateful for her assassin buffer and then just as quickly ashamed. Her father had destroyed Marshall's family and probably stolen every last one of his birthrights and wealth. She did not deserve to be spared his anger or pain.

Diving Eagle was right. She had the power to stop all of this — and the weak heart of a coward.

Tiana bowed her head and focused on her feet, less interested in watching her step than trying to sink into herself and think. Her mind drifted to Arthur and Aveline in the city and the quiet promise she had made to Aveline to fetch her friend, if she were in danger.

The more she thought, the more she began to realize the truth of her situation. There was only one real threat to anyone for a thousand miles, and it was not her father or the skinwalker or anyone else.

It was she, if her cowardice won, and she did not stop the one person she feared the most.

Of all the thoughts running through her mind, she could not help wishing to talk to Arthur. Her older brother had always understood the world, and conveyed it to her in a way she understood, and with such confidence, she never doubted he knew exactly what to do at all times.

They reached the hunting village some time later. Tiana sensed the skinwalker's agitated magic half a mile from the village and was not surprised to find him waiting for them, standing at the cages where her brother and Marshall had been imprisoned.

She sneaked a look over her shoulder, concerned about Marshall.

His eyes were on the ground, his features drawn. He appeared despondent, lost, and her heart felt as if it broke anew to recall what her father had done to him. Blinking away tears, Tiana returned her attention to what lay ahead. The skinwalker did not have to tell her aloud or telepathically he was waiting only for her; she felt him beckon her with his energy.

"Please do not place my friend in a cage again," she said quietly to the Native ahead of her.

Diving Eagle glanced back. "He will be treated as a guest, alongside the engineer."

"Thank you."

With a brusque nod, Diving Eagle left the column to speak to several other warriors in hushed tones.

She wiped her eyes and continued walking toward the skinwalker. Rocky trailed her silently, and she paused a safe distance from the form changing Native. At his feet was the basket of pups.

"What is that sound?" Marshall asked loudly.

Tiana turned to see him standing in the middle of space between the tree and forest. He twisted around once, features in deep consternation.

"I hear nothing," Rocky said. "You feeling well?"

"Someone keeps calling my name." Marshall leveled another glare on Tiana. "If you are toying with me, Hanover ..." He let the threat die.

"I am not," Tiana said. She glanced towards the skinwalker, who lifted the pup. "But perhaps one of them is."

Marshall frowned. "Who?"

Black Wolf approached him and lifted the covering off the basket.

"Ah, the babes," Marshall said, peering into it. His expression softened. "They've grown so much already."

"Which one speaks to you?" the skinwalker prodded.

Marshall hesitated before selecting the brindle one. "The sound I hear. It is him?"

"They are growing old enough to begin speaking, to call to the souls they were sent to lead," Black Wolf replied.

"I did not know your family suffered deformities," Tiana murmured to Marshall.

At the sound of her voice, Marshall's features shuttered once more. "You know nothing of my family, Hanover." He held the pup to his chest, turned, and stalked away.

Black Wolf appeared amused, while Tiana's heart tumbled a few feet lower than it had been. She sighed and waited as the skinwalker returned to the tree.

"You were right," he said. "I do need your help."

"I know," she replied.

"I'm leaving today. I believe you will leave tomorrow. They don't entirely trust us together," he said, eyes on Diving Eagle.

"They should know we are not willing partners."

"Maybe they know something they have not shared."

She studied him. "What would that be?"

"The form we saw in your vision. The person in rags. It's a skinwalker," Black Wolf replied.

Her brow furrowed. "Why would there be a skinwalker in a vision of me fighting my father?"

"I don't know, but I have the feeling those around us might have an idea."

She followed his gaze, which rested on the chief's tent.

"We are all his pawns," Black Wolf said.

"He is not wrong to do what he must to protect his people," she murmured. "My father has murdered more people than even you."

"You will become like him," said a faint voice.

Tiana's heart skipped a beat, and she glanced at the vengeful spirit that had materialized beside the basket of pups. The child squatted beside the spirit guides.

"I will not," Tiana said, voice trembling.

"Maybe you should," Black Wolf suggested. "Maybe that is how you finish this."

She shook her head. "No. I do not care what you or your vengeful spirit say."

"If you do not die, you will be alone forever. None of these is for you," the spirit said and looked from the basket to the skinwalker.

"Leave, spirit," he growled without looking at it.

Tiana frowned. "Is that your fear? Being alone?" she asked.

"My spirit wolf was my companion for a hundred years."

Though he expressed no emotion, Tiana understood the vengeful spirit's purpose enough to pity the skinwalker. How was it possible for a man who murdered everyone he met, without regret, to miss his companion? The sense she would not ever understand anyone disturbed her. People were complex and took great pains to hide who they really were.

Understanding anyone was impossible.

"What you should be focused on is what your father might want with a skinwalker," Black Wolf said. "The half-breed is in the city."

Unease slid through her. She had enough reason to worry about Aveline without the added connection to her vision. "Do you go there to help her, too?" she asked.

"I'm hoping for a glorious death," he replied with a wry smile. "There's no better guarantee of dying than going to your city."

"But some part of you wants to save the last remaining member of your tribe," she insisted. "You helped her once. Will you let her die in the city now?"

He shrugged. "If helping her is in my power, I will. If my fate is to walk into the city and die on the spot, then I will do that, too."

"Your life has climaxed in this place and time. I cannot imagine what you survived to reach this point. You do not strike me as someone who is content to let fate decide what happens."

"I'm not letting *fate* decide what happens to me," he replied. "I'm letting *you* decide what happens. I will do everything in my power to murder your father, but if I fail, you will determine what happens next, whether he survives or I do, and what happens to those you care about."

She listened. No part of her wanted to humor the claims of a mass murderer with no conscience ... except that he made sense. His wisdom, rarely dispensed, was nonetheless irrefutably sound. That a skinwalker could be the smartest person she had ever met, and her father had once been a good man, left her wanting to scream out of frustration from trying to relate to those around her.

The skinwalker looked past her and pushed himself away from the tree. He snatched the basket and reached in to pluck one of the pups from its depths.

"This belongs to Diving Eagle. He will not admit to possessing magic and refuses to claim his spirit wolf." He handed the pup to her.

Tiana took it, and the tension slid from her at the feel of the soft, warm pup in her hands.

"Make sure he has his wolf before he comes to the city," the skinwalker said. "I'm leaving now." He walked past her.

"What about the other spirit pups? You are not taking them with you, are you?" she asked, turning to watch him go.

"We are all destined to go to the city, even the remaining spirit guide," he replied without stopping or turning.

Tiana could not help thinking Diving Eagle's father was not the only one carefully guarding his secrets. She glanced at the pup with a smile and placed it in the pouch beside its sister before looking around for the Native who would not claim his pup.

Diving Eagle was surrounded by several warriors, deep in discussion.

"We should rest," Rocky advised. "I think we'll be gone in the morning."

"Back to the city," she whispered.

"Back to the city," he confirmed. "You wouldn't happen to have a plan, would you?"

She shook her head.

"We'll call it an adventure," he said, smiling. "Come on. Let's check on Jose and find some food."

Tiana trailed him. She hoped they weren't relying on her to know what to do, because she did not. Diving Eagle would. She rested a hand on the pouch containing the pups and allowed her eyes to find the Native again.

He was watching her from across the village center. He did not hold her gaze long but returned his attention to the others.

Tiana's eyes lingered a beat longer as she considered the promise she had made to him – not to be a coward – and what might happen if she were not strong enough to do what everyone wanted her to.

Diving Eagle was not likely to be forgiving, no matter what Rocky believed about the Native liking her. He had given her a choice, and she made her decision.

I hope things do not become as bad as I think they will, she thought as she followed Rocky towards the tent he and Jose had shared.

With any luck, the skinwalker would murder her father before she reached the city.

Seconds before she reached the tent, she heard her name and turned.

Diving Eagle approached, his hard features difficult to read and confident stride quick. She dropped her gaze, as she usually did around him, and noticed the bracelet around his wrist.

It was identical to the one his father had given her. Curious, she debated whether or not she should ask him about it and decided to wait to see if he were irritated with her about anything.

"I am leaving with Black Wolf," he told her when he reached her. "You will travel tomorrow with the bulk of our army."

She looked up at the mention of the army. "Do you not want me with you to ensure the skinwalker behaves?"

"He has accepted his fate," Diving Eagle responded. "We will be scouting for any traps and assessing our ability to enter the city undetected."

"You know if he accompanies you, it is for his purpose, not yours," she murmured.

"As long as he goes."

Familiar concern trickled through her. "What is your plan?" she asked. "Exactly."

"I will do whatever I must to remove your father from power."

"I know that. But what about the people of the city? The skinwalker cares for no one's life but his."

"What about them?"

She released a breath. "Thousands of innocent people live there."

"If they stay out of our way, they will not be harmed by me or anyone with me."

Tiana studied him. Her insides either felt like they were twisting or fluttering when he was around. Dared she believe him on his claim?

Had she met anyone yet she would trust with the lives of a hundred thousand people?

"Do you swear to honor these words?" she pressed. "You will harm only those who prevent you from reaching my father?"

"You want my word," he said.

"I do. I have given you mine that I will help you face my father."

It was Diving Eagle's turn to reflect. A tiny instinct, of whose accuracy she was uncertain, whispered that sparing the people had never been Diving Eagle's plan.

"Please," she said. "They are my people. They have suffered more under my father's madness than anyone outside the city."

"Our concern," he said slowly, "has always been the Hanover's, although, it would be easier for us to wipe out the city all together."

"Is that the kind of man you are?" she asked, genuinely confused and angry. "The kind of chief you will become? One who rules as my father does, with a knife in one hand a torch in the other?"

"Tiana, this war –"

"– is about to be over. You have an entire life to lead afterwards, to continue your father's legacy of peace. Do not make the mistake of becoming like *my* father instead!" she said with emotion she was certain would draw his criticism.

Diving Eagle said nothing for a long moment, gazing at her in what she took to be judgmental silence.

"I ask for this promise for your sake as well as the sake of everyone in the city. You can end this war and walk away from all of it. I cannot. Ever. The magic of the Hanover's runs through my blood as does the madness. If it costs me my mind to save your people from my father, I will give it gladly. I only ask that you spare mine!" Speaking to him often left her close to tears, and today was no exception.

Diving Eagle said nothing. Taking his quiet as a negative sign, Tiana spun and walked away before he saw her cry.

"Tiana," he called more softly. "I give you my word."

She stopped, suspecting she had heard wrong.

"As long as they do not impede me, I will spare them," he stated.

She faced him again, startled.

He approached once more. "I care nothing for your people, but I do not want you to view me in the same light as your father."

"You are better," she seconded.

"In truth, I am not, but I want you to believe I am." His rare, faint smile left her wondering what she had missed.

This time, the quiet stretching between them was charged in a way she did not entirely understand. Wanting to break the tension,

Tiana reached into the pouch and withdrew the white spirit wolf with a black star on its belly.

"This will help you find your way," she said and held it out.

Diving Eagle hesitated, as if accepting the pup was to admit he was not so different from the Hanover's he loathed. Finally, he reached out to take the pup from her.

Tiana turned away once more and entered the tent. Rocky stood near the entrance, smiling. She assumed he had been discreetly watching over her, as usual.

"I told you he liked you," he teased.

"You would be wrong," she replied.

This time, she almost understood why he thought so. Diving Eagle, in few words per usual, had admitted to wanting her to think of him in a good way. He had also made her a promise he clearly did not want to make. She recalled Rocky's claim, that the Native had followed her into the forest and confronted a skinwalker without any concern for himself. She had seen this as yet another act of bravery, one she was not likely to mirror, given her cowardice.

What if Rocky's insight was correct, and Diving Eagle had pursued her not because bravery was in his nature, but because he was concerned? Was it possible for him to care for her, a Hanover? Or was he wary of her power, should he refuse to promise to protect her people?

Further, was his promise a lie? Would he keep his oath, once he reached the city?

"How do people do this?" she expressed in frustration.

"What?" Rocky asked.

"Survive this world. Believe anything anyone else says. Trust someone. All of it!"

"You learn and have faith," he replied.

She shook her head. Maybe it was better she was destined to go mad. Maybe then, she would fit into the world.

SEVENTEEN

THE ONLY CONCERN in the world that could override the Hanover leader's persistent message in Aveline's mind was discovering her mother was alive.

The older woman slept fitfully. Aveline's head lifted from her paws each time her mother shifted or thrashed. Her tail flicked of its own accord, and her senses were filled with the pungent scent of refuse and smoke that filled the streets. Smells had never been this strong as a human. Every once in a while, Aveline caught a whiff of something that made her gag.

She sneezed and tossed her head. The sounds were another issue all together. Somewhere in the decrepit building where they took refuge, a family of rats scurried. Cockroaches tap-danced in the walls, while the movement of any person or animal within the ward filled her head with an even more intense pounding than before. Every movement sounded as if it was right beside her, though, after two days as a panther, she had begun to understand sound – like smell and sight – had nuances and depth she never needed to understand as a human.

Even so, she was unable to sleep, and it was not only the quiet chaos of her surroundings filling her senses. In this form, it was easier to touch the mind of another or perhaps, the mind of someone like her.

Her mother's mind was ... messy. Too messy for Aveline to pick up specific thoughts, unless Walks With A Limp steered specific thoughts towards her. Images too brief to make out, unfamiliar scents, noises, loud discordant music and other seemingly random fragments of memories swam in her mother's mind.

Aveline could make no sense of it and wondered if her mother could.

Of all the questions she had, she wanted to know most of all why her father had lied all those years about her mother.

The frail Native tossed and turned and then stilled again. Earlier in the day, Aveline had dragged in half a carcass of a goat from a butcher's nearby for food while they hid. The animal was left hanging in back of the butcher's shop while its blood drained into the street.

Her mother had eaten the entire thing – without transforming into an animal to do it – and then fallen into a restless sleep for the rest of the day and into the night.

Aveline rose and shifted forward, following the scent of blood remaining on her mother. She licked her mother's hands clean and the clothing and blood from the floor. Her mother did not stir.

Aveline shook the voice of the Hanover leader out of her head once more and paced to the door. She nudged it open and stepped out onto the collapsed porch, pausing to let her senses gauge the danger in creeping out into the night.

No heartbeats pummeled her brain, though her sensitive nose picked up on the scent of humans in the next ward. This one was abandoned, partially burnt out and partially collapsed.

Easing out the door, Aveline glanced towards the sky, which was blocked by thick smoke, before sliding into the shadows. Her stomach growled, but her destination was not food. She loped instead through familiar streets towards the pyramid. When the pounding of heartbeats in the populated wards became too much, she altered her course to take a different route.

Her tactic worked – until she realized the wards surrounding the center of the outer city were where everyone else had fled to. Forced to retreat by the noise in her head, she backtracked to the point where she could bear the pain.

The top and one side of the pyramid were visible. Her eyes went to the top, and questions filled her once again.

Why did you lie to me, Father? She asked and looked toward the smoke obscured sky. Was he watching her? Was he ashamed of his lie or proud she had learned the truth on her own? And what did he think of the woman he loved? Had he known she was imprisoned?

Aveline sat on her haunches, ears flickering in response to movement. The chill and drizzle could not penetrate her fur, though the scent of wet animal made her nose wrinkle. Her thoughts went to Arthur, who was in prison or dead in the pyramid, and to Tiana, who was lost in the forest. How had the Hanover children turned out differently than their father?

What of Karl? Was Arthur in a cell next to the man she blamed for her father's death?

She focused hard on trying to change her form and released a frustrated growl. Tiana's father had transformed her with a touch, and she could do nothing to turn back into a human.

"Because you are only half skinwalker, you will never be able to transform on your own."

The sound of her mother's voice was quiet. Aveline had known she approached without any of her senses picking up on physical cues. It was more of a shift within her, a spark of energy in her mind that warned her about her mother.

Her mother stopped to stand beside her and rested a hand on Aveline's head.

"What are you doing here?" her mother asked. "You cannot think to face the Hanover leader on your own."

Aveline yowled softly in protest.

"Concentrate on the words," her mother advised.

In this form, I can take him, she replied.

"Then why are you not there?"

Aveline looked up at her. *Why were you there?*

Her mother's eyes were on the pyramid. A strange light burned within them, one Aveline did not believe was healthy.

Why did my father lie? She asked more loudly through her mind.

"He had no choice. Your father ..." The light in Walks With A Limp's eyes faded, replaced by affection. "... he was the most honorable man I had ever met. He raised you well, as I knew he would."

I need to know, Aveline insisted. *What happened that he could never tell me? Why the secrets about you?*

"What did he tell you about me?"

That he fell in love with you on sight and bought you at a slave auction.

"He was always a romantic." Her mother smiled, the first genuine smile Aveline had seen. "I loved him and he loved me. If I did not believe him to be the man he was, I would not have left you with him. Isn't that enough for you?"

Aveline shook her head vehemently.

"Very well. Let us find more food first. I will reveal everything."

Her mother started forward, towards a building Aveline sensed was crammed full with people.

Aveline voiced her objection again.

Hurts, she said.

"There is much you need to learn about what you are," her mother said over her shoulder. "Stay here. I will find us food."

Aveline paced unhappily, concerned for her mother in her frail state. Walks With A Limp disappeared around a corner, and Aveline waited.

Moments later, her mother reappeared with a sack thrown over her shoulder. She hunched at the weight. Aveline smelled no blood, though the dirty sack contained too many scents for her to judge what it contained.

"Come with me," her mother said.

Aveline trailed her through the city and back to the abandoned ward. The moment Aveline put distance between her and the nearest human, she relaxed. Her mother's own presence in her mind was one of energy, coupled with a faint, fluttering heartbeat Aveline could not quite make sense of. Her mother had solid form; why was her heartbeat erratic? Was this, as well as her messy mind, an indication she was ill?

They reached the building and entered. Aveline needed no light to see her surroundings as clear as day. Licking her lips, she sat in the room.

Her mother settled the bag in the middle and lit a candle.

"You fed me earlier. You are welcome to the first bite," Walks With A Limp said and motioned to the sack. She tugged the tie loose.

Aveline nudged and pawed the sack open.

Her mother laughed.

"That is a human way," she said. "Tear through it. You are an animal."

Aveline's nose wrinkled. The sack smelled of years of use – dirt, excrement, spoiled foods and too many other unpleasant scents she found unappealing. She pawed it off the food inside and stopped cold. Her breath caught.

What is this? She asked and looked up at her mother.

"Food."

Aveline gazed at the unmoving body of a child around the age of four. Blood marred his neck from two puncture wounds. He was dead but still warm, a fresh kill. Aveline stared, stuck in the memory of the children she had seen being hauled off for meat when she was taken to a brothel.

Her mother shifted forward with a knife and gripped the boy's wrist.

Aveline swiped her hand away with a growl.

You eat humans? She demanded.

"I eat anything," her mother replied. "A human is meat like any other." She reached for the boy again. "This is what you are, Avi. You are an animal."

Aveline hesitated before swiping her mother's hand away again.

Exasperated, Walks With A Limp looked at her. "You're not one of them. What do you care if we eat him? He is already dead."

Aveline gagged at the thought, repulsed by the images in her head of eating a person. She coughed and then took two steps over the dead boy's body to protect him from her mother.

Is this what you are? She asked, baffled and horrified. *Is this what a skinwalker is? An animal with no respect for life?*

"In my two hundred and twenty years, I have loved one man and learned one lesson. Survival knows no boundaries."

Aveline gazed into her mother's eyes. The strange light was back, and her mother's mind was chaotic. A new thought entered her mind, one she would never have considered before.

Perhaps her father did not tell her about her mother, because her mother was a monster. As Aveline thought, the inconsistent versions of events regarding her family's checkered past began to fall into place.

The Devil's Massacre. It was not my father who committed it, was it? She asked, mind racing.

Her mother looked away and sat back. "We agreed to tell you it was. It supported his reputation among his kind and hid the truth from everyone, including you."

What truth? Aveline did not leave her protective position over the dead boy.

"Of what you were. Of what happened. Of how I ended up in the hands of a Hanover twice."

Tell me!

Walks With A Limp sighed. "Your father may have fallen in love with me on sight, but he did not buy me at an auction. He found me in the street. I had escaped a Hanover, with the help of a Hanover. I lived a hundred years in that attic, enslaved to four consecutive Hanover's. When I was freed, I knew nothing of the world, for it had changed in the century I was hidden away. I panicked and I ran into the inner city. Your father found me. He was kind and fair, and he took me in."

Aveline listened in breathless anticipation to hear the secrets she had always yearned to understand.

"He hid me away for a couple of years. You were born during that time, and we adopted a little boy named Rockwell. How is he? Is he alive?"

He became the best assassin, second only to my father, Aveline replied.

"I knew he would. He was a tough little boy and sharp," her mother said, smiling again. "It is the only time in my life where I was truly happy. But it didn't last. I slipped up. I didn't hide my presence in the city from the Hanover leader well enough, and he sent his Shield members after me. When I saw them coming to take everything from me, I lost control. I massacred a thousand people in three days. The Hanover leader cornered me in a building, and I destroyed everyone who came for me. Until the Hanover wizened up and sent your father with a message. My children would be spared, if I turned myself in."

My father did not betray you to the Hanover leader, did he? Aveline demanded, anger trickling through her.

"No. Your father agreed to deliver the message and wanted me to help him kill the Hanover leader. But I knew what he did not, that no one could protect my children from the Hanover leader, not even the top assassin in the city. I told your father I would work with him to destroy the Hanover leader, and then I surrendered in exchange for your safety."

Sorrow replaced Aveline's anger.

"Your father was heartbroken, I am certain. But my deal with the Hanover leader saved your life. It is said skinwalkers are selfish creatures, but what else was I supposed to do? I could not trade your life for mine."

Aveline studied her mother. While true affection existed in the mind of Walks With A Limp, it was a drop of water among a lake filled with fractured emotions, thoughts, and images. The woman her mother had been no longer existed.

He cares for no one's life, not even his own daughter. Why did he agree to spare two children from the inner city? Aveline asked.

"The mind of a Hanover is not one even I can understand," was the soft response. "But here you are, my beautiful daughter. Your father raised you well." Her mother drew a deep breath. "I no longer sense him. What happened?"

He was poisoned. Aveline replied carefully. Aveline did not want to find out how unstable her mother was by revealing the full truth.

"By Karl."

Aveline's mouth dropped open.

Her mother was not surprised. "The Hanover leader planted Karl to work with your father long ago. I believe your father managed to sway his loyalties, but a man with fickle loyalties will not always remain true to anyone for long."

Father knew Karl was loyal to the Hanover chief?

"He did. This was how the Hanover leader kept me from trying to escape again. He had someone close to you."

When my father decided to go after the Hanover leader ...

"Karl acted."

With the blessing of the council, so it did not look as obvious whom he worked for.

Aveline's loathing of her father's betrayer grew. She had dissected Wilhelm – Karl's brother's – tale of what happened many times and always felt something was missing. That Karl was already working for the Hanover chief both secured his place as her enemy and filled the gap her instincts had been trying to explain away. Wilhelm had not been in a position to understand the relationship between Karl and the Hanover leader, but Walks With A Limp was.

Karl had spent his years befriending Aveline while knowing he could be called upon to murder her at a moment's notice.

More questions percolated from the depths of her mind, but

Aveline was near her limit. She reached down and gently gripped the dead boy's arm in her mouth then dragged the child out reach of her mother. She tugged him out of the building altogether and into the street.

Lifting her head, she could not shake the image of the children sold for meat from her mind, or the second image of her mother feasting on the flesh of those children. As much as she wanted to believe her father had lied to keep her safe from Karl and the Hanover chief, Aveline began to suspect her father had lied to protect her just as much from her own mother, the woman who committed the Devil's Massacre.

She glanced down at the boy, and new anger stirred. Her mother had murdered the boy with the intent of eating him. Was this Aveline's true legacy? She had always hoped to become like her father, but what if she was destined to become more like her mother? Or like Black Wolf?

She stood, warring with herself, before shaking off the confusion and anger and dragging the boy away. Somewhere, a mother would awaken in the morning and wonder where her child was. Dared Aveline return the child to where he belonged?

She gazed up towards the sky, wishing her father could help her. Finally, she decided that, sometimes, it was better not to know the truth, especially when it was this terrible. If a skinwalker could not bear to lose her daughter, a human would bear the pain many more times.

Aveline went towards the populated part of the city once more and dragged the boy inside another building near the edge of a crowded ward. She laid him out to the best of her ability and sat beside him to pray. She hoped her father was watching through the clouds and smoke, so he could guide the tiny spirit into the spirit world where it belonged.

"Thank you."

Aveline whirled and stared at the translucent phantom of the child behind her.

"He gave me a message for you," the little boy said.

Aveline blinked rapidly, not believing her eyes.

"He said you must help seal the breach."

Who? Aveline managed to focus long enough to send the word to the ghost.

"And he misses you."

Sorrow unfurled within her. *My father?*

The boy nodded.

Aveline's eyes grew tight, and tears blurred her eyes. *Tell him I miss him, too.*

"I will see him soon. But I must go now. She owns me until her death and then we will both be free." As he said the words, the boy faded.

Wait! Aveline hurried towards him.

By the time she reached him, he had completely vanished.

She stared into the empty space, not understanding anything other than the spirit had spoken to her father. Aveline went to the dead boy and shook him gently, hoping to encourage his spirit to speak to her again.

It did not.

She left the building and returned to the place where her mother hid. She sniffed the air before entering, afraid to discover her mother had claimed another human life and eaten it in Aveline's absence.

Her mother was seated inside where Aveline left her. Aveline met her gaze and paused in the doorway. She did not feel connected to the woman inside the destroyed room, and she did not fully grasp how her father had fallen in love with someone like this.

"What is it?" Walks With A Limp asked. "You are troubled."

Rather than reveal the truth of her thoughts, Aveline slinked into the room and sat. *I saw a spirit.*

"Ah. That's normal," her mother said. "The spirits of every life you take are yours to keep until your death."

Keep?

"They will accompany you forever. Sometimes you see them, and sometimes they speak to you. But you do not have to listen to them. They often talk just to talk."

Aveline blew air hard through her nose. She looked around without seeing any spirits and thought about how many people she had killed thus far. A dozen perhaps, mainly Shield members.

Is this the curse of being a skinwalker? She asked.

"An inconvenience. They want to be free, but they belong to you. If you tell them to stay quiet and leave you be, they will."

But are they not people? Shouldn't I care about what they say?

"Why?"

Aveline did not send her mother a response. Instead, she turned way and made a show of rearranging her small nest. She walked in a few circles to flatten any objects that might poke her before settling down. Her mind, however, was as far from this room as possible.

She was nothing like her mother or the other skinwalker she had met. Was this because her father was human? Or how he raised her? To kill when hired or necessary and to act with honor even in those circumstances by killing quickly.

She could not help comparing herself to Tiana, whose father was a monster not unlike Walks With A Limp. She had always pitied Tiana, but comprehending exactly what the Hanover daughter had gone through daily left Aveline feeling closer to Tiana than her own mother.

"Someone will come for us soon," her mother assured her.

Aveline was not certain she wanted to know who this person was. She rested her head on her paws and watched her mother get comfortable on the other side of the room. Privately, Aveline vowed not to let her mother hurt anyone else needlessly, even if that meant she remained with the unstable skinwalker she did not trust.

EIGHTEEN

BLACK WOLF SAT ATOP A MULE, frowning as he looked out over the grasslands. If his spirit wolf were still alive, he would be able to teleport to the city and not waste two days traveling on horseback. If he were not obligated to wait for the normal humans, he could run to the city in half the time in one of his animal forms.

As it was, he was bored and trapped with the lesser people accompanying him.

The basket with the remaining pup was tied securely to his pommel. Dusk was fast approaching, and the smoke surrounding the city completely obscured it from view.

Diving Eagle drew abreast of him. How he knew not to allow normal horses near him, Black Wolf did not know. The chief's son was smarter than he seemed at times, though nowhere as interesting as the chief himself.

"Do not dare tell me we are stopping for the night," Black Wolf said, irritated.

"We are not," Diving Eagle confirmed. "We are awaiting allies."

Black Wolf rolled his eyes. "You don't need them. You have me."

"We have waited five hundred years for this. We will not be hasty."

While there was probably wisdom in this approach, Black Wolf could appreciate none of it. He was anxious to meet his fate, to find the pups their homes, and meet the man every Native and non-Native for a thousand miles spoke about in whispers. The skinwalker was not accustomed to working with others or bending his wishes to another's schedule and priorities.

"Catch up when you find them," he said moodily and nudged his mule forward. "I'm not waiting."

Diving Eagle issued a flurry of orders to those with him before following. To his credit, he did not order Black Wolf to stop or slow but fell into step beside him.

"Are you entering the city?" Black Wolf asked. "Or do I go alone?"

"We may have an agreement, but I do not trust you to go alone."

Black Wolf said nothing, amused the Native thought to keep an eye on him when they both understood who would win in an altercation.

They rode into the night. Diving Eagle turned out to be a competent, quiet companion capable of hunting quickly and determined to reach the city with minimal breaks, which were more for the sakes of the mules than their own. The western Native sneaked to feed his pup at intervals. The Hanover girl had delivered the pup as Black Wolf assumed she would, and Diving Eagle did not refuse the animal when it came from her.

Did the two of them understand why? Black Wolf did not think either of them really did, and his glance fell often to the turquoise bracelet Diving Eagle wore. Nothing less than absolute destruction was going to deter, and hopefully stop, the Hanover chief. How Black Wolf pushed her to that point, he did not yet know. Diving Eagle would either be a place to start or one of many reasons for her to act when she would otherwise not.

Before dawn, they left the road leading to the city and halted at a small pond. The sturdy mules lowered their heads to drink, and Black Wolf stared towards Lost Vegas. Halfway there, the smoke still obscured the city of legend. He could not help being disappointed not to be able to see it yet. However, the fog was also befitting the city shrouded in strange rumors and myth.

Can you hear me? He asked without turning to face his companion.

Diving Eagle stilled in his movement. There was a pause before he began moving once more without answering.

"Do your western tribes not believe in spirit guides?" Black Wolf asked.

"We do."

"And that they come in animal forms?"

"Yes."

"I don't think I've ever met anyone more reluctant to be claimed by a spirit guide." Black Wolf faced the western Native.

Diving Eagle was holding his pup, which was trying to stand. "If I did not believe it was an honor, I would not have brought it." He peered at the wolf with a conflicted expression.

"Him," Black Wolf corrected him. "He made the effort to take this form. Respect that. He can feel your resentment, too."

Diving Eagle lowered the pup and settled one of his piercing looks on Black Wolf. A lesser man would be intimidated, but Black Wolf feared nothing in this world.

"He says my name over and over and the word Star," Diving Eagle asked. "I believe he wishes it to be his name."

"He will learn to say more as he grows older," Black Wolf said.

"I do not resent *him*," the chief's son added. "Since you entered our hunting village, promising great wealth, we have been cursed. You changed the course we were on."

"Or I put you on the course you were meant to be on," Black Wolf replied. "If you want to win this war, you can't continue to nurse your hurt pride. You're not the first man I tricked or lied to."

Diving Eagle shook his head, carefully replaced the pup in a pouch at his waist, and stalked over to the mules.

"Do you have any sort of plan?" Diving Eagle asked.

"I don't need plans."

"If you fail, and the Hanover chief realizes his danger, you will ruin any chance of us succeeding."

Black Wolf had never had a reason to consider how his actions impacted others and brooded silently, uncertain if even this situation warranted him caring what happened to anyone else if he somehow managed not to succeed.

They mounted their mules once more and returned to the road.

"Of all the rumors about the Hanover chief, which are true?" he asked finally. "Your brother spoke of spirit soldiers and entire armies disappearing before they could reach the city. I have heard too many different versions of events to believe any of them."

"If he is like his daughter, there are no limits to his abilities."

"But there is a price. No one can use power of this magnitude without paying a price," Black Wolf replied. "That price could limit his willingness to use magic or to unleash everything he is capable of."

"You speak of the Hanover madness," Diving Eagle's voice was quieter.

"In part. This level of unnatural ability must have another price as well."

"Do you pay a price for slaughtering innocents?"

"I will. Someday," Black Wolf replied. "But it does not stop me."

"The Hanover's cannot be of this world," Diving Eagle said. "They cannot be meant for this world, either."

Black Wolf smiled, not caring if the Native saw it. Diving Eagle was torn in what he felt for Tiana Hanover. But the truth was, there was no hope for the girl. If she survived a confrontation with her father, she would not survive much longer with her right mind.

Diving Eagle halted suddenly. Black Wolf twisted to see what his companion did before halting his horse as well. The western Native had turned his mule towards the forest. A column of smoke – black at its center swirled with yellow, red, and blue – rose from the forest.

"My father has crossed over," Diving Eagle said. "I felt it last night but hoped ..." He fell quiet and watched.

"He will witness the revenge of your people from the spirit world," Black Wolf said. "You should be pleased. He could not see what you do otherwise." Unconcerned, he nudged his mule forward and began walking once more. "They're waiting for us."

After a pause, Diving Eagle followed. "Who?"

Black Wolf did not answer. He had felt the presence of the skin-walker beckoning him towards the city for three days now, since sharing the vision with the Hanover girl. It was stronger this day. The compulsion to ride without stopping grew stronger the closer he came. He had not known how to categorize the unusually strong presence in his mind, but the closer they came to Lost Vegas, the more he believed it was a distress call. The skinwalker in the vision was in trouble. But it was not the half-breed he had saved, Aveline. This was a different person, someone older than he was.

"I do have a plan," Black Wolf said after some consideration. "But you will not like it."

"I do not expect to."

He snorted, always amused by the Diné's blunt honesty. "I learned the history of the bracelet you wear. Do you know who possesses the other one?" he asked.

Diving Eagle glanced down.

"The Hanover girl."

Diving Eagle's jaw clenched.

"Your fates are bound. Your father believes it to be so," Black Wolf continued.

"What is your plan?" Diving Eagle snapped.

"Go with her when she faces her father."

"I will not abandon my warriors or my people or my plan."

"I'm not asking you to." Black Wolf smiled. "You and she both wish to face her father. Why not do it together?"

"Because I have a duty to my people, and because –"

"That bracelet is where your duty lies. If your father thought otherwise, he would not have given it to you."

Sullen silence followed his words. Black Wolf said no more. He did not have to. He had planted the seed and yanked the first bud free of the soil. The rest was up to Diving Eagle.

NINETEEN

THE TICKLE of grass against Tiana's face tugged her out of deep sleep. She had been dreaming about being trapped back in her tiny room with Aveline. It was not a vision, but a normal dream, one that slipped away as her eyes opened. The pup's warm body was cradled in her hand as it slumbered. She gazed at the lightening sky above her for a long moment then sat up quickly.

She had gone to sleep inside a tent, with Rocky a few feet away. She blinked and twisted to see around her. She was nowhere near a tent but on the ground in waist-high grass. Tiana rose up on her knees, and her breath caught.

Smoke from her father's human sacrifices obscured the city from view. It rolled off the city into the sky above and added to the blanket of fog surrounding it. She was less than a few miles from Lost Vegas.

How many people had he hurt? How many more would die?

How was she the right person to stop him?

Her pup stirred and awoke. It whispered her name telepathically. Rarely did it say more, though it had screamed into her mind the moment Black Wolf tried to kill her. The disabled pup lifted its head in jerky, wobbling movements towards her and peered at her through eyes that did not quite yet understand how to focus.

Tiana smiled and held the pup closer to her body so the early morning chill did not reach it. She was about to puzzle over how she arrived here when she saw the basket of bottles at her back.

"I have a feeling you brought us here," she said and reached for one to feed the pup. "I did not know you had this ability."

Tiana. Was all her pup said. The tiny wolf ate hungrily and then settled against her to sleep.

She tucked it into a deep pocket and picked up the bottles. Tiana stood and gazed around. The four roads – one in each cardinal direction – leading away from the city were nowhere in sight. With the familiar forest at her back, she guessed she was on the north side still, in the expanses of prairie land stretching between the roads.

Smoke rose from the forest as well, a multi-colored column far less ominous than the billowing clouds surrounding Lost Vegas. Tiana returned her attention to the city. Her insides were twisting, and she fought the urge to run away or curl up on the ground and cry. The panic inside her held her prisoner for some time, squeezing her chest and making her head spin.

She sat down again and struggled to regain her composure. She was where she was meant to be. If she ever hoped to make it to the Freelands, she had to first ensure her father never came after her or harmed anyone else. One confrontation, and she was free – permanently.

But the thought did not calm her the way it should have. If anything, a sense of doom settled into her gut, as if some part of her knew she would never be free.

She stood and began walking towards the city. Arthur and Aveline were inside. Hopefully, she would arrive in time to stop her father from hurting either of them.

Tiana walked towards the city. Not long after she began, she saw two figures on horseback, their presences marking the road leading from the north. She angled towards it and continued walking. Not soon after she spotted them, they saw her and stopped. Tiana slowed, not wanting to draw attention to herself before she entered the city. One of the riders raised an arm and waved. Curious, she focused on them and allowing their presences to register with her mind.

Black Wolf. Diving Eagle.

She missed a step as she debated whether or not she really wanted to face them. With a sigh, she pressed on. If she could not face her allies, how would she find the courage to face her father?

Tiana walked through the high grasses until she reached the road and paused. The mules grew restless at her presence without moving. Black Wolf did not appear surprised to see her, while Diving Eagle frowned.

"How did you get here?" the chief's son asked.

"Her wolf," Black Wolf answered for her. "Teleporting is one of their capabilities."

"I did not ask her to bring me," she said. "I assumed she wanted me to be here. Perhaps to meet you both."

"You can accompany us into the city," Black Wolf decided.

"That is not the plan," Diving Eagle countered.

"It is my plan."

"It is not mine!"

She looked between the two of them, sensing tension.

Black Wolf made a derisive sound. Diving Eagle dismounted and approached, standing in front of her.

"My allies are a day behind us. We wait and use the element of surprise then enter the city," he explained. "It's safer that way."

Tiana's gaze went to the city. "I need to go now," she said. "I have to find my brother and Aveline before you make your move, or they will be in greater danger."

"Tiana, you should not enter the city at all," Diving Eagle's voice was quieter. "You do not know what your father has planned for you."

Nothing good, she thought. "If you do not plan to attack until tomorrow, then I will be certain to return by then," she said. She started to turn away, but he rested a hand on her arm. When Aveline touched her, she did not notice. Not so with Diving Eagle. His simple touch felt unusually intimate.

Tiana looked up into his dark eyes.

"You do not have to do this," he said.

"Find my brother and friend?"

"No."

Tiana flushed, embarrassed he had somehow read her intentions. It was not the first time he understood words she did not speak. "How do you do that?" she muttered.

"My father has gone to the spirit world and passed his gift to me."

She stepped back, fear flashing through her. "You can see what he did."

"Yes."

She stood perfectly still while he gazed into her eyes, waiting to be judged.

"If I saw the madness, you would not be alive," he said, amused.

"That brings me little comfort," she admitted. "Do you see what your father did?"

"I can never know that answer," he replied. "But I can see you believe you will never leave the city, once you enter it."

Tiana swallowed hard. She did not want to acknowledge this fear, let alone hear someone else speak of it aloud. "I hate that place," she said with rare vehemence. "It will not let me go. Ever!"

"Freedom is not what you want."

"I do not like this new gift of yours," she replied and lowered her eyes. "How can you know the secrets of my mind when I do not?"

"This is no secret," he replied. "If you valued freedom above all, you wouldn't have agreed to return with me. Which means you value something more than freedom. It's logic not magic."

"Maybe I do." Her thoughts were on her brother and Aveline. "Maybe I want to be more than a duty to someone, to be accepted for what I am, maybe even cared about. Genuinely."

Diving Eagle said nothing.

"I am sorry for your father's passing and any pain you are in," she added. "He gave me a gift before I left. I will return it, if you desire." She pulled the small pouch out of the satchel containing the feather and bracelet. She handed it to Diving Eagle.

He opened it and paused, staring into the depths. For a long moment, he did not seem to breathe.

"If they are of value to you, it is only right you keep them," she voiced.

Diving Eagle withdrew the feather and shifted forward, pinning it to her hair. When he reached up, his sleeve fell away from his wrist, and she spotted the turquoise bracelet circling it. He withdrew the identical bracelet from the pouch and took her hand gently, sliding it over her fingers to her wrist.

"My father's foresight is beyond my understanding," he said and dropped his hands.

She touched the feather in her hair, affected by the quiet reverence in his tone when he mentioned his father.

"These were gifts," Diving Eagle lowered his arms. "You must keep them."

At his quietness, she lifted her gaze again. His hard, planed features were impossible to read.

"He knew what you were when you met him, and I am only now understanding."

"What am I?" she ventured, uncertain she would like his answer but desperate to know his thoughts about her without understanding why.

"You're a warrior."

"Do warriors fear the battles they face?"

"At first, yes. But when you fight for a cause greater than yourself, you discover strength you did not know."

She listened, fascinated by his insight. "Do all warriors wear these to battle?" she asked, lifting her wrist while her eyes went to his wrist.

Diving Eagle looked away. "Only one warrior ever has."

"Did he win?"

"At great cost."

Tiana nodded. The idea she was entering the city for the last time left her wanting to weep for the Freelands, and freedom, she would never see. She fought herself, refusing to allow someone as brave as Diving Eagle witness her tears.

"I cannot go with you now," he said. "But if you stay until this evening, I can. I do not want to see you hurt."

If ever she had heard these words, she never thought they would come from him. Part of her felt the war with her father would be over long before the Native led his people into the city for the attack. At the very least, she *hoped* this to be true. The Diné had lost one chief this day. They would not lose another if she could help it.

Tiana shook her head. "I have to go," she said softly. "For them. For me. For you." She glanced over her shoulder. Black Wolf had already ridden away without waiting, unconcerned with anyone's agenda but his own.

"I will say a prayer for you," Diving Eagle replied. "Take my horse." He pulled a knife and sheath free from the small of his back and handed it to her. "If you find your father before I do, drive this through his heart."

She accepted it with no small amount of surprise.

"It is has been purified and blessed. Do not use it on you," he added firmly.

She accepted it.

Tiana waited for Diving Eagle to say more. He did not. She turned away from him. He helped her mount and handed her the reins to the mule. Wishing she knew what to say, Tiana wracked her mind for the right words. None revealed themselves.

She nudged the horse forward and started towards the city she loathed. She sneaked a look over her shoulder. Diving Eagle was watching her, frowning and troubled. Tiana straightened and toyed with the bracelet. That it was important enough for him to wear one, too, meant more than she thought it should.

The butterflies in her stomach turned to stone when her focus shifted ahead of her, to the city surrounded by smoke. Black Wolf did not wait for her or stop. She did not share his eagerness for death.

Drawing abreast of him, she glanced over to see if he were as worried as she was. If anything, the skinwalker seemed pleased. The skinwalker was forever on his own version of events. She did not ask why he smiled and instead, focused on not turning and fleeing the closer they went towards her father.

Black Wolf pulled a cloak off the back of his horse and tossed it to her. "He will sense you, but let's pretend he might not notice you crossing the threshold into the city."

Tiana accepted it and pulled it on then tugged up the hood. Her father's capabilities were less well known than her own, which she did not understand much at all. But if he were able to track people like she could, he was probably already aware she was close. What was his plan?

"If he senses me, can he sense you?" she asked.

"I don't know," the skinwalker said.

"How do I find my brother and Aveline, if my father knows I'm here?"

"I have an idea."

She waited.

The skinwalker did not expand on his claim but continued riding with a small smile on his face.

Had he, too, gone mad? He understood how magic worked better than she did, but his goals ... she had never understood what he wanted at all.

A little lost, Tiana decided to stick with him until she had a better plan for finding Arthur and Aveline. Her brother's presence in her mind came from the direction of their home, but Aveline? She stretched out her senses, seeking her friend without feeling her at all.

They entered the shroud of smoke and fog. Only the darker color of the ground was visible; she could not even see the skinwalker. Tiana covered her mouth and nose, disgusted by the idea she was breathing in what remained of the people her father had burned. The clouds were thick enough, it took her five minutes to pass through them before they began to thin, and the city materialized.

The smoke here as more of a fog that hung low enough for wisps of it to cling to buildings and horses. The city was quiet. The few people in the streets did not remain outside long and darted between buildings.

Tiana and Black Wolf walked slowly into Lost Vegas. The scent of wood and flesh burning made her nose wrinkle. Tiana tugged her shirt up over her nose and left it there. The skinwalker appeared unconcerned. Instead, his gaze was pinned to the west of them. As soon as they reached the first intersection, he turned left.

"You sense or seek someone?" she asked.

"Yes."

"Not my father," she murmured, noting their direction was opposite of the side of the city where her brother was located.

Black Wolf led them deep into the inner city, past entire wards of buildings recently turned to ash, and through narrow streets tucked between dilapidated buildings where no one spoke or emerged to challenge the strangers.

He drew to a halt in front of a sagging building that appeared to be abandoned and dismounted.

Tiana studied it critically. Before she could ask him what he sensed, when she felt nothing, Black Wolf reached up and hauled her off the mule. He released her when she was on the ground then took both mounts and tied them to a column at the front of the building. He walked in.

Tiana shivered. It was unnaturally quiet and foggy. She hurried after the skinwalker into the building. The wooden flooring was cracked and sunken in and creaked loudly when she moved across it. She peered into two rooms, both of which were trashed and dark and smelled of something awful. Tiana followed the skinwalker more closely as he moved through the building. He paused at points before continuing.

They reached the last doorway in the bottom floor, and he stopped again. A crooked door filled most of the space of the doorway. She sensed his magic flex and roll outwards.

As if in response, something from behind the door growled low and deep. Tiana inched away, not certain she could trust the skinwalker not to lead her into a trap of some sort. He opened the door, displaying the dark room beyond, and motioned for her to enter.

Tiana hesitated, looking at him hard.

"It's not in my interest to murder you before you help me complete my mission," he said and took her arm. He pushed her through the doorway.

Tiana. This time, it was not her pup that called her name.

"Aveline?" she replied, puzzled. "Are you –" Before she could complete the sentence, something large, warm and fuzzy had tackled her to the ground. Tiana hit with a thump and grunt. The weight on her lifted, and a large muzzle pushed at her insistently. The animal purred loudly and pawed at her.

Tiana sat up, struggling to differentiate between the animal and the rest of the objects in the dark room. A flicker of energy soared away from her to the ceiling before erupting in dazzling light.

The black panther pawing and nudging her became visible. Tiana froze then recognized the necklace dangling from the animal's neck.

"Avi!" she exclaimed and wrapped her arms around the panther. She hugged her friend hard.

Aveline nuzzled and pushed her again, made circles and leapt in the air in place.

"She is stuck." The second voice was unfamiliar.

Tiana climbed to her feet amid Aveline's excited activity and gazed at the middle-aged Native woman standing halfway across the room. She was surrounded by trash, broken furniture and other refuse – but she stood apart from everything, untouched by the refuse of this world. Realizing she was staring, Tiana blinked.

"What do you mean stuck?" she asked.

"The Hanover leader turned her into a beast. She cannot turn back on her own." The woman's sharp eyes were in direct opposition of her frail form and wild hair.

"Skinwalker," Black Wolf said. He pushed Aveline aside, an elder setting a boundary. His attention remained on the woman. "You summoned me."

"I did."

"What is going on?" Tiana asked, glancing between the two of them.

"The form we saw at the end of your vision. It was her," Black Wolf replied.

Mother, Aveline said into Tiana's head.

Tiana gasped.

"I am her mother," the middle-aged skinwalker stated. "I have spent the past hundred years imprisoned by that family."

"Is he as fierce an opponent as I have heard?" Black Wolf asked.

"No one can face him."

Black Wolf smiled.

"I was as foolish as you once," the female skinwalker said. "Listen to me when I say no skinwalker can defeat him."

"I can," Black Wolf said. "With her help." He motioned to Tiana. "She is his heir."

The female skinwalker's face hardened when she looked at Tiana. "Then you are more of a fool than I thought. Hanover enslave skinwalkers. The Hanover's are powerful, but they lack what we have: one foot in the spirit world. They use us to maintain a crack in the barrier between our world and the spirit world. You think you have brought her here, but she has brought you to use you."

Tiana felt three pairs of eyes on her. "I do not understand any of this," she voiced.

Aveline gave a mournful moan Tiana did not understand, but her mother seemed to.

"I don't care what you think on this topic," the skinwalker said.

"You cannot understand what one of our kind endures at the hand of the Hanover's. The three of us are the last of the skinwalkers."

"The spirit armies are real," Black Wolf said thoughtfully.

"Whole armies have also disappeared directly into the spirit world when they attack the Hanover's," the female skinwalker said. "And yes, he can call upon the spirits of soldiers to fight for him, but it is rare for even a Hanover. The cost is great."

"I am not like my father or his predecessors," Tiana said quietly. "I want Hanover rule to end."

"It cannot end when someone with your power exists."

Tiana swallowed hard. Deep down, she knew this. But it was difficult to admit to herself how true it was. "It is why I came to the city. I have to end this. All of it," she whispered.

Aveline nudged her. Tiana managed to smile down at the panther.

"I will never trust a Hanover," Aveline's mother said. "Did you steal that from her as well?" She indicated the bracelet Tiana wore.

Tiana glanced down at the bracelet she had found among Aveline's belongings in her room. It bore the same symbol as the one on the skinwalker's medallion around his neck.

"I took it for safekeeping," she said.

Aveline was looking at her.

"It was in an envelope you carried to my room," Tiana explained. "It belonged to your mother."

"It was all I left with her father," Walks With A Limp snapped. "Leave it to a Hanover to steal my Avi's only memory of me."

Tiana frowned and removed the bracelet. She placed it around Aveline's paw, and the furry assassin nudged her.

"I am sorry," Tiana said to her.

Aveline nuzzled the bracelet. This time, she sent Tiana a picture in her mind. She saw Arthur and the secret passages.

"My brother freed you," Tiana said. "We are not like our father." She reached out to Aveline and buried her hands in the panther's soft fur. Without knowing how, Tiana closed her eyes and willed Aveline to return to her human form. The fur beneath her hands grew shorter and vanished, until her palms rested on the bare back of her friend.

Tiana opened her eyes.

Aveline rested on the floor, naked and shaking. Tiana covered her with her cloak and stepped back, thrilled to see her friend again.

"I ... trust her," Aveline said. She hugged the cloak around her and stood, facing Tiana. "You're late." She looked down at the bracelet around the wrist of her bear paw, and a flicker of unhappy emotion crossed her features before vanishing.

If Tiana had to guess, Aveline was not pleased to have her bracelet back. Tiana smiled. "I did my best."

"Where's Rocky?"

"Quiet. Tell me more about these Hanover abilities," Black Wolf said in irritation.

Aveline took Tiana's arm and led her away, where they could talk. In as few words as possible, Tiana explained where Rocky was and about the attack planned the next morning.

"Your brother's in prison," Aveline reported. "How do you plan on disabling your father before the Natives attack the city?"

Tiana shrugged.

Aveline glanced towards her mother and then back. Rather than happy, she appeared pensive. "She might know how to help," she said. "She's serious about vengeance on the Hanover's. I don't care if your father is killed, but you and Arthur are different."

"Arthur is," Tiana allowed. "But Aveline, if I die, too, we must consider it an option. My father was once a good man. Our deformities corrupt us."

Aveline shook her head. "I don't believe that. Even if it's true, you can choose not to use your power. Whatever we decide to do, you won't end up like your father."

Tiana did not have the heart to object when she saw the determination in her friend's eyes. "We will need to act quickly," she said. "Tomorrow morning, the Diné will attack the city. My father likely already knows I'm here, and I have to save Arthur."

"My mother says she can block his ability to find us."

"I noticed that, too," Tiana said. "Black Wolf can absorb my magic. I think your mother knows more about my father's capabilities than anyone else in existence. We will need her help. Do you think she will agree to help?"

"She's different than I thought she would be," Aveline whispered. "Very strong, which I admire. But ... she's too much like him." She lifted her chin towards Black Wolf. "Even if she does, I don't think we can trust her."

"I don't think we can trust anyone. When Black Wolf is focused on the same purpose as we are, he is an unparalleled ally," Tiana said. "We had better hope your mother shares our purpose."

"She wants your father dead. Let's hope that's enough," Aveline said with a small smile. "We've been hiding here for two days, waiting for you. She told me details about my father I didn't know. He was a good man, and his last mission was to try to murder your father."

"Your family shares a hobby," Tiana said.

Aveline looked at her. "Did you tell a joke?"

Tiana smiled.

"You're not the scared little girl I met months ago," Aveline said with some pride. "When this is over, I'll take you to the Freelands. I promise."

Tiana's smile faded. She would never see the Freelands. She had held onto the sliver of desperate hope until she stepped into the city and felt the thrumming energy of her father's magic. If she lived through this, she risked becoming him, and destroying the lives of thousands of innocent people. Her best chance of not becoming mad was to die in the confrontation with her father, leaving Arthur to help the city recover and negotiate peace with the Natives.

When Aveline glanced her way again, Tiana forced a smile.

"I would like that," she said. "But we will have to fetch Rocky and Jose first."

"I am so sorry I dragged Jose into all this." Aveline sighed, eyes on the two skinwalkers deep in discussion. "I don't like the way she looks at you," Aveline said.

Tiana glanced at her friend's long lost mother. The female skin-walker was gazing at Tiana with the intensity Black Wolf had when they first met, as if she were mentally peeling off her skin.

"This isn't how I thought she would be," Aveline said, a note of sorrow in her voice. "I think we should leave."

"Without them?"

"Now." Aveline took her arm and started towards the door. "I'm going to get some real clothes," she called to the others. "If we stay, she'll try to kill you. Let's get you somewhere safe, and then I'll talk to her alone about helping us."

They walked outside. Aveline went to the first horse and raided the saddlebags, tossing her cloak to change quickly.

"Mount up," she told Tiana. "I need to tell you something about your brother."

Tiana untied both the mules from the post and mounted hers. "What about him? Is he safe?"

"Not even close." Aveline finished dressing and hauled herself on top of the mule with a frown. "What is that?"

Tiana saw her reach for the basket tied to Black Wolf's horse and smiled. "You have a spirit wolf. Do you hear it?"

"I do." Aveline lifted the remaining black pup and peered at it. It squeaked and squirmed in her hand. "Can it say anything other than my name?"

"I don't think so. Maybe when they're older," Tiana replied. "But they can teleport."

"You're better at this magic stuff." Aveline hesitated then handed her pup to Tiana. "I'll tell you what your brother got himself into on the way."

Tiana tucked Aveline's pup into the satchel with her own and followed her, concerned.

TWENTY

LATER, when they were safe and hiding, Aveline told her everything.

Tiana thought long and hard about the news about Arthur that Aveline shared with her. The uncle she did not know existed, her father's assassination attempt imprisonment of Arthur, the skinwalker enslaved in the attic ...

How long she sat, she did not know. The day grew on while she battled herself silently. She understood the problem, and she understood the solution. But executing it? Diving Eagle had no problem amassing the courage he needed to perform his duties, but she did.

Aveline was quiet as well, playing with the pups on the floor of the tiny shed where they hid from the world. At long last, Tiana blinked out of her thoughts and shifted to the floor.

"I have to surrender," she voiced.

Aveline froze and looked up. "To your father?"

Tiana nodded.

"I'll go with you."

"Aveline –"

"Either we're in this together, or you aren't going."

Tiana hesitated. She was not surprised by Aveline's insistence.

She had a backup plan. "Then I think we should find my brother before we go," she said.

"Easy. He's in prison."

"No, he is not. I sense him in the inner city. Is it possible my father moved him?"

Aveline shook her head. "He might have escaped somehow, maybe with the help of your uncle, assuming he's on Arthur's side."

"Do you think it wise for us to find Arthur first?" Tiana asked. It was hard to manipulate someone, harder still to do it to Aveline. "I need him to know Diving Eagle's plans. If my uncle has a small army willing to fight for home, maybe he and Diving Eagle can work together."

"They can't take on your father."

"With me and the skinwalkers they can," Tiana pointed out. She dared not reveal her real plan to Aveline. "If all of us are together in the same place and time, we can face my father."

Aveline was watching her. "I don't know what happened to you, but you've changed since we met," she said slowly. "Why didn't you accept Diving Eagle's offer to go to the Freelands and escape all of this?"

"I could not leave knowing you and my brother are in danger. It would not be right. I would spend my life thinking about how I should have been brave, like you, and done the right thing," Tiana answered honestly. "If I escape, you all must be safe, too."

"All or nothing."

Tiana nodded. She played with her pup, hoping her friend did not notice she was holding her breath and nervous. Aveline appeared thoughtful before she finally spoke again.

"Why don't I go get your brother and bring him here? If your uncle set him up, he might be waiting for you to rescue him."

"If you think it is best," Tiana replied. "But I will be there when everyone faces my father."

"I think you will have to be," Aveline agreed. She picked up her pup. "Where is your brother?"

Tiana focused hard on the mental image of his presence. Aveline tilted her head and closed her eyes. She smiled.

"Got it. Kind of a useful ability, isn't it?"

Tiana nodded. "Be careful."

Aveline tucked her spirit pup in her pocket and left, closing the door securely behind her. Tiana waited a full five minutes, feeding her wolf again, before she tucked it away in her satchel. She stood and slipped out of the shed silently. She did not have to check her mind to know in which direction her father was; he was like a bur in her skull. His presence, and overwhelming energy, were unmistakable.

Tiana mounted her mule and walked silently into the foggy street. It was afternoon, and the sun appeared as a glowing disk in the sky. No one was out as she walked the streets of the inner city. Her journey took two hours through unfamiliar wards and roads. Her nerves began to fray when the pyramid came into sight ahead of her, its ominous shape piercing the fog. She crossed a bridge and passed a market and continued onward. Each step she took closer to her destiny left her a little less optimistic she would ever leave.

She hid the mule near the pyramid, in case she had a chance to escape.

Five minutes later, she stood at the base of the pyramid. Tiana took a deep breath and lowered the hood of her cloak. She had no way of knowing how she would be received by anyone.

I am here. She sent the message towards her former home without knowing if her father could or would receive it. Tiana waited a moment and then walked into the pyramid.

If anything, her appearance did not cause the raucous she expected but quite the opposite. The wealthy members of the outer city stopped in place to stare at her. She no longer cared if they saw her deformed eyes. She was there to save them all from the man in the uppermost reaches of the pyramid. What they thought of her did not concern her.

The Shield did not rush her. If anything, several of them fell into step behind her in what she recognized as a protective layer, the way they used to loosely surround Arthur.

Come home. The quiet command in her head was unmistakably her father's.

Tiana missed a step and caught herself quickly. Over and over, she heard Black Wolf's claim about her power knowing no limits, and Diving Eagle's challenge not to be a coward. By the time she entered the elevator reserved for Hanover's only, she trembled beneath the cloak. But she continued on, aware the lives of her friends were in her hands.

Tiana left the elevator and entered the apartment alone. Her guards remained outside the apartment door. She had never walked down this hallway alone except for the time she escaped. She took in the paintings lining the corridor of her predecessors, the Hanover men who had ruled Lost Vegas for four hundred and fifty years. At the end of the hall was her father's portrait and beside it, room for one more.

Tiana's eyes lingered on the empty space and she stopped.

It was right that no picture hung here. In fact, if she were as strong as every man who preceded her, no picture ever would, for the Hanover tyranny ended with her. She drew a deep breath and continued through the apartments. The opulence of the next rooms was lost on her; she could think only of confronting her father for the first time in her life.

Tiana reached the door to his private quarters and paused. It was cracked open. She pushed it the rest of the way open to reveal her father seated across the room from her, at a small table with two chairs. He sipped amber liquid from a rare glass tumbler.

Swallowing hard, Tiana closed the door and went to the table. She assumed her seat and clenched her hands in her lap, her heart hammering hard and fast.

Edwin Hanover lowered his tumbler and gazed at her. He appeared pleased, which unsettled her more.

"I came home," she said quietly.

"You want to negotiate."

It should not have surprised her that he already knew part of what was in her mind. Tiana nodded.

"Arthur, Aveline, the skinwalkers, the Diné. I want them all to be left alone and free to leave the city," she said in a voice that quivered. "I will stay as your heir."

Her father poured himself another drink. "This is not entirely about what I alone would do to them."

"I ... know my mind will be consumed by the same madness that consumes the minds of every Hanover leader. If they are outside the city, they will be safe from you and me."

"If your brother had not freed the skinwalker, I would not be concerned about letting then all go," her father said. "But he has, which threatens my grip on the city. I will agree to your terms, if you turn over one of the skinwalkers. I do not care which one."

Tiana started to object. Her father stood.

"One skinwalker for the lives of everyone you care about," he said. "Think about it."

He walked out of his quarters.

Tiana watched him, feeling helpless to stop him or make him understand she had no intention of turning over anyone to him, even Black Wolf, who would probably be thrilled by the challenge.

When the door closed, Tiana sagged. Her insides were in knots, her mind racing and heart pounding hard enough it felt as if it might explode through her chest. Aveline, Arthur, the skin-walkers and Diving Eagle were outside of her father's influence – for now. She had to keep his attention focused on her and away from them.

But how did she do that? She wracked her mind and went to the door, intent on distracting him, no matter what it took. Wrenching the door open, she said the only thing she could think of.

"Why did you spare me?"

He stopped. Without turning, he answered. "Which time?"

"The first, when I was a child. You burned someone else's body in my place. I would not have survived if not for Arthur. If you meant to imprison and forget me, why spare me?"

For a moment, she did not think he would respond. "Someone convinced me it was better to have two potential heirs than one."

"Is the family legacy the only reason?"

"Legacy. Power. What else is there?" He faced her.

She felt the urge to wilt but did not, instead taking a moment to collect herself before she spoke again. "I guess I want to know ... were you ever like Arthur and me? Did you ever love anyone?"

He raised an eyebrow. "Love. It is a weakness, one you cannot afford if you are to lead the city."

"But you had to have cared for someone at some point. Your parents, your wives, us."

"If I did, I cannot remember it."

Speechless, Tiana watched him walk away. This time, she did not try to stop him. If Marshall Cruise were right, and her father was once normal and capable of caring for another, then that part of him had been swallowed his madness.

A small piece of hope within her felt as if it shriveled and died. She had fantasized many possible scenarios of the fate she could not fully face. In one of these fantasies, she had seen herself successfully appealing to the side of her father that loved his children or at the very least, had at one point been capable of caring for someone else and convincing him to go with her to the Freelands.

If he cared for no one, he was no more human than the skin-walker. Of all the things she was capable of, turning her father into a caring human was not among them.

Was she destined to become like him? How long had it taken for him to lose himself? How much magic had he used? Did he know it was happening? Did he care? Would she be aware when she crossed the threshold to become the threat the others believed she could be?

Amid the questions she could never answer, and the confusion crippling her, was one fact she would never doubt. She had one chance to end this, before she became like her father.

Tiana went to the door leading to the tiny, wooden room where she had spent her life. She lifted a hand and removed the door through telekinesis then stepped into it. With the same small effort, she yanked the boards from the window and stood before it, gazing out into the early evening. At one point, several weeks ago, she had been able to glimpse the distant forest from her window.

But now, her visibility stretched to the nearest street and no further. Smoke and ash obscured everything. She closed her eyes to locate her friends and Arthur. Aveline was hidden, and she believed her friend had been earnest in her attempt to find Arthur, who was in the inner city. Black Wolf was not hiding from her this time, and she was not surprised to feel him near the pyramid. She marked his location mentally and checked in on Diving Eagle, who remained outside Lost Vegas. Her father was present in the pyramid, for now.

I intend to keep it that way, she thought.

Tiana opened her eyes. She had entered Lost Vegas suspecting she would never leave again and mourned the loss of the forest, grasslands, and open skies already. It was only fitting she ended up where it all began, in the tiny room her father had put her in and hoped to forget her.

Without knowing for certain if her plan would work, she visualized a shield over the pyramid and encapsulating the location of Black Wolf, who she was also determined would not leave the city again after all the lives he had taken. She used the same method to contain Black Wolf.

A burst of energy left her, and she sagged, drained. It felt as if she had stayed up most the night and rose early, before she was ready, for several days in a row. Drained and fatigued, she leaned against the window, yearning already to return to the peaceful forest.

Her pup squeaked from within the pouch. Tiana smiled and sank down beneath the window, back against the wall. She withdrew the pup and one of the bottles it had thought to bring with it. The tiny creature lifted its wobbly head to gaze at her.

"I hope we both survive this, but if I do not, you will have to choose another person to guide," she whispered. "Or maybe go with Aveline."

Aveline. The tiny voice in her mind repeated.

Tiana laughed and rested her head against the wall. "Yes, Aveline. She will protect you until you are big enough to protect her."

The pup returned to repeating Tiana's name over and over tele-pathically. Tiana smiled. The voice in her head did not quiet again until the wolf subsided into sleep once more.

"Now we wait," Tiana said and glanced towards the gray fog visible through the window above her. With her father trapped in her bubble, she hoped to give her brother time to escape the city. In the meantime, she needed rest to prepare for the confrontation with her father.

Quick footsteps echoed down the hall. Tiana placed the pup carefully in her satchel and prepared to face her father's anger. With her energy gone, she could only hope he was not too angry and that she possessed the strength to contain him, and not to die, before she was recovered enough to kill him.

It was a terrible plan, but it was all she could think of to do.

TWENTY-ONE

ARTHUR FELT the shift in the world around him without understanding what it was. The energy coursing through him, a low, constant hum, ceased suddenly. He sat up, alarmed by the strange silence replacing it.

His uncle, wearing his own face, straightened from his position bent over a table, conspiring with other members of his inner circle.

As if the city itself experienced the sudden release of magic, the smoke and ash choking the streets floated upward, towards the sky. Within minutes, the streets were clear again.

Arthur watched the transformation from the window of the building in which his uncle had taken him. Only one person could alter the energy his father had thrown upon the city.

"Tiana," he whispered.

Where in the city was she? Was she safe?

"Look." His uncle joined him and pointed.

The fog had lifted from each direction but one. In the center of a dome, the pyramid rose ominously, surrounded by white clouds and gray ash.

A figure crossed the window. Arthur looked once and then back.

Aveline. Her stride was sure while her gaze was on the pyramid. She appeared grim, if not angry.

Arthur rushed to the door it. He waved his uncle's guards off and opened it.

"What are you doing here?" he demanded.

Aveline faced him. "Looking for you."

"Tiana?"

Aveline shook her head. "I want to say safe, but I'm pretty sure she sent me here so she could distract me." She entered, gazing warily at the men working with Arthur's uncle. "Are you a prisoner?" The question was accompanied by the expansion of her bear claw into a bear arm.

"No. He broke me out of prison. I am somewhat satisfied with his explanation for abandoning me to my father's men," Arthur replied ruefully. "I will explain, but first, are you well?"

Aveline gazed at him quizzically, as if no one had asked her this question before. "Don't I look well?" she retorted.

Arthur suppressed a smile. "You do. Where is Tiana?"

"If I had to guess, with your father," Aveline said. "She gave me a message and sent me to find you."

Arthur frowned.

"She said the Diné are planning to attack the city tomorrow morning at dawn. She thinks you and your uncle, assuming he's not a traitor, might benefit from working with the Diné to counter your father."

"Hmm. It is not out of the question," Arthur said with a glance over his shoulder at his uncle, who was listening closely. "But what is Tiana's plan?"

"I am certain she just challenged your father," his uncle replied. "The Diné were the only allies I could not sway to my cause. If this is true, then we need to find them before they attack. I've waited too long to have my plan foiled by that particular tribe of Natives."

"Diving Eagle?" Arthur asked Aveline.

She nodded.

"They will not wait, uncle. They will attack as planned. If you wish to join them, they will probably not object, but do not expect them to listen to reason," Arthur advised.

"Are you volunteering to take me to them?" his uncle asked, gaze sharp.

"Diving Eagle and I know each other well enough he may listen before caging me," Arthur replied, amused. He returned his focus to Aveline. "What of the skinwalkers?"

"They're set on vengeance."

"Find Tiana. Stay with her."

Aveline nodded. "That was my plan after delivering the message. I don't think the skinwalkers have any intention of letting a single Hanover survive. You're forewarned." She glanced past him to settle a glare on his uncle. She turned to leave.

"Aveline," Arthur called. His failure as a brother to the half-sister he had never known left him wishing he could do or say something more. As much as he did not want to send Aveline into danger, he also believed Tiana and Aveline had a better chance of surviving if they were together. "Be careful."

She nodded and trotted off towards the fog-filled dome over the pyramid.

Arthur turned to his uncle. "We need to leave now, if you are serious about intercepting Diving Eagle."

His uncle was quiet, considering, before he nodded. He glanced towards one of the men awaiting his command, who dashed off, out of the building.

Five minutes later, Simon and Arthur, flanked by a guard of four, were on horseback and headed towards the north side of the city. Unable to guess what Tiana was planning, and hoping Aveline's street sense prevailed, Arthur could not take his eyes off the dome until they turned their backs to it. Doom was heavy in his stomach, along with the uncertainty of how Diving Eagle was going to react to any mention of postponing his plans.

SEVERAL HOURS LATER, he had confirmation his instinct had been correct.

The size of Diving Eagle's army was impossible to gauge. His men, and those of his allies, hid in the grasses around the city. Only one fire was created, and Arthur stood in front of it, listening to his uncle's useless attempts to convince Diving Eagle not to attack at dawn.

Exasperated, his uncle threw his hands up and walked away. Arthur hid a smile. He was not the first man to try to sway the obstinate Diné warrior off his position. The young chief stood with two warriors behind him and Marshall, whose presence reminded Arthur of every wrong his family had committed.

"I was sorry to hear of your father's passing," Arthur said, replacing his uncle in front of the agitated Diné chief. "He was good to my sister, for which I am grateful."

Diving Eagle's gaze shifted from Simon to Arthur.

"I am certain your council did not hesitate to choose you as his successor."

Diving Eagle studied him before replying. "I come from a long line of Diné chiefs. My family has the support of our people."

"I imagine that could change if you do not succeed," Arthur pointed out gently, not wanting to add fuel to the Native's resistance. "Believe me when I say, none of us can afford to fail in removing my father from power. We are in this together."

Diving Eagle drew a deep breath. "What do you want of me, Hanover?"

"Tiana is operating independently of us all. I have a feeling we are her backup plan, if she fails to stop my father," Arthur continued with a glance towards the city.

All smoke and ash had cleared, leaving the city exposed, vulnerable. The exception: a hazy cloud encased in the dome around the pyramid.

"Is she alive?" Diving Eagles tone was quieter, and far less harsh, than it had been discussing their next moves with Arthur's uncle.

"She is," Arthur confirmed. He gazed at Diving Eagle, whose focus had shifted towards the dome as well. The new tension visible in the young chief was of a different kind. He showed signs of impatience with Arthur's uncle, but his irritation became more apparent. He paced now, a caged animal waiting to be unleashed against his greatest enemy.

For a long moment, Arthur studied the Native, assessing the instincts whispering there was more to this war for Diving Eagle than long-awaited vengeance.

"You knew her plan, did you not?" Arthur asked softly.

"I suspected."

"And you let her go anyway?"

Diving Eagle's pacing stopped, and he pinned Arthur with a glare.

Arthur's uncle turned to listen, hands on hips.

"Duty first. I understand," Arthur continued. "It is what I told myself every time I saw the new scars on her body and overheard my father discussing his desire to burn her. I assumed, when I had the power, I would save her."

"She does not need saving," Diving Eagle replied.

"No, she does not. Not now anyway. But she will need help. If I have one regret, it is not understanding how much power I had to help her when I chose to look away instead."

"I will not delay my attack tomorrow."

"I am not asking you to. I am asking you to compromise with my uncle. Tiana is giving us a window, at the cost of her own safety and possibly, life. We ought to use it. Work with a Hanover. It is all I am asking. If you will not bend on your schedule, then bend on your allies and the tactics of your plan. Accept my uncle's assistance. He knows every hiding place, every way to move stealthily, and every inch of the city. What better to surprise my father and his Shield than with an insurgency?"

Diving Eagle did not flatly refuse, as he had with Arthur's uncle.

Arthur shifted to the side and motioned his uncle forward.

"The attack will occur at dawn," he said firmly to his uncle. "But how it is carried out must incorporate both plans." This was directed to Diving Eagle. "Failure to agree on this puts all our efforts, and the lives of everyone in the city, at risk."

Diving Eagle and his uncle stared long and hard at one another.

"I will agree to the timing," his uncle stated.

"Very well," Diving Eagle replied.

Arthur released the breath he was holding. "Good. Now, you two talk." He stepped out of the ring of light and warmth and approached Marshall. "May I have a moment of your time?"

Marshall nodded and led him away.

When they were far enough away from the fire not to disturb the two untrusting allies, Marshall faced him.

Arthur studied him briefly. "By now you must know about your family."

"I do," was the cold response. "Did you know when we were traveling with the skinwalker?"

"Yes."

Marshall hissed a curse and strode a few feet away, back to Arthur, and rested his interlaced hands on his head.

"My family is the source of much pain in this world." Arthur trailed him. "Apologizing will not make a difference to you, I fear, and neither will the favor I must ask you."

"Favor?" Marshall demanded, whirling. "You dare ask me to do anything for you after everything we have been through?"

Arthur listened to the angry outburst with patience born from understanding. "I have determined, and my uncle agrees, that no Hanover should remain in the city after we have freed it from my father. Assuming any of us survive, we will embrace exile with open arms."

Marshall appeared ready to speak then stopped himself and crossed his arms.

"The favor I wish to ask of you is that you take my place," Arthur said.

"What are you talking about?"

"The city was founded by Cruises and stolen by my ancestors. It is time we make this right," Arthur continued. "Reclaim your place, your family's legacy."

Marshall faced him once more. Surprise crossed his features. "You would do that? Walk away?"

"For the sake of everyone my family has hurt? Yes. You may hate me, but I count you among the very few genuine friends I have," Arthur said, throat tight. "I could never right the wrongs of my ancestors, but I can ensure no Hanover interferes with Lost Vegas, or anyone else, ever again. I believe there will never be peace with the Natives or anyone else, if a Hanover remains in charge of the city."

Marshall did not respond. Anger burned in his eyes.

Arthur took a step back. He had hoped ... what he had hoped was foolish, given his own wrongs against the Cruise heir. He turned away, wishing Marshall would say something.

When the Cruise heir did not, Arthur returned to the bonfire. To his satisfaction, Diving Eagle and his uncle were deep in discussion, while their lieutenants listened closely.

A smile touched his lips. Arthur glanced towards the city once more. The dread hovering around him warned him it was not likely for any Hanover to leave the city alive. Perhaps this was how he was meant to save the city. Not to rule as a better Hanover, but to ensure no Hanover ever ruled again.

"Lost Vegas is your home. I would not throw you out," Marshall said from behind him.

"No Hanover will remain in the city," Arthur said firmly.

Marshall drew abreast of him. "If so, this is your choice, not mine."

Arthur glanced at him, not expecting the graciousness from a man who owed him nothing.

"I know you are not your father, and neither is your sister. I know your father is the one who massacred my family, and I suspect part of the reason is that he knew my father had sided with your uncle against him," Marshall said. "All that aside ... why did you not tell me the truth?"

"Because I thought you would abandon me when I needed your help," Arthur responded.

"I could have abandoned you at any point the past few weeks. I chose to stay, in spite of everything."

Arthur glanced at him. "I know. It was wrong of me to hide the truth."

"It was wrong of you to believe my friendship so shallow."

"I learned not to trust anyone at a young age. It is not an excuse, but I do not think I know how to trust someone. Not my sister. Not Warner. Not you." Arthur shook his head.

"Where will you go?"

"The Freelands, with Tiana."

"And if she is mad?"

Arthur had been dwelling on this same dilemma. His father was beyond saving. "I have to believe she is different for a reason. She will not become like our father and his fathers. She is stronger."

"For all our sakes, I hope you are right," Marshall said.

At the dark note in his voice, Arthur looked at his friend. "We both know a Hanover is never wrong," he teased.

Marshall snorted.

"Will you ensure Warner makes it home, if I do not survive?" Arthur's voice was hushed. "He is being cared for now by Chases Deer's people. But he deserves to return home."

"I will see to it," Marshall promised.

A wave of energy rolled outward from the city, and the ground beneath them rumbled in response.

Arthur's breath caught in his throat. The eyes of those near the fire went to the dome.

Arthur started towards his horse. The energy wave ignited his worry once more, and he was no longer satisfied waiting until dawn to help his sisters. His place was with them.

"Arthur!" Simone called after him.

Arthur ignored him. He had spent his entire life waiting – and he was done. It was the eve of his father's downfall and possibly, the last night of his own life. With the various visions of grim futures replaying in his head, Arthur had the sudden urge to be in the city once more. He would not spend this night, like so many others, wishing he had done more for his sisters. They would do this together. All of them.

Someone caught his arm, and Arthur whirled, yanking away.

Diving Eagle lifted his hands to show he was not there to attack.

"Plan your war," Arthur said. "I am going after my sisters."

"Do not go alone," Diving Eagle said.

"Your place is here. Mine is there," Arthur said. "If Tiana fails to defeat my father, I might be able to distract him long enough for you to act. My uncle has a plan of how to steal my father's power."

There was a pause, and he could almost see Diving Eagle's mind working. The strange sense there was more to this than revenge returned. Arthur was not about to remain long enough to ask why mentioning Tiana's name altered Diving Eagle's expression.

Before Arthur could mount, and Diving Eagle could speak, a loud curse sounded from behind them. They both turned to see Chases Deer standing where no one had been seconds before. She looked around wildly before whirling to face him.

Diving Eagle muttered words in his tongue Arthur guessed were curses.

"What have you done?" Chases Deer demanded, marching towards him. "How did you bring me here?"

"I did not," Diving Eagle snapped.

"It was sorcery, and your kind are known to hold such magic!"

"It was not him," Marshall said, joining them. He pointed to the place where she had been standing. "Your guide brought you."

"My ... guide." Chases Deer returned to the spot and knelt. When she rose, she held a wolf pup in her hands.

Arthur smiled. "Did you think it was a normal wolf?"

She shot him a dirty look.

"Your family carries some level of sorcery as well," Diving Eagle snapped. "I always knew your speed to be unnatural."

For once, the warrior woman did not respond.

Diving Eagle shook his head and faced Arthur. "I believe she is meant to accompany you, for she has no use to me."

"No use?" Chases Deer retorted. "I am worth five of your warriors!"

"I do not think I need a companion," Arthur replied, uncertain he could manage anyone as stubborn as Chases Eagle.

"She goes with you, or you do not go," Diving Eagle told him in a growl before facing Chases Eagle. "And you, if you wish me to marry you as your father intends, then stay here. We can have the ceremony tonight."

At her offended look, Arthur covered his surprised laugh with a cough. The Diné chief could be brutal in word and deed, but he showed the signs of being an effective leader.

Chases Deer strode towards the horse waiting beside Arthur's. "I would never disrespect my own people by mixing our blood with that of you barbarians," she said to the Diné chief.

Diving Eagle ignored her with effort great enough to amuse Arthur, despite his circumstances.

"You," Diving Eagle pointed at Marshall. "I am finished with men from the city disrupting my plans. The city or the cage. Your choice."

Even Marshall knew better than to challenge the dangerous note in the Native's voice. Arthur sensed Diving Eagle was at his end with the more diplomatic approach required of a chief and close to resorting to his former methods of ensuring compliance.

As if suspecting the same, Marshall moved faster than Arthur had ever seen a Cruise move and mounted a third horse brought to them by one of Diving Eagle's warriors.

"As I ordered. You will not go alone," Diving Eagle said to Arthur.

Arthur mounted. Another wave of energy pierced him, and he shuddered.

"You may want to move your plans up," he advised Diving Eagle. "If anything happens to Tiana, I do not know that you will have a chance to act at all."

The eyes of the Native and Simon were on the city.

Arthur wheeled his horse and urged it onward. The stallion bolted, carrying him towards his destiny.

TWENTY-TWO

BLACK WOLF HAD NEVER MET someone more driven to violence than he was. Walks With A Limp was not just violent, she was twice his age. Her energy was agitated, unstable. He had never met another skinwalker, aside from the mother he barely remembered, and an ancient man on his deathbed, but he began to think there was more wrong with Walks With A Limp than he would ever know.

"The little bitch has trapped us here," the female skinwalker said. She threw herself against the invisible shield that kept them – and the Hanover leader – close to the pyramid. The world outside the dome was clear, quiet, while smoke swirled angrily inside.

"She needs our help," he replied.

"She wants to murder us."

Black Wolf shook his head. If he had not experienced Tiana's vision with her, he would not understand her plan. She would challenge the Hanover chief and toss him into the spirit realm, before the city and its surroundings were sucked into the abyss.

But to do that, she would need a skinwalker with one foot on the other side in order to keep that doorway open. Black Wolf was thrilled by the chance to not only face the Hanover chief, but to drag both Hanover's to their deaths in the next world. That his long journey would come to such a noble end was fitting for a man unlike any other.

Assuming the scared little Hanover girl could follow through with it.

His eyes went to the pyramid. He did not hide his presence from her, which was how she had created the barrier right beside him, with him trapped inside with her. Some part of her understood she needed the help of her enemy.

"Do what you wish. I am going to find her," he said and strode away from the other skinwalker.

"We are stronger together."

"I do not intend to leave. If you value your life, do not follow me." Black Wolf replied.

Walks With A Limp ceased her nervous movement.

His choice made, Black Wolf did not pay attention to her and strode down the street towards the pyramid. As if a dam had broken, a flood of people soon swarmed him, wealthy members of the outer city fleeing the pyramid.

The sudden onslaught of hundreds of heartbeats against his brain drove him to his knees. He staggered and dropped, unable to stop the ripple of transformation that went through him.

Not yet. With great effort, Black Wolf stopped the change from consuming him. He needed to conserve his energy for the coming battle. He hunkered down beside a building, waiting for the mad rush to stop. From the corner of his eye, he saw the people flee out of the dome. The Hanover was freeing them while keeping him contained.

When the people were gone, he relaxed, head in his hands. His mind righted itself.

"How have you never learned to control it?" Walks With A Limp asked, standing over him. "Did your mother not show you?"

"She died before I transformed." Black Wolf stood.

"If you are going to collapse into a weak ball whenever we cross a human, you will need my help." Walks With A Limp began walking towards the pyramid. "We will reach the Hanover bitch together. My gut tells me my daughter is already there."

Black Wolf trailed her. He found himself looking around for his spirit wolf. Not finding her, sorrow slid through him. It was not the first time he had sought her out only to recall she would never advise or help him again.

"Did you have a guide?" he asked the frail but determined skin-walker ahead of him.

"I did. We were separated not long before I came to this godfor-saken city. I feel ... I know he has died since then. I should have, too, but the Hanover chief kept me alive."

They reached the base of the pyramid and stopped to look up. In all his travels, Black Wolf had never seen a place like this one. Several guards surrounded the sacred place belonging to the wealthy, but they appeared to be busy with the remaining city dwellers. Several more people trickled out of the great building and ran past them, towards the dome's barrier.

He strode forward and into the building, stopping once more when he witnessed the mini-village at the center of the pyramid whose walls were lined with rooms and doors. The interior was ablaze with light from electricity, and the scent of kitchen fare wafted towards him from the direction of a stairwell nearby. He took in the abandoned lower floors in a cross between amazement and amusement.

"This way." Walks With A Limp was already twenty feet ahead of him.

Black Wolf followed her towards an elevator.

The quick ascent to the top of the pyramid turned his stomach. He could not help wishing his spirit guide were there to experience the elevator. When the door opened, they were greeted by two dead guards who had been struck down at their stations before either could challenge the intruder.

He did not need to look twice to recognize the gashes on the men that could only have been caused by a bear claw.

"Aveline is here." Walks With A Limp paused in front of the door in front of them. "I had hoped she would have stayed away."

"She and the Hanover are bonded. Neither would leave the other." Black Wolf pushed past her and opened the door.

"That's what I'm afraid of."

The world beyond the door was more wondrous than what he had already seen of the pyramid. After a hundred years, he knew wealth and quality when he saw it, and the Hanover's personal residence was by far, the wealthiest he had ever seen. Black Wolf walked through the apartments, appraising all he saw with the expert eye of a man who had hocked and traded his entire life. He did not plan on surviving, but if by some chance he did, he would take everything he could carry from the Hanover's before leaving the pyramid.

Walks With A Limp's eyes, however, remained fixed on their destination. She walked as if in a trance, her line of movement straight whereas his wandered all over the apartment to assess the wealth he found. When it was clear she would not wait for him, Black Wolf trotted away from a china cabinet filled with delicate dishware from the Old World and down a hall.

He sensed Tiana – but not her father. In fact, he was unable to locate the Hanover chief at all inside the pyramid or bubble the girl had created over part of the city.

Walks With A Limp strode to the very end of the apartment and into a tiny room. Black Wolf trailed.

"You should not be here, Aveline," Walks With A Limp said to her daughter, who knelt beside the still form of the Hanover girl.

Black Wolf went to the pair and knelt, assessing the Hanover girl's condition. He did not doubt she was alive. If she were not, the dome would not remain in place. She was bloodied and unconscious. The scars he had noted across her body had all opened – an indication of a magic attack rather than purely physical one. The pool of blood beneath her was spreading fast.

"I don't know what to do," Aveline voiced with a wary glance at him. "I tried to bind a wound, but it popped open again."

"Leave her. If the Hanover chief has finished her off, then let us leave while we can," Walks With A Limp said, unconcerned.

Black Wolf gave a mirthless half smile at Aveline's exasperated expression. When it became clear the female skinwalker was not about to help her daughter, he spoke.

"This cannot be fixed by human means," he explained. Black Wolf took Aveline's paw and hand and placed them on the Hanover girl's bloody body.

"Why are you helping her? Isn't it better to have one Hanover dead instead of two alive to murder us?" Walks With A Limp demanded. She began to pace again, her unstable energy brushing over both of them. "We can still leave the city, Aveline. We can find Karl before we go and exact your revenge."

Aveline shifted away from Tiana, eyes on her mother. "Karl."

"The man who killed your father, my love. He is in the city somewhere."

Aveline hesitated. Her eyes drifted towards Tiana, and she shook her head.

Walks With A Limp frowned.

Black Wolf did not know if her distress stemmed from years of mistreatment at the hands of the Hanover chief, or if she were born unstable. In truth, he did not care, as long as she did not interfere in his plans.

"This may be your only chance for revenge," Walks With A Limp said.

"I'm not leaving her," Aveline said quietly and then met Black Wolf's gaze. "What do I do?"

Black Wolf leaned over Tiana's body, seeking the tiny presence he sensed. Tiana's spirit wolf was tucked safely away in a satchel in a dark corner. He retrieved it and opened it, pulling the pup out.

"Little guide. You are young, but you must do your duty," he whispered to the pup. The tiny creature lifted its head to gaze in his direction.

Tiana, it said.

Black Wolf set it on the Hanover girl's chest. "She is too small to heal the way she will when she is grown. You must help her. Focus your thoughts and energy on the Hanover girl, and let her guide send the energy where it needs to go."

Aveline's look softened when she took in the pup. She drew a deep breath and closed her eyes.

While a half-skinwalker did not retain the power of a full breed, Black Wolf understood the bond between the two girls to be unique, and suspected the reason was not what either of them thought.

"This is a mistake," Walks With A Limp said.

"Then leave!" Aveline snapped.

"You would send your mother away?"

Aveline sighed.

Black Wolf waited, unable to gauge what had passed between mother and daughter. As he watched, the gaping wounds across the Hanover girl's body began to heal. At first, it was slow, as if the pup had not yet figured out what to do. When it did, the wounds closed quickly.

Within minutes, Tiana was healed. Black Wolf picked up the pup and held it, aware it would be drained from the effort.

Aveline opened her eyes and leaned back. She wiped her bloodied hands on her pants before pushing hair out of Tiana's face to see her features clearly.

The Hanover girl's eyes fluttered open. She stared at the ceiling for a long moment before turning her head towards them.

"I am so sorry about lying to you, Aveline," she said, distraught.

"Don't worry about that now. You're safe," Aveline told her.

"None of us are safe," Tiana replied. She pushed herself up into a seated position. Her features were drawn, and dark circles lined the undersides of her eyes. Her voice trembled, and tears filled her eyes.

"You won't face him alone again," Aveline vowed. "I don't know what these two are doing," she waved her hands in the direction of Black Wolf and her mother, "but I'm here with you until this is over."

The Hanover girl smiled and took her friend's hand, squeezing it. "I am always happy to see you, Aveline."

"Where is your father?" Black Wolf asked. "I cannot sense him."

The Hanover girl frowned. "I cannot either."

"Then we know where," Walks With A Limp said. She looked upward. "That place has hidden skinwalkers for four centuries."

Tiana stood, with Aveline's assistance.

"He's hurt," she said. "But nothing compared to what he did to me."

"Is Tiana stronger than him?" Aveline asked, eyes on her mother. "Is this a matter of putting them in a room for a confrontation, with us to prevent him from hurting her?"

"In theory, the heir should be stronger. Every heir kills his predecessor and takes his place when he is ready," Walks With A Limp replied.

"When he is ready," Black Wolf echoed the words. "This girl may never be ready." He motioned to the slender, Ghoul-eyed waif.

"I am ready," Tiana insisted softly.

"Can you control your power?" Walks With a Limp snapped. "Can you block his?"

The Hanover girl did not respond.

"You are black powder without a spark," the female skinwalker continued. "You are a child trying to fight an adult's war."

"She can do it," Aveline said firmly. "She's stronger than she looks and smarter than any of us!"

"He cannot pass my shield," Tiana added.

"We both know what must happen," Black Wolf said. "One of the reasons you did not allow me to leave either."

The Hanover girl nodded.

"What?" Aveline asked.

"We have to widen the barrier between this world and the next, or open one, if it has closed," was the quiet response.

"Absolutely not!" Walks With A Limp exclaimed. "To do so is pure madness."

"We shared a vision," Black Wolf said. "It must be done."

"All we must do is kill him. We do not need to place all of this world in danger to rid it of one man."

"He is not a man. Not anymore," Tiana responded. "No one here can kill him, including me. Even combined, I do not think we can. He held you captive for fifteen years, did he not? If you could not escape him, how can you kill him?"

Walks With A Limp lowered her head. It was impossible to miss the malice in her eyes as she gazed at the Hanover girl.

"She did escape him once. But your father threatened to kill me if she tried again," Aveline answered.

Black Wolf considered the full skinwalker closely, trying to determine what she hid. After a moment, he turned to Aveline.

"What did you feel when you found her?" he asked.

"Feel?" she shrugged. "An insane amount of energy."

"My father was not there when you found your mother, was he?" Tiana asked, puzzling over the skinwalker's silence as well.

Aveline shook her head. "I assumed it was her sending out all the energy. But I think it was the attic."

"I should have known." Black Wolf chuckled.

Tiana glanced at him. "You are thinking what I am," she stated.

"The place where you found her exists in the next world," he confirmed. His focus shifted to Aveline. "Your mother is a skinwalker, a creature not belonging fully to either world but existing in whichever world she is born, or placed. She can cross between them if need be."

"If my father can walk between them," the Hanover girl's eyes were on the ceiling. "So can I."

Walks With A Limp was gazing at her daughter, anger in her eyes, but also concern. After a hesitation, she spoke to the Hanover girl.

"Your father maintained the tear between this world and the

spirit world," she said. "It enhances your power. If you close it, yours will diminish."

The Hanover girl started to smile. "So will his."

"It has been open since the Old World ended. The Hanover's have been guardians who abused their positions," Walks With A Limp said.

"A breach of this nature cannot exist without an anchor," Black Wolf said. "It is not natural. Something must be keeping it open."

"Skinwalkers. With one of us stuck in the breach, it could not close."

"Then why is it open now?" Tiana asked.

"It is closing. Slowly. Your father may be trying to do exactly what you wish to – widen it," Walks With A Limp replied. "That is the danger, that he can throw you into the other side before you can do so to him. Or worse. One of you could destroy this world all together if it is sucked into the next."

Black Wolf left, tired of waiting. He strode into the hallway and paused briefly, until he was able to feel from which direction the energy of the breach came. The pulse of energy was stronger than he had felt from his spirit guide.

He followed his instincts and strode into an opulent bedroom. Ignoring the wealth around him this time, he stopped to feel for the direction again.

"This way." Aveline brushed by him and walked down the hallway, into a small room. A painting covering the hidden entrance had been removed from the wall and propped up next to the door. "There's a passageway between the walls that leads to the attic."

Aveline stopped quickly.

"He is expecting us," Tiana said, her breath catching audibly.

Black Wolf pushed past them into the room and observed the gaping opening in the wall.

"We cannot walk in there without considering what might be on the other side," the Hanover girl said and rubbed the scars on her arms.

Black Wolf listened to them debate, his eyes on the corner of the hearth. Blood covered the corner and dripped onto the marble flooring beneath it. More blood smeared the flooring in front of the door.

He took some heart in knowing his enemy could bleed but was just as quickly perplexed as to how anyone knew a skinwalker could hold open the breach let alone identify a tear between worlds and know how to exploit it.

A human – a true human – could never know this. A skinwalker? His kind had the ability, though no skinwalker in their millennia of history had tried, likely because they knew better.

It was not the first time Black Wolf's eyes fell to Tiana, and he wondered what kind of creature she was. He had believed her to be a spirit when they first met and told her once she was not of this world, half in jest, half to aggravate her. But the longer he stood in the room, the more he began to believe none of the Hanover's were originally from this world.

And what of the half-skinwalker capable of entering and leaving the next world? As a half-human, Aveline should never have been able to enter it at all. Which meant her father was not the human she thought he was.

Black Wolf glanced at Walks With A Limp, who watched the two girls interact with clear disapproval.

The two of them came to a decision and approached the wall, hand in hand.

Black Wolf watched, curious to see if his hunch was correct.

Aveline walked through, but Tiana bounced off an invisible barrier.

"He's blocked you," Aveline said with a frown. "This won't work if we can't all face him together."

They both looked to him.

Black Wolf approached, using his senses to assess what his eyes could not.

"He has not blocked it," he said slowly. "You cannot enter." This he addressed to Tiana.

"Why not?" she asked. "I am his heir."

"Your connection to this world is too strong," Black Wolf said. He did not have the time to tell her what he believed to be the truth.

Tiana's face fell.

"But I can cross." Aveline jumped from one side of the doorway to the other.

Black Wolf glanced towards Walks With A Limp, who turned away and strode out.

"Mother!" Aveline called. "You can't leave!"

Walks With A Limp did not respond.

"What she did not tell you is that your father was not a human," Black Wolf said. "You and the Hanover's are bound by more than duty."

Tiana's eyes were riveted to his, while Aveline stared after her mother, upset again.

"My twin," Tiana said.

"Different mothers, same father," Black Wolf confirmed.

Aveline looked from one to the other. "There's no chance in hell! My father was an assassin. My mother met him when she escaped from this place, and I was born ..."

"Sometime after," Black Wolf said, enjoying the confusion of the girls.

"She said ... Karl was there to spy. But what if ..." Aveline shook her head. "Why are we listening to you at all?"

"Because he knows things, whether or not he should." Unlike Aveline, Tiana started to smile. "You are a Hanover, Aveline."

"Absolutely not!"

"You are my sister."

Aveline's gaze shifted from Black Wolf to Tiana, who smiled.

"I always wanted a sister," Tiana said. "That must be why Arthur found you."

Aveline opened her mouth to speak, stopped, and then whirled.

"I'm going to kill him, if any of you wish to come!" She held out her arm to Tiana. "No offense, but I will never be a Hanover. Now, turn me into a panther."

Tiana still smiled, undeterred by Aveline's vehement refusal to admit their relationship. She touched Aveline, who morphed instantly into her animal form. The panther entered the wall.

Black Wolf waited, sensing the pacing skinwalker in the hall. Aveline's bond to Tiana kept her here when she would otherwise not stay. Walks With A Limp would feel the same.

Seconds later, a tigress the size of a bear padded into the room. She snapped her teeth at Tiana and went to the hole in the wall. She followed Aveline towards the breach to flush out the man they both hated.

Black Wolf trailed her in his human form. He had never been in the presence of three skinwalkers at once. Had anyone? Their tribe was one of loners, and he could not help being excited by the prospect of hunting with two others.

"Bring him here," Tiana said as he passed her. "We must do this together."

He waved her off and entered the darkness.

At last, he was about to meet the Hanover leader spoken about for thousands of miles outside of Lost Vegas.

TWENTY-THREE

ARTHUR BARRELED INTO THE CITY, accompanied by Marshall and Chases Deer. The streets were vacant, dark and clear, the sky above filled with stars. Urgency lit his blood on fire, along with the energy radiating off the dome at the far end of the city. Every hour it took to travel was one hour less he had to find his sisters and help them.

He reached the dome several hours after leaving Diving Eagle and slowed to a halt. Arthur looked up at the transparent barrier trapping his sister and father within it. Would it allow him to enter?

He dismounted.

"Arthur, wait!" Marshall called.

On slower steeds, he and Chases Deer lagged behind.

Arthur strode through the dome and stopped on the other side. Smoke obscured his vision, and he shuddered once more. The power within the dome was greater than any he had experienced. It crawled through his body and scraped against his skin.

He shook off the strange sensations, preferring to meet whatever threat awaited him without endangering the other two. Arthur ran towards the pyramid, the only structure in the city with electricity or light at all. It glowed eerily inside its globe.

His father's personal guard, a phalanx of soldiers four deep, came into view too late for him to avoid being spotted. They materialized out of the fog, protecting the entrances to the pyramid.

Arthur slid to a halt in the mud and debated what to do before drawing the only weapons – two knives – he had grabbed from his uncle. A light breeze brushed his neck, and suddenly, Chases Deer was beside him.

He jumped, surprised.

She glared at him, as if daring him to mention her inhuman speed.

"If at all possible, do not let Marshall get hurt," he said.

She gave a curt nod of her head and drew a pistol with one hand and a sword with another.

Before the soldiers could charge them, Arthur darted forward. Whether it was the poor visibility inside the dome, or the extra charge of energy in his blood, he cut down the first two Shield members with little effort. Chases Deer fired her weapon and slashed at those within reach. Arthur's instincts – always fast to warn him of danger – kept him one step ahead of every blow headed towards him.

They fought off half a dozen Shield soldiers before Arthur glanced towards the direction in which Marshall stood. The Cruise heir, more thoughtful and less athletic than Arthur, was grappling with one soldier and about to try to face off with a second.

Arthur finished fighting the soldier in front of him and slapped Chases Deer on the arm as he darted past her. He motioned to Marshall and dashed away from the soldiers closing in around the Native warrior.

Marshall was knocked to the ground within seconds of the second soldier joining the fight against him. Arthur launched himself forward and stabbed the first attacker through the neck before rolling to his feet and slicing the other's stomach open.

Marshall watched, surprised.

Arthur leaned down and dragged Marshall to his feet.

"Your father teach you to gut a man like an animal?" Marshall asked, voice trembling.

"Part of the Hanover charm," Arthur said with a quick smile. "This is not civilized warfare, Marshall. If you cannot fight then stay out of the way so I do not have to rescue you again." Without waiting to see how offended his friend would be by the words, Arthur threw himself back into the fray. He fought his way to Chases Deer's side once more, pleased to see the damage the warrior had done in his absence.

Her movement was supernatural, blows too fast to follow with the eye while her legs moved so quickly, they were blurred by the motion. She moved with the speed of a hummingbird.

A cry went up from Shield members on the opposite side of the company Arthur and Chases Deer fought. He glanced towards them, expecting reinforcements, when he saw them all pointing upward, toward the sky.

Arthur followed their looks and arms between blows and then stepped away from the fight.

A gaping hole was in the side of the pyramid. Far above the fray, near the top of the dome, was a figure plummeting down towards the ground. Arthur watched for a split second until his instincts told him the figure's trajectory.

He grabbed Chases Deer's arm and hauled her away fast enough for them both to stumble and fall. A split second later, a bundle of fur and claws smashed into the ground where they had been standing.

The skinwalker's bear form was unmistakable. Arthur scrambled away, uncertain if Black Wolf had an ounce of control. He pulled Chases Deer with him.

"The only explanation for a flying bear is that my father threw him," Arthur said and pointed towards the hole in the side of the pyramid, through which light shone.

The skinwalker stood and shook off the fall with no apparent damage. It faced off against the shocked soldiers around him before his eyes settled on Arthur. The skinwalker's gaze was crazed with no sign he recognized Arthur at all.

"Very slowly stand up and step back," Arthur said to Chases Deer.

The fierce warrior did not argue and instead, mirrored his movement as they inched away.

"When I say run, use that speed of yours. Go anywhere away from here."

The skinwalker appeared to be waiting. Finally, one of the soldiers made a move to flee. Whipping around, Black Wolf tackled the man and tore his head off with one bite.

"Now," Arthur said.

He and Chases Deer sprinted away. The skinwalker, busy with the other soldiers, ignored them.

Arthur darted around a cart loaded as if the owners had been packing to leave permanently and ducked down. Chases Deer sat beside him. The sounds of the creature tearing into the soldiers soon ceased, when all the men had run or died.

Arthur's senses tingled a warning. "Give me your pup," he whispered urgently to Chases Deer.

She pulled the small wolf out of a pouch and handed it to him. "Do we run?"

"Absolutely not." Arthur lifted the animal. "In fact, do not move, even to breathe."

The small wolf squirmed in his hands and lifted its head in the direction of the skinwalker.

"Tell him to leave us be," Arthur whispered to the guide.

The skinwalker circled the cart and bared his teeth when he spotted them. The blood of those he killed soaked his fur. He started forward and then stopped, eyes going to the pup. His growl turned softer, and he ceased baring his teeth. He leaned forward to nudge the tiny pup gently. The wolf yelped at him in complaint, and the skinwalker took a step back and moved away. He disappeared from view, and Arthur heard the scream of his next victim.

"I am sorry I doubted you," Chases Deer said, accepting her pup back.

Arthur stood and leaned around the cart in time to see the massive bear loping into the interior of the pyramid.

"He cleared our path," Arthur observed.

"Just in time."

He glanced at the warrior. She lifted her chin towards the sky, which had begun to lighten.

"If we wait, Diving Eagle will have his army here soon," Chases Deer.

"They will be massacred," Arthur said. He started towards the pyramid.

"We're not going in there, are we?" she called. "Not without support?"

"We are here to stop this war before it starts." He stopped to swipe weapons from a dismembered soldier. "I thought you hated Diving Eagle's methods anyway."

"I would want him by my side in war and nowhere else," she replied curtly. "Even then, I would not trust him to know when to stop."

Arthur tossed her a pistol. "You do not believe him to be capable of being a good man? Not at all?"

She joined him, and they trotted towards the pyramid.

"I do not know what kind of man he is or what kind of leader he will become. But I know he is loyal to his people, and he backs his oaths with blood." She spoke the words reluctantly, as if complimenting the Diné chief caused her personal pain. "I will not marry him. Or you."

"I read those letters from my father and yours," Arthur said. "You need not fear marrying me. You are not my kind."

She stopped cold and raised her gun. "Because I am Native?"

"No." Arthur ignored her. "Because my lover lies dying in your medical clinic. If I am to marry anyone, it will be him."

Chases Deer was silent. He continued into the pyramid and

towards the elevator that would take them to his family's apartment. The Native warrior joined him.

"I will convince my father not to marry me off," she stated.

"Diving Eagle is chief now. If he does not wish to marry you, I imagine he will not feel obligated."

"Let us pray this is so."

Arthur glanced at her, surprised by how vehement their rivalry was.

"I'm going with you."

They both turned to face Marshall.

"This is my city, too," he said before Arthur could object.

"If you insist," Arthur said, sensing Marshall's resolve.

"I cannot trust you Hanover's to finish this."

Arthur returned his attention to the elevator. The doors slid open, and he entered. "Perhaps you can marry Marshall, Chases Deer. He will run the city after all. You already have something in common: your hatred for my family."

She scowled. Marshall did not appear amused either.

Arthur released the breath he held when the doors closed, and the lift whisked them upward.

"What resistance will we face?" Chases Deer asked, reloading her pistol.

"I cannot begin to imagine," Arthur replied. "Two, maybe three skinwalkers, my father, Tiana, if she is mad."

Marshall reached over and took one of Chases Deer's guns.

"Add it to my ransom balance," he said at her sharp look.

"I will never see my money, will I?" she grumbled.

The doors of the elevator slid open. Arthur stepped out cautiously, paused to listen, and then passed the dead guards to step into the hallway.

"If all those people are up here, why can we not hear them?" Marshall whispered.

Arthur had been wondering the same. The apartment was silent. Quiet was not the normal state of a skinwalker, from what he knew of them. He reached the common living areas. The lightening sky was visible through the hole in the side of the pyramid. The wealth his family had collected over many generations lay in shambles.

They entered the second hallway leading to the private quarters. Arthur's instincts were as calm as the apartment.

"Marshall, check there. Chases Deer, there." He pointed to the rooms belonging to Tiana and Matilda.

Arthur opened the door to his father's room, prepared to pounce, lest his father be lying in wait inside.

"Arthur!" The alarmed note in Marshall's shout sent both Arthur and Chases Deer scrambling to reach him.

The Native beat Arthur by four strides to the door in whose doorway Marshall stood.

"What is ..." Arthur stopped and stared. His breath caught in his throat.

The hole. The one from his dream that swallowed the city. It gaped at the base of the pyramid and had sucked his old room, the side of the pyramid, the smoke trapped in the dome, and one building into it.

Beside it, facing it with her arms extended, was Tiana. The three skinwalkers in their animal forms – panther, bear, tigress – were behind her, standing between her and the form of his father. As Arthur watched, Aveline dived in front of a bolt of lightning meant for Tiana. It knocked the panther to the ground. Aveline leapt to her feet and resumed her protective stance.

A rumbled filled the air, followed by the sound of another building collapsing. The hole gaped wider, swallowing half a ward this time.

"Look!" Chases Deer pointed.

Two wards over, outside the dome, a mix of Natives and his uncle's men were making their way towards the pyramid, oblivious to the danger. Arthur's attention returned to Tiana. She was struggling to contain the hole.

"Warn Simon and Diving Eagle," Arthur said, backpedaling

quickly.

"And you?" Marshall called.

"I'm going to Tiana."

Arthur sprinted through the apartment and to the elevator. He did not wait for them but descended and sent the lift back up before bolting to the nearest entrance. He stopped in his tracks when he reached it. The hole was racing towards this direction. Whirling, Arthur ran as fast as he could to one of the other entrances, refusing to think about the certain death following him.

He left the pyramid and snaked through the nearby ward to reach Tiana and Aveline. The intensity of energy increased as he grew nearer. Another building collapsed, and then two. Arthur broke free of them just as the building behind him began to implode. He darted into the street, behind his father. Two of the skinwalkers were down while Aveline was on her feet, waiting for the next strike. Arthur's eyes lingered on the half-sister he had never known about. He drew his knife and approached slowly and stealthily behind his father, whose focus was on the four challengers. Edwin's arms were up. Invisible power pulsed away, towards Tiana and the skinwalkers, rippling the air as it did so.

"They're warned." Chases Deer was at his side.

"Holy ..." Arthur hissed. "Can you not do that? I swear my heart leapt from my body!"

Her eyes were on the expanding hole. "Diving Eagle insisted on continuing this way. I will watch for him."

"Go. Get out of this mess." Arthur motioned her away and crept forward once more. When he was within several feet, he gripped his knife more tightly and lifted onto his tiptoes, preparing to attack. He took a deep breath and sprang forward, shoving the knife into his father's side.

Edwin stumbled. His hands dropped, releasing the hold on the others, and he whirled. Arthur raised the knife to stab his father again but felt himself flung upward and over, towards the hole. The ground and sky flipped over and over in his view.

Before he could be dropped into the next world, he smacked into an invisible wall. Arthur shook his head, dizzy from the journey. He was upside down, dangling helplessly above the blackness.

Arthur, the voice in his head was Tiana's. He twisted until he could see her. Bloodied and pale, Tiana stood at the edge of the hole, one hand lifted towards him to keep him from falling.

A roar and a shout sounded, drawing both of their attentions.

The tigress skinwalker had managed to break the hold Edwin had on them and tackled him. She shredded the Hanover leader's shoulder before he flung her off with magic towards a building. Tiana's focus left the hole completely as she stopped the skinwalker from smashing into the building. Arthur was brought down gently, as was the skinwalker.

A flash of lightning sizzled by Aveline and slammed into Tiana's side, splattering blood around her.

She went down with a gasp.

Fear raced through him. Arthur dropped the last four feet to the ground and rushed to his sister's side. Aveline and Black Wolf took up defensive positions, absorbing the power flung towards Tiana.

"Tiana!" Arthur exclaimed, gathering his sister's small body into his arms.

Her eyes opened, revealing the black depths belonging to her real mother.

He smiled.

She blinked and pushed at him. Arthur helped her sit, ignoring the buildings falling on either side of the street as the hole widened.

"You came," she murmured. "I wanted you to stay safe, outside the city."

"I belong here, with you and Aveline," he replied firmly. "We will face him together."

Tiana wrapped her arms around him in a tight hug. "I do not know if I can save you."

Aveline drew near and nudged Tiana's arm.

"We belong here together," Arthur said. He looped an arm

around Aveline's neck and pulled her in for a quick hug. "All of us." The large cat purred then wiggled free to face the threat.

Arthur stood, helping Tiana up as well.

The three of them faced their father, who, for once, did not appear as if he were in control of anything. Black Wolf's massive frame appeared in front of them. He growled before turning away to confront the Hanover leader.

"Tell me how to help," Arthur said urgently to Tiana.

"He is blocking them and widening the tear," Tiana said. "I cannot stop the tear while he does this." Her eyes were glazed, and Arthur sensed his sister was already close to spent.

"It stands to reason he cannot defend himself and widen the tear, if you are fighting him," he said. "If this were a typical battle, I would remove the greatest threat to *you* so that you can remove the greatest threat to us."

As she listened, her eyes went to their father. "You always know what to do."

Arthur was about to remind her he was all but helpless in a battle where he was neither the heir nor a skinwalker. Tiana walked away from him and lifted her arms. Hidden from view behind the skinwalkers, Arthur felt the energy coalesce and swirl around her before a blast of power rippled outward, ricocheting off buildings and shaking the earth.

It knocked the three skinwalkers off their feet, earning her a glare from the tigress. Only then did Arthur see their father. She had flung him down the street. He was staggering to his feet, temporarily disabled.

"Go," she whispered to the skinwalkers. They needed no second encouragement and bolted towards their common enemy. Tiana sent another blast, this one better aimed, and it shoved their father even farther away.

The buildings on either side of them imploded in a hail of dust and pebbles. The pyramid leaned and groaned, falling halfway into the hole with its tip propped up on the outer edge of the hole.

The sight of their home on the brink of destruction caused both of them to pause. Tiana's features were ashen.

Arthur recovered first and nudged his sister. "Hurry. I will warn you if our father tries to attack again," he said. "Pull the hole away from that direction first." He pointed to the ward through which his uncle and Diving Eagle's warriors were likely to come.

Tiana returned to the edge of the tear between this world and the next and lifted her arms again.

Arthur stood to the side, glancing between the skinwalkers and hole. The skinwalkers managed to pounce and begin mauling his father before Edwin Hanover repulsed them with his telekinesis. But they did not go far, as if he was weakening.

The tear began to retreat towards its center, away from the forces of Simon and Diving Eagle. Arthur watched with no small amount of surprise. His sister, the sweet, naïve, tiny girl who barely survived this far, was more powerful than anyone he had met. Pride bubbled within him to know she was more special than he had originally believed.

His eyes went to their father, who was climbing to his feet, bloodied and furious. Aveline loped back towards Tiana and resumed her protective stance in front of Arthur and Tiana. The other two skinwalkers remained down the street, pacing and stalking the Hanover leader.

"Good!" he called to Tiana above the roaring wind being sucked into the hole. "Now, can you hold it there and put our father down again?"

Tiana nodded and stepped back with one foot, until she was in a position to extend one arm towards their father. She knocked him back again. Before the skinwalkers could pounce, their father rebuffed them and sent several streaks of lightning arcing down the street towards Tiana. Aveline blocked the first and was knocked to the ground.

Arthur tackled Tiana to the ground. Immediately, his head exploded into light and dark. Unable to identify whether her power, or the lightning had hit him, he rolled to the side and lay still. Pain pierced him and he fought to remain conscious.

"Arthur!" Tiana cried.

Arthur shook his head to clear his vision. She knelt beside him. Covered in dirt and mud, Aveline stood over him protectively.

"I am well," he said and forced a smile. He started to sit – and gasped as pain ricocheted within him. Warmth soaked his side, and he reached for the spot. His hand came away bloody.

Tiana was gazing at him, stricken.

"It is minor," he assured her. "Go back to what you were doing. Stabilize the tear and disable our father so the skinwalkers can eliminate him."

She hesitated then stood, returning to her stance.

Arthur did not let her see his grimace of pain. He tugged his shirt up and stared. His father had put a hole in his side, much larger than would be caused by a bullet. Blood poured down his leg and hip. He lowered the shirt.

Aveline was watching him, understanding in her large eyes.

Keep quiet. He directed the words towards her and indicated Tiana with a nod of his head.

She resumed her defensive position. Arthur rose with effort, determined to help his sisters in what ways he could.

Tiana was maintaining the hold on both her father and the tear – but gaining no real ground with either. Before he could advise her on how to change her tactic, Arthur found himself floating upward. He was not alone. Aveline lifted off the ground and began to thrash wildly. Down the street, the tigress skinwalker, who was closest to the Hanover chief, was midair as well.

Aveline's growl of frustration drew Tiana's gaze, and she gasped.

"Focus!" Arthur ordered her. "He is trying to distract you!"

All three airborne people were tossed towards the center of the hole.

Tiana's attention shifted away from both her tasks. Arthur felt himself yanked away, back to safety, Aveline beside him. The tigress roared from her position midair above the gaping hole.

Arthur's feet touched the ground. He saw Tiana's body shift as her power went from him to the tigress.

Two more bolts of lightning smashed into Tiana, and she fell to the ground, unconscious.

The tigress dropped and disappeared into the hole. Aveline gave a mournful cry.

Arthur hurried to Tiana's side, as did Aveline.

How much longer can she do this? Aveline's concern was one Arthur shared.

"Just a little longer," he replied. "She has no choice. My father will destroy the known world if she does not." The hair on the back of his neck rose, tickling, and his instincts whispered a warning. Arthur knew the danger before he turned. He grabbed the pouch that had been positioned beside Tiana's feet. It contained a knife and two pup. He gently pulled the pup speaking her name free.

Arthur placed it on Tiana's chest, and Aveline nuzzled it awake.

"Work your magic, little guide," he said to the pup. His words for Aveline were grimmer. "Wake her. Make sure she finishes this at any cost." He grabbed the knife and tucked it between his belt and pants at the small of his back.

Aveline looked up when he stood. *You have no power, no weapons. What are you doing?* She asked.

"I am already dead, Avi," he said and motioned to the wound in his side. "The least I can do is buy you both some time." He paused. "I hope you can forgive me for not knowing you existed, for not taking care of you, and for treating you terribly when we first met. I am proud to have you as my sister."

Don't go, Aveline answered.

"He will kill you both if I don't," Arthur replied. "Wake her."

He turned towards their father and began to walk down the street. Black Wolf in his bear form lay unmoving at the foot of a building near Edwin, and Arthur swallowed hard. From an alley nearby, Chases Deer and Marshall stood. Arthur stretched his senses, feeling for the presences of his uncle's men and praying this time, Simon would not fail him.

Simon was close, along with Diving Eagle and hundreds of others. They were hidden behind the rows of buildings flanking the street. All the warriors and soldiers for a thousand miles could not defeat Edwin Hanover, but maybe they could distract him until Tiana had recovered.

Arthur flung open his arms to show he was unarmed, doubting it mattered at this point.

"Father," he said, moving towards the man whose gaze fell on him without recognition. "Tiana is done. I can do nothing. If we surrender now, will you stop the tear before it destroys our city?"

Edwin regarded Arthur for a long moment, as if debating whether he would attack or speak. As if sensing Arthur spoke the truth, he lowered his arms and took a step forward.

"It is because of you I am doing this," his father said. "You were meant to be my heir."

"I do not have that ability," Arthur replied. "And Tiana is ... weak, as you have always said."

"No Hanover dynasty, no city."

"It is not that simple!" Arthur exclaimed. From the corner of his eye, he saw Black Wolf stand and shake himself off. The skinwalker was bleeding and lethargic but on his feet, which was all Arthur cared about.

Arthur moved closer to his father. He purposely kept his mind on Tiana and the city, in case his father's gifts extended to mind reading.

"Do you not care that you might destroy everything? This entire world?" he pressed.

"We are not from this world, Arthur."

"Our family came here for a reason, did they not?" Arthur countered. "We have killed so many to ensure our dynasty here on this world. You cannot expect me to believe you would give up this easily. Please reconsider -"

"I will not!" Edwin boomed.

Arthur's instincts whispered an instant before he saw the movement in his peripheral. His father felt it as well, and they turned simultaneously.

A flurry of arrows and gunshots rang out, smashing into the protective bubble around Edwin. The Hanover leader slammed the warriors belonging to Simon and Diving Eagle into a building and then lifted them into the air, hurling them towards the hole.

Black Wolf slammed into Edwin from behind, driving the Hanover leader to the ground. Lightning erupted from Edwin in response. It passed through the skinwalker and smashed erratically into the surroundings, into buildings, soldiers and the sky. Fire shot through Arthur once again before he was able to dive to the ground. He lay still, panting. His ears rang and his body twitched from the power his father flung in an effort to dislodge the skinwalker.

"Arthur!" The voice was distant, from somewhere in the darkness swallowing his mind. He saw the blurry face of Marshall bent over him, while Chases Deer stood guard. Marshall dragged him into the relative safety of an alley. "Stay with me!"

Arthur could not move for a long moment. At last, he managed to roll onto his stomach and planted his palms into the pool of blood forming within him.

Come out, Hanover. The voice of Black Wolf was loud in his mind.

Arthur grimaced. He wanted to fall into unconsciousness, to let his battered body rest.

It is time you pay the price for the deal we made, Black Wolf continued.

"Help me up," Arthur said, dazed.

"You need a healer!" Chases Deer snapped.

Arthur drew the knife from the small of his back and forced himself to his feet. He wobbled, unable to see straight and uncertain his body would carry him back out into the street.

"What are you doing?" Marshall gripped his arm to halt his staggering walk.

"Tiana needs help," Arthur replied and yanked away. The movement sent him careening into the wall.

"You are in no position ... Arthur! Arthur!"

"Stay here," Arthur replied.

Ignoring them, Arthur barreled recklessly into the street once more. The skinwalker was down again and struggling to rise. No one but Aveline stood between Tiana and their father, who appeared to be in little better shape than Arthur.

Arthur had always known Black Wolf would demand a price for the favor he asked of him weeks ago. He never expected to be happy to repay the favor, and he never guessed he would do so while saving the lives of his sisters as well as the skinwalker.

Arthur reached the middle of the street and tossed his head back. How had he never noticed how blue the sky was in morning?

"Father!" he shouted.

Edwin whirled to face Arthur once more.

In the background, Arthur saw Aveline helping Tiana up. Tiana leaned heavily against the panther, and Arthur wished with all his heart that he was enough to distract his father.

Arthur pulled out the knife. "Let's finish this! You and me. Right here!"

"I am finished with you, Arthur!" came the cold response.

Arthur braced himself for the lightning, hoping he was far enough gone not to feel it when it hit. Two strikes burnt through him, and his mouth fell open in silent agony. Every nerve ending was on fire, every drop of blood screaming.

He dropped to his knees, the knife sliding from his hand.

Take him down, he said, hoping Aveline or Tiana or the skinwalker – or all of them – heard him.

Blackness swallowed his mind.

Arthur fell to the ground.

TWENTY-FOUR

TIANA STOOD in shock as her brother dropped. Her mind was slow from the blows, her body aching and too hot.

Arthur. Aveline's mournful thought was accompanied by a soft purr.

Arthur's presence disappeared from Tiana's mind, indicating he no longer lived. She stood in disbelief, unable to process what she had seen.

Her father turned away from Arthur's lifeless body without a flicker of concern for his son.

Her uncle's army, along with Diving Eagle's warriors, poured out from their hiding places behind the buildings and into the street behind Edwin. Diving Eagle was not among them. She had his presence marked in her mind, so she could track him without thought. He and quite a few others were moving towards them from a different direction, near the edge of the tear.

Marshall emerged from an alley and went to Arthur. He gently maneuvered her brother's body to see if Arthur still lived then lowered his head in silent prayer.

You must end this, Aveline told her with a nudge. *No matter who he kills. Your father will destroy the lives of everyone.*

Tiana blinked out of her shock, unaware of the tears on her cheeks. Air thrashed around her as it was sucked into the hole behind her, which was growing again. But the tear between worlds no longer mattered. She replayed Arthur's death in her mind, over and over.

Take him out, Tiana! Aveline yelled into her mind. She took off at a lope and then a sprint, headed toward their father.

"Wait ..." Tiana called. Her limbs were heavy as she took a step forward, her mind slow to understand the world. Everything around her appeared to speed up, while she struggled to keep up let alone react. Her surroundings took on a surreal feeling, and she began to wonder if this were a vision or dream. If it were real, would she not feel pain and loss and sorrow? Would she not be able to act instead of watch?

Aveline raced towards their father, only to be repulsed and flung into the air once more and thrown towards the hole. The panther disappeared, following her mother into the void. Aveline's presence disappeared from Tiana's mind.

Tiana observed without comprehending what she saw.

Sensing the attackers gathering behind him, Edwin turned to confront the men with a sneer, ignoring the caged skinwalker waiting to end him.

Tiana closed her eyes and then opened them. Half the army was in the air, flying towards the void. They disappeared into the widening tear, their energies gone from her mind as well. The pyramid that had been her home listed and then toppled into the hole, followed by several more buildings. An entire ward. More soldiers.

I cannot do this. Tiana was sinking into herself, imploding. Ready to hide forever in her room. More lives disappeared from her mind. She closed her eyes and willed herself to awaken from the nightmare.

"Tiana!" someone gripped her arms.

She looked up into Diving Eagle's face, barely recognizing him.

He assessed her quickly then withdrew a knife and took her arm, turning the soft underside towards the sky.

Hot, sharp pain sliced through her denial and shock. She drew a breath, unable to recall when she had last noticed the feel of air in her lungs. His scent reached her senses next: sweat, man, leather.

Diving Eagle lowered the bloodied knife. He released her arm and cupped her cheek with his free hand. In that moment, he was all that seemed real, his warm touch, the roughness of his calloused hand, the intensity of his gaze, and how, even now standing beside the abyss, he was not afraid.

"While it is true I am here as a duty to my people, I am also here because ... my heart tells me I belong here. With you." Did he say the words aloud, or had she read them from his mind? "Fight, Tiana. Only you can do this."

Hot tears filled her eyes. The trickle of reality turned into a flood: the whirlwind of air, energy radiating from the tear, staggering sorrow, images of those she loved dying, screams as her father struck down more of his opponents. Pain. Fear.

Fury stronger than anything she had ever felt before.

Wiping her eyes, Tiana turned away from Diving Eagle and singled out her father among the many forms down the street. She did not try to fight his energy this time and instead, did as she had done when she arrived to the city. She formed a dome over him and him alone, cutting off his ability to harm anyone. She started down the street, intent on finishing him, as Arthur had told her to, when the faint presence of Diving Eagle vanished suddenly from her mind.

Tiana whirled. The tear had widened, following her, and swallowed the Native warrior and street in her wake.

Agony twisted her gut when she began to feel all she had lost, and she froze, gazing into the void following her. It had expanded in three other directions into the neighboring wards and took up nearly half the city. Arthur, Aveline, Diving Eagle and countless others had already given their lives so that she had the chance to act. She squeezed blood from the arm Diving Eagle had cut until new pain pierced her thoughts.

Why did his loss hurt as much as Arthur's and Aveline's? She had always admired him for his bravery, strength, and courage. Was there more to what she felt? Was her destiny intertwined with his, as much as hers had been with Arthur's and Aveline's?

Did it matter when the world was collapsing around her?

A heavy paw rested on her shoulders.

You are weak. I can channel power into you, Black Wolf said into her mind.

With a glance at her father trapped in his dome, Tiana faced the void again and focused on closing it.

She closed her eyes. She envisioned the tear closing. The power pushed back, and she found herself drawing heavily off of the skin-walker beside her. Where his magic came from, she did not know, but she absorbed it as fast as he could give it to her.

The tear rebuffed her efforts. Tiana rested her hands on the invisible wall separating her from the next world and began to physically push as well as push with her mind. It began to give, resisted and then retreated once more.

Close to the end of her strength, her fury turned to hot rage when she considered all the lives she had let her father claim this day.

Aveline. Arthur. Diving Eagle. She repeated their names over and over.

Tears ran down her face. Rather than fight the pain, Tiana let it and the anger consume her, until she was lost in the emotion. A wailing scream tore out of her lungs, the cry of a Ghoul in pain. The tear trembled beneath her palms and suddenly, silence encased her surroundings.

Panting, Tiana's lungs and throat burned, and she opened her eyes.

Black Wolf laughed. "That's it!" he exclaimed. "This is why you alone can do this. Look!"

She did so and for a moment, was lost as to what had happened.

The world around her appeared frozen at first, people caught mid stride or stuck in the air on their way towards the void. As she looked more closely, however, she realized they were moving, albeit very deliberately.

"The Ghouls," Black Wolf said. "This is how they capture their prey. They freeze it in place with their minds. Their power is but a drop in a rainstorm compared to yours. Have you never wondered why you have the eyes of a Ghoul?"

She looked around, baffled by the strangeness of her surroundings. Her entire body shook from effort and emotion, and she felt ready to collapse in place. "You think my mother was a Ghoul?" she asked.

"How else could you have done this?" he countered. "This gift to paralyze with the mind belongs to the Ghouls alone. Combined with your Hanover power, you have paralyzed the world."

Her eyes fell to Black Wolf, and her breath caught. "You are letting me drain you," she said.

He was human from the waist up, gaunt where he had been strong before, with sunken eyes and sickly features.

"Quickly. Close the tear while you can," he said, ignoring her observation.

The idea her mother was a Ghoul was too much for her to consider. Tiana's eyes lingered on him before she returned to her duty. He rested his hand on her shoulder again. She thanked him silently.

The hole, similar to everything else, was expanding at a crawl, inches per minute instead of feet.

Exhausted, with more tears blinding her, Tiana rested her hands on the wall and concentrated on closing the void once more.

It responded more quickly this time. Buoyed by the difference, she allowed the skinwalker's power to flow through her as she closed the tear. When the hole between this world and the next was little bigger than a horse, the task became abruptly difficult again, and the world began to return to its normal passage of time.

"Your power comes from there. You are losing power as you close the void," Black Wolf explained.

Dizziness and tunnel vision formed. Tiana shook her head, refusing to stop when she was so close. She drew more from the skinwalker. Except this time, his magic felt different. Older.

"This is you," she whispered, hesitating. "I am draining your life not your magic."

"I am glad to give it." His voice was raspy. "Not because I care for you or your cause, but because I will be known as the skinwalker who saved the world."

Tiana was unable to help the hoarse, hysterical laugh that bubbled up in response. "If this is your wish, then I will grant it."

"In a direct confrontation, I would have won."

More tears filled her eyes. The creature who had killed tens of thousands without a drop of remorse was not worth her second thought, let alone worth the sorrow in her heart. And yet she felt his loss even before he was gone. For all that he was, he had chosen to be more than anyone thought he could be.

Tiana closed her eyes once more. She pulled his life force from his body and pushed it towards the tear. Seconds later, Black Wolf's hand left her shoulder as he slid to the ground. The bulk of her power ceased with the closing of the hole.

Tiana collapsed, exhausted and weak from the fight. She lay still, crying quietly, unable to help the tears when she thought of those she had lost. She wept until too tired to cry more and her head pulsed.

"I cannot pretend to understand this, but I am grateful to you for what you have done."

Lost everyone I love? Destroyed half the city? Tiana did not move at Marshall's voice.

He bent and lifted her off the ground.

Tiana roused herself, aware the final blow had to be dealt, and hating herself for not wanting to do it. Good or bad, her father was all that remained of her world. Marshall released her when she was steady on her feet. She trailed him towards the dome in which she had trapped her father. The soldiers and Natives parted for them, and she ignored everyone.

"Is this everyone?" she asked, looking around. At one point, she had sensed hundreds of fighters.

"Yes," Marshall's voice was hushed. "Chases Deer, your uncle, and most of his men are gone. They came with a thousand."

Tiana stopped, uncertain she had heard him correctly. No more than sixty remained around her. What of the people who lived in the city? How many more lives were lost? If she had been stronger, or acted sooner, or not frozen up when she did, or ...

Her father stood proud and defiant, and her doubt and sorrow fizzled in the face of his complete unconcern for what he had done. Because he had done this, she realized. He had tried to pull this city, and the rest of the human world, into the next world rather than lose his hold over it.

I am not like him. This thought surprised her. Her mind was hers. Her power was hers, even if Hanover blood ran through her veins. It did not control whether or not she hurt rather than helped, for this was a choice, one her father had made the same way she had. When tested, he harmed others.

But she had not. Relief trickled through her, followed by the bitterness of knowing those who might understand were gone, victims of a man she should have faced much sooner.

"You would have destroyed it all," she said to him. She was too tired to be angry anymore.

"The tear can be reopened," he said staunchly. "You can regain your power."

Tiana did not reply to the statement even she judged as ridiculous. The skinwalkers, including Aveline, were all dead. No tear could be opened without one.

Her father no longer radiated the energy he had. She tested her own ability, not about to be caught off guard by any remaining tricks of her father. She lifted the knife Diving Eagle had given her from its place shoved in Marshall's pocket. It floated to her, confirming that, while she could not feel her power, a fraction of it remained.

Tiana started forward, towards her father, hand gripping the hilt hard. She had never killed a man in cold blood, and she was not certain she could, even one as deserving as this one.

Marshall caught her wrist, stopping her.

Tiana looked up at him.

"No," he said firmly. "Arthur would never allow you to become like your father. I cannot either."

"No Hanover will leave the city," she whispered. "You cannot let me, either, Marshall."

Marshall's features softened. "Your brother was right. As always. You are not like your father. You do not need to live in his shadow anymore." He pried the knife from her fingers as he spoke. "You are free, Tiana, from this day forward, with the exception of this decision."

She let the knife go reluctantly. The effort of holding it, and staying upright when she wanted to collapse and sleep for days, was too much for her. "I am sorry for your loss, Marshall. I do not know how you live with this pain," she whispered.

"I do not know either, but somehow I do," he replied sadly. "Today changes everything for both of us."

He stepped away from her, towards her father.

Tiana expelled what energy remained around Marshall and willed the dome to allow him to enter. Her father tried to lash out at him, first with power that bounced off him, and then with a punch. Weakened by the skinwalkers, Edwin's blow did not even glance off Marshall, and he was too slow to recover. Marshall wrapped his hand in the Hanover leader's hair and yanked his head back. He placed the knife to it.

Tiana closed her eyes. The energy humming in the air around them vanished, and her father's body hit the ground.

Seconds later, so did Tiana's. She heard Marshall's quiet voice calling her name but did not care to listen. Her heart aching, her soul hurting, her body pushed beyond its limits, she wanted nothing else than to join Arthur and Aveline in the next world.

AS HER LUCK would have it, she did not awaken in the next world. Tiana's head hurt, and she smelled the combination of mud and blood that had dried on her clothing. The ache at her core, however, was the final assurance she remained alive when she did not want to be.

Grass tickled her face, and nearby, a tree creaked in a cool breeze. The scent of pine and flowers lay just beneath the smells remaining from her battle, and a creek gurgled in the distance.

She opened her eyes, not recognizing her surroundings, other than she was in the forest. Whose forest, she could not tell.

The warm puddle at the middle of her chest caused her to lift her head. Her wolf lay on her, its belly to the sky, and its breathing deep and regular. The moment she saw the basket of bottles beside her thigh, she understood who had brought her here.

Tiana picked up her wolf and sat, not at all eager to face the day or anyone else. Listless, unable to stop the mental replay of all that had happened in the city, she was too exhausted to cry for those she had lost. All she could do was ... sit. And hold her pup. Something was jammed in her ribs, and she shifted away.

The knife. She sighed. Her father's dried blood remained on the blade and hilt. Tiana pulled it free from her waistband.

"Tiana."

Her brow furrowed, and she twisted. Tiana's mouth dropped open. "I did die!" she managed in a rasping voice.

Diving Eagle shook his head.

"Then you are a spirit," she said. Unlike the malicious spirit that plagued Black Wolf, Diving Eagle appeared solid. He was dressed in clean clothing, the war paint gone from his face. Around one wrist, he wore the turquoise bracelet.

She checked for hers self-consciously. The bracelet was present, as was the necklace that matched her sister's. At the reminder Aveline was gone, Tiana's gaze dropped to the ground. Why was the necklace so bright when Aveline was dead?

Tiana surveyed her surroundings for any sign of her sister's spirit. When she saw none, she drew a sharp breath and stood.

"This is for you, if you can have it as a spirit." She held out the knife.

Diving Eagle accepted it. He withdrew it from its sheath, his eyes on the blood crusting the knife.

"I believe your Hanover vengeance to be complete, with one exception." She knelt in front of him and placed her pup on the ground. "I am ready."

He was silent.

"You must rid this world of Hanover blood," she said. "For all we know, the madness could take me at any moment."

Diving Eagle crouched, holding the knife.

She held her breath, waiting for the deathblow and praying it was fast, and not about to debate whether or not any Hanover deserved a quick death.

He tilted her chin up until she was forced to meet his gaze. "You are not mad," he said, reading her eyes in a way that left her uncomfortable. "You are not linked to the next world anymore. Perhaps that was the source of Hanover madness."

"I am still a Hanover," she murmured. "Your blood enemy."

"You saved my people and yours. As far as I am concerned, you are free."

"What is freedom without those I care about?" Her chin trembled. Did he know she had felt his death like a knife through her heart? "I am so sorry I could not save you."

He looked away and dropped his knees to the ground. "How can you apologize for the loss of one life when you saved tens of thousands, to include the lives of my people?" He sheathed the knife as he spoke.

"It is not one but three. Aveline, Arthur, and you. One is too many. Three is ... unbearable. And the lives of everyone else who fought my father? What I have done, or did not do, is unforgiveable." She reached for the knife and pulled it from the sheath. Tiana stared at the blade covered with her father's blood. It was only fitting she used this knife.

Tiana pulled up one sleeve and sat back. This time, she would cut deep enough on both arms for her blood to drain. It would be a slow death, but once it was over, she would be with Arthur and Aveline forever.

"Tiana, stop." Diving Eagle gripped both wrists.

"I can't stay here alone," she said, throat tight.

"You are not alone, Tiana," he continued. "I am not a spirit, and neither is Aveline."

She looked up, surprised. "You fell into the tear. I felt you both die."

"My wolf guide brought me back. He said it was not my time. Aveline's pup returned her here as well."

Her pulse quickened, and for the first time, she understood why Diving Eagle affected her as he did. She had not fully realized she cared for him until he was suddenly gone.

"Arthur?" she asked hopefully.

"No."

Her emotions somersaulted within her, flying between despair for Arthur and exhilaration for Aveline. Tears stung her eyes again. She wiped them away, but more formed, blurring her vision.

"I did not kill you," she repeated. She touched his arm to reassure herself he was indeed not a spirit. "I did not kill Aveline."

Overwhelmed, Tiana flung her arms around Diving Eagle and hugged him, not caring how harshly he dared judge her for being over-emotional. His strong arms circled her, and he pulled her into him rather than rejecting her. His familiar scent was calming, his support of her weary frame far greater than any she could muster.

"The six of us chosen by the pups are connected, whether or not we wish to be," he said quietly. "I believe we are meant to make the world better than the one we were raised in. Without the rivalries, war and blood feuds."

She listened to his steady heartbeat and his voice, calming. "Is that possible? To make our world better?"

"I am holding a Hanover in my arms and have no desire to kill her. If this is possible, anything is."

She smiled despite the pain settling deep in her breast at the thought of never seeing Arthur again.

"Marshall Cruise has asked me to meet with him to discuss trade and peace agreements," the Native chief continued.

"Will you go?" she asked.

"Our war is over. My father would say peace is long overdue, and we need the trade agreements."

She pulled away to look at him, relieved the stubborn warrior acknowledged it was time for peace.

"Aveline has expressed an interest in returning to the city," he said.

"You have spoken to her already?" She frowned. "How long have I been unconscious?"

"Your father was slain two days ago. Marshall saw you vanish, and no one could find you. Aveline and I returned yesterday. Our pups told us you would reappear when you were healed."

She glanced down at herself and patted her side and stomach, where her father's lightning had struck her. Through her exhaustion, she had not realized she was no longer in physical pain.

"What was the next world like?" she asked.

"I recall only darkness. We were not meant to be there. I believe we were not permitted to see the spirit realm for that reason."

Pensive, Tiana chewed her lower lip. "I cannot go back to the city," she said. "I do not want to. I had hoped Aveline would stay with me."

"I do not think she means to remain there. She has her own vengeance to seek. After that, it is her choice and yours where you go," he said.

Tiana's mind was on where she went while Aveline pursued her vengeance, for not one cell in Tiana's body wanted to return to Lost Vegas.

"You can stay," the quiet, measured note in Diving Eagle's tone was not lost on her. As before, he had guessed the thoughts she did not think it possible for him to know.

"With you?" she asked before she could stop herself. "I meant, with everyone. You ... all. In the forest or ..." Her face flamed hot with embarrassment, and she entertained the idea of taking the knife and ending her misery and awkwardness once and for all.

"With me," he clarified with his normal candid brevity.

"Does your council not despise me?"

"Not after I revealed who defeated the Hanover leader. They declared you and Aveline, and any descendants bearing your blood, honored guests of ours. If you leave this area for the Freelands, you will always have a home here when you return."

Home. Tiana had never before realized she did not know what that meant. She had grown up in a closet, but it was never home. Home meant a comfortable place where she was accepted and wanted, where people she cared for reciprocated her love, where she was free to be herself, Ghoulish eyes, Hanover magic and all.

She had always thought escape was what she wanted, to be free somewhere where no one could judge her. But what if she could be free somewhere where people accepted her?

The ensuing silence was intolerable, filled with wired tension and racing thoughts, with her heart beating in her ears and the sense of being fevered and wishing for snow or a cold rain.

Diving Eagle was tense, as if his invitation had revealed more than he was comfortable revealing.

"I hope you told your council you were the key. I could not have done it without you," she murmured. "If you had not been there ..." She shook her head, recalling her temporary break with reality.

"You have always had the strength and courage," he replied. "You are the only one who could not see it."

"You did not always think so," she countered.

"As blinded as I was for vengeance, I couldn't deny it for long. It's not easy to question the truths you have believed your entire life. I resisted acknowledging what was in front of me. I let my pride judge you before I understood you," he replied. "I intend ... *hope* to be better, and make better decisions, for my people. They have entrusted me with leading them, and I will not be resistant to change or hasty to judge." He paused, and his voice grew even softer. "I lied and deceived you. I hurt you, and I am sorry for it."

"You also put your life in danger for mine more than once, even if you were not certain what you felt," she pointed out.

"We are alike in that."

Warmth blossomed within her. It was different, new. Happy. For the first time in her life, she was not afraid of what the day would bring, or what happened when her father found her. She was free to choose her path, free to feel what she wanted to feel, free of the Hanover curse.

Tiana looked around her and noticed the flowers, the pine needles, the blue sky peeking down at her with renewed interest. She had fallen in love with the forest the first time she set foot in it. This could be her home, if she chose, and Aveline and Diving Eagle could be her family. The thoughts filled her with unexpected joy, though a pang of sorrow remained. Arthur had not had the chance she did to become who he wished to be.

At the long silence, Diving Eagle shifted to his feet and held out his hand. Tiana accepted it, and he pulled her up easily.

"Aveline is here." He stepped aside, indicating a dirt path leading towards a small clearing visible through the trees.

Tiana started past him and paused, facing him again. "I would like to stay here. With you," she said. "I want to help you and Marshall rebuild our world. I want a Hanover to help repair all the damage other Hanover's have done." She paused, thinking. "Just please do not ask me to return to the city."

"I will not." Diving Eagle started to smile, the first real smile she had ever seen from him. The tension slid from his features and for once, he did not look as if the weight of the world rested on his shoulders.

"And, you must promise me, if I do turn mad, you will drive that knife through my heart," she added.

"If it brings you peace, then I agree," he said. "But I feel you will never face your family's madness."

"I am not so sure," she said. "I trust you, with everything."

"It's an honor to gain your trust, Tiana."

Satisfied, Tiana turned and walked towards the clearing. Aveline was not alone in the meadow. Rocky was with her, along with Jose and Warner, whose midsection was bandaged but whose face shone with life once more.

Tiana had eyes for no one else but Aveline. She bolted and threw herself into her sister's arms. Aveline lost her balance with a laugh, and they toppled into the grass.

Sitting up, Tiana hugged Aveline again. When her trembling stopped, Tiana pulled away. Aveline was smiling.

"You are really returning to the city?" Tiana asked.

"For a short time. But ... I don't think I want to stay there. Marshall will not ban me even though I am a Hanover by birth, but it does not seem right for any of us with that man's blood in our veins to remain," Aveline replied. "Jose is needed to re-establish the electricity, and Warner will return to lead the new Shield once he heals."

Tiana glanced towards her brother's longtime lover. "The skin-walker is gone. His magic has left the wound?"

Aveline nodded. "I'll stay until I find Karl or his body. Then ... I avoided learning about my Native heritage for too long. Once I have found my father's betrayer, I think I will learn about this side of me." She lifted her bear claw.

"I am sorry about your mother. And Arthur," Tiana whispered. "I am sorry I could not save them."

"You saved all of us." Aveline hugged her. "We are sisters. What you always wanted."

More warmth filled Tiana.

"Though I'm not too happy to learn my real father was a Hanover," Aveline added with a small laugh. "Did you retain any of your power?"

"Some," Tiana replied.

"Good. You can use it to keep a certain Diné chief in line and make sure he doesn't decide to declare war on Marshall."

"I do not think I will need to use it." Tiana smiled and glanced towards Diving Eagle. She tilted her head and looked past the Native. The translucent, spirit form of Black Wolf lingered in the forest. Her mixed feelings about the creature remained. In the end, when it mattered, he chose to help rather than harm, and this was how she wanted to remember him.

She lifted a hand to him. He raised his in return.

"I really hope we aren't haunted for eternity," Aveline said, looking towards the apparition.

"He can do no harm now," Tiana replied. She returned her attention to her sister. "I think we are entering a period of peace. The first this city has known since the Old World. I am glad we are both here to see it."

"Me, too."

The two of them held one another in silence.

Despite her exhaustion and tragedy of losing Arthur, Tiana could not recall starting her day with more hope than she felt in the clearing that morning.

TWENTY-FIVE

BLACK WOLF HAD NOT BEEN INVITED to the spirit realm after his death. He had not expected to be. He watched the reunion of the Hanover sisters, pleased to have died on his terms and more than a little pleased to have been right about Tiana.

"The judgment has been made." The vengeful spirit in the form of the boy materialized at his side. "One hundred years for every life you took."

Black Wolf shrugged. "Unlike you, I do not care if I am a lost spirit trapped here."

"You have learned nothing!" the boy complained. "But perhaps you will after you have served your time."

Wandering alone for the next two million years was not the best news Black Wolf had ever received. But he had never deluded himself into believing he would not face some consequences for his actions, even if this knowledge never stopped him from massacring anyone.

"And, against our better judgment, we are granting you one concession," the spirit said reluctantly. "Your only selfless act in a lifetime was to sacrifice your life to save others. We granted her request to serve your penance with you."

Black Wolf's guide, in her wolf form, materialized beside the boy.

Black Wolf smiled and then laughed. She leapt towards him, and he caught her in his arms. He swung her around and hugged her hard, thrilled he was able to feel her soft fur again and smell her woodsy scent.

"This is no penance at all," he retorted to the vengeful boy.

"Do not make us regret this," the boy said and then disappeared.

Black Wolf lowered the spirit wolf to the ground. She did not wait him to choose a destination but trotted into the forest, as eager to explore as he was.

Black Wolf glanced one last time towards the Hanover girls and their companions. With a smile, he turned and followed his guide into the woods.

ALSO BY LIZZY FORD

Young Adult Fiction

Non-Series Title

The Door (teen sci-fi)

Between (paranormal) (2019)

Esme (teen paranormal)

Halloween

Thanksgiving

Christmas

Lost Vegas Series – young adult post-apocalyptic

Aveline

Tiana

Arthur

Black Wolf

Lost Vegas Series Omnibus

Spell Realm Series – young adult romantic fantasy

Water Spell

Dragon Spell (2019)

Moon Spell (2019)

Sword Spell (2020)

Omega Series – teen dystopia with Greek Gods

Omega

Theta

Alpha (2019)

Omega Beginnings Miniseries – individual episodes

Alessandra

Mismatch

Phoibe

Lantos

Theodosia

Niko

Cleon

Herakles

Omega Beginnings Miniseries Omnibus

Theta Beginnings Miniseries

Silent Queen

Mercenary

Shadow Titan

People's Champion

Theta Beginnings Miniseries Omnibus

Anshan Saga – new adult science fiction romance

Kiera's Moon

Kiera's Sun

Witchlings – young adult paranormal

Dark Summer

Autumn Storm

Winter Fire

Spring Rain

Broken Beauty Novellas – new adult dramatic fiction

Broken Beauty

Broken World

Broken Chains

Foretold Trilogy – young adult fantasy

Elle's Journey

Shadow Rising (2019)

Journey West (2019)

Voodoo Nights - young adult paranormal

Cursed

Erotic Romance

Non-Series Titles

Star Kissed (erotic sci-fi)

A Night Worth Dying For (short story, contemporary erotic thriller)

Trial Series – erotic paranormal romance

Trial by Moon

Trial by Thrall

Trial by Blood

Trial by Heart

Trial Series Omnibus

Heart of Fire – sexy dragon shifter

Charred Heart

Charred Tears

Charred Hope

Incubatti Duet – Buffy meets 50 Shades

Zoey Rogue

Zoey Avenger

Writing as SE Reign, erotica writer

101 Nights Box Set (featuring all seven serials)

Adult Sweet Romance

(no graphic sex scenes)

Non-Series Titles – 2014 - 2018

White Tree Sound

Black Moon Draw (fantasy romance)

Highlander Enchanted (historical romance)

Last Resort (2019)

History Interrupted – Time Travel Romantic Adventures

West

East

North

South (2019)

Super Villainess Chronicles – twisted superhero romance

It's Not Easy Being Evil

It's Not Easy Being Good

Starwalkers Serials (with Julia Crane) – new adult science fiction serial

Severed

Trapped

Exiled

Revealed

Escaped

Ascended

Starwalkers – Omnibus

Sons of War – contemporary military romance

Semper Mine

Soldier Mine

SEAL Mine

Rhyn Trilogy – new adult paranormal with demons

Katie's Hellion

Katie's Hope

Rhyn's Redemption

Rhyn Eternal – Death finds love

Gabriel's Hope

Deidre's Death

Darkyn's Mate

The Underworld

Twisted Fate

Twisted Karma

Sammy's Demon

Untitled (2019)

War of Gods – paranormal with gods, guardians and exceptional humans

Damian's Oracle

Damian's Assassin

Damian's Immortal

The Grey God

Damian Eternal

Xander's Chance

The Black God

Hidden Evil – paranormal with angels and four horsemen

Hear No

See No

Speak No

Unnamed Series

Unnatural (TBD)

Short Stories

Santa's Ninja Elves: Natasha

Santa's Ninja Elves: Hunter

Snow Whisperers (retired)

Non-Series Titles – 2011 - 2013

A Demon's Desire (paranormal romance)

The Warlord's Secret (fantasy romance)

Maddy's Oasis (contemporary romance)

Rebel Heart (sci-fi romance)

ABOUT THE AUTHOR

I breathe stories. I dream them. If it were possible, I'd eat them, too. (I'm pretty sure they'd taste like cotton candy.) I can't escape them - they're everywhere! Which is why I write! I was born to bring the crazy worlds and people in my mind to life, and I love sharing them with as many people as I can.

I'm also the bestselling, award winning, internationally acclaimed author of over sixty titles and counting. I write speculative fiction in multiple subgenres of romance and fantasy, contemporary fiction, books for both teens and adults, and just about anything else I feel like writing. If I can imagine it, I can write it!

I live in the desert of southern Arizona with a pack of spoiled dogs.

Connect with Lizzy

Website: LizzyFord.com
Facebook: www.Facebook.com/LizzyFordBooks
Twitter @LizzyFord2010
Instagram: @LizzyFordAuthor

www.ingramcontent.com/pod-product-compliance
Lightning Source LLC
Chambersburg PA
CBHW022245020726
47496CB00004B/1076